Lois C. Witherspoon
8808 Mount Mc Saula Road
Charlevoix, MI 49720
Monday, January 14, 2008.

Book *of the* Dead

Also by Patricia Cornwell

Book *of the* Dead

Patricia Cornwell

**Doubleday Large Print
Home Library Edition**

G. P. PUTNAM'S SONS
NEW YORK

This Large Print Edition, prepared especially for Doubleday Large Print Home Library, contains the complete, unabridged text of the original Publisher's Edition.

G. P. PUTNAM'S SONS
Publishers Since 1838
Published by the Penguin Group
Penguin Group (USA) Inc., 375 Hudson Street, New York, New York 10014, USA • Penguin Group (Canada), 90 Eglinton Avenue East, Suite 700, Toronto, Ontario M4P 2Y3, Canada (a division of Pearson Penguin Canada Inc.) • Penguin Books Ltd, 80 Strand, London WC2R 0RL, England • Penguin Ireland, 25 St Stephen's Green, Dublin 2, Ireland (a division of Penguin Books Ltd) • Penguin Group (Australia), 250 Camberwell Road, Camberwell, Victoria 3124, Australia (a division of Pearson Australia Group Pty Ltd) • Penguin Books India Pvt Ltd, 11 Community Centre, Panchsheel Park, New Delhi– 110 017, India • Penguin Group (NZ), 67 Apollo Drive, Rosedale, North Shore 0632, New Zealand (a division of Pearson New Zealand Ltd) • Penguin Books (South Africa) (Pty) Ltd, 24 Sturdee Avenue, Rosebank, Johannesburg 2196, South Africa

Penguin Books Ltd, Registered Offices: 80 Strand, London WC2R 0RL, England

ISBN 978-0-7394-8792-1

Printed in the United States of America

This is a work of fiction. Names, characters, places,
and incidents either are the product of the author's
imagination or are used fictitiously, and any resem-
blance to actual persons, living or dead, businesses,
companies, events, or locales is entirely coincidental.

While the author has made every effort to provide accurate telephone numbers and Internet addresses at the
time of publication, neither the publisher nor the author
assumes any responsibility for errors, or for changes that
occur after publication. Further, the publisher does not
have any control over and does not assume any responsibility for author or third-party websites or their content.

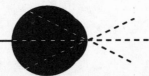

**This Large Print Book carries the
Seal of Approval of N.A.V.H.**

Acknowledgments

I am especially grateful to Dr. Staci Gruber, Assistant Professor of Psychiatry, Harvard Medical School, and Associate Director of the Cognitive Neuroimaging Laboratory, McLean Hospital.

This book is dedicated
to my publisher,
Ivan Held.

Rome

Water splashing. A gray mosaic tile tub sunk deep into a terra-cotta floor.

Water pours slowly from an old brass spout, and darkness pours through a window. On the other side of old, wavy glass is the piazza, and the fountain, and the night.

She sits quietly in water, and the water is very cold, with melting ice cubes in it, and there is little in her eyes—nothing much there anymore. At first, her eyes were like hands reaching out to him, begging him to save her. Now her eyes are the bruised blue of dusk. Whatever was in them has almost left. Soon she will sleep.

"Here," he says, handing her a tumbler that was handblown in Murano and now is filled with vodka.

He is fascinated by parts of her that have never seen the sun. They are pale like limestone, and he turns the spigot almost off, and the water is a trickle now, and he watches her rapid breathing and hears the chattering of her teeth. Her white breasts float beneath the surface of the water, delicate like white flowers. Her nipples, hard from the cold, are tight pink buds. Then he thinks of pencils. Of chewing off nubby pink erasers when he was in school, and telling his father and sometimes his mother that he didn't need erasers because he didn't make mistakes. When in truth, he liked to chew. He couldn't help it, and that also was the truth.

"You'll remember my name," he says to her.

"I won't," she says. "I can forget it." Chattering.

He knows why she says it: If she forgets his name, her destiny will be rethought like a bad battle plan.

"What is it?" he asks. "Tell me my name."

"I don't remember." Crying, shaking.

"Say it," he says, looking at her tan arms, pebbly with goose bumps, the blond hair on them erect, her young breasts and the darkness between her legs underwater.

"Will."

"And the rest of it?"

"Rambo."

"And you think that's amusing," he says, naked, sitting on the lid of the toilet.

She shakes her head vigorously.

Lying. She made fun of him when he told her his name. She laughed and said Rambo is make-believe, a movie name. He said it's Swedish. She said he isn't Swedish. He said the name is Swedish. Where did she think it came from? It's a real name. "Right," she said. "Like Rocky," she said, laughing. "Look it up on the Internet," he said. "It's a real name," he said, and he didn't like that he had to explain his name. This was two days ago, and he didn't hold it against her, but he was aware of it. He forgave her because despite what the world says, she suffers unbearably.

"Knowing my name will be an echo," he says. "It makes no difference, not in the least. Just a sound already said."

"I would never say it." Panic.

Her lips and nails are blue, and she shivers uncontrollably. She stares. He tells her to drink more, and she doesn't dare refuse him. The slightest act of insubordination, and she knows what happens. Even one small scream, and she knows what happens. He sits calmly on the lid of the toilet, his legs splayed so she can see his excitement, and fear it. She doesn't beg anymore or tell him to *have his way with her,* if that's the reason she's his hostage. She doesn't say this anymore because she knows what happens when she insults him and implies that if he had a *way* it would be *with her.* Meaning she wouldn't give it willingly and want it.

"You realize I asked you nicely," he says.

"I don't know." Teeth chattering.

"You do know. I asked you to thank me. That's all I asked, and I was nice to you. I asked you nicely, then you had to do this," he says. "You had to make me do this. You see"—he gets up and watches his nakedness in the mirror over the smooth marble sink—"your suffering makes me do this," his nakedness in the mirror says. "And I don't want to do this. So you've hurt me. Do you understand you've critically hurt me by making me do this?" his nakedness in the mirror says.

She says she understands, and her eyes scatter like flying shards of glass as he opens the toolbox, and her scattered gaze fixes on the box cutters and knives and fine-tooth saws. He lifts out a small bag of sand and sets it on the edge of the sink. He pulls out ampules of lavender glue and sets them down, too.

"I'll do anything you want. Give you anything you want." She has said this repeatedly.

He has ordered her not to say it again. But she just did.

His hands dip into the water, and the coldness of the water bites him, and he grabs her ankles and lifts her up. He holds her up by her cold, tan legs with their cold, white feet and feels her terror in her panicking muscles as he holds her cold ankles tight. He holds her a little longer than last time, and she struggles and flails and thrashes violently, cold water splashing loudly. He lets go. She gasps and coughs and makes strangling cries. She doesn't complain. She's learned not to complain—it took a while, but she's learned it. She's learned all of this is for her own good and is grateful for a sacrifice that will change his life—not hers, but his—in a way that isn't good. Wasn't good. Can never be good. She should be grateful for his gift.

He picks up the trash bag he filled with ice from the ice maker in the bar and pours the last of it in the tub and she looks at him, tears running down her face. Grief. The dark edges of it showing.

"We used to hang them from the ceiling over there," he says. "Kick them in the sides of their knees, over and over. Over there. All of us coming into the small room and kicking the sides of their knees. It's excruciatingly painful and, of course, crippling, and, of course, some of them died. That's nothing compared to other things I saw over there. I didn't work in that prison, you see. But I didn't need to, because there was plenty of that type of behavior to go around. What people don't understand is it wasn't stupid to film any of it. To photograph it. It was inevitable. You have to. If you don't, it's as if it never happened. So people take pictures. They show them to others. It only takes one. One person to see it. Then the whole world does."

She glances at the camera on the marble-top table against the stucco wall.

"They deserved it anyway, didn't they?" he says. "They forced us to be something we weren't, so whose fault was it? Not ours."

She nods. She shivers, and her teeth chatter.

"I didn't always participate," he says. "I did watch. At first it was difficult, perhaps traumatic. I was against it, but the things they did to us. And because of what they did, we were forced to do things back, so it was their fault that they forced us, and I know you see that."

She nods and cries and shakes.

"The roadside bombs. Kidnapping. Much more than you hear about," he says. "You get used to it. Just like you're getting used to the cold water, aren't you?"

She isn't used to it, only numb and on her way to hypothermia. By now her head pounds and her heart feels as if it will explode. He hands her the vodka, and she drinks.

"I'm going to open the window," he says. "So you can hear Bernini's fountain. I've heard it much of my life. The night's perfect. You should see the stars." He opens the window and looks at the night, the stars, the fountain of four rivers, and the piazza. Empty at this hour. "You won't scream," he says.

She shakes her head and her chest heaves and she shivers uncontrollably.

"You're thinking about your friends. I know that. Certainly they're thinking about you. That's too bad. And they aren't here. They aren't anywhere to be seen." He looks at the deserted piazza again and shrugs. "Why would they be here now? They've left. Long ago."

Her nose runs and tears spill and she shakes. The energy in her eyes—it's not what it was when he met her, and he resents her for ruining who she was to him. Earlier, much earlier, he spoke Italian to her because it changed him into the stranger he needed to be. Now he speaks English because it no longer makes a difference. She glances at his excitement. Her glances at his excitement bounce against it like a moth against a lamp. He feels her there. She fears what's there. But not as much as she fears everything else—the water, the tools, the sand, the glue. She doesn't comprehend the thick black belt coiled on the very old tile floor, and she should fear it most of all.

He picks it up and tells her it's a primitive urge to beat people who can't defend themselves. Why? She doesn't answer. Why? She stares at him in terror, and the light in her eyes is dull but crazed, like a mirror shattering right in front of him. He tells her to stand, and she does, shakily, her knees almost collapsing. She stands in the frigid water and he turns off the spout. Her body reminds him of a bow with a taut string because she's flexible and powerful. Water trickles down her skin as she stands before him.

"Turn away from me," he says. "Don't worry. I'm not going to beat you with the belt. I don't do that."

Water quietly laps in the tub as she turns away from him, facing old, cracked stucco and a closed shutter.

"Now I need you to kneel in the water," he says. "And look at the wall. Don't look at me."

She kneels, facing the wall, and he picks up the belt and slides the end of it through the buckle.

Chapter 1

Ten days later. April 27, 2007. A Friday afternoon.

Inside the virtual-reality theater are twelve of Italy's most powerful law enforcers and politicians, whose names, in the main, forensic pathologist Kay Scarpetta can't keep straight. The only non-Italians are herself and forensic psychologist Benton Wesley, both consultants for International Investigative Response (IIR), a special branch of the European Network of Forensic Science Institutes (ENFSI). The Italian government is in a very delicate position.

Nine days ago, American tennis star Drew

Martin was murdered while on vacation, her nude, mutilated body found near Piazza Navona, in the heart of Rome's historic district. The case is an international sensation, details about the sixteen-year-old's life and death replayed nonstop on television, the crawls at the bottom of the screen doing just that—crawling by slowly and tenaciously, repeating the same details the anchors and experts are saying.

"So, Dr. Scarpetta, let's clarify, because there seems to be much confusion. According to you, she was dead by two or three o'clock that afternoon," says Captain Ottorino Poma, a medico legale in the Arma dei Carabinieri, the military police heading the investigation.

"That's not according to me," she says, her patience beginning to fray. "That's according to you."

He frowns in the low lighting. "I was so sure it was you, just minutes ago, talking about her stomach contents and alcohol level. And the fact they indicate she was dead within hours of when she was seen last by her friends."

"I didn't say she was dead by two or three o'clock. I believe it is you who continues to say that, Captain Poma."

At a young age he already has a wide-spread reputation, and not an entirely good one. When Scarpetta first met him two years ago in the Hague at the ENFSI's annual meeting, he was derisively dubbed the Designer Doctor and described as extraordinarily conceited and argumentative. He is handsome—magnificent, really—with a taste for beautiful women and dazzling clothes, and today he is wearing a uniform of midnight blue with broad red stripes and bright silver embellishments, and polished black leather boots. When he swept into the theater this morning, he was wearing a red-lined cape.

He sits directly in front of Scarpetta, front row center, and rarely takes his eyes off her. On his right is Benton Wesley, who is silent most of the time. Everyone is masked by stereoscopic glasses that are synchronized with the Crime Scene Analysis System, a brilliant innovation that has made the Polizia Scientifica Italiana's Unità per l'Analisi del Crimine Violento the envy of law enforcement agencies worldwide.

"I suppose we need to go through this again so you completely understand my position," Scarpetta says to Captain Poma, who now rests his chin on his hand as if he is having an intimate conversation with her over a glass of wine. "Had she been killed at two or three o'clock that afternoon, then when her body was found at approximately eight-thirty the following morning, she would have been dead at least seventeen hours. Her livor mortis, rigor mortis, and algor mortis are inconsistent with that."

She uses a laser pointer to direct attention to the three-dimensional muddy construction site projected on the wall-size screen. It's as if they are standing in the middle of the scene, staring at Drew Martin's mauled, dead body and the litter and earth-moving equipment around it. The red dot of the laser moves along the left shoulder, the left buttock, the left leg and its bare foot. The right buttock is gone, as is a portion of her right thigh, as if she had been attacked by a shark.

"Her lividity . . ." Scarpetta starts to say.

"Once again I apologize. My English isn't so good as yours. I'm not sure of this word," Captain Poma says.

"I've used it before."

"I wasn't sure of it then."

Laughter. Other than the translator, Scarpetta is the only woman present. She and the translator don't find the captain amusing, but the men do. Except Benton, who hasn't smiled once this day.

"Do you know the Italian for this word?" Captain Poma asks Scarpetta.

"How about the language of ancient Rome?" Scarpetta says. "Latin. Since most medical terminology is rooted in Latin." She doesn't say it rudely, but is no-nonsense because she's well aware that his English becomes awkward only when it suits him.

His 3-D glasses stare at her, reminding her of Zorro. "Italian, please," he says to her. "I never was so good in Latin."

"I'll give you both. In Italian, 'livid' is *livido,* which means bruised. 'Mortis' is *morte,* or death. Livor mortis suggests an appearance of bruising that occurs after death."

"It's helpful when you speak Italian," he says. "And you do it so well."

She doesn't intend to do it here, although she speaks enough Italian to get by. She prefers English during these professional discussions because nuances are tricky, and the translator intercepts every word anyway. This difficulty with language, along with political pressure, stress, and Captain Poma's relentless and enigmatic antics, add to what already is rather much a disaster that has nothing to do with any of these things. But rather, the killer in this case defies precedents and the usual profiles. He confounds them. Even the science has become a maddening source of debate—it seems to defy them, lie to them, forcing Scarpetta to remind herself and everyone else that science never tells untruths. It doesn't make mistakes. It doesn't deliberately lead them astray or taunt them.

This is lost on Captain Poma. Or perhaps he pretends. Perhaps he isn't serious when he refers to Drew's dead body as uncooperative and argumentative, as if he has a relationship with it and they are squabbling. He asserts that her postmortem changes may say one thing, and her blood alcohol and stomach contents say another, but contrary to what Scarpetta believes, food and drink should always be trusted. He is serious, at least about that.

"What Drew ate and drank is revealing of truth." He repeats what he said in his impassioned opening statement earlier today.

"Revealing of a truth, yes. But not *your* truth," Scarpetta replies, in a tone more polite than what she says. "Your truth is a misinterpretation."

"I think we've been over this," Benton says from the shadows of the front row. "I think Dr. Scarpetta has made herself perfectly clear."

Captain Poma's 3-D glasses—and rows of other 3-D glasses—remain fixed on her. "I regret if I bore you with my reexamination, Dr. Wesley, but we need to find sense in this. So please indulge me. April seventeenth, Drew ate very bad lasagna and drank four glasses of very bad Chianti between eleven-thirty and twelve-thirty at a tourist trattoria near the Spanish Steps. She paid the bill and left, then at the Piazza di Spagna parted company with her two friends, who she promised to rejoin at Piazza Navona within the hour. She never appeared. That much we know to be true. What remains a mystery is everything else." His thick-framed glasses look at Scarpetta, then he turns in his seat and speaks to the rows behind him. "Partly because our esteemed colleague from the United States now says she's convinced Drew didn't die shortly after lunch or even that same day."

"I've been saying this all along. Once again, I'll explain why. Since it seems you are confused," Scarpetta says.

"We need to move on," Benton says.

But they can't move on. Captain Poma is so respected by the Italians, is such a celebrity, he can do whatever he wants. In the press he is called the Sherlock Holmes of Rome, even though he is a physician, not a detective. Everyone, including the Comandante Generale of the Carabinieri, who sits in a back corner and listens more than he speaks, seems to have forgotten that.

"Under normal circumstances," Scarpetta says, "Drew's food would have been fully digested several hours after she ate lunch, and her alcohol level certainly wouldn't have been as high as the point-two determined by toxicological testing. So, yes, Captain Poma, her stomach contents and toxicology suggest she died shortly after lunch. But her livor mortis and rigor mortis suggest—rather emphatically, let me add—that she died possibly twelve to fifteen hours after she ate lunch at the trattoria, and these postmortem artifacts are the ones we should pay the most attention to."

"So here we are. Back to lividity." He sighs. "This word I have so much trouble with. Please explain it again, since I seem to have so much trouble with what you call post-mortem *artifacts*. As if we are archaeologists digging up ruins." Captain Poma's chin rests on his hand again.

"Lividity, livor mortis, postmortem hypostasis, all the same thing. When you die, your circulation quits and the blood begins to accumulate in the small vessels due to gravity, rather much like sediment settling in a sunken ship." She feels Benton's 3-D glasses looking at her. She dares not look at him. He isn't himself.

"Continue, please." Captain Poma underlines something several times on his legal pad.

"If the body remains in a certain position long enough after death, the blood will settle accordingly—a postmortem artifact we call livor mortis," Scarpetta explains. "Eventually, livor mortis becomes fixed, or set, turning that area of the body purplish-red, with patterns of blanching from surfaces pressing against it or constricting it, such as tight clothing. Can we see the autopsy photograph, please?" She checks a list on the podium. "Number twenty-one."

The wall fills with Drew's body on a steel table in the morgue at Tor Vergata University.

She is facedown. Scarpetta moves the laser's red dot over the back, over the purplish-red areas and blanching caused by lividity. The shocking wounds that look like dark red craters she has yet to address.

"Now, if you'll put the scene up, please. The one that shows her being placed into the body bag," she says.

The three-dimensional photograph of the construction site fills the wall again, but this time there are investigators in white Tyvek suits, gloves, and shoe covers lifting Drew's limp, naked body into a sheet-lined black pouch on top of a stretcher. Around them, other investigators hold up additional sheets to block the view from the curious and the paparazzi at the perimeter of the scene.

"Compare this to the photograph you just saw. By the time she was autopsied some eight hours after she was found, her lividity was almost completely set," Scarpetta says. "But here at the scene, it's apparent that lividity was in its early stages." The red dot moves over pinkish areas on Drew's back. "Rigor was in its early stages as well."

"You rule out the early onset of rigor mortis due to a cadervic spasm? For example, if she strenuously exerted herself right before death? Maybe she struggled with him? Since you've not mentioned this phenomenon so far?" Captain Poma underlines something on his legal pad.

"There's no reason to talk about a cadervic spasm," Scarpetta says. *Why don't you throw in the kitchen sink?* she's tempted to ask. "Whether she strenuously exerted herself or not," she says, "she wasn't fully rigorous when she was found, so she didn't have a cadervic spasm. . . ."

"Unless rigor came and went."

"Impossible, since it became fully fixed in the morgue. Rigor doesn't come and go and then come again."

The translator suppresses a smile as she relays this in Italian, and several people laugh.

"You can see from this"—Scarpetta points the laser at Drew's body being lifted onto the stretcher—"her muscles certainly aren't stiff. They're quite flexible. I estimate she'd been dead less than six hours when she was found, possibly considerably less."

"You're a world expert. How can you be so vague?"

"Because we don't know where she'd been, what temperatures or conditions she was exposed to before she was left in the construction site. Body temperature, rigor mortis, livor mortis can vary greatly from case to case and individual to individual."

"Based on the condition of the body, are you saying it's *impossible* she was murdered soon after she had lunch with her friends? Perhaps while she was walking alone to Piazza Navona to join them?"

"I don't believe that's what happened."

"Then once again, please. How do you explain her undigested food and point-two alcohol level? They imply she died soon after she ate lunch with her friends—not some fifteen, sixteen hours later."

"It's possible not long after she left her friends, she resumed drinking alcohol and was so terrified and stressed, her digestion quit."

"What? Now you're suggesting she spent time with her killer, possibly as much as ten, twelve, fifteen hours with him—that she was drinking with him?"

"He might have forced her to drink, to keep her impaired and easier to control. As in drugging somebody."

"So he forced her to drink alcohol, perhaps all afternoon, all night, and into the

early morning, and she was so frightened
her food didn't digest? That's what you're offering us as a plausible explanation?"

"I've seen it before," Scarpetta says.

The animated construction site after dark.

Surrounding shops, pizzerias, and ris-
torantes are lit up and crowded. Cars and motor scooters are parked on the sides of the
streets, on the sidewalks. The rumble of traffic
and the sounds of footsteps and voices fill the
theater.

Suddenly, the lighted windows go dark.
Then silence.

The sound of a car, and the shape of it. A
four-door black Lancia parks at the corner of
Via di Pasquino and Via dell'Anima. The driver's door opens and an animated man gets
out. He is dressed in gray. His face has no
features and, like his hands, is gray, from
which everyone in the theater is to infer that
the killer hasn't been assigned an age, race,
or any physical characteristics. For the sake
of simplicity, the killer is referred to as male.
The gray man opens the trunk and lifts out a
body wrapped in a blue fabric with a pattern
that includes the colors red, gold, and green.

"The sheet wrapped around her is based

on silk fibers collected from the body and in the mud under it," Captain Poma says.

Benton Wesley says, "Fibers found all over the body. Including in the hair, on the hands, the feet. Certainly an abundance of them were adhering to her wounds. From this we can conclude she was completely wrapped from head to toe. So, yes, obviously we have to consider a large piece of colorful silk fabric. Perhaps a sheet, perhaps a curtain . . ."

"What's your point?"

"I have two of them: We shouldn't assume it was a sheet, because we shouldn't assume anything. Also, it's possible he wrapped her in something that was indigenous to where he lives or works, or where he held her hostage."

"Yes, yes." Captain Poma's glasses remain fixed on the scene filling the wall. "And we know there are carpet fibers which are also consistent with carpet fibers in the trunk of a 2005 Lancia, which is consistent also with what was described driving away from that area at approximately six a.m. The witness I mentioned. A woman in a nearby apartment got up to see about her cat because it was—what is the word . . . ?"

"Yowling? Meowing?" the translator says.

"She got up because of her cat yowling and happened to look out her widow to see a dark luxury sedan driving away from the construction site as if in no hurry. She said it turned right on dell'Anima, a one-way street. Continue, please."

The animation resumes. The gray man lifts the colorfully wrapped body out of the car trunk and carries it to a nearby aluminum catwalk that is barricaded only by a rope, which he steps over. He carries the body down a wooden plank that leads into the site. He places the body to one side of the plank, in the mud, and squats in the dark and quickly unwraps a figure that turns into the dead body of Drew Martin. This is no animation, but a three-dimensional photograph. One can see her clearly—her famous face, the savage wounds on her slender, athletic, naked body. The gray man balls up the colorful wrapping and returns to his car. He drives off at a normal rate of speed.

"We believe he did carry the body instead of dragging it," Captain Poma says. "Because these fibers were only on the body and on the soil beneath it. There were no others, and although this isn't proof, it certainly does indicate he didn't drag her. Let me remind you, this scene has been mapped with the laser mapping system, and the perspective you're seeing and the position of objects and the body are completely precise. Obviously, only people or objects that weren't video-taped or photographed—such as the killer and his car—are animated."

"How heavy was she?" the minister of the interior asks from the back row.

Scarpetta replies that Drew Martin weighed one hundred and thirty pounds, then converts that to kilograms. "He had to be reasonably strong," she adds.

Animation resumes. Silence and the construction site in early-morning light. The sound of rain. Windows in the area remain dark, the businesses closed. No traffic. Then the whine of a motorcycle. Getting louder. A red Ducati appears on Via di Pasquino, the rider an animated figure in a rain slicker and a full-face helmet. He turns right on dell'Anima and suddenly stops, and the bike drops to the pavement with a loud thud, and the engine quits. The startled rider steps over his bike and hesitantly steps onto the aluminum catwalk, his boots loud on metal. The dead body below him in the mud looks more shocking, more gruesome, because it's a three-dimensional photograph juxtaposed to the motorcyclist's rather stilted animation.

"It's now almost half past eight, the weather, as you can see, overcast and raining," Captain Poma says. "Please move ahead to Professor Fiorani at the scene. That would be image fourteen. And now Dr. Scarpetta, you can, if you will, examine the body at the scene with the good professor, who isn't here this afternoon, I'm sorry to say, because, can you guess? He's at the Vatican. A cardinal died."

Benton stares at the screen behind Scarpetta, and it knots her stomach that he is so unhappy and won't look at her.

New images—video recordings in 3-D—fill the screen. Blue lights strobing. Police cars and a midnight-blue Carabinieri crime scene van. More Carabinieri with machine guns guarding the perimeter of the construction site. Plainclothes investigators inside the cordoned-off area, collecting evidence, taking photographs. The sounds of camera shutters and low voices and crowds on the streets. A police helicopter thud-thuds overhead. The professor—the most esteemed forensic pathologist in Rome—is covered in white Tyvek that is muddy. Close on, his point of view: Drew's body. It's so real in the stereoscopic glasses, it's bizarre. Scarpetta feels as if she can touch Drew's flesh and her gaping dark red wounds that are smeared with mud and glistening wet from the rain. Her long blond hair is wet and clings to her face. Her eyes are tightly shut and bulging beneath the lids.

"Dr. Scarpetta," Captain Poma says. "You may examine her, please. Tell us what you see. You have, of course, studied Professor Fiorani's report, but as you look at the body itself in three-dimension and are placed at the scene with it, please give us your own opinion. We won't criticize you if you disagree with Professor Fiorani's findings."

Who's considered as infallible as the Pope he embalmed several years earlier.

The laser's red dot moves where Scarpetta points, and she says, "The position of the body. On the left side, hands folded under the chin, legs slightly bent. A position I believe is deliberate. Dr. Wesley?" She looks at Benton's thick glasses looking past her, at the screen. "This is a good time for you to comment."

"Deliberate. The body was positioned by the killer."

"As if she's praying, perhaps?" says the chief of the state police.

"What was her religion?" asks the deputy director of the Criminal Police National Directorate.

A peppering of questions and conjectures from the barely lit theater.

"Roman Catholic."

"She didn't practice it, I understand."

"Not much."

"Perhaps some religious connection?"

"Yes, I wonder that, too. The construction site is so close to Sant'Agnese in Agone."

Captain Poma explains, "For those unfamiliar"—he looks at Benton—"Saint Agnes was a martyr tortured and murdered at the age of twelve because she wouldn't marry a pagan like me."

Peals of laughter. A discussion about the murder having a religious significance. But Benton says no.

"There's sexual degradation," he says. "She's displayed, and she's nude and dumped in plain view in the very area where she was supposed to meet her friends. The killer wanted her found, he wanted to shock people. Religion isn't the overriding motive. Sexual excitement is."

"Yet we found no evidence of rape." This said by the head of the Carabinieri forensic labs.

He goes on to say through the translator that it appears the killer left no seminal fluid, no blood, no saliva, unless it was washed away by rain. But DNA from two different sources was collected from under her fingernails. The profiles have proved useless so far because, unfortunately, he explains, the Italian government doesn't allow DNA samples to be taken from criminals, as it's considered a violation of their human rights. The only profiles that can be entered into an Italian database at this time, he says, are those obtained from evidence, not from individuals.

"So there's no database to search in Italy," Captain Poma adds. "And the most we can say right now is the DNA collected from under Drew's fingernails doesn't match the DNA of any individual in any database outside Italy, including the United States."

"I believe you've ascertained that the sources of DNA collected from under her nails are males of European descent—in other words, Caucasian," Benton says.

"Yes," the lab director says.

"Dr. Scarpetta?" Captain Poma says. "Please continue."

"May I have autopsy photo number twenty-six, please?" she says. "A posterior view during the external examination. Close-up of the wounds."

They fill the screen. Two dark red craters with jagged edges. She points the laser, and the red dot moves over the massive wound where the right buttock used to be, then to a second area of flesh that has been excised from the back of the right thigh.

"Inflicted by a sharp cutting instrument, possibly with a serrated blade, that sawed through muscle and superficially cut the bone," she says. "Inflicted postmortem, based on the absence of tissue response to the injuries. In other words, the wounds are yellowish."

"Postmortem mutilation rules out torture, at least torture by cutting," Benton adds.

"Then what explanation? If not torture?" Captain Poma asks him, both men staring at each other like two animals that are natural enemies. "Why else would a person inflict such sadistic, and, I would suggest, disfiguring, wounds on another human being? Tell us, Dr. Wesley, in all your experiences have you seen anything like this before, perhaps in other cases? Especially when you were such a famous profiler with the FBI?"

"No," Benton says curtly, and any reference to his former career with the FBI is a calculated insult. "I've seen mutilation. But I've never seen anything quite like this. Especially what he did to her eyes."

He removed them and filled the sockets with sand. Afterward, he glued her eyelids shut.

Scarpetta points the laser and describes this, and Benton is chilled again. Everything about this case chills him, unnerves and fascinates him. What is the symbolism? It's not that he's unfamiliar with the gouging out of eyes. But what Captain Poma suggests is far-fetched.

"The ancient Greek combat sport pankration? Perhaps you've heard of it," Captain Poma says to the theater. "In pankration, one uses any means possible to defeat his enemy. It was common to gouge out the eyes and kill the person by stabbing or strangulation. Drew's eyes were gouged out, and she was strangled."

The general of the Carabinieri asks Benton, through the translator, "Then maybe there's a connection to pankration? That the killer had this in his mind when he removed her eyes and strangled her?"

"I don't think so," Benton says.

"Then what explanation?" the general asks, and like Captain Poma, he wears a splendid uniform but with more silver and ornamentation around the cuffs and high collar.

"A more interior one. A more personal one," Benton says.

"From the news, perhaps," the general says. "Torture. The Death Squads in Iraq that pull out teeth and gouge out eyes."

"I can only suppose that what this killer did is a manifestation of his own psyche. In other words, I don't believe what he did to her is an allusion to anything even remotely obvious. Through her wounds, we get a glimpse into his inner world," Benton says.

"This is speculation," Captain Poma says.

"It's a psychological insight based on many years of working violent crimes," Benton replies.

"But it's your intuition."

"We ignore intuition at our peril," Benton says.

"May we have the autopsy picture that shows her anteriorly during the external examination?" Scarpetta says. "A close-up of her neck." She checks the list on the podium. "Number twenty."

A three-dimensional image fills the screen: Drew's body on a stainless-steel autopsy table, her skin and hair wet from washing.

"If you look here"—Scarpetta points the laser at the neck—"you notice a horizontal ligature mark." The dot moves along the front of the neck. Before she can continue, she's interrupted by Rome's head of tourism.

"Afterwards, he removed her eyes. After death," he says. "Versus while she was alive. This is important."

"Yes," Scarpetta replies. "Reports I've reviewed indicate the only premortem injuries are contusions on the ankles and contusions caused by strangulation. The photograph of her dissected neck, please? Number thirty-eight."

She waits, and images fill the screen. On a cutting board, the larynx and soft tissue with areas of hemorrhage. The tongue.

Scarpetta points out, "Contusions to the soft tissue, the underlying muscles, and fractured hyoid due to strangulation clearly indicate damage inflicted while she was still alive."

"Petechiae of her eyes?"

"We don't know if there were conjunctival petechiae," Scarpetta says. "Her eyes are absent. But reports do indicate some pe-techiae of eyelids and face."

"What he did to her eyes? You're familiar with this from anything else in your experi-ences?"

"I've seen victims whose eyes were gouged out. But I've never seen or heard of a killer filling eye sockets with sand and then sealing the eyelids shut with—in this instance—an adhesive that according to your report is a cyanoacrylate."

"Superglue," Captain Poma says.

"I'm keenly interested in the sand," she says. "It doesn't appear to be indigenous to the area. More important, scanning electron microscopy with EDX found traces of what appears to be gunshot residue. Lead, anti-mony, and barium."

"Certainly it isn't from the local beaches," Captain Poma says. "Unless many people shoot each other and we don't know it."

Laughter.

"Sand from Ostia would have basalt in it," Scarpetta says. "Other components from volcanic activity. I believe all of you have a copy of the spectral fingerprint of the sand recovered from the body and a spectral fingerprint of sand from a beach area in Ostia."

The sounds of paper rustling in the theater. Small flashlights click on.

"Both analyzed with Raman spectroscopy, using an eight-point-milliwatt red laser. As you can see, sand from the local beaches of Ostia and sand found in Drew Martin's eye sockets have very different spectral fingerprints. With the scanning electron microscope, we can see the sand's morphology, and backscattered electron imaging shows us the GSR particles we're talking about."

"The beaches of Ostia are very popular with tourists," Captain Poma says. "But not so much this time of year. People from here and the tourists usually wait until it's warmer. Late May, even June. Then many people from Rome especially crowd them, since the drive is maybe thirty, maybe forty minutes. It's not for me," as if anybody asked his personal feelings about the beaches of Ostia. "I find the black sand of the beaches ugly, and I would never go in the water."

"I think what's important here is where is

the sand from, which seems to be a mystery," Benton says, and it's late afternoon now and everyone is getting restless. "And why sand at all? The choice of sand—this specific sand—means something to the killer, and it may tell us where Drew was murdered, or perhaps where her killer is from or spends time."

"Yes, yes," Captain Poma says with a hint of impatience. "And the eyes and very terrible wounds mean something to the killer. And thankfully, these details aren't known to the public. We've managed to keep them away from journalists. So if there is another similar murder, we will know it isn't a copy."

Chapter 2

The three of them sit in a candlelit corner of Tullio, a popular trattoria with a travertine facade, near the theaters, and an easy walk from the Spanish Steps.

Candlelit tables are covered in pale gold cloths, and the dark-paneled wall behind them is filled with bottles of wine. Other walls are hung with watercolors of rustic Italian scenes. It's quiet here except for a table of drunk Americans. They're oblivious and pre-occupied, as is the waiter in his beige jacket and black tie. No one has any idea what Benton, Scarpetta, and Captain Poma are discussing. If anyone comes close enough to hear, they change their conversation to harmless topics and tuck photographs and reports back into folders.

Scarpetta sips a 1996 Biondi Santi Brunello that is very expensive but not what she would have picked had she been asked, and usually she is asked. She returns her glass to the table without removing her eyes from the photograph beside her simple Parma ham and melon, which she will follow with grilled sea bass, then beans in olive oil. Maybe raspberries for dessert, unless Benton's deteriorating demeanor takes away her appetite. And it might.

"At the risk of sounding simple," she is quietly saying, "I keep thinking there's something important we're missing." Her index finger taps a scene photograph of Drew Martin.

"So now you don't complain about going over something again and again," Captain Poma says, openly flirtatious now. "See? Good food and wine. They make us smarter." He taps his head, mimicking Scarpetta tapping the photograph.

She is pensive, the way she gets when she leaves the room without going anywhere.

"Something so obvious we're completely

blind to it, everyone's been blind to it," she continues. "Often we don't see something because—as they say—it's in plain view. What is it? What is she saying to us?"

"Fine. Let's look for what's in plain view," says Benton, and rarely has she seen him so openly hostile and withdrawn. He doesn't hide his disdain of Captain Poma, now dressed in perfect pinstripes. His gold cuff links engraved with the crest of the Carabinieri flash when they catch the light of the candle.

"Yes, in plain view. Every inch of her exposed flesh—before anybody touched it. We should study it in that condition. Untouched. Exactly as he left it," Captain Poma says, his eyes on Scarpetta. "How he left it is a story, is it not? But before I forget, to our last time together in Rome. At least for now. We should drink a toast to that."

It doesn't seem right to raise their glasses with the dead young woman watching, her naked, savaged body right there on the table, in a sense.

"And a toast to the FBI," says Captain Poma. "To their determination to turn this into an act of terrorism. The ultimate soft target—an American tennis star."

"It's a waste of time to even allude to such a thing," Benton says, and he picks up his glass, not to toast but to drink.

"Then tell your government to stop suggesting it," Captain Poma says. "There, I will say this bluntly since we're alone. Your government is spreading this propaganda from behind the scenes, and the reason we didn't discuss this earlier is because the Italians don't believe anything so ridiculous. No terrorist is responsible. The FBI to say such a thing? It's stupid."

"The FBI isn't sitting here. We are. And we aren't the FBI, and I'm weary of your references to the FBI," Benton replies.

"But you were FBI most of your career. Until you quit and disappeared from sight as if you were dead. For some reason."

"If this were an act of terrorism, someone would have claimed responsibility by now," Benton says. "I'd rather you don't mention the FBI or my personal history again."

"An insatiable appetite for publicity and your country's current need to scare the hell out of everybody and rule the world." Captain Poma refills their wineglasses. "Your Bureau of Investigation interviewing witnesses here in Rome, stepping all over Interpol, and they're supposed to work with Interpol, have their own representatives there. And they fly in these idiots from Washington who don't know us, much less how to work a complex homicide—"

Benton interrupts him. "You should know by now, Captain Poma, that politics and jurisdictional infighting are the nature of the beast."

"I wish you would call me Otto. As my friends do." He moves his chair closer to Scarpetta, and with him comes the scent of his cologne, then he moves the candle. He glances in disgust at the table of obtuse, hard-drinking Americans and says, "You know, we try to like you."

"Don't try," Benton says. "No one else does."

"I've never understood why you Americans are so loud."

"Because we don't listen," Scarpetta says. "That's why we have George Bush."

Captain Poma picks up the photograph near her plate, studies it as if he's never seen it before. "I'm looking at what's in plain view," he says. "And all I see is the obvious."

Benton stares at the two of them sitting so close, his handsome face like granite.

"It's better to assume there's no such thing as *obvious*. It's a word," Scarpetta says, sliding more photographs out of an envelope. "A reference to one's personal perceptions. And mine may be different from yours."

"I believe you demonstrated that quite exhaustively at state police headquarters," the captain says, while Benton stares.

She looks at Benton, a lingering look that communicates her awareness of his behavior and how unnecessary it is. He has no reason to be jealous. She has done nothing to encourage Captain Poma's flirtations.

"In plain view. Well, then. Why don't we start with her toes," Benton says, barely touching his buffalo mozzarella and already on his third glass of wine.

"That's actually a good idea." Scarpetta studies photographs of Drew. She studies a close-up of Drew's bare toes. "Neatly manicured. Nails painted recently, consistent with her getting a pedicure before she left New York." She repeats what they know.

"Does that matter?" Captain Poma studies a photograph, leaning so close to Scarpetta that his arm is touching hers, and she feels his heat and smells his scent. "I don't think so. I think it matters more what she was wearing. Black jeans, a white silk shirt, a black silk–lined black leather jacket. Also, black panties and a black bra." He pauses. "It's curious her body didn't have any fibers from these, just the fibers from the sheet."

"We don't know for a fact it was a sheet," Benton reminds him sharply.

"Also, her clothing, her watch, necklace, leather bracelets, and earrings haven't been found. So the killer took these things," the captain says to Scarpetta. "For what reason? Perhaps souvenirs. But we will talk about her pedicure, since you think it important. Drew went to a spa on Central Park South right after she got to New York. We have details of this appointment, charged to Drew's credit card—her father's credit card, actually. From what I'm told, he was most indulgent with her."

"I think it's been well established she was spoiled," Benton says.

"I think we should be careful using words like that," Scarpetta says. "She earned what she had, is the one who practiced six hours a day, trained so hard—had just won the *Family Circle* Cup and was expected to win other . . ."

"That's where you live," Captain Poma says to her. "Charleston, South Carolina. Where the *Family Circle* Cup is played. Odd, isn't it. That very night she flew to New York. And from there to here. To this." He indicates the photographs.

"What I'm saying is money can't buy championship titles, and spoiled people usually don't work as passionately as she did," Scarpetta says.

Benton says, "Her father spoiled her but couldn't be bothered with parenting. Same with her mother."

"Yes, yes," Captain Poma agrees. "What parents permit a sixteen-year-old to travel abroad with two eighteen-year-old friends? Especially if she'd been acting moody. Up and down."

"When your child becomes more difficult, it gets easier to give in. Not resist," Scarpetta says, thinking about her niece, Lucy. When Lucy was a child, God, their battles. "What about her coach? Do we know anything about that relationship?"

"Gianni Lupano. I spoke to him, and he said he was aware she was coming here and wasn't happy about it because of major tournaments in the next few months, such as

Wimbledon. He wasn't helpful and seemed angry with her."

"And the Italian Open here in Rome next month," Scarpetta points out, finding it unusual the captain didn't mention it.

"Of course. She should train, not run off with friends. I don't watch tennis."

"Where was he when she was murdered?" Scarpetta asks.

"New York. We've checked with the hotel where he said he stayed, and he was registered at that time. He also commented she had been moody. Down one day, up the next. Very stubborn and difficult and unpredictable. He wasn't sure how much longer he could work with her. Said he had better things to do than put up with her behavior."

"I'd like to know if mood disorders run in her family," Benton says. "I don't suppose you bothered to ask."

"I didn't. I'm sorry I wasn't astute enough to think of it."

"It would be extremely useful to know if she had a psychiatric history her family's been secretive about."

"It's well known she'd struggled with an eating disorder," Scarpetta says. "She's talked openly about it."

"No mention of a mood disorder? Nothing from her parents?" Benton continues his cool interrogation of the captain.

"Nothing more than her ups and downs. Typical teenager."

"Do you have children?" Benton reaches for his wine.

"Not that I know of."

"A trigger," Scarpetta says. "Something was going on with Drew that no one's telling us. Perhaps what's in plain view? Her behavior's in plain view. Her drinking's in plain view. Why? Did something happen?"

"The tournament in Charleston," Captain Poma says to Scarpetta. "Where you have your private practice. What is it they call it? The *Lowcountry*? What is *Lowcountry*, exactly?" He slowly swirls his wine, his eyes on her.

"Almost sea level, literally low country."

"And your local police have no interest in this case? Since she played a tournament there just maybe two days before she was murdered?"

"Curious, I'm sure—" Scarpetta starts to say.

"Her murder has nothing to do with the

Charleston police," Benton interrupts. "They have no jurisdiction."

Scarpetta gives him a look, and the captain watches both of them. He's been watching their tense interaction all day.

"No jurisdiction hasn't stopped anybody from showing up and flashing their badges," Captain Poma says.

"If you're alluding to the FBI again, you've made your point," says Benton. "If you're alluding to my being former FBI again, you've definitely made your point. If you're alluding to Dr. Scarpetta and me—we were invited by you. We didn't just show up, Otto. Since you've asked us to call you that."

"Is it me or is this not perfect?" The captain holds up his glass of wine as if it is a flawed diamond.

Benton picked the wine. Scarpetta knows more about Italian wines than he does, but tonight he finds it necessary to assert his dominance, as if he has just plummeted fifty rungs on the evolutionary ladder. She feels Captain Poma's interest in her as she looks at another photograph, grateful the waiter doesn't seem inclined to come their way. He's busy with the table of loud Americans.

"Close-up of her legs," she says. "Bruising around her ankles."

"Fresh bruises," Captain Poma says. "He grabbed her, maybe."

"Possibly. They aren't from ligatures."

She wishes Captain Poma wouldn't sit so close to her, but there's nowhere else for her to move unless she pushes her chair into the wall. She wishes he wouldn't brush against her when he reaches for photographs.

"Her legs are recently shaven," she goes on. "I would say shaven within twenty-four hours of her death. Barely any stubble. She cared about how she looked even when she was traveling with friends. That might be important. Was she hoping to meet someone?"

"Of course. Three young women looking for young men," Captain Poma says.

Scarpetta watches Benton motion for the waiter to bring another bottle of wine.

She says, "Drew was a celebrity. From what I've been told, she was careful about strangers, didn't like to be bothered."

"Her drinking doesn't make much sense," Benton says.

"Chronic drinking doesn't," Scarpetta says. "You can look at these photographs and see she was extremely fit, lean, superb muscle development. If she'd become a heavy drinker, it would appear it hadn't been going on long, and her recent success would indicate that as well. Again, we have to wonder if something recently had happened. Some emotional upheaval?"

"Depressed. Unstable. Abusing alcohol," Benton says. "All making the person more vulnerable to a predator."

"And that's what I think happened," Captain Poma says. "Randomness. An easy target. Alone at the Piazza di Spagna, where she encountered the gold-painted mime."

The gold-painted mime performed as mimes do, and Drew dropped another coin into his cup, and he performed once more to her delight.

She refused to leave with her friends. The last thing she ever said to them was, "Beneath all that gold paint is a very handsome Italian." The last thing her friends ever said to her was, "Don't assume he's Italian." It was a valid comment, since mimes don't speak.

She told her friends to go on, perhaps visit the shops of Via dei Condotti, and she promised to meet them at the Piazza Navona, at the fountain of rivers, where they waited and waited. They told Captain Poma they tasted free samples of crispy waffles made of eggs and farina and sugar, and giggled as Italian boys shot them with bubble guns, begging them to buy one. Instead, Drew's friends got fake tattoos and encouraged street musicians to play American tunes on reed pipes. They admitted they had gotten somewhat drunk at lunch and were silly.

They described Drew as "a little drunk," and said she was pretty but didn't think she was. She assumed people stared because they recognized her, when often it was because of her good looks. "People who don't watch tennis didn't necessarily recognize her at all," one of the friends told Captain Poma. "She just didn't get how beautiful she was."

Captain Poma talks on through their main course, and Benton, for the most part, drinks, and Scarpetta knows what he thinks—she should avoid the captain's seductions, should somehow move out of range, which in truth would require nothing less than her leaving the table, if not the trattoria. Benton thinks the captain is full of shit, because it defies common sense that a medico legale would interview witnesses as if he is the lead detective in the case, and the captain never mentions the name of anyone else involved in the case. Benton forgets that Captain Poma is the Sherlock Holmes of Rome, or, more likely, Benton can't stomach the thought, he is so jealous.

Scarpetta makes notes as the captain recounts in detail his long interview with the gold-painted mime, who has what appears to be an infallible alibi: He was still performing in his same spot at the base of the Spanish Steps until late afternoon—long after Drew's friends returned to look for her. He claimed to vaguely remember the girl, but he had no idea who she was, thought she was drunk, and then she wandered off. In summary, he paid little attention to her, he said. He is a mime, he said. He acted like a mime at all times, he said. When he's not a mime, he works at night as a doorman at the Hotel Hassler, where Benton and Scarpetta are staying. At the top of the Spanish Steps, the Hassler is one of the finest hotels in Rome, and Benton insisted on staying there in its penthouse for reasons he has yet to explain.

Scarpetta has barely touched her fish. She continues to look at the photographs as if for the first time. She doesn't contribute to

Benton and Captain Poma's argument about why some killers grotesquely display their victims. She adds nothing to Benton's talk of the excitement these sexual predators derive from the headline news or, even better, from lurking nearby or in the crowd, watching the drama of the discovery and the panic that follows. She studies Drew's mauled naked body, on its side, legs together, knees and elbows bent, hands tucked under the chin.

Almost as if she's sleeping.

"I'm not sure it's contempt," she says.

Benton and Captain Poma stop talking.

"If you look at this"—she slides a photograph closer to Benton—"without the usual assumption in mind that this is a sexually degrading display, you might wonder if there's something different. Not about religion, either. Not praying to Saint Agnes. But the way she's positioned." She continues to say things as they come to her. "Something almost tender about it."

"Tender? You're joking," Captain Poma says.

"As in sleeping," Scarpetta says. "It doesn't strike me that she's displayed in a sexually degrading way—victim on her back, her arms, her legs spread, et cetera. The more I look, I don't think so."

"Maybe," Benton says, picking up the photograph.

"But nude for everyone to see," Captain Poma disagrees.

"Take a good look at her position. I could be wrong, of course, just trying to open my mind to other interpretations, putting aside my prejudices, my angry assumptions that this killer is filled with hate. It's just a feeling I'm getting. The suggestion of a different possibility, that maybe he wanted her found but his intention wasn't to sexually degrade," she says.

"You don't see contempt? Rage?" Captain Poma is surprised, seems genuinely incredulous.

"I think what he did made him feel powerful. He had a need to overpower her. He has other needs that at this moment we can't possibly know," she says. "And I'm certainly not suggesting there's no sexual component. I'm not saying there isn't rage. I just don't think these are what drive him."

"Charleston must feel very lucky to have you," he says.

"I'm not sure Charleston feels anything of the sort," she says. "At least, the local coroner most likely doesn't."

The drunk Americans are getting louder. Benton seems distracted by what they're saying.

"An expert like yourself right there. Very lucky is how I would consider it if I were the coroner. And he doesn't avail himself of your talents?" Captain Poma says, brushing against her as he reaches for a photograph he doesn't need to look at again.

"He sends his cases to the Medical University of South Carolina, has never had to contend with a private pathology practice before. Not in Charleston or anywhere. My contracts are with some of the coroners from outlying jurisdictions where there's no access to medical examiner facilities and labs," she explains, distracted by Benton.

He indicates for her to pay attention to what the drunk Americans are saying.

". . . I just think when it's undisclosed this and undisclosed that, it's fishy," one of them pontificates.

"Why would she want anybody to know? I don't blame her. It's like Oprah or Anna

Nicole Smith. People find out where they are, they show up in droves."

"How sickening. Imagine being in the hospital . . ."

"Or in Anna Nicole Smith's case, in the morgue. Or in the damn ground . . ."

". . . And mobs of people out there on the sidewalk, yelling out your name."

"Can't take the heat, get out of the kitchen, is what I say. Price you pay for being rich and famous."

"What's going on?" Scarpetta asks Benton.

"It would seem our old friend Dr. Self had some sort of emergency earlier today and is going to be off the air for a while," he replies.

Captain Poma turns around and looks at the table of noisy Americans. "Do you know her?" he asks.

Benton says, "We've had our run-ins with her. Mainly, Kay has."

"I believe I read something about that when I was researching you. A sensational, very brutal homicide case in Florida that involved all of you."

"I'm glad to know you researched us," Benton says. "That was very thorough."

"Only to make myself familiar before you

came here." Captain Poma meets Scarpetta's eyes. "A very beautiful woman I know watches Dr. Self regularly," he says, "and she tells me she saw her on the show last fall. It had something to do with her winning that very big tournament in New York. I admit I don't pay much attention to tennis."

"The U.S. Open," Scarpetta says.

"I'm not aware Drew was on her show," Benton says, frowning as if he doesn't believe him.

"She was. I've checked. This is very interesting. Suddenly, Dr. Self has a family emergency. I've been trying to get in touch with her, and she has yet to respond to my inquiries. Perhaps you could intercede?" he says to Scarpetta.

"I seriously doubt that would be helpful," she says. "Dr. Self hates me."

They walk back, following Via Due Macelli in the dark.

She imagines Drew Martin walking these streets. She wonders who she encountered. What does he look like? How old is he? What did he do to inspire her trust? Had they met before? It was daylight, plenty of people out, but so far no witnesses have come forward with convincing information that they saw anybody who fit her description at any time after she left the mime. How can that be possible? She was one of the most famous athletes in the world, and not one person recognized her on the streets of Rome?

"Was what happened random? Like a lightning strike? That's the question we seem no closer to answering," Scarpetta says as she and Benton walk through the balmy night, their shadows moving over old stone. "She's by herself and intoxicated, perhaps lost on some deserted side street, and he sees her? And what? Offers to show her the way and leads her where he can gain complete control of her? Perhaps where he lives? Or to his car? If so, he must speak at least a little English. How could no one have seen her? Not one person."

Benton says nothing, their shoes scuffing on the sidewalk, the street noisy with people emerging from restaurants and bars, very loud, with motor scooters and cars that come close to running them over.

"Drew didn't speak Italian, scarcely a word of it, so we're told," Scarpetta adds.

The stars are out, the moon soft on Casina Rossa, the stucco house where Keats died of tuberculosis at age twenty-five.

"Or he stalked her," she goes on. "Or perhaps he was acquainted with her. We don't know and probably never will unless he does it again and is caught. Are you going to talk to me, Benton? Or shall I continue my rather fragmented, redundant monologue?"

"I don't know what the hell's going on between the two of you, unless this is your way of punishing me," he says.

"With who?"

"That goddamn captain. Who the hell else?"

"The answer to the first part is nothing's going on, and you're being ridiculous to think otherwise, but we'll get back to that. I'm more interested in the punishment part of your statement. Since I have no history of punishing you or anyone."

They begin climbing the Spanish Steps, an exertion made harder by hurt feelings and too much wine. Lovers are entwined, and rowdy youths are laughing and boisterous and pay them no mind. Far away, what seems a mile high, the Hotel Hassler is lit up and huge, rising over the city like a palace.

"One thing not in my character," she resumes. "Punishing people. Protect myself and others, but not punish. Never people I care about. Most of all"—out of breath—"I would never punish you."

"If you intend to see other people, if you're interested in other men, I can't say I blame you. But tell me. That's all I ask. Don't put on displays like you did all day. And tonight. Don't play fucking high school games with me."

"Displays? Games?"

"He was all over you," Benton says.

"And I was all over everywhere else trying to move away from him."

"He's been all over you for all day long. Can't get close enough to you. Stares at you, touches you right in front of me."

"Benton . . ."

"And I know he's this good-looking, well, maybe you're attracted to him. But I won't tolerate it. Right in front of me. Goddamn it."

"Benton . . ."

"Same with God knows who. Down there in the Deep South. What do I know?"

"Benton!"

Silence.

"You're talking crazy. Since when, in the

history of the universe, have you ever worried about my cheating on you? Knowingly."

No sound but their footsteps on stone, their labored breathing.

"Knowingly," she repeats, "because the one time I was with someone else was when I thought you were . . ."

"Dead," he says. "Right. So you're told I'm dead. Then a minute later you're fucking some guy young enough to be your son."

"Don't." Anger begins to gather. "Don't you dare."

He is quiet. Even after the bottle of wine he drank all by himself, he knows better than to push the subject of his feigned death when he was forced into a protected witness program. What Benton put her though. He knows better than to attack her as if she's the one who was emotionally cruel.

"Sorry," he says.

"What's really the matter?" she says. "God, these steps."

"I guess we can't seem to change it. As you say about livor and rigor. Set. Fixed. Let's face it."

"I won't face whatever *it* is. As far as I'm concerned, there's no *it*. And livor and rigor are about people who are dead. We're not dead. You just said you never were."

Both of them are breathless. Her heart is pounding.

"I'm sorry. Really," he says, referring to what happened in the past, his faked death and her ruined life.

She says, "He's been too attentive. Forward. So what?"

Benton is used to the attention other men pay to her, has always been rather unperturbed by it, even amused, because he knows who she is, knows who he is, knows his enormous power and that she has to deal with the same thing—women who stare at him, brush against him, want him shamelessly.

"You've made a new life for yourself in Charleston," he says. "I can't see your undoing it. Can't believe you did it."

"Can't believe . . . ?" And the steps go up and up forever.

"Knowing I'm in Boston and can't move south. Where does that leave us."

"It leaves you jealous. Saying 'fuck,' and you never say 'fuck.' God! I hate steps!" Unable to catch her breath. "You have no reason to be threatened. It's not like you to feel threatened by anyone. What's wrong with you?"

"I was expecting too much."

"Expecting what, Benton?"

"Doesn't matter."

"It certainly does."

They climb the endless flight of steps and stop talking, because their relationship is too much to talk about when they can't breathe. She knows Benton is angry because he's scared. He feels powerless in Rome. He feels powerless in their relationship because he's in Massachusetts, where he moved with her blessing, the chance to work as a forensic psychologist at the Harvard-affiliated McLean Hospital too good to ignore.

"What were we thinking?" she says, no more steps, and she reaches for his hand. "Idealistic as ever, I suppose. And you could return a little energy with that hand of yours, as if you want to hold mine, too. For seventeen years we've never lived in the same city, much less the same house."

"And you don't think it can change." He laces his fingers through hers, taking a deep breath.

"How?"

"I suppose I've entertained this secret fantasy you'd move. With Harvard, MIT, Tufts. I guess I thought you might teach. Perhaps at a medical school or be content to be a part-time consultant at McLean. Or maybe Boston, the ME's office. Maybe end up chief."

"I could never go back to a life like that," Scarpetta says, and they are walking into the hotel's lobby that she calls Belle Époque because it is from a beautiful era. But they are oblivious to the marble, the antique Murano glass and silk and sculptures, to everything and everyone, including Romeo—that really is his name—who during the day is a gold-painted mime, most nights a doorman, and of late, a somewhat attractive and sullen young Italian who doesn't want any further interrogations about Drew Martin's murder.

Romeo is polite but avoids their eyes and, like a mime, is completely silent.

"I want what's best for you," Benton says. "Which is why, obviously, I didn't get in your way when you decided to start your own practice in Charleston, but I was upset about it."

"You never told me."

"I shouldn't tell you now. What you've done is right and I know it. For years you've felt you really don't belong anywhere. In a sense, homeless, and in some ways unhappy ever since you left Richmond—worse, sorry to remind you, were fired. That goddamn piss-ant governor. At this stage in your life, you're doing exactly what you should." As they board the elevator. "But I'm not sure I can stand it anymore."

She tries not to feel a fear that is indescribably awful. "What do I hear you saying, Benton? That we should give up? Is that what you're really saying?"

"Maybe I'm saying the opposite."

"Maybe I don't know what that means, and I wasn't flirting." As they get out on their floor. "I never flirt. Except with you."

"I don't know what you do when I'm not around."

"You know what I don't do."

He unlocks the door to their penthouse suite. It is splendid with antiques and white marble and a stone patio big enough to entertain a small village. Beyond, the ancient city is silhouetted against the night.

"Benton," she says. "Please, let's don't fight. You're flying back to Boston in the morning. I'm flying back to Charleston. Let's don't push each other away so it somehow makes it easier to be away from each other."

He takes off his coat.

"What? You're angry that I've finally found a place to settle down, started again in a place that works for me?" she says.

He tosses his coat over a chair.

"In all fairness," she says, "I'm the one who has to start all over again, create something out of nothing, answer my own phone, and clean up the damn morgue myself. I don't have Harvard. I don't have a multimillion-dollar apartment in Beacon Hill. I have Rose, Marino, and sometimes Lucy. That's it, so I end up answering the phone myself half the time. The local media. Solicitors. Some group that wants me as a luncheon speaker. The exterminator. The other day, it was the damn Chamber of Commerce—how many of their damn phone directories do I want to order. As if I want to be listed in the Chamber of Commerce directory as if I'm a dry cleaner or something."

"Why?" Benton says. "Rose has always screened your calls."

"She's getting old. She can do but so much."

"Why can't Marino answer the phone?"

"Why anything? Nothing's the same. Your making everyone think you were dead fractured and scattered everyone. There, I'll say it. Everybody's changed because of it, including you."

"I had no choice."

"That's the funny thing about choices. When you don't have one, nobody else does, either."

"That's why you've put down roots in Charleston. You don't want to choose me. I might die again."

"I feel as if I'm standing all alone in the middle of a fucking explosion, everything flying all around me. And I'm just standing here. You ruined me. You fucking ruined me, Benton."

"Now who's saying 'fuck'?"

She wipes her eyes. "Now you've made me cry."

He moves closer to her, touches her. They sit on the couch and gaze out at the twin bell towers of Trinità dei Monti, at the Villa Medici on the edge of the Pincian Hill, and far beyond, Vatican City. She turns to him and is struck again by the clean lines of his face,

his silver hair, and his long, lean elegance
that is so incongruous with what he does.

"How is it now?" she asks him. "The way
you feel, compared to back then? In the beginning."

"Different."

"Different sounds ominous."

"Different because we've been through so
much for so long. By now it's hard for me to
remember not knowing you. It's hard for me to
remember I was married before I met you.
That was someone else, some FBI guy who
played by the rules, had no passion, no life,
until that morning I walked into your conference room, the important so-called profiler,
called in to help out with homicides terrorizing
your modest city. And there you were in your
lab coat, setting down a huge stack of case
files, shaking my hand. I thought you were the
most remarkable woman I'd ever met,
couldn't take my eyes off of you. Still can't."

"Different." She reminds him of what he
said.

"What goes on between two people is different every day."

"That's okay as long as they feel the
same way."

"Do you?" he says. "Do you still feel the same way? Because if . . ."

"Because if what?"

"Would you?"

"Would I what? Want to do something about it?"

"Yes. For good." He gets up and finds his jacket, reaches into a pocket, and comes back to the couch.

"For good, as opposed to for bad," she says, distracted by what's in his hand.

"I'm not being funny. I mean it."

"So you don't lose me to some foolish flirt?" She pulls him against her and holds him tight. She pushes her fingers through his hair.

"Maybe," he says. "Take this, please."

He opens his hand, and in his palm is a folded piece of paper.

"We're passing notes in school," she says, and she's afraid to open it.

"Go on, go on. Don't be a chicken."

She opens it, and inside is a note that says, *Will you?* and then a ring. It's an antique, a thin platinum band of diamonds.

"My great-grandmother's," he says, and he slides it over her finger, and it fits.

They kiss.

"If it's because you're jealous, that's a terrible reason," she says.

"I just happened to have it with me after it's been in a safe for fifty years? I'm really asking you," he says. "Please say you will."

"And how do we manage? After all your talk about our separate lives?"

"For Christ's sake, for once don't be rational."

"It's very beautiful," she says of the ring. "You better mean it, because I'm not giving it back."

Chapter 3

Nine days later, Sunday. A ship's horn is mournful out at sea.

Church steeples pierce the overcast dawn in Charleston, and a solitary bell begins to ring. Then a cluster of them joins in, clanging in a secret language that sounds the same around the world. With the bells comes the first light of dawn, and Scarpetta begins to stir about in her master suite, as she wryly refers to her living area on the second floor of her early-nineteenth-century carriage house. Compared to the somewhat sumptuous homes of her past, what she has is a very odd departure.

Her bedroom and study are combined, the space so crowded she can barely move without bumping into the antique chest of drawers or bookcases, or the long table draped with a black cloth that bears a microscope and slides, latex gloves, dust masks, camera equipment, and various crime scene necessities—all eccentric in their context. There are no closets, just side-by-side wardrobes lined with cedar, and from one of them she selects a charcoal skirt suit, a gray-and-white-striped silk blouse, and low-heeled black pumps.

Dressed for what promises to be a difficult day, she sits at her desk and looks out at the garden, watching it change in the varying shadows and light of morning. She logs into e-mail, checking to see if her investigator, Pete Marino, has sent her anything that might confound her plans for the day. No messages. To double-check, she calls him.

"Yeah." He sounds groggy. In the background, an unfamiliar woman's voice complains, "Shit. Now what?"

"You're definitely coming in?" Scarpetta makes sure. "I got word late last night we have a body on the way from Beaufort, and I'm assuming you'll be there to take care of it. Plus, we have that meeting this afternoon. I left you a message. You never called me back."

"Yeah."

The woman in the background says in the same complaining voice, "What's *she* want this time?"

"I'm talking within the hour," Scarpetta firmly tells Marino. "You need to be on your way now or there will be no one to let him in. Meddicks' Funeral Home. I'm not familiar with it."

"Yeah."

"I'll be in around eleven to finish up what I can with the little boy."

As if the Drew Martin case isn't bad enough. Scarpetta's first day back to work after she returned from Rome brought in another horrible case, the murder of a little boy whose name she still doesn't know. He has moved into her mind because he has nowhere else to go, and when she least expects it, she sees his delicate face, emaciated body, and curly brown hair. And then the rest of it. What he looked like when she was done. After all these years, after thousands of cases, a part of her hates the necessity of what she must do to the dead because of what someone did to them first.

"Yeah." That's all Marino has to say.

"Petulant, rude . . ." she mutters as she makes her way downstairs. "I'm so goddamn tired of this." Blowing out in exasperation.

In the kitchen, her heels are sharp on the terra-cotta tile floor that she spent days on her hands and knees laying in a herringbone pattern when she moved into the carriage house. She repainted the walls plain white to capture light from the garden, and restored the cypress ceiling beams that are original to the house. The kitchen—the most important room—is precisely arranged with the stainless-steel appliances, copper pots and pans (always polished as bright as new pennies), cutting boards, and handcrafted German cutlery of a serious chef. Her niece, Lucy, should be here any minute, and it pleases Scarpetta very much, but she's curious. Lucy rarely calls and invites herself for breakfast.

Scarpetta picks out what she needs for egg-white omelets stuffed with ricotta cheese and white cap mushrooms sautéed in sherry and unfiltered olive oil. No bread, not even her flat griddle bread grilled on the terra-cotta slab—or *testo*—she hand-carried from Bologna back in the days when airport security didn't consider cookware a weapon. Lucy is on an unforgiving diet—in training, as she puts it. For what, Scarpetta always asks. For life, Lucy always says. Preoccupied by whipping egg whites with a whisk and ruminating about what she must deal with today, she's startled by an ominous thud against an upstairs window.

"Please, no," she exclaims in dismay, setting down the whisk and running to the door.

She disarms the alarm and hurries out to the garden patio where a yellow finch flutters helplessly on old brick. She gently picks it up, and its head lolls from side to side, eyes half shut. She talks soothingly to it, strokes its silky feathers as it tries to right itself and fly, and its head lolls from side to side. It's just stunned, will suddenly recover, and it falls over and flutters and its head lolls from side to side. Maybe it won't die. Foolish wishful thinking for someone who knows better, and she carries the bird inside. In the locked bottom drawer of the kitchen desk is a locked metal box, and inside that, the bottle of chloroform.

· · ·

She sits on the back brick steps and doesn't get up as she listens to the distinctive roar of Lucy's Ferrari.

It turns off King Street and parks on the shared driveway in front of the house, and then Lucy appears on the patio, an envelope in hand.

"Breakfast isn't ready, not even coffee," she says. "You're sitting out here and your eyes are red."

"Allergies," Scarpetta says.

"The last time you blamed allergies— which you don't have, by the way—was when a bird flew into a window. And you had a dirty trowel on the table just like that." Lucy points to an old marble table in the garden, a trowel on top of it. Nearby, beneath a pit-tosporum, is freshly dug earth covered by broken pieces of pottery.

"A finch," Scarpetta says.

Lucy sits next to her and says, "So it appears Benton's not coming for the weekend. When he is, you always have a long grocery list on the counter."

"Can't get away from the hospital." The small, shallow pond in the middle of the garden has Chinese jasmine and camellia petals floating in it like confetti.

Lucy picks up a loquat leaf knocked down from a recent rain, twirls it by the stem. "I hope that's the only reason. You come back from Rome with your big news and what's different? Nothing that I can tell. He's there, you're here. No plans to change that, right?"

"Suddenly you're the relationship expert?"

"An expert on ones that go wrong."

"You're making me sorry I told anyone," Scarpetta says.

"I've been there. It's what happened with Janet. We started talking about commitment, about getting married when it finally became legal for perverts to have more rights than a dog. Suddenly, she couldn't deal with being gay. And it was over before it began. And not in a nice way."

"Not nice? How about unforgivable?"

"I should be the unforgiving one, not you," Lucy says. "You weren't there. You don't know what it's like to be there. I don't want to talk about it."

A small statue of an angel that watches over the pond. What it protects, Scarpetta has yet to discover. Certainly not birds. Maybe not anything. She gets up and brushes off the back of her skirt.

"Is this why you wanted to talk to me," she

says, "or did it just happen to pop into your mind while I was sitting here feeling awful because I had to euthanize another bird?"

"It's not why I called you last night and said I need to see you," Lucy says, still playing with the leaf.

Her hair, cherrywood-red with highlights of rose-gold, is clean and shiny and tucked behind her ears. She wears a black T-shirt that shows off a beautiful body earned by punishing workouts and good genetics. She's going somewhere, Scarpetta has a suspicion, but she's not going to ask. She sits down again.

"Dr. Self." Lucy stares at the garden, the way people stare when they aren't looking at anything except what's bothering them.

It's not what Scarpetta expected her to say. "What about her?"

"I told you to keep her close, always keep your enemies close," Lucy says. "You didn't pay attention. Haven't cared that she disparages you every chance she gets because of that court case. Says you're a liar and a professional sham. Just Google yourself on the Internet. I track her, forwarded her bullshit to you, and you barely look at it."

"How could you possibly know whether I barely look at something?"

"I'm your system administrator. Your faithful IT. I know damn well how long you keep a file open. You could defend yourself," Lucy says.

"From what?"

"Accusations that you manipulated the jury."

"What court's about. Manipulating the jury."

"That you talking? Or am I sitting with a stranger?"

"If you're hog-tied, tortured, and can hear the screams of your loved ones being brutalized and killed in another room, and you take your own life to escape their fate? That's not a goddamn suicide, Lucy. That's murder."

"What about legally?"

"I really don't care."

"You sort of used to."

"I sort of didn't. You don't know what's been in my mind when I've worked cases all these years and often found myself the only advocate for the victims. Dr. Self wrongly hid behind her shield of confidentiality and didn't divulge information that could have prevented profound suffering and death. She deserves worse than she got. Why are we talking about this? Why are you getting me upset?"

Lucy meets her eyes. "What do they say?

Revenge is best served cold? She's in contact with Marino again."

"Oh, God. As if this past week hasn't been hell enough. Has he completely lost his mind?"

"When you came back from Rome and spread the word, did you think he was going to be happy about it? Do you live in outer space?"

"Clearly, I must."

"How can you not see it? Suddenly he goes out and gets drunk every night, gets a new trashy girlfriend. He's really picked one this time. Or don't you know? Shandy Snook, as in Snook's Flamin' Chips?"

"Flamin' what? Who?"

"Greasy, oversalted potato chips flavored with jalapeño and red pepper sauce. Made her father a fortune. She moved here about a year ago. Met Marino at the Kick 'N Horse this past Monday night, and it was love at first sight."

"He tell you all this?"

"Jess told me."

Scarpetta shakes her head, has no idea who Jess is.

"Owns the Kick 'N Horse. Marino's biker hangout, and I know you've heard him talk about it. She called me because she's worried about him and his latest trailer-park paramour, worried about how out of control he's getting. Jess says she's never seen him like this."

"How would Dr. Self know Marino's e-mail address unless he contacted her first?" Scarpetta asks.

"Her personal e-mail address hasn't changed since he was her patient in Florida. His has. So I think we can figure out who wrote who first. I can find out for sure. Not that I have the password for the personal e-mail account on his home computer, although minor inconveniences like that have never stopped me. I'd have to . . ."

"I know what you'd have to do."

"Have physical access."

"I know what you'd have to do, and I don't want you to. Let's don't make this any worse than it is."

"At least some of the e-mails he's gotten from her are now on his office desktop for all the world to see," Lucy says.

"That makes no sense."

"Of course it does. To make you angry and jealous. Payback."

"And you noticed them on his desktop because?"

"Because of the little emergency last night. When he called me and said he'd been notified that an alarm was going off, indicating the fridge was malfunctioning, and he wasn't anywhere near the office and could I check. He said if I need to call the alarm company, the number's on the list taped to his wall."

"An alarm?" she says, baffled. "No one notified me."

"Because it didn't happen. I get there and everything's status quo. The fridge is fine. I go into his office to get the number of the alarm company so I can check to be sure everything really is okay, and guess what's on his desktop."

"This is ridiculous. He's acting like a child."

"He's no child, Aunt Kay. And you're going to have to fire him one of these days."

"And manage how? I can barely manage now. I'm already short-staffed, without a single eligible person on the horizon to hire."

"This is just the beginning. He's going to get worse," Lucy says. "He's not the person you once knew."

"I don't believe that, and I could never fire him."

"You're right," Lucy says. "You couldn't. It would be a divorce. He's your husband. God knows you've spent a hell of a lot more time with him than you have with Benton."

"He most assuredly isn't my husband. Don't goad me, please."

Lucy picks up the envelope from the steps and hands it to her. "Six of them, all from her. Coincidentally, starting on this past Monday, your first day back at work from Rome. The same day we saw your ring and, great sleuths that we are, figured out it wasn't from Cracker Jacks."

"Any e-mails from Marino to Dr. Self?"

"He must not want you to see whatever he wrote. I recommend you bite on a stick." Indicating the envelope and what's inside it. "How is he? She misses him. Thinks about him. You're a tyrant, a has-been, and he must be miserable working for you, and what can she do to help him?"

"Will he never learn?" Mostly, it's depressing.

"You should have kept the news from him. How could you not know what it would do to him?"

Scarpetta notices the purple Mexican petunias climbing the north garden wall. She notices the lavender lantana. They look a bit parched.

"Well, aren't you going to read the damn things?" Lucy indicates the envelope again.

"I'm not going to give them that power right now," Scarpetta says. "I have more important things to deal with. That's why I'm dressed in a damn suit and going into the damn office on a damn Sunday when I could be working in my garden or even going for a damn walk."

"I ran a background check on the guy you're meeting with this afternoon. Recently, he was the victim of an assault. No suspect. And related to this, he was charged with a misdemeanor for possession of marijuana. The charge was dropped. Beyond that, not even a speeding ticket. But I don't think you should be alone with him."

"What about the brutalized little boy all alone in my morgue? Since you haven't said anything, I assume your computer searches are still coming up empty-handed."

"It's like he didn't exist."

"Well, he did. And what was done to him is one of the worst things I've ever seen. Maybe it's time we go out on a limb."

"And do what?"

"I've been thinking about statistical genetics."

"I still can't believe no one's doing it," Lucy

says. "The technology's there. It's been there. It's all so stupid. Alleles are shared among relatives, and, as is true of any other database, it's all a function of probability."

"A father, mother, sibling would have a higher score. And we'd see it and focus on it. I think we should try it."

"If we do, what happens if it turns out this little kid was killed by a relative? We use statistical genetics in a criminal case, and what happens in court?" Lucy says.

"If we figure out who he is, then we'll worry about court."

Belmont, Massachusetts. Dr. Marilyn Self sits before a window in her room with a view.

Sloping lawns, forests and fruit trees, and old brick buildings harken back to a genteel era when the wealthy and famous could disappear from their lives, briefly or for as long as needed, or in some hopeless cases, forever, and be treated with the respect and pampering they deserved. At McLean Hospital, it's perfectly normal to spot famous actors, musicians, athletes, and politicians strolling the cottage-style campus, designed by the famous landscape architect Frederick Law Olmsted, whose other famous projects include New York's Central Park, the grounds of the U.S. Capitol, the Biltmore Estate, and Chicago's 1893 World's Fair.

It isn't perfectly normal to spot Dr. Marilyn Self. But she doesn't intend to be here much longer, and when the public eventually finds out the truth, her reasons will be clear. To be safe and sequestered, and then, as has always been the story of her life, a destiny. What she calls *a meant-to-be.* She'd forgotten Benton Wesley works here.

Shocking Secret Experiments: Frankenstein.

Let's see. She continues to script her first show when she returns to the air. *While in seclusion to guard my life, I unwittingly and unwillingly became an eyewitness—worse, a guinea pig—to clandestine experiments and abuse. In the name of science. It is as Kurtz said in* Heart of Darkness—*"The horror! The horror!" I was subjected to a modern form of what was done in asylums during the darkest days of the darkest times when people who didn't have the proper tools were considered subhuman and treated like . . . Treated like . . . ?* The right analogy will come to her later.

Dr. Self smiles as she imagines Marino's

ecstasy when he discovered she had written back to him. He probably believes that she (the most famous psychiatrist in the world) was happy to hear from him. He still believes she cares! She's never cared. Even when he was her patient in her less prominent Florida days, she didn't care. He was little more than a therapeutic amusement, and yes (she admits it), a dash of spice, because his adoration of her was almost as pathetic as his besotted sexual obsession with Scarpetta.

Poor, pathetic Scarpetta. Amazing what a few well-placed calls can do.

Her mind races. Her thoughts are nonstop inside her room at the Pavilion, where meals are catered and a concierge is available, should one wish to go to the theater or a Red Sox game or a health spa. The privileged patient at the Pavilion gets rather much whatever he or she wants, which in Dr. Self's case is her own e-mail account and a room that happened to be occupied by another patient named Karen when Dr. Self was admitted nine days ago.

The unacceptable room assignment was, of course, remedied easily enough without administrative intervention or delay on Dr.

Self's first day when she entered Karen's room before dawn and awakened her by gently blowing on her eyes.

"Oh!" Karen exclaimed in relief when she realized it was Dr. Self, not a rapist, hovering over her. "I was having a strange dream."

"Here. I brought you coffee. You were sleeping like the dead. Perhaps you stared too long at the crystal light fixture last night?" Dr. Self looked up at the shadowy shape of the Victorian crystal light fixture above the bed.

"What!" Karen exclaimed in alarm, setting down her coffee on the antique bedside table.

"One must be most careful about staring at anything crystal. It can have a hypnotic effect and put you into a trancelike state. What was your dream?"

"Dr. Self, it was so real! I felt someone's breath in my face and I was scared."

"Do you have any idea who? Perhaps someone in your family? A family friend?"

"My father used to rub his whiskers against my face when I was little. I could feel his breath. How funny! I'm just now remembering that! Or maybe I'm imagining it. Sometimes I have a problem knowing what's real." Disappointed.

"Repressed memories, my dear," Dr. Self

said. "Don't doubt your inner Self [said slowly]. It's what I tell all my followers. Don't doubt your what, Karen?"

"Inner Self."

"That's right. Your inner Self [said very slowly] knows the truth. Your inner Self knows what's real."

"A truth about my father? Something real I don't remember?"

"An unbearable truth, an unthinkable reality you couldn't face back then. You see, my dear, everything really is about sex. I can help you."

"Please help me!"

Patiently, Dr. Self led her back in time, back to when she was seven, and with some insightful guidance navigated her back to the scene of her original psychic crime. Karen finally, for the first time in her pointless, used-up life, recounted her father crawling into bed with her and rubbing his exposed erect penis against her buttocks, his boozy breath in her face, and then a warm, wet stickiness all over her pajama bottoms. Dr. Self went on to direct poor Karen to the traumatic realization that what happened wasn't an isolated incident, because sexual abuse, with rare exception, is repeated, and her mother must have been aware, based on the condition of little Karen's pajamas and the bedcovers, meaning her mother turned a blind eye to what her husband was doing to their younger daughter.

"I remember my father bringing me hot chocolate in bed once and I spilled it," Karen finally said. "I remember the warm stickiness on my pajama bottoms. Maybe that's what I'm remembering and not . . ."

"Because it was safe to think it was hot chocolate. And then what followed?" No answer. "If you spilled it? Whose fault was it?"

"I spilled it. It was my fault," Karen says, tearfully.

"Perhaps why you've abused alcohol and drugs ever since? Because you feel what happened is your fault?"

"Not ever since. I didn't start drinking or smoking pot until I was fourteen. Oh, I don't know! I don't want to go into another trance, Dr. Self! I can't bear the memories! Or if it wasn't real, now I think it is!"

"It's just as Pitres wrote in his *Leçons cliniques sur l'hystérie et l'hypnotisme* in 1891," Dr. Self said as the woods and lawn beautifully materialized in the dawn—a view that soon would be hers. She explained delirium and hysteria, and intermittently looked up at the crystal light fixture over Karen's bed.

"I can't stay in this room!" Karen cried. "Won't you please trade rooms with me?" she begged.

Lucious Meddick snaps a rubber band on his right wrist as he parks his shiny black hearse in the alley behind Dr. Scarpetta's house.

Intended for horses, not huge vehicles, what kind of nonsense is this? His heart is still pounding. He's a nervous wreck. Damn lucky he didn't scrape against trees or the high brick wall that separates the alley and old houses along it from a public garden. What kind of ordeal is this to put him through, and already his brand-new hearse is feeling out of alignment, was pulling to one side as it bumped over pavers, kicking up dust and dead leaves. He climbs out, leaving the engine rumbling, noticing some old lady staring out her upstairs window at him. Lucious smiles at her, can't help but think it won't be long before the old bag needs his services.

He presses the intercom button on a formidable iron gate and announces, "Meddicks'."

After a long pause, which requires him to make the announcement again, a woman's strong voice sounds through the speaker: "Who is this?"

"Meddicks' Funeral Home. I have a delivery. . . ."

"You brought a delivery *here*?"

"Yes, ma'am."

"Stay inside your vehicle. I'll be right there."

The southern charm of General Patton, Lucious thinks, somewhat humiliated and irked as he climbs back into his hearse. He rolls up his window and thinks of the stories he's heard. At one time Dr. Scarpetta was as famous as Quincy, but something happened when she was the chief medical examiner. . . . He can't remember where. She got fired or couldn't take the pressure. A breakdown. A scandal. Maybe more than one of each. Then that highly publicized case in Florida a couple years back, some naked lady strung up from a rafter, tortured and tormented until she couldn't take it anymore and hung herself with her own rope.

A patient of that TV talk-show shrink. He

tries to remember. Maybe it was more than one person tortured and killed. He's quite sure Dr. Scarpetta testified and was key in convincing the jury to find Dr. Self guilty of something. And in a number of articles he's read since, she has referred to Dr. Scarpetta as "incompetent and biased," a "closet lesbian," and a "has-been." Probably true. Most powerful women are like men or at least wish they were men, and when she started out, there weren't many women in her profession. Now there must be thousands of them. Supply and demand, nothing special about her anymore, no-sirree-bob, women all over the place—young ones—getting ideas from TV and doing the same thing she does. That and all the other stuff said about her sure as heck would explain why she moved to the Lowcountry and works out of a tiny carriage house—a former stable, let's be honest—which certainly isn't what Lucious works out of, not hardly.

He lives in the upstairs of the funeral home the Meddick family has owned in Beaufort County for more than a hundred years. The three-story mansion on a former plantation still has the original slave cabins, sure isn't some itty-bitty carriage house on an old narrow alleyway. Shocking, downright shocking. It's one thing to embalm bodies and prepare them for burial in a professionally outfitted room in a mansion, quite another to do autopsies in a carriage house, especially if you're dealing with floaters— *greenies*, he calls them—and others who are hard as hell to make presentable to families, no matter how much D-12 deodorant powder you use so they don't stink up the chapel.

A woman appears behind her two sets of gates, and he begins to indulge in his favorite preoccupation, voyeurism, scrutinizing her through the dark-tinted side window. Metal clanks as she opens and shuts the first black gate, then the outer one—tall with flat, twisted bars centered by two J-curves that look like a heart. As if she has a heart, and by now he's sure she doesn't. She's dressed in a power suit, has blond hair, and he calculates she's five-foot-five, wears a size-eight skirt, a size-ten blouse. Lucious is darn near infallible when it comes to his deductions about what people would look like naked on an embalming table, jokes around about having what he calls "x-ray eyes."

Since she so rudely ordered him not to

get out of his vehicle, he doesn't. She knocks on his dark window, and he starts to get flustered. His fingers twitch in his lap, try to rise to his mouth as if they have a will of their own, and he tells them *no.* He snaps himself hard with the rubber band around his wrist and tells his hands to *stop it.* He snaps the rubber band again and grips the wood-grain steering wheel to keep his hands out of trouble.

She knocks again.

He sucks on a wint-o-green Life Saver and rolls down his window. "You sure got a strange location to be hanging out your shingle," he says with a big practiced smile.

"You're in the wrong place," she tells him, not so much as a *good morning* or *nice to meet you.* "What in the world are you doing here?"

"Wrong place, wrong time. That's what keeps people like you and me in business," Lucious replies with his toothy smile.

"How did you get this address?" she says in the same unfriendly tone. She seems like she's in a real big hurry. "This isn't my office. This certainly isn't the morgue. I'm sorry for your inconvenience, but you need to leave right now."

"I'm Lucious Meddick from Meddicks' Funeral Home in Beaufort, right outside of Hilton Head." He doesn't shake her hand, doesn't shake anybody's hand if he can avoid it. "I guess you could call us the resort of funeral homes. Family-run, three brothers, including me. The joke is when you call for *a Meddick,* it doesn't mean the person's still alive. Get it?" He jerks his thumb toward the back of the hearse, says, "Died at home, probably a heart attack. Oriental lady, old as dirt. I reckon you've got all the information on her already. Your neighbor up there some kind of spy or something?" He looks up at the window.

"I talked to the coroner about this case last night," Scarpetta says in the same tone. "How did you get this address?"

"The coroner . . ."

"He gave you *this* address? He knows where my office is. . . ."

"Now, hold on. First off, I'm new when it comes to deliveries. Was bored to death sitting at a desk and dealing with bereft families, decided it was time to hit the road again."

"We can't have this conversation here."

Oh, yes, they will, and he says, "So I

bought me this 1998 V-twelve Cadillac, dual carburetors, dual exhaust, cast aluminum wheels, flagstaffs, violet beacon, and canyon black bier. Couldn't be more fully loaded unless the fat lady in the circus was in it."

"Mr. Meddick, Investigator Marino's on his way to the morgue. I just called him."

"Second of all, I've never delivered a body to you. So I had no idea where your office is until I looked it up."

"I thought you said the coroner told you."

"That's not what he told me."

"You really need to leave. I can't have a hearse behind my house."

"See, this Oriental lady's family wants us to handle the funeral, so I told the coroner it may as well be me for transport. Anyway, I looked up your address."

"Looked it up? Looked it up where? And why didn't you call my death investigator?"

"I did, and he never bothered to call me back so I had to look up your location, like I said." Lucious snaps the rubber band. "On the Internet. Listed with the Chamber of Commerce." He cracks the sliver of Life Saver between his back teeth.

"This is an unlisted address and has never been on the Internet, nor has it ever been confused with my office—the morgue—and I've been here two years. You're the first person to do this."

"Now, don't get huffy with me. I can't help what's on the Internet." He snaps the rubber band. "But then if I'd been called earlier in the week when that little boy was found, I would have delivered his body and now we wouldn't have this problem. You walked right past me at the scene and ignored me, and had you and me worked that one together, sure as shooting you would have given me the right address." He snaps the rubber band, pissed off she's not more respectful.

"Why were you at that scene if the coroner didn't ask you to transport the body?" She's getting very demanding, staring at him now like he's a troublemaker.

"My motto is 'Just Show Up.' You know, like Nike's 'Just Do It.' Well, mine's 'Just Show Up.' Get it? Sometimes when you're the first one to show up, that's all it takes."

He snaps the rubber band, and she stares pointedly at him doing it, then looks at the police scanner inside his hearse. He runs his tongue over the transparent plastic retainer he wears on his teeth to stop him from biting his nails. Snaps the rubber band around his wrist. Snaps it hard, like a whip, and it hurts like hell.

"Head to the morgue now, please." She looks up at the neighbor looking down at them. "I'll make sure Investigator Marino meets you." She steps away from the hearse, suddenly noticing something at the back of it. She stoops to take a closer look. "The day just gets better," she says, shaking her head.

He climbs out and can't believe it. "Shit!" he exclaims. "Shit! Shit! Shit!"

Chapter 4

Coastal Forensic Pathology Associates, on the fringes of the College of Charleston.

The two-story brick building antedates the Civil War, and it slants a little, having shifted on its foundation during the earthquake of 1886. Or this is what the Realtor told Scarpetta when she bought the place for reasons Pete Marino still doesn't understand.

There were nicer buildings, brand-new ones she could have afforded. But for some reason, she, Lucy, and Rose decided on a place that demanded more work than Marino had in mind when he took the job here. For months, they stripped away layers of paint and varnish, knocked out walls, replaced windows and slate tiles on the roof. They scavenged for salvage, most of it from funeral homes, hospitals, and restaurants, eventually ending up with a more-than-adequate morgue that includes a special ventilation system, chemical hoods, a backup generator, a walk-in cooler and a walk-in freezer, a decomposition room, surgical carts, gurneys. The walls and floor are sealed with epoxy paint that can be hosed down, and Lucy installed a wireless security and computer system as mysterious to Marino as the da Vinci Code.

"I mean, who the hell would want to break into this joint?" he says to Shandy Snook as he punches in a code that deactivates the alarm for the door leading from the bay into the morgue.

"I bet a lot of people would," she says. "Let's roam around."

"Nope. Not down here." He steers her to another alarmed door.

"I want to see a dead body or two."

"Nope."

"What you afraid of? Amazing how scared

you are of her," Shandy says, one creaking step at a time. "It's like you're her slave."

Shandy says that constantly, and each time it angers Marino more. "If I was afraid of her, I wouldn't let you in here, now would I, no matter how much you've been driving me crazy about it. There's cameras all the hell over the place, so why the hell would I do this if I'm scared of her?"

She looks up at a camera, smiles, and waves.

"Quit it," he says.

"Like, who's gonna see it? No one here but us chickens, and no reason for the Big Chief to look at the tapes, right? Otherwise, we wouldn't be in here, right? You're afraid of her as shit. It makes me sick, a big man like you. Only reason you let me in is because that numbnut funeral-home guy had a flat tire. And the Big Chief won't be in for a while, and nobody's ever going to look at the tapes." She waves at a camera again. "You wouldn't have the guts to give me a tour if anybody might find out and tell the Big Chief." She smiles and waves at another camera. "I look good on camera. You ever been on TV? My daddy used to be on TV all the time, made his own commercials. I've been in some of them, could probably make a career of being on TV, but who wants people staring at them all the time?"

"Besides you?" He swats her ass.

The offices are on the first floor, Marino's the classiest he's ever had, with heart-of-pine floors, chair rails, and fancy molding. "See, back in the eighteen hundreds," he tells Shandy as they walk in, "my office was probably the dining room."

"Our dining room in Charlotte was ten times this big," she says, looking around and chewing gum.

She's never been in his office, never inside the building. Marino wouldn't dare ask permission, and Scarpetta wouldn't give it. But after a late decadent night with Shandy, she ripped into him again about being Scarpetta's slave and his mood turned spiteful. Then Scarpetta called to tell him Lucious Meddick had a flat tire and would be late, and then Shandy had to rag on him about that, too, go on and on about Marino's rushing around for nothing and he may as well give her a tour like she's been asking him to do all week. After all, she's his girlfriend and should at least see where he works. So he told her to follow him on her motorcycle north on Meeting Street.

"These are genuine antiques," he brags. "From junk shops. The Doc refinished them herself. Something, huh? The first time in my life I ever sat at a desk older than me."

Shandy settles in the leather chair behind his desk, starts opening the dovetailed drawers.

"Me and Rose have spent a lot of time wandering around, trying to figure out what's what, and pretty much decided her office was once the master bedroom. And the biggest space, the Doc's office, was what they called the *sitting room*."

"Kinda stupid." Shandy stares inside a desk drawer. "How can you find anything in here? Looks like you just cram shit in your drawers because you can't be bothered filing."

"I know exactly where everything is. Got my own filing system, stuff sorted according to drawers. Sort of like the Dewey decibel system."

"Well, where's your card catalogue then, big fella?"

"Up here." He taps his shiny shaved head.

"Don't you have any good murder cases in here? Maybe some pictures?"

"Nope."

She gets up, readjusts her leather pants. "So the Big Chief's got the *sitting room.* I want to see it."

"Nope."

"I got a right to see where she works, since she seems to own you."

"She don't own me, and we're not going in there. Nothing for you to see in there anyway, except books and a microscope."

"Bet she's got some good murder cases in that *sitting room* of hers."

"Nope. We keep sensitive cases locked up. In another words, ones you'd think was good."

"Every room's for *sitting*, isn't it? So why was it called a *sitting room*?" She won't shut up about it. "That's stupid."

"Back in the old days, it was called a sitting room to differentiate it from the parlor," Marino explains, proudly looking around his office, at his certificates on the paneled walls, at the big dictionary he never uses, at all the other untouched reference books Scarpetta has passed down to him when she gets the newest revised editions. And, of course, his bowling trophies—all neatly arranged and brassy-bright on built-in shelves. "The parlor was this real formal room right inside the front door, where you stuck people you didn't want staying around very long, whereas the opposite is true of the sitting room, which is the same thing as a living room."

"Sounds to me like you're glad she got this place. No matter how much you complain about it."

"Not half bad for an old joint. I'd rather have something new."

"Your old joint's not half bad, either." She grabs him until he aches. "Fact, feels new to me. Show me her office. Show me where the Big Chief works." She grabs him again. "You having a hard time because of her or me?"

"Shut up," he says, moving her hand away, annoyed by her puns.

"Show me where she works."

"I told you no."

"Then show me the morgue."

"No can do."

"Why? Because you're so fucking scared of her? What's she gonna do? Call the morgue police? Show it to me," she demands.

He glances up at a tiny camera in a corner of the hallway. No one will see the tapes. Shandy's right. Who would bother? No reason. He gets that feeling again—a cocktail of spitefulness, aggression, and vengefulness that makes him want to do something awful.

Dr. Self's fingers *click-click* on her laptop, new e-mails constantly landing (agents, lawyers, business managers, network executives, and special patients and very select fans).

But nothing new from *him.* The Sandman. She can scarcely stand it. He wants her to think he's done the unthinkable, to torment her with anxiety, with terror, by making her think the unthinkable. When she opened his last e-mail on that fated Friday during her midmorning break at the studio, what he'd sent to her, the last thing he sent, was life-altering. At least temporarily.

Don't let it be true.

How foolish and gullible she was to answer him when he sent the first e-mail to her personal address last fall, but she was intrigued. How was it possible he got her personal and very, very private e-mail address? She had to know. She wrote him back and asked. He wouldn't tell her. They began a correspondence. He is unusual, special. Home from Iraq, where he had been profoundly traumatized. Bearing in mind that he would make a fabulous guest on one of her shows, she developed a therapeutic relationship with him online, having no idea he might be capable of the unthinkable.

Please don't let it be true.

If only she could undo it. If only she'd never answered him. If only she hadn't tried to help him. He's insane, a word she rarely uses. Her claim to fame is that everyone is capable of change. Not him. Not if he did the unthinkable.

Please don't let it be true.

If he did the unthinkable, he's a hideous human being beyond repair. The Sandman. What does that mean, and why didn't she demand he tell her, threaten that if he refused she'd have no further contact with him?

Because she's a psychiatrist. Psychiatrists don't threaten their patients.

Please don't let the unthinkable be true.

Whoever he really is, he can't be helped by her or anyone else on earth, and now he may have done what she never expected. He may have done the unthinkable! If he has, there's only one way for Dr. Self to save her-SELF. She decided this at her studio on a day she'll never forget when she saw the photograph he sent her and realized she could be in serious danger for a multitude of reasons, and this necessitated her telling her producers she had a family emergency she couldn't divulge. She would be off the air, hopefully no longer than several weeks. They would have to fill in with her usual replacement (a mildly entertaining psychologist who is no competition but deludes himself into thinking he is). Which is why she can't afford to be away longer than several weeks. Everyone wants to take her place. Dr. Self called Paulo Maroni (said it was another referral and was put straight through) and (in disguise) climbed into a limousine (couldn't possibly use one of her own drivers) and (still disguised) boarded a private jet, and secretly checked herself into McLean, where she is safe, is hidden, and, she hopes, will find out soon enough that the unthinkable hasn't happened.

It's all a sick ruse. He didn't do it. Crazy people make false confessions all the time.

(What if it's not?)

She has to consider the worst-case scenario: People will blame her. They'll say it's because of her that the madman fixated on Drew Martin after she won the U.S. Open last fall and appeared on Dr. Self's shows. Incredible shows and exclusive interviews. What remarkable hours she and Drew shared on the air, talking about positive thinking, about empowering oneself with the proper tools, about actually making a decision to win or lose and how this enabled Drew, at barely sixteen, to pull off one of the biggest upsets in tennis history. Dr. Self's award-winning series *When to Win* was a phenomenal success.

Her pulse picks up as she returns to the other side of horror. She opens the Sandman's e-mail again, as if looking at it again, as if looking at it enough, will somehow change it. There's no text message, only an attachment, a horrifying high-resolution image of Drew naked and sitting in a gray mosaic tile tub sunk deep into a terra-cotta floor. The water level is up to her waist, and when Dr. Self enlarges the image, as she has so many times, she can make out the goose bumps on Drew's arms, and her blue lips and fingernails, suggesting the water running out of an old brass spout is cold. Her hair is wet, the expression on her pretty face hard to describe. Stunned? Pitiful? In shock? She looks drugged.

The Sandman told Dr. Self in earlier e-mails that it was routine to dunk naked prisoners in Iraq. Beat them, humiliate them, force them to urinate on each other. You do what you got to do, he wrote. After a while it's normal, and he didn't mind taking pictures. He didn't mind much until *that one thing* he did, and he has never told her what *that one thing* is, and she's convinced it began his transformation into a monster. Assuming he's done the unthinkable, if what he sent her isn't a ruse.

(Even if it's a ruse, he's a monster for doing this to her!)

She studies the image for any sign of fakery, enlarging and reducing it, reorienting it, staring. *No, no, no,* she continues reassuring herself. *Of course it's not real.*

(What if it is?)

Her mind chews on itself. If she's held accountable, her career will be shot out of the air. At least temporarily. Her millions of followers will say it's her fault because she should have seen it coming, should never have discussed Drew in e-mails with this anonymous patient who calls himself the Sandman and who claimed to watch Drew on TV and read about her and thought she

seemed like a sweet girl but unbearably isolated, and was sure he would meet her and
she would love him and have no more pain.

If the public finds out, it will be Florida all
over again, only worse. Blamed. Unfairly. At
least temporarily.

"I saw Drew on your show and could feel
her unbearable suffering," the Sandman
wrote. "She will thank me."

Dr. Self stares at the image on her screen.
She'll be castigated for not calling the police
immediately when she got the e-mail exactly
nine days ago, and no one will accept her
reasoning, which is perfectly logical: If what
the Sandman sent is real, it's too late for her
to do anything about it; if it's all a sick ruse
(something put together with one of those
photo-enhancement software packages),
what's the point in divulging it and perhaps
putting the idea in some other deranged person's head?

Darkly, her thoughts turn to Marino. To
Benton.

To Scarpetta.

And Scarpetta walks into her mind.

Black suit with wide pale blue pinstripes
and a matching blue blouse that makes her
eyes even bluer. Her blond hair short; she

wears very little makeup. Striking and strong, sitting straight but at ease in the witness stand, facing the jurors. They were mesmerized by her as she answered questions and explained. She never looked at her notes.

"But isn't it true almost all hangings are suicidal, therefore suggesting it's possible she actually took her own life?" One of Dr. Self's attorneys paced the Florida courtroom.

She'd finished testifying, had been released as a witness, and was unable to resist watching the proceedings. Watching her. Scarpetta. Waiting for her to misspeak or make a mistake.

"Statistically, in modern times, it's true that most hangings—as far as we know—are suicides," Scarpetta replies to the jurors, refusing to look at Dr. Self's attorney, answering him as if he's talking over an intercom from some other room.

"'As far as we know'? Are you saying, Mrs. Scarpetta, that . . ."

"Dr. Scarpetta." Smiling at the jurors.

They smile back, riveted, so obviously enamored. Smitten with her while she hammers away at Dr. Self's credibility and decency without anybody realizing it's all manipulation and untruths. Oh, yes, lies. A murder, not a suicide. Dr. Self indirectly is to blame for murder! It isn't her fault. She couldn't have known those people would be murdered. Just because they disappeared from their home didn't mean anything bad had happened to them.

And when Scarpetta called her with questions after finding a prescription bottle with Dr. Self's name on it as the prescribing physician, she was completely right to refuse to discuss any patient or former patient. How could she have known that anyone would end up dead? Dead in an unspeakable way. It wasn't her fault. Had it been, there would have been a criminal case, not just a lawsuit filed by greedy relatives. It wasn't her fault, and Scarpetta deliberately made the jury believe otherwise.

(The courtroom scene fills her head.)

"You mean, you can't determine whether a hanging was a suicide or a homicide?" Dr. Self's attorney gets louder.

Scarpetta says, "Not without witnesses or circumstances that make it clear what happened. . . ."

"Which was?"

"That a person couldn't possibly have done this to himself."

"Such as?"

"Such as being found hanging from a tall light post in a parking lot, no ladder. Hands tightly bound behind the back," she says.

"A real case, or are you just making this up as you go along?" Snidely.

"Nineteen sixty-two. A lynching in Birmingham, Alabama," she says to the jurors, seven of whom are black.

Dr. Self returns from the other side of horror and closes the image on her screen. She reaches for the phone and calls Benton Wesley's office, and her instincts immediately tell her that the unfamiliar woman who answers is young, overestimates her importance, has an entitlement attitude, and therefore is probably from a wealthy family and was hired by the hospital as a favor and is a thorn in Benton's side.

"And your first name, Dr. Self?" the woman asks, as if she doesn't know who Dr. Self is, when everyone at the hospital knows.

"I'm hoping Dr. Wesley has finally gotten in," Dr. Self says. "He's expecting my call."

"He won't be in until about eleven." As if Dr. Self is no one special. "May I ask what you're calling about?"

"That's quite all right. And you are? I don't

believe we've met. Last time I called, it was someone else."

"No longer here."

"Your name?"

"Jackie Minor. His new research assistant." Her tone turns grand. She probably hasn't finished her Ph.D. yet, assuming she ever will.

Dr. Self charmingly says, "Well, thank you very much, Jackie. And I assume you took the job so you could assist in his research study, what is it they call it? Dorsolateral Activation in Maternal Nagging?"

"DAMN?" Jackie says in surprise. "Who calls it that?"

"Why, I believe you just did," Dr. Self says. "The acronym hadn't occurred to me. You're the one who just said it. You're quite witty. Who was the great poet . . . Let me see if I can quote it: 'Wit is the genius to perceive and the metaphor to express.' Or something like that. Alexander Pope, I believe. We'll meet soon enough. Very soon, Jackie. As you probably know, I'm part of the study. The one you call DAMN."

"I knew it was someone important. Which is why Dr. Wesley ended up staying here this weekend and asked me to come in. All they put is *VIP* on the schedule."

"It must be quite demanding working for him."

"Absolutely."

"With his worldwide reputation."

"That's why I wanted to be his RA. I'm interning to be a forensic psychologist."

"Brava! Very good. Perhaps I'll have you on my show someday."

"I hadn't thought about it."

"Well, you should, Jackie. I've been thinking quite a lot about expanding my horizons into *The Other Side of Horror*. The other side of crime that people don't see—the criminal mind."

"That's all anybody's interested in anymore," Jackie agrees. "Just turn on the TV. Every single show is about crime."

"So, I'm just at the brink of thinking about production consultants."

"I'd be happy to accommodate a conversation with you about that anytime."

"Have you interviewed a violent offender yet? Or perhaps sat in on one of Dr. Wesley's interviews?"

"Not yet. But I absolutely will."

"We'll meet again, Dr. Minor. It is *Dr.* Minor?"

"As soon as I take my quals and find time

to really focus on my dissertation. We're already planning my hooding ceremony."

"Of course you are. One of the finest moments in our lives."

In centuries past, the stucco computer lab behind the old brick morgue was a quarters for horses and grooms.

Fortunately, before there was an architectural review board that could put a stop to it, the building was converted into a garage/storage facility that is now, as Lucy calls it, her make-do computer lab. It's brick. It's small. It's minimal. Construction is well in the works on a massive facility on the other side of the Cooper River, where land is plentiful and zoning laws are toothless, as Lucy puts it. Her new forensic labs, when completed, will have every instrument and scientific capability imaginable. So far they manage fairly well with fingerprint analysis, toxicology, firearms, some trace evidence, and DNA. The Feds haven't seen anything yet. She will put them to shame.

Inside her lab of old brick walls and firwood flooring is her computer domain, which is secured from the outside world by bullet- and hurricane-proof windows, the shades always drawn. Lucy sits before a work station that is connected to a sixty-four-gigabyte server with a chassis built of six U mountable racks. The kernel—or operating system interfacing the software with the hardware—is of her own design, built with the lowest assembly language so she could talk to the motherboard herself when she was creating her cyberworld—or what she calls the Infinity of Inner Space (IIS), pronounced IS, the prototype of which she sold for a staggering sum that's indecent to mention. Lucy doesn't talk about money.

Along the top of the walls are flat video screens constantly displaying every angle and sound captured by a wireless system of cameras and embedded microphones, and what she's witnessing is unbelievable.

"You stupid son of a bitch," she says loudly to the flat screen in front of her.

Marino is giving Shandy Snook a tour of the morgue, different angles of them on the screens, their voices as clear as if Lucy is with them.

Boston, the fifth floor of a mid-nineteenth-century brownstone on Beacon Street. Benton Wesley sits at his desk gazing out his window at a hot-air balloon drifting above the common, above Scotch elms as old as America. The white balloon slowly rises like a huge moon against the downtown skyline.

His cell phone rings. He puts on his wireless earpiece, says, "Wesley," and hopes like hell it's not some emergency that has to do with Dr. Self, the current hospital scourge, perhaps the most dangerous one ever.

"It's me," Lucy says in his ear. "Log on now. I'm conferencing you."

Benton doesn't ask why. He logs on to Lucy's wireless network, which transfers video, audio, and data in real time. Her face fills the video screen of the laptop on his desk. She looks fresh and dynamically pretty, as usual, but her eyes are sparking with fury.

"Trying something different," she says. "Connecting you to security access so you can see what I'm seeing right now. Okay? Your screen should split into four quadrants to pick up four angles or locations. Depending on what I choose. That should be enough for you to see what our so-called friend Marino is doing."

"Got it," Benton says as his screen splits, allowing him to view, simultaneously, four areas of Scarpetta's building scanned by cameras.

The buzzer in the morgue bay.

In the upper-left corner of the screen, Marino and some young, sexy but cheap-looking woman in motorcycle leather are in the upstairs hallway of Scarpetta's office, and he's saying to her, "You stay right here until she gets signed in."

"Why can't I go with you? I'm not afraid." Her voice—husky, a heavy southern accent—is transmitted clearly through the speakers on Benton's desk.

"What the hell?" Benton says to Lucy over the phone.

"Just watch," she comes back. "His latest girl wonder."

"Since when?"

"Oh, let's see. I think they started sleeping together this past Monday night. The same night they met and got drunk together."

Marino and Shandy board the elevator, and another camera picks them up as he says to her, "Okay. But if he tells the Doc, I'm cooked."

"Hickory-dick-or-y-Doc, she's got you by the cock," she says in a mocking singsong.

"We'll get a gown to hide all your leather,

but keep your mouth shut and don't do nothing. Don't freak out or do nothing, and I mean it."

"It's not like I've never seen a dead body before," she says.

The elevator doors open and they step out.

"My father choked on a piece of steak right in front of me and my family," Shandy says.

"The locker room's back there. The one on the left." Marino points.

"Left? Like when I'm facing which way?"

"The first one when you go around the corner. Grab a gown and do it quick!"

Shandy runs. In one section of the screen, Benton can see her inside the locker room—Scarpetta's locker room—grabbing a blue gown out of a locker—Scarpetta's gown and locker—and hastily putting the gown on—backward. Marino waits down the hall. She runs back to him, the gown untied and flapping.

Another door. This leading into the bay where Marino's and Shandy's motorcycles are parked in a corner, barricaded by traffic cones. A hearse is inside, the engine's rumbling echoing off old brick walls. A funeral home attendant climbs out, lanky and gawky in a suit and tie as black and shiny as his hearse. He unfolds his skinny self like a stretcher, as if he's turning into what he does for a living. Benton notices something weird about his hands, the way they're clenched like claws.

"I'm Lucious Meddick." He opens the tailgate. "We met the other day when they fished that dead little boy out of the marsh." He pulls on a pair of latex gloves, and Lucy zooms in on him. Benton notices a plastic orthodontic retainer on his teeth, and a rubber band around his right wrist.

"Closer on his hands," Benton tells Lucy.

She zooms in more as Marino says, as if he can't stand the man, "Yeah, I remember."

Benton notices Lucious Meddick's raw fingertips, says to Lucy, "Severe nail biting. A form of self-mutilation."

"Anything new on that one?" Lucious is asking about the murdered little boy who Benton knows is still unidentified in the morgue.

"None of your business," Marino says. "If it was for public semination, it would be in the news."

"Jesus," Lucy says in Benton's ear. "He sounds like Tony Soprano."

"Looks like you lost a hubcap." Marino points to the back left tire of the hearse.

"It's a spare." Lucious is snippy about it.

"Kinda ruins the effect, don't it," Marino says. "Tricked out with all that shine, then a wheel with ugly lug nuts."

Lucious huffily opens the tailgate and slides the stretcher over rollers in back of the hearse. Collapsible aluminum legs clack open and lock in place. Marino doesn't offer assistance as Lucious rolls the stretcher and its black-pouched body up the ramp, bangs it against the door frame, cusses.

Marino winks at Shandy, who looks bizarre in her open surgical gown and black leather motorcycle boots. Lucious impatiently abandons the pouched body in the middle of the hall, snaps the rubber band on his wrist, and says in an irritable raised voice, "Got to take care of her paperwork."

"Keep it down," Marino says. "You might wake somebody up."

"I don't got time for your comedy club." Lucious starts to walk off.

"You ain't going nowhere until you help me transfer her from your stretcher to one of our state-of-the-art gurneys."

"Showing off." Lucy's voice sounds in Benton's earpiece. "Trying to impress his potato-chip tramp."

Marino rolls a gurney out of the cooler, scratched up and rather bandy-legged, one of the wheels slightly cockeyed like a bedraggled grocery store buggy. He and an angry Lucious lift the pouched body from the stretcher, place it on the gurney.

"That lady boss of yours is a piece of work," Lucious says. "The b-word comes to mind."

"Nobody asked your opinion. You hear anybody ask his opinion?" To Shandy.

She stares at the pouch, as if she didn't hear him.

"It's not my fault she's got her addresses mixed up on the Internet. She acted like it was my problem showing up, trying to do my job. Not that I can't get along with anybody. You got a particular funeral home you recommend to your clients?"

"Get a fucking ad in the Yellow Pages."

Lucious heads to the small morgue office, walking fast, hardly bending his knees, reminding Benton of a pair of scissors.

One quadrant of the screen shows Lucious inside the morgue office, fussing with paperwork, opening drawers, rummaging, finding a pen.

Another quadrant of the screen shows Marino saying to Shandy, "Didn't anyone know the Hinelick maneuver?"

"I'll learn anything, baby," she says. "Any maneuver you want to show me."

"Seriously. When your father was choking on—" Marino starts to explain.

"We thought he was having a heart attack or a stroke or a seizure," she interrupts him. "It was so awful, grabbing himself, falling to the floor and cracking his head, his face turning blue. No one knew what to do, had no idea he was choking. Even if we had, we couldn't have done anything except what we did, call nine-one-one." She suddenly looks as if she might start crying.

"Sorry to tell you, but you could have done something," Marino says. "I'm gonna show you. Here, turn around."

Done with his paperwork, Lucious hurries out of the morgue office, walks right past Marino and Shandy. They pay him no mind as he enters the autopsy suite unattended. Marino wraps his huge arms around her waist, makes a fist, his thumb against her upper abdomen, just above her navel. He grasps his fist with his other hand and gives a gentle upward thrust, just enough to show her. He slides his hands up and fondles her.

"Good God," Lucy says in Benton's ear. "He's got a hard-on in the fucking morgue."

In the autopsy suite, the camera picks up Lucious walking to the large black log on a countertop, the Book of the Dead, as Rose politely calls it. He starts signing in the body with the pen he took from the morgue office desk.

"He's not supposed to do that." Lucy's voice in Benton's ear. "Only Aunt Kay is supposed to touch that log. It's a legal document."

Shandy says to Marino, "See, it's not hard being in here. Well, maybe it is." Reaching back, grabbing him. "You sure know how to cheer a girl up. And I do mean up. Whoa!"

Benton says to Lucy, "This is unbelievable."

Shandy turns around in Marino's arms and kisses him—kissing him on the mouth right there in the morgue—and for an instant, Benton thinks they might have sex in the hallway.

Then, "Here, you try it on me," Marino says.

In another quadrant of his screen, Benton watches Lucious thumbing through the morgue log.

When Marino turns around, his arousal is apparent. Shandy can barely get her arms all the way around him, starts to laugh. He puts his huge hands over hers, helps her push, says, "No kidding. You ever see me choking, you push just like this. Hard!" He shows her. "Point is to force the air out so whatever's caught in there flies out, too." She slides her hands down and grabs him again, and he pushes her away and turns his back to Lucious as he emerges from the autopsy suite.

"She figured out anything about that dead little boy?" Lucious snaps the rubber band around his wrist. "Well, I guess not, since he's entered in the Dead Log as 'undetermined.'"

"He was undetermined when he was brought in. What you been doing, snooping through the book?" Marino looks ridiculous, his back to Lucious.

"Obviously, she can't handle such a complicated case. Too bad I didn't bring him in here. I could have been of assistance. I know more about the human body than any doctor." Lucious moves to one side and stares down in the direction of Marino's crotch. "Well, hello," he says.

"You don't know shit and can shut up

about that dead boy," Marino says nastily. "And you can shut up about the Doc. And you can get the hell out of here."

"You mean that little boy from the other day?" Shandy says.

Lucious rattles off with his stretcher, leaving the body he just delivered on the gurney in the middle of the hall, in front of the stainless-steel cooler door. Marino opens it and pushes the uncooperative gurney inside, his arousal still obvious.

"Christ," Benton says to Lucy.

"He on Viagra or something?" Her voice in his ear.

"Why the hell don't you get a new cart or whatever you call that thing?" Shandy says.

"The Doc don't waste money."

"So she's cheap, too. Bet she doesn't pay you shit."

"If we need something, she gets it, but she don't waste money. Not like Lucy, who could buy China."

"You always stick up for the Big Chief, don't you? But not like you stick up for me, baby." Shandy fondles him.

"I think I'm going to throw up." Lucy's voice.

And Shandy walks inside the cooler to

get a good look at what's inside. The cold air blowing is audible through Benton's speakers.

And a camera in the bay picks up Lucious sliding behind the wheel of his hearse.

"She a murder?" Shandy asks about the latest delivery, then looks at another pouched body in a corner. "I want to know about the kid."

Lucious rumbles away in his hearse, the bay door loudly clanking shut behind him, sounding like a car wreck.

"Natural causes," Marino says. "Old Oriental woman. Eighty-five or something."

"How come she got sent here if she died of natural causes?"

"Because the coroner wanted to send her in. Why? Hell if I know. The Doc just said for me to be here. Hell if I know. Sounds like a cut-and-dried heart attack to me. I'm getting a whiff of something." He makes a face.

"Let's look," Shandy says. "Come on. Just a quick peek."

Benton watches them on-screen, watches Marino unzip the pouch and Shandy recoil in disgust, jump back, cover her nose and mouth.

"What you deserve." Lucy's voice as she

zooms in on the body: decomposing, bloated by gases, the abdomen turning green. Benton knows that odor all too well, a putrid stench unlike any other that clings to the air and the roof of your mouth.

"Shit," Marino complains, zipping up the pouch. "She's probably been lying around for days and the damn Beaufort County coroner didn't want to fool with her. Got a noseful, did you?" He laughs at Shandy. "And you thought my job was a piece of cake."

Shandy moves closer to the small black pouched body parked in a corner all by itself. She stands very still, staring down at it.

"Don't do it." Lucy sounds in Benton's ear, but she's talking to Marino's image on the screen.

"Bet I knows what's in this little bag," Shandy says, and it's hard to hear her.

Marino steps outside the cooler. "Out, Shandy. Now."

"Whatcha gonna do? Lock me in here? Come on, Pete. Open up this little bag. I know it's that dead boy you and that funeral creep were just talking about. I heard all about that boy on the news. So he's still here. How come? Poor little thing all alone and cold in a refrigerator."

"He's lost it," Benton says. "Completely lost it."

"You don't want to see that," Marino says to her, walking back inside the cooler.

"Why not? That little boy found at Hilton Head. The one all over the news," she repeats herself. "I knew it. Why's he still here? They know who did it?" She holds her position by the little black pouch on its gurney.

"We don't know a damn thing. That's why he's still here. Come on." He motions to her, and it's difficult to hear both of them.

"Let me see him."

"Don't do it." Lucy's voice, talking to Marino's image on the screen. "Don't fuck yourself, Marino."

"You don't want to," he says to Shandy.

"I can handle it. I got a right to see him, because you're not supposed to have secrets. That's our rule. So prove right now you don't keep secrets from me." She can't take her eyes off the pouch.

"Nope. With stuff like this, the secret rule don't count."

"Oh, yes it does. Better hurry, I'm turning as cold as a dead body in here."

"Because if the Doc ever found out . . ."

"There you go again. Scared of her like

she fucking owns you. What's so bad you don't think I can handle it?" Shandy says furiously, almost screaming as she holds herself because of the cold. "I bet he doesn't stink as bad as that old lady."

"He's been skinned and his eyeballs are gone," Marino tells her.

"Oh, no," Benton says, rubbing his face.

Shandy exclaims, "Don't mess with me! Don't you dare joke with me! You let me see him right now! I'm sick and tired of you always turning into a damn wimp when *she* tells you something!"

"Nothing funny about it, you got that right. What goes on in this place ain't no joke. I keep trying to tell you that. You got no idea what I deal with."

"Well, isn't that something. To think your Big Chief would do something like that. Skinning a little kid and cutting out his eyes. You always said she treats the dead real nice." Hatefully. "Sounds like a Nazi to me. They used to skin people and make lampshades."

"Sometimes the only way you can tell if darkish or reddish areas are really bruises is to look at the underside of the skin so you can make sure what you're looking at is broken blood vessels—in other words, bruises or what we call contusions—instead of it be-ing from livor mortis," Marino pontificates.

"This is unreal." Lucy sounds in Benton's ear. "So now he's the chief medical examiner."

"Not unreal," Benton says. "Massively in-secure. Threatened. Resentful. Overcom-pensating and decompensating. I don't know what's going on with him."

"You and Aunt Kay are what's going on with him."

"From what?" Shandy stares at the little black pouch.

"From when your circulation stops, and the blood settles and can make your skin look red in places. Can look a whole lot like fresh bruises. And there can be other rea-sons for things that look like injuries, what we call postmortem artifacts. It's compli-cated," Marino says with self-importance. "So to make sure, you peel back the skin, you know, with a scalpel"—he makes swift cutting motions in the air—"to see the under-side of it, and in this case, they were bruises, all right. The little guy's covered with them from head to toe."

"But why would you take out his eyeballs?"

"Further study, looking for more hemor-rhages like you find in shaking baby syndrome, things like that. Same with his brain. It's fixed in formalin in a bucket, not here but at a medical school where they do special studies."

"Oh my God. His brain's in a bucket?"

"It's just what we do. Fixing it in this chemical so it don't decompose and can be looked at better. Sort of like embalming."

"You sure know a lot. You should be the doctor around here, not *her*. Let me look."

All this inside the cooler, the door wide open.

"I've been doing this practically longer than you're old," Marino says. "Sure, I could've been a doctor, but who the hell wants to go to school that long? Who'd want to be her, either? She's got no life. Nobody but dead people."

"I want to see him," Shandy demands.

"Damn, don't know what it is," Marino says. "Can't be inside a damn cooler without dying for a cigarette."

She digs in a pocket of the leather vest under her gown, pulls out a pack, a lighter. "I can't believe someone would do that to a little kid. I have to see him. I'm here, so show me." She lights up two cigarettes and they smoke.

"Manipulative, borderline," Benton says. "He's picked real trouble this time."

Marino rolls out the tray, rolls it out of the cooler.

Unzipping the pouch. Plastic rustling. Lucy zooms in tight on Shandy blowing out smoke, staring wide-eyed at the dead little boy.

An emaciated little body sliced in neat straight lines from chin to genitals, from shoulders to hands, from hips to toes, his chest open like a hollowed-out watermelon. His organs are gone. His skin is reflected back from his body and spread out in flaps that reveal scores of dark purple hemorrhages of varying ages and severity, and tears and fractures to cartilage and bone. His eyes are empty holes, and through them is the inside of his skull.

Shandy screams, "I hate that woman! I hate her! How could she do this to him! Gutted and skinned like a shot deer! How can you work for that psycho bitch!"

"Calm down. Quit yelling." Marino zips up the pouch and rolls it back inside the cooler. He shuts the door. "I warned you. There's some things people don't need to see. They can get a post-trauma stress condition from stuff like this."

"Now I'll see him forever in my head, looking just like that. Sicko bitch. Damn Nazi."

"You keep your mouth shut about this, you hear me?" Marino says.

"How can you work for someone like that?"

"Shut up. I mean it," Marino says. "I helped with the autopsy, and I'm sure as hell no Nazi. That's what happens. People get fucked over twice when they get murdered." He takes Shandy's surgical gown, hastily folds it. "That little kid was probably murdered the day he was born. No one giving a rat's ass about him, and this is the result."

"What do you know about life? You people think you know everything about everyone when all you see is what's left when you cut them up like a butcher."

"You're the one who wanted to come in here." Marino is getting angry. "So shut up about it, and don't call me a butcher."

He leaves Shandy in the hallway, returns the gown to Scarpetta's locker. He sets the alarm. The camera in the bay captures them, the huge bay door screeching and clanking up.

Lucy's voice. Benton will have to be the one to inform Scarpetta about Marino's tour, about a betrayal that could destroy her if the media ever found out. Lucy's headed to the airport, won't be back until late tomorrow. Benton doesn't ask. He's pretty sure she already knows, even if she hasn't told him. Then she tells him about Dr. Self, about her e-mails to Marino.

Benton doesn't comment. He can't. On his video screen, Marino and Shandy Snook ride off on their motorcycles.

Chapter 5

The clatter of metal wheels on tile.

The walk-in freezer door opens with a reluctant suck. Scarpetta is impervious to the frigid air, the stench of frozen death as she rolls in the steel cart bearing the small black body bag. Attached to the zipper pull is a toe tag, and written on it in black ink: *Unknown,* with the date, *4/30/07,* and the signature of the funeral home attendant who transported the body. In the morgue log Scarpetta entered *Unknown* as a *male, five to ten years old,* a *homicide* from *Hilton Head Island,* a two-hour drive from Charleston. His race is mixed:

thirty-four percent sub-Saharan African and sixty-six percent European.

Entries into the log are always made by her, and she is outraged by what she discovered when she arrived hours earlier and found this morning's case had already been entered, presumably by Lucious Meddick. Unbelievably, he took it upon himself to decide the elderly woman he transported is a *natural* death caused by *cardiac and respiratory arrest.* The presumptuous moron. Everybody dies of cardiac or respiratory arrest. Whether shot or hit by a car or a baseball bat, death occurs when the heart and lungs quit. He had no right or reason to conclude the death is natural. She hasn't done the autopsy yet, and it isn't his responsibility or legal jurisdiction to determine a goddamn thing. He's not a forensic pathologist. He should never have touched the morgue log. She can't fathom why Marino would have allowed him to enter the autopsy suite and then left him unattended.

Her breath fogs out as she removes a clipboard from a cart and fills in *Unknown's* information and the time and date. Her frustration is as palpable as the cold. Despite her obsessive efforts, she doesn't know where the little boy died, although she suspects it isn't far from where he was found. She doesn't know his exact age. She doesn't know how his killer transported the body but hypothesizes it was by boat. No witnesses have come forward, and the only trace evidence she recovered is white cotton fibers assumed to be from the sheet the Beaufort County coroner wrapped him in before zipping him inside a pouch.

The sand and salt and bits of shells and plant debris in the boy's orifices and on his skin are indigenous to the marshland where his nude decomposing body was facedown in pluff mud and saw grass. After days of using every procedure she can conjure up to make his body talk to her, he has offered but a few painful revelations. His tubular stomach and emaciation say he was starved for weeks, possibly months. Mildly deformed nails indicate new growth of different ages and suggest repeated blunt-force trauma or some other type of torture to his tiny fingers and toes. Subtle reddish patterns all over his body tattle to her that he was brutally beaten, most recently with a wide belt that had a large square buckle. Incisions, a reflecting back of skin, and microscopic analysis revealed hemorrhaging into soft tissue from the crown of his head to the soles of his little feet. He died of internal exsanguination—bled to death without externally shedding a drop—a metaphor, it seems, for his invisible and miserable life.

She has preserved sections of his organs and injuries in jars of formalin and sent off his brain and eyes for special examination. She's taken hundreds of photographs, and notified Interpol in the event he's been reported missing in another country. His fingerprints and footprints have been entered into the Integrated Automated Fingerprint Identification System (IAFIS) and his DNA profile into the Combined DNA Index System (CODIS)—all of his information entered into the National Center for Missing and Exploited Children database. Of course, now Lucy is searching the Deep Web. So far, there are no leads, no matches, suggesting he wasn't abducted, wasn't lost, didn't run away and end up in the hands of a sadistic stranger. Most likely he was beaten to death by a parent or some other relative, guardian, or so-called caregiver who left his body in a remote area to hide his or her crime. It happens all the time.

Scarpetta can do nothing more for him medically or scientifically, but she won't give him up. There will be no defleshing and packing his bones in a box—no pauper's grave. Until he's identified, he will stay with her, transferred from the cooler to a time capsule of sorts, a polyurethane insulated freezer chilled to minus-sixty-five degrees centigrade. If need be, he can stay with her for years. She shuts the freezer's heavy steel door and walks out into the bright deodorized hallway, untying her blue surgical gown and pulling off her gloves. Her disposable shoe covers make a quick, quiet *whish* on the spotless tile floor.

From her room with a view, Dr. Self talks to Jackie Minor again, since Benton has yet to bother returning her call and it is now almost two p.m.

"He's well aware we need to take care of this. Why do you think he's here this weekend and asked you to come in? Do you get overtime, by the way?" Dr. Self doesn't show her ire.

"I knew there was a VIP all of a sudden. That's all any of us are usually told when it's somebody famous. We get a lot of famous people here. How did you find out about the study?" Jackie inquires. "I'm supposed to ask because I'm supposed to keep track so we can figure out what's the most effective form of advertising. You know, newspaper and radio ads, posting notices, word of mouth."

"The recruitment notice in the admissions building. I saw it first thing when I checked in what now seems a very long time ago. And it occurred to me, why not? I've decided to leave soon, very soon. It's a pity your weekend is ruined," Dr. Self says.

"Truth be told, it's a good thing. It's hard finding volunteers who meet the criteria, especially the normals. Such a waste. At least two out of three turn out not to be normal. But think about it. If you were normal, why would you want to come here and . . ."

"Be part of a science project." Dr. Self finishes Jackie's lamebrain thought. "I don't believe you can sign up as a *normal*."

"Oh, I didn't mean to say you're not . . ."

"I'm always open to learning something new, and I have an unusual reason for being here," Dr. Self says. "You're aware of how confidential this is."

"I heard you're sort of hiding here for security reasons."

"Did Dr. Wesley tell you that?"

"A rumor. And confidentiality is a given, according to HIPAA, which we have to abide by. It must be safe for you to leave, if you are."

"One can only hope."

"Are you aware of the details of the study?"

"What I vaguely recall from the recruitment notice," Dr. Self says.

"Dr. Wesley hasn't gone over it with you?"

"He was just notified Friday when I informed Dr. Maroni, who's in Italy, that I wanted to volunteer for the study, but it would have to be taken care of immediately because I've decided to check out. I'm sure Dr. Wesley intends to brief me thoroughly. I don't know why he hasn't called. Perhaps he hasn't gotten your message yet."

"I told him, but he's a very busy, important person. I know he has to tape the VIP's mother today, meaning your mother. So I'm assuming he plans to do that first. Then I'm sure he'll talk to you."

"It must be so hard on his personal life. These studies and whatnot that keep him here on weekends. I suppose he must have a lover. A handsome, accomplished man like him certainly wouldn't be alone."

"He has someone down south. In fact, her niece was here about a month ago."

"How interesting," Dr. Self says.

"She came here for a scan. Lucy. Some secret agent type, or tries to look like one anyway. I know she's a computer entrepreneur, is friends with Josh."

"Involved in law enforcement," Dr. Self ponders. "Some type of secret operative, highly technically trained. And independently wealthy, I presume. Fascinating."

"She didn't even speak to me other than to introduce herself as Lucy and shake my hand and say hi and chat. She hung out with Josh, then was in Dr. Wesley's office for quite a while. With the door shut."

"What did you think of her?"

"She's really stuck on herself. Of course, I didn't spend time with her. She was hanging out with Dr. Wesley. With the door shut." She makes that point again.

Jealous. How perfect. "How nice," Dr. Self says. "They must be very close. She sounds very unusual. Is she pretty?"

"I thought she was rather masculine, if you get my drift. Dressed all in black and kind of muscular. A firm handshake like a guy. And she looked right into my eyes with this intense gaze. Like her eyes were these green laser beams. It made me very uncomfortable. I didn't want to be alone with her, now that I think about it. Women like that . . ."

"I hear you saying she was attracted to you and wanted sex with you before she flew back on, what? A private jet, let me guess," Dr. Self says. "Where did you say she lives?"

"Charleston. Like her aunt. I think she did want sex with me. My God. How could I not have realized that at the time, when she shook my hand and looked into my eyes. And oh, yes. She asked me if I had long hours, as if maybe she wanted to know what time I got off work. She asked me where I'm from. She got personal. I just didn't see it at the time."

"Perhaps because you were afraid to see it, Jackie. She does sound very appealing and charismatic, the sort who almost hypnotically lures a straight woman into bed, and after an extremely erotic experience . . . ?" A pause. "You do understand why two women having sex, even if one of them is straight or both are, isn't at all uncommon."

"Absolutely not."

"Do you read Freud?"

"I've never felt an attraction to another woman. Not even my roommate in college. And we lived together. If there was that latent predisposition, a lot more would have happened."

"Everything is about sex, Jackie. Sexual desire goes all the way back to infancy. What is it that both male and female infants get, that later is denied the female?"

"I don't know."

"The nurturing at mother's breast."

"I don't want that kind of nurturing and don't remember anything about it and only care about boobs because men like them. They're important for that reason, and I only notice them for that reason. I think I was bottle-fed, anyway."

"I do agree with you, though," Dr. Self says. "Rather odd she came all the way up here for a scan. I certainly hope there's nothing wrong with her."

"I just know she comes in a couple times a year."

"A couple times a year?"

"That's what one of the techs said."

"How tragic if there's something wrong with her. You and I both know it isn't routine for someone to have brain scans several times a year. If at all. What else do I need to know about my scan?"

"Has anyone bothered to ask if you have a problem going into the magnet?" Jackie asks with the seriousness of an expert.

"A problem?"

"You know. If it might cause you a problem."

"Not unless after it's over I can no longer tell north from south. Another very astute point you're making, though. I do have to wonder what it does to people. I'm not sure that's really been determined. MRI hasn't been commonly used all that long, now has it."

"The study uses *fMRI*. Functional MRI, so we can watch your brain working while you listen to the tape."

"Yes, the tape. My mother will so enjoy making that tape. Now, what else do I have to look forward to?"

"The protocol is to start with the SCID. Let me explain, the Structured Clinical Interview for *DSM-Three-R*."

"I'm quite familiar. Especially with *DSM-Four*. The latest revision."

"Sometimes Dr. Wesley lets me do the SCID. We can't scan you until we get that out of the way, and it can be a lengthy process going through all those questions."

"I'll discuss that when I see him today. And if it's appropriate, inquire about Lucy. No, I suppose I shouldn't. But I do hope nothing's wrong with her. Especially since it seems she's very special to him."

"He's booked up with other patients, but I could probably find time to SCID you."

"Thank you, Jackie. I'll talk to him about it the minute he calls me. And have there been averse reactions to his fascinating study? And who funded the grant? I believe you said your father?"

"We've had a few people who were claustrophobic. So we couldn't scan them after all that work. Imagine," Jackie says, "I go to all the trouble to SCID them and tape their mothers . . ."

"Tape them over the phone, I presume. You've done quite a lot in one short week."

"Much cheaper and more efficient. No need to see these people in person. It's just a standard format, what you need them to talk about on tape. I'm not allowed to discuss grant funding, but my father's into philanthropy."

"The new show I'm developing. Did I mention I'm just on the brink of thinking about production consultants? You indicated Lucy is somehow involved with law enforcement? Or a special agent? She might be another one to consider. Unless there's something wrong with her. And she's had her brain scanned here how many times?"

"I'm sorry to say I've not watched your show much. Because of my schedule, I can only watch TV at night."

"My shows are aired repeatedly. Morning, noon, and night."

"Scientifically exploring the criminal mind and its behavior versus interviewing people who wear guns and just go around arresting them is really the right idea. Your audience would love it," Jackie says. "Love it a lot more than most of what's on these talk shows. I think getting an expert to interview one of these sexually violent psychopathic killers on your show would make your ratings go up."

"From which I am to infer that a psychopath who rapes or sexually abuses and kills might not necessarily be violent. That is an extraordinarily original concept, Jackie, which next makes me wonder if, for example, only sociopathic sexual murderers are also violent. And following that hypothesis, we next have to ask what?"

"Well . . ."

"Well, we have to ask where compulsive sexual homicide fits. Or is it all about vernacular? I say potato, you say spud."

"Well . . ."

"How much Freud have you read, and do you pay attention to your dreams? You should write them down, keep a journal by your bed."

"Of course, in classes, well, not the journal and dreams. I didn't do that in classes," Jackie says. "In real life, nobody's into Freud anymore."

Eight-thirty p.m., Rome time. Seagulls swoop and cry in the night. They look like large white bats.

In other cities near the coast, the gulls are a nuisance during the day but vanish after dark. Certainly this is true in America, where Captain Poma has spent considerable time. As a young boy, he frequented foreign lands with his family. He was to become a man of the world who spoke other languages fluently and had impeccable manners and an excellent education. He was to amount to something, his parents said. He watches two fat, snowy gulls on a windowsill near his table, eyeing him. Maybe it's the beluga caviar they want.

"I ask you where she is," he says in Italian. "And your answer is to inform me of a man I should know about? But you won't give me details? Now I'm extremely frustrated."

"What I said was the following," replies Dr. Paulo Maroni, who has known the captain for years. "Dr. Self had Drew Martin on her show, as you know. Weeks later, Dr. Self began getting e-mails from someone very disturbed. I know this, because she referred him to me."

"Paulo, please. I need details about this disturbed person."

"I was hoping you had them."

"I'm not the one who introduced the subject."

"You're the one working the case," Dr. Maroni says. "It appears I have more information than you do. That's depressing. So there's nothing."

"I wouldn't want to admit it publicly. We're no further along. That's why it's vital you tell me about this disturbed person. And I feel you are toying with me in a very strange way."

"For more details, you must talk to her. He isn't her patient, and she can talk about him freely. Assuming she's cooperative." He reaches for the silver plate of blini. "And that's a big assumption."

"Then help me find her," Captain Poma says. "Because I have a feeling you know where she is. That's why you suddenly called me and invited yourself to a very expensive dinner."

Dr. Maroni laughs. He could afford a roomful of the very best Russian caviar. That's not why he's having dinner with the captain. He knows something and has complex reasons, a scheme. This is typical of him. He's gifted in his understanding of human proclivities and motivations, possibly the most brilliant man the captain knows. But he's an enigma, and his definition of truth is his own.

"I can't tell you where she is," Dr. Maroni says.

"Which doesn't mean you don't know. You're playing your word games with me, Paulo. It's not that I'm lazy. It's not that I haven't tried very hard to find her. Ever since I learned she was acquainted with Drew, I've talked to people who work for her and am always told the same story that's been on the news. She had a mysterious family emergency. No one knows where she is."

"Logic would tell you it's impossible no one knows where she is."

"Yes, logic does tell me that," the captain says, spreading caviar on a blini and handing it to him. "I have a feeling you'll help me find her. Because as I say, you know, which is why you called me and now we're playing word games."

"Her staff has forwarded your e-mails requesting a meeting or at least a telephone conversation?" Dr. Maroni asks.

"So they say." The gulls fly away, interested in another table. "I won't reach her through the normal channels. She has no intention of acknowledging me, because the last thing she would want is to become a factor in the investigation. People might assign responsibility to her."

"As they probably should. She's irresponsible," Dr. Maroni says.

The wine steward appears to refill their glasses. The Hotel Hassler's rooftop restaurant is one of Captain Poma's favorites. The view is beautiful and he never tires of it, and he thinks about Kay Scarpetta and wonders if she and Benton Wesley ever ate here. Probably not. They were too busy. They strike him as too busy for what matters in life.

"You see? The more she's avoided me, the more I think she has a reason," the captain adds. "Maybe it's this disturbed man she referred to you. Please tell me where to find her, because I think you know."

Dr. Maroni says, "Did I mention we have regulations and standards in the United States, and lawsuits are the national sport?"

"Her staff's not going to tell me if she's a patient at your hospital."

"I would never tell you, either."

"Of course not." The captain smiles. Now he knows. He has no doubt.

"I'm so glad not to be there at the moment," Dr. Maroni then says. "We have a very difficult VIP at the Pavilion. I hope Benton Wesley can adequately handle her."

"I must talk to her. How can I make her think I found out from a source other than you?"

"You didn't find out anything from me."

"I found out from somebody. She'll demand I tell her."

"You found out nothing from me. In fact, you're the one who said it. And I haven't verified it."

"May we discuss it hypothetically?"

Dr. Maroni drinks his wine. "I prefer the Barbaresco we had last time."

"You would. It was three hundred euros."

"Full-bodied but very fresh."

"The wine? Or the woman you were with last night?"

For a man his age who eats and drinks whatever he pleases, Dr. Maroni looks good and is never without a woman. They offer themselves to him as if he is the god Priapus, and he's faithful to no one. Usually, he leaves his wife in Massachusetts when he comes to Rome. She doesn't seem to mind. She's well taken care of, and he isn't demanding about his sexual desires because she no longer meets them and he no longer is in love with her. This is a destiny the captain refuses to accept. He's romantic, and he wonders about Scarpetta again. She doesn't need to be taken care of and wouldn't permit it. Her presence in his thoughts is like the light of the candles on the tables and the lights of the city beyond the window. He is moved by her.

"I can contact her at the hospital. But she'll demand to know how I found out about her being there," the captain says.

"The VIP, you mean." Dr. Maroni dips a mother-of-pearl spoon into the caviar, scoops out enough for two blini. He spreads the caviar over one and eats it. "You mustn't contact anyone at the hospital."

"What if Benton Wesley's my source? He was just here and is involved in the investigation. And now she's his patient. It irritates me we talked about Dr. Self the other night and he didn't divulge she's his patient."

"You mean the VIP. Benton isn't a psychiatrist, and the VIP technically isn't his patient. Technically, the VIP is my patient."

The captain pauses as the waiter appears with the *primi piatti.* Risotto with mushrooms and Parmesan. Basil-flavored minestrone with quadrucci pasta.

"Anyway, Benton would never divulge a confidence like that. You may as well ask a stone," Dr. Maroni says when the waiter is gone. "My guess is the VIP will be gone soon. Where she goes will be the important question for you. Where she's been is important only because of motive."

"Dr. Self's show is filmed in New York."

"VIPs can go where they please. If you find out where she is and why, you might discover where she would go next. A more likely source would be Lucy Farinelli."

"Lucy Farinelli?" The captain is baffled.

"Dr. Scarpetta's niece. As it happens, I'm

doing her a favor, and she comes to the hospital fairly often. So she could hear rumors from the staff."

"And what? She told Kay, who next told me?"

"Kay?" Dr. Maroni eats. "Then you are on friendly terms with her?"

"I hope so. Not so friendly with him. I don't think he likes me."

"Most men don't like you, Otto. Only homosexuals. But you see my point. Hypothetically. If the information comes from an outsider—Lucy, who tells Dr. Scarpetta, who tells you"—Dr. Maroni eats the risotto with enthusiasm—"then there are no ethical or legal concerns. You can begin to follow the trail."

"And the VIP knows Kay's working with me on the case, since she was just here in Rome and it's been in the news. So this VIP will believe Kay indirectly is the source, and then there's no trouble. That's very good. Perfect."

"The *risotto ai funghi* is almost perfect. What about the minestrone? I've had it before," Dr. Maroni says.

"Excellent. This VIP. Without compromising confidentiality, can you tell me why she's a patient at McLean?"

"Her reason or mine? Personal safety is her reason. Mine is so she could take advantage of me. She has both axis one and axis two pathology. Rapid-cycling bipolar and refuses to acknowledge it, much less take a mood stabilizer. Which personality disorder would you like me to discuss? She has so many. I regret to say that people with personality disorders rarely change."

"So something caused a breakdown. Is this the VIP's first hospitalization for psychiatric reasons? I've been doing research. She's against medication and thinks all of the problems in the world can be managed by following her advice. What she calls *tools*."

"The VIP has no known history of hospitalization prior to this. Now you're asking the important questions. Not where she is. But why. I can't tell you where she is. I can tell you where the VIP is."

"Something was traumatic to your VIP?"

"This VIP received an e-mail from a madman. Coincidentally, the same madman Dr. Self told me about last fall."

"I must talk to her."

"Talk to who?"

"All right. May we discuss Dr. Self?"

"We'll change our conversation from the VIP to Dr. Self."

"Tell me more about this madman."

"As I said, someone I saw several times at my office here."

"I won't ask the name of this patient."

"Good, because I don't know it. He paid cash. And he lied."

"You have no idea about his real name?"

"Unlike you, I don't get to do a background check on a patient or demand proof of his true identity," Dr. Maroni says.

"Then what was his false name?"

"I can't tell you."

"Why did Dr. Self contact you about this man? And when?"

"Early October. She said he was sending e-mails to her and she thought it best to refer him elsewhere. As I've said."

"Then she's at least somewhat responsible, if she acknowledged a situation was beyond her capabilities," Captain Poma says.

"This is where, perhaps, you don't understand her. She would never begin to think anything is beyond her capabilities. She couldn't be bothered with him, and it appealed to her maniacal ego to refer him to a Nobel Prize–winning psychiatrist who is on the faculty of Harvard Medical School. It was gratifying to inconvenience me, as she's done many times before. She has her reasons. If nothing else, she probably knew I would fail. He isn't treatable." Dr. Maroni studies his wine as if there is an answer in it.

"Tell me this," Captain Poma says. "If he's untreatable, then don't you agree this also justifies what I'm thinking? He's a very abnormal man who may be doing very abnormal things. He's sent her e-mails. He may have sent her the e-mail she mentioned to you when she was admitted at McLean."

"You mean the VIP. I never said Dr. Self is at McLean. But if she were, you certainly should find out exactly why. It seems that's what matters. I'm repeating myself like a broken record."

"He might have sent the VIP the e-mail that disturbed her enough to make her hide at your hospital. We must locate him and at least be sure he isn't a murderer."

"I have no idea how to do that. As I said, I couldn't begin to tell you who he is. Only that he's an American and served in Iraq."

"What did he say was his purpose in coming to see you here in Rome? That's a long way for an appointment."

"He was suffering from PTSD. He seems to have connections in Italy. He told a very unsettling story about a young woman he spent a day with last summer. A body discovered near Bari. You remember the case."

"The Canadian tourist?" the captain says, surprised. "Shit."

"That's the one. Only she was unidentified at first."

"She was nude, badly mutilated."

"Not like Drew Martin, from what you've told me. The same thing wasn't done to the eyes."

"She was also missing large areas of flesh."

"Yes. At first it was assumed she was a prostitute who'd been thrown from a moving car or was hit by one, thus explaining these wounds," Dr. Maroni says. "The autopsy showed otherwise, was done very competently, even if it was performed in very primitive conditions. You know how these things go in remote areas that have no money."

"Especially if it's a prostitute. She was autopsied in a cemetery. Had the Canadian tourist not been reported missing about this same time, she may have been buried in the cemetery, unidentified," Captain Poma recalls.

"It was determined the flesh had been removed by some type of knife or saw."

"And you aren't going to tell me everything you know about this patient who paid cash and lied about his name?" the captain protests. "You must have notes you could share with me?"

"Impossible. What he told me is no proof."

"What if he's this killer, Paulo?"

"If I had more evidence, I'd tell you. I have only his twisted tales and the uneasy feeling I got when I was contacted about the murdered prostitute who turned out to be the missing Canadian."

"You were contacted? What? For your opinion? That's news to me."

"It was worked by the state police. Not the Carabinieri. I give my free advice to many people. In summary, this patient never came to see me again, and I couldn't tell you where he is," Dr. Maroni says.

"Couldn't or won't."

"I couldn't."

"Don't you see how it's possible he's Drew

Martin's killer? He was referred to you by Dr. Self, and suddenly she hides at your hospital because of an e-mail from a madman."

"Now you're perseverating and back to the VIP. I've never said Dr. Self is a patient at the hospital. But motivation for hiding is more important than the hiding place itself."

"If only I could dig with a shovel inside your head, Paulo. No telling what I'd find."

"Risotto and wine."

"If you know details that could help this investigation, I don't agree with your secrecy," the captain says, and then he says nothing because the waiter is heading toward them.

Dr. Maroni asks to see the menu again, even though he has tried everything on it by now because he dines here often. The captain, who doesn't want a menu, recommends the grilled Mediterranean spiny lobster, followed by salad and Italian cheeses. The male seagull returns alone. He stares through the window, ruffling his bright white feathers. Beyond are the lights of the city. The gold dome of Saint Peter's looks like a crown.

"Otto, if I violate confidentiality with so little evidence and am mistaken, my career is finished," Dr. Maroni finally says. "I don't have a legitimate reason to expose further details about him to the police. It would be most unwise of me."

"So you introduce the subject of who may be the killer and then close the door?" Captain Poma leans into the table and says in despair.

"I didn't open that door," Dr. Maroni says. "All I did was point it out to you."

Lost in her work, Scarpetta is startled when the alarm on her wristwatch goes off at quarter of three.

She finishes suturing the Y incision of the decomposing elderly woman whose autopsy was unnecessary. Atherosclerotic plaque. Cause of death, as expected, arteriosclerotic coronary vascular disease. She pulls off her gloves and drops them in a bright red biohazard trash can, then calls Rose.

"I'll be up in a minute," Scarpetta tells her. "If you could contact Meddicks', let them know she's ready for pickup."

"I was just coming down to find you," Rose says. "Worried you might have accidentally locked yourself in the fridge." An old joke. "Benton's trying to reach you. Says for you to check your e-mail when, and I quote, you are alone and composed."

"You sound worse than you did yesterday. More congested."

"I might have a bit of a cold."

"I heard Marino's motorcycle a little while ago. And someone's been smoking down here. In the fridge. Even my surgical gown reeks of it."

"That's odd."

"Where is he? Be nice if he could have found time to help me out down here."

"In the kitchen," Rose says.

Fresh gloves, and Scarpetta pulls the elderly woman's body from the autopsy table into a sheet-lined sturdy vinyl bag on top of a gurney, which she rolls into the cooler. She hoses off her work station, places tubes of vitreous fluid, urine, bile, and blood, and a carton of sectioned organs into a refrigerator for later toxicological testing and histology. Bloodstained cards go under a hood to dry— samples for DNA testing that are included in each case file. After mopping the floor and cleaning surgical instruments and sinks and gathering paperwork for later dictation, she's ready to attend to her own hygiene.

At the back of the autopsy suite are drying cabinets with HEPA and carbon filters for bloody, soiled clothing before it is packaged as evidence and sent to the labs. Next is a storage area, then a laundry room, and finally the locker room, divided by a glass-block wall. One side for men, the other for women. At this early stage of her practice in Charleston, it's just Marino assisting her in the morgue. He has his side of the locker room and she has the other, and it always feels awkward to her when both of them are showering at the same time and she can hear him and see changes in light through the thick green translucent glass as he moves about.

She enters her side of the locker room, shuts and locks the door. She removes her disposable shoe covers, apron, cap, and face mask, and drops them in a biohazard trash can, then tosses her surgical gown in a hamper. She showers, scrubbing herself with antibacterial soap, then blow-dries her hair and changes back into her suit and pumps. Returning to the corridor, she walks the length of it to a door. On the other side is the steep flight of worn oak stairs that lead directly up to the kitchen where Marino is popping open a can of Diet Pepsi.

He looks her up and down. "Aren't we dressed fancy," he says. "You forget it's Sunday and think you got court? So much for my ride to Myrtle Beach." A long night of carousing shows on his flushed, stubbly face.

"Count it as a gift. Another day of being alive." She hates motorcycles. "Besides, the weather is bad and supposed to get worse."

"Eventually I'm gonna get you on the back of my Indian Chief Roadmaster and you'll be hooked, be begging for more."

The idea of straddling his big motorcycle, her arms around him, her body pressed against him, is a complete turnoff, and he knows it. She's his boss, and in many ways always has been for the better part of twenty years, and that no longer seems all right with him. Certainly both of them have changed. Certainly they've had their good times and bad. But over recent years and especially of late, his regard for her and his job has become increasingly unrecognizable, and now this. She thinks of Dr. Self's e-mails, wonders if he assumes she's seen them. She thinks of whatever game Dr. Self is engaging him in—a game he won't understand and is destined to lose.

"I could hear you come in. Obviously, you parked your motorcycle in the bay again," she says. "If it gets hit by a hearse or a van," she reminds him, "the liability's yours and I won't feel sorry for you."

"It gets hit, there'll be an extra dead body wheeled in, whatever dumbshit funeral home creepy-crawler didn't look where he was going."

Marino's motorcycle, with its sound barrier–breaking pipes, has become yet one more point of contention. He rides it to crime scenes, to court, to emergency rooms, to law offices, to witnesses' homes. At the office, he refuses to leave it in the parking lot and tucks it in the bay, which is for body deliveries, not personal vehicles.

"Has Mr. Grant gotten here yet?" Scarpetta says.

"Drove up in a piece-of-shit pickup truck with his piece-of-shit fishing boat, shrimp nets, buckets, other crap in back. One big son of a bitch, pitch-black. I've never seen black people as black as they are around here. Not a drop of cream in the coffee. Not like our ole stomping grounds in Virginia where Thomas Jefferson slept with the help."

She's in no mood to engage in his provocations. "Is he in my office, because I don't want to make him wait."

"I don't get why you dressed up for him

like you're meeting with a lawyer or a judge or going to church," Marino says, and she wonders if what he really hopes is that she dressed up for him, perhaps because she read Dr. Self's e-mails and is jealous.

"Meeting with him is as important as meeting with anyone else," she says. "We always show respect, remember?"

Marino smells like cigarettes and booze, and when "his chemistry's off," as Scarpetta understates it all too often these days, his deep-seated insecurities shift his bad behavior into high gear, a problem made quite threatening by his physical formidability. In his mid-fifties, he shaves off what is left of his hair, typically wears black motorcycle clothing and big boots, and, as of the past few days, a gaudy necklace with a silver dollar dangling from it. He is fanatical about lifting weights, his chest so broad he's known to brag that it takes two x-rays to capture his lungs on film. In a much earlier phase of his life, based on old photographs she's seen, he was handsome in a virile, tough way, and might still be attractive were it not for his crassness, slovenliness, and hard living that at this point in his life can't be blamed on his difficult upbringing in a rough part of New Jersey.

"I don't know why you still entertain the fantasy that you'll fool me," Scarpetta says, shifting the conversation away from the ridiculous subject of how she is dressed and why. "Last night. And clearly in the morgue."

"Fool you about what?" Another gulp from the can.

"When you splash on that much cologne to disguise cigarette smoke, all you do is give me a headache."

"Huh?" He quietly belches.

"Let me guess, you spent the night at the Kick 'N Horse."

"The joint's full of cigarette smoke." He shrugs his massive shoulders.

"And I'm sure you didn't add to it. You were smoking in the morgue. In the fridge. Even the surgical gown I put on smelled like cigarette smoke. Were you smoking in my locker room?"

"Probably drifted in from my side. The smoke, I mean. I might have carried my cigarette in there, in my side. I can't remember."

"I know you don't want lung cancer."

He averts his eyes the way he does when

a certain topic of conversation is uncomfortable, and he chooses to abort it. "Find anything new? And I don't mean the old lady, who shouldn't have been sent here just because the coroner didn't want to deal with a stinky decomp. But the kid."

"I've put him in the freezer. There's nothing more we can do right now."

"I can't stand it when it's kids. I figure out who did that little kid down there, I'll kill him, tear him to pieces with my bare hands."

"Let's don't threaten to kill people, please." Rose is in the doorway, an odd expression on her face. Scarpetta isn't sure how long she's been standing there.

"It ain't no threat," Marino says.

"That's exactly why I mentioned it." Rose steps into the kitchen, dressed as neat as a pin—her old-fashioned expression—in a blue suit, her white hair tucked back in a French twist. She looks exhausted, and her pupils are contracted.

"You lecturing me again?" Marino says to her with a wink.

"You need a good lecture or two. Or three or four," she says, pouring herself a cup of strong black coffee, a "bad" habit she quit about a year ago and now, apparently, has resumed. "And in case you've forgotten"—she eyes him above the rim of her coffee mug—"you have killed people before. So you shouldn't make threats." She leans against the countertop and takes a deep breath.

"I told you. It ain't no threat."

"You sure you're all right?" Scarpetta asks Rose. "Maybe you're getting more than a little cold. You shouldn't have come in."

"I had a little chat with Lucy," Rose says. To Marino, "I don't want Dr. Scarpetta alone with Mr. Grant. Not even for a second."

"Did she mention he passed his background check?" Scarpetta says.

"You hear me, Marino? Not for one second do you leave Dr. Scarpetta alone with that man. I don't give a hoot about his background check. He's bigger than you are," says the ever-protective Rose, probably upon the ever-protective Lucy's instructions.

Rose has been Scarpetta's secretary for almost twenty years, following her from pillar to post, in Rose's words, and through thick and thin. At seventy-three, she's an attractive, imposing figure, erect and keen, daily drifting in and out of the morgue armed with phone messages, reports that must be signed right this minute, any matter of business she decides can't wait, or simply a reminder—no, an order—that Scarpetta hasn't eaten all day and take-out food—healthy, of course—awaits her upstairs and she *will* go eat it now and she *won't* have another cup of coffee because she drinks too much coffee.

"He's been in what appears to be a knife fight." Rose continues to worry.

"It's in his background check. He was the victim," Scarpetta says.

"He looks very violent and dangerous, and is the size of a freighter. It concerns me greatly that he wanted to come here on a Sunday afternoon, perhaps hoping he'd find you alone," she says to Scarpetta. "How do you know he isn't the one who killed that child?"

"Let's just hear what he has to say."

"In the old days, we wouldn't do it like this. There would be a police presence," Rose insists.

"This isn't the old days," Scarpetta replies, trying not to lecture. "This is a private practice, and we have more flexibility in some ways and less in others. But in fact, part of our job has always been to meet with anyone who might have useful information, police presence or not."

"Just be careful," Rose says to Marino. "Whoever did this to that poor little boy knows darn well his body's here and Dr. Scarpetta's working on it, and usually when she works on something, she figures it out. He could be stalking her, for all we know."

Usually Rose doesn't get this overwrought.

"You've been smoking," Rose then says to Marino.

He takes another big gulp of Diet Pepsi. "Should've seen me last night. Had ten cigarettes in my mouth and two in my ass while I was playing the harmonica and getting it on with my new woman."

"Another edifying evening at that biker bar with some woman whose IQ is the same as my refrigerator. Sub-Zero. Please don't smoke. I don't want you to die." Rose looks troubled as she walks over to the coffeemaker and starts filling the pot with water to make a fresh pot. "Mr. Grant would like coffee," she says. "And no, Dr. Scarpetta, you can't have any."

Chapter 6

Bulrush Ulysses S. Grant has always been called Bull. Without any prompting, he begins the conversation by explaining the origin of his name.

"I 'spect you're wondering about the S part of my name. That's it. Just an S and a period," he says from a chair near Scarpetta's shut office door. "My mama knows the S in General Grant's name is for Simpson. But she was afraid if she stuck Simpson in there, it would be a lot for me to write out. So she left it at S. Explaining it takes longer than writing it out, you ask me."

He's neat and clean in freshly pressed

gray work clothes, and his sneakers look as if they just came out of the washing machine. A frayed yellow baseball cap with a fish on it is in his lap, his big hands politely folded on top of it. The rest of his appearance is frightening, his face, neck, and scalp savagely slashed with a crisscross of long, pink gashes. If he ever saw a plastic surgeon, it wasn't a good one. He will be badly disfigured for life, a patchwork of keloid scars that make Scarpetta think of Queequeg in *Moby-Dick*.

"I know you just moved here not all that long ago," Bull says, to her surprise. "In that old carriage house that backs up to the alley between Meeting and King."

"How the hell do you know where she supposedly lives, and what business is it of yours?" Marino aggressively interrupts him.

"I used to work for one of your neighbors." Bull directs this to Scarpetta. "She passed on a long time back. I guess it would be more accurate to say I worked for her maybe fifteen years, then 'bout four years ago her husband passed. After that, she got rid of most of her help, I think had money anxiousness, and I had to find me something else. Then she passed, too. What I'm telling you is

I know the area where you live like the back of my hand."

She looks at the pink scars on the backs of his hands.

"I know your house. . . ." he adds.

"Like I said . . ." Marino starts in again.

"Let him finish," Scarpetta says.

"I know your garden real good 'cause I dug the pond and poured the cement, and took care of the angel statue looking over it, kept her nice and clean. I built the white fence with finials on one side. But not the brick columns and wrought iron on the other. That was before my time and probably so overgrowed with wax myrtle and bamboo when you bought the place, you didn't know it was there. I planted roses, Europa, California poppies, and Chinese jasmine, and I fixed things around the house."

Scarpetta is stunned.

"Anyhow," Bull says, "I been doing things for half the people up and down your alley-way and on King Street, Meeting Street, Church Street, all over. Since I was a boy. You wouldn't know it because I keep to my own business. That's a good thing if you don't want folks around here to take offense to you."

She says, "Like they do to me?"

Marino shoots her a disdainful look. She's being too friendly.

"Yes, ma'am. They sure can be like that around here," Bull says. "Then you put all them spiderweb decals on all the windows, and that don't help, 'specially because of what you do for a living. One of your neighbors, if I'm honest, calls you Dr. Halloween."

"Let me guess. That would be Mrs. Grimball."

"I wouldn't take no seriousness to it," Bull says. "She calls me Olé. 'Cause of me being called Bull."

"The decals are so birds don't fly into the glass."

"Uh-huh. Never have figured out how we know exactly what birds see. Like do they see what's s'posed to be a spiderweb and head the other way even though I never have seen a bird caught up in a spiderweb like it's a bug or something. It's like saying dogs is color-blind or got no sense of time. How do we know?"

"What business is it of yours to be anywhere near her house?" Marino says.

"Looking for work. When I was a boy, I helped out Mrs. Whaley, too," Bull says to

Scarpetta. "Now, I'm sure you've heard of Mrs. Whaley's garden, the most famous one here in Charleston, down there on Church Street." He smiles proudly, pointing in the general direction, wounds on his hand flashing pink.

He has them on his palms, too. Defensive injuries, Scarpetta thinks.

"That was a real privilege working for Mrs. Whaley. She was real good to me. She wrote a book, you know. They keep copies of it right there in the window of that bookstore at the Charleston Hotel. She signed a copy for me once. I still got it."

"What the shit's going on here?" Marino says. "You come to the morgue to talk to us about that dead little boy, or is this a damn job interview and stroll through memory lane?"

"Sometimes things fit together in mysterious ways," Bull says. "My mama always says that. Maybe something good come out of the bad. Maybe something good could come out of what happened. And what happened is bad, all right. Like a movie in my head playing all the time, seeing that little boy dead in the mud. Crabs and flies crawling on him." Bull touches a scarred index finger to his scarred, furrowed brow. "Up there, I see it when I shut my eyes. The police in Beaufort County says you're still getting established down here." He scans Scarpetta's office, slowly taking in all her books and framed degrees. "You look pretty established to me, but I probably could've done you better." His attention drifts to recently installed cabinets, where she locks up sensitive cases and ones that haven't gone to court yet. "Like that black walnut door ain't flush with the one beside it. Not hung straight. I could fix it easy enough. You see any doors hung crooked in your carriage house? No, ma'am, you don't. Not ones I hung back then when I helped out over there. Can do 'bout anything, and if I don't know, I'm sure willing to learn. So I said to myself, maybe I should just ask. No harm in asking."

"So maybe *I* should just ask," Marino says. "You kill that little boy? Kind of a coincidence you found him, right?"

"No, sir." Bull looks at him, looks him straight in the eye, his jaw muscles flexing. "I go all over these parts cutting sweetgrass, fishing, shrimping, digging clams, and picking oysters. Let me ask you"—he holds Marino's stare—"if I killed that boy, why would I be the one to find him and call for the police?"

"You tell me. Why would you?"

"I sure wouldn't."

"That reminds me. How'd you call anyone?" Marino says, leaning farther forward in his chair, hands the size of bear paws on his knees. "You got yourself a cell phone?" As if a poor black man wouldn't have a cell phone.

"I called nine-one-one. And like I said, why would I if I was the one who killed that boy?"

He wouldn't. Furthermore, although Scarpetta isn't going to say it to him, the victim is a child-abuse homicide with old healed fractures, scarring, and obvious food deprivation. So unless Bulrush Ulysses S. Grant was the boy's caretaker or foster parent, or kidnapped him and kept him alive for months or years, he certainly isn't the one who killed him.

Marino says to Bull, "You called here saying you want to tell us what happened this past Monday morning, almost a week ago to the day. But first. Where do you live? Because as I understand it, you don't live in Hilton Head."

"Oh, no, sir, I sure don't." Bull laughs. "Believe that's a little beyond my means. Me and my family got us a little place northwest of here off five twenty-six. I do a lot of fishing and other things in these parts. Haul my boat in the back of my truck, drive it places, and put it in the water. Like I say, shrimping, fishing, oysters, depending on the season. I got me one of these flat-bottom boats don't weigh more than a feather and can make it up the creeks, long as I know the tides and don't get stuck high and dry out there with all them skeeters and no-see-ums. Cotton-mouths and rattlers. Gators, too, but that's mostly in the canals and creeks where there's woods and the water's brackish."

"The boat you're talking about is the one in the back of that truck you parked in the lot?" Marino asks.

"That's right."

"Aluminum with what? Five-horsepower engine?"

"That's right."

"I'd like to take a look at it before you drive off. You got any objections to my looking inside your boat and truck? I'm assuming the police already did."

"No, sir, they didn't. When they got there and I told them what I knew, they said I could go. So I headed back to the put-in where my truck was. By then all kinds of people was there. But you go on and help yourself. I got nothing to hide."

"Thank you, but it's not necessary." Scarpetta gives Marino a look. He knows damn well they don't have jurisdiction to search Mr. Grant's truck or boat or anything else. That's for the police to do, and they didn't think it necessary.

"Where did you put your boat in the water six days ago?" Marino says to Bull.

"Old House Creek. There's a boat landing and little store where if I've had me a good day, I sell some of what I catch. Especially if I get lucky with shrimps and oysters."

"You see anybody suspicious in the area when you parked your truck this past Monday morning?"

"Can't say I did, but don't know why I would. By then the little boy was already where I found him and had been for days."

"Who said days?" Scarpetta asks.

"The funeral home man in the parking lot."

"The one who drove the body here?"

"No, ma'am. The other one. He was there with his big hearse. Don't know what he was doing there. Except talking."

"Lucious Meddick?" Scarpetta asks.

"Meddicks' Funeral Home. Yes, ma'am. According to his thinking, that little boy was dead for two, three days by the time I found him."

That damn Lucious Meddick. Presumptuous as hell, and wrong. April 29 and 30, the temperatures ranged between seventy-five and eighty degrees. Had the body been in the marsh for even one full day, it would have begun to decompose and suffer substantial damage from predatory animals and fish. Flies are quiet at night but would have laid eggs in daylight, and he would have been infested with maggots. As it was, by the time the body arrived at the morgue, rigor mortis was well developed but not complete, although that particular postmortem change would have been somewhat lessened and slowed due to malnourishment and subsequent poor muscle development. Livor mortis was indistinct, not yet fixed. There was no discoloration due to putrefaction. Crabs, shrimp, and the like were just getting started on the ears, nose, and lips. In her estimation, the boy had been dead less than twenty-four hours. Maybe much less than that.

"Go on," Marino says. "Tell us exactly how you found the body."

"I anchored my boat and got out in my boots and gloves, carrying my basket and a hammer . . ."

"A hammer?"

"For breaking up coons."

"Coons?" Marino says with a smirk.

"Coon oysters are stuck together in clusters, so you break them apart and knock loose any dead shells. Coons is mostly what you get, hard to find select ones." He pauses, says, "Don't seem you folks know much about oystering. So let me explain. A select oyster is a single one like you get on the half-shell in a restaurant. That's the kind you want but are hard to find. Anyhow, I started picking about noon. The tide was fairly low. And that's when I caught me a glance of something in the grass that looked like muddy hair, got closer, and there he was."

"Did you touch him or move him?" Scarpetta asks.

"No, ma'am." Shaking his head. "Once I saw what it was, I got right back in my boat and called nine-one-one."

"Low tide started around one in the morning," she says.

"That's so. And by seven it was high again—as high as it was going to get. And by the time I was out there, it was pretty low again."

"If it was you," Marino says, "and you wanted to get rid of a body using your boat, would you do it at low tide or high tide?"

"Whoever done it probably put him there when the tide was fairly low, put him in the mud and grass on the side of that little creek. Otherwise, the body would have been carried on out by the current if the tide was real high. But you put him in a place like the one I found him in, he's most likely gonna stay right there unless it's a spring tide at a full moon when the water can get up to ten feet. In that case, he might have been carried out, could have ended up anywhere."

Scarpetta has looked it up. The night before the body was found, the moon was no more than a third full, the skies partly cloudy.

"A smart place to dump a body. In a week, he wouldn't have been much more than scattered bones," Marino says. "It's a miracle he was found, don't you think?"

"It wouldn't take long out there to be nothing but bones, and it was a good chance no one would ever find him, that's true," Bull says.

"Thing is, when I mentioned high versus

low tide, I didn't ask you to speculate about what someone else would have done. I asked what you would have done," Marino says.

"Low tide in a small boat that doesn't have much draw, so you could get into places no more'an a foot deep. That's what I would've done. But I didn't." He stares Marino in the eye again. "I didn't do nothing to that little boy except find him."

Scarpetta gives Marino another pointed glance, has had enough of his interrogating and intimidating. She says to Bull, "Is there anything else you can remember? Anybody you saw in the area? Anybody you may have seen in the area who got your attention?"

"I keep thinking about that, and the only thing that comes to mind is about a week ago I was at this same landing, Old House Creek, in the market there selling shrimps, and when I was leaving I noticed this person tying up a boat. A bass boat. What got my attention is he didn't have nothing in it you might use for shrimping, oystering, fishing, so I just figured he liked being out in his boat. Didn't care about fishing or nothing, just liked being on the water, you know. I admit I didn't like the way he stared at me.

Gave me a funny feeling. Like he'd seen me somewhere."

"You get a description?" Marino asks. "See what he was driving? A truck, I assume, for hauling his boat?"

"He had a hat pulled low, sunglasses. Don't seem he was real big, but I couldn't tell you. And I had no reason to look hard and didn't want him thinking I was looking at him. That's how things get started, you know. My recollection is he had on boots. Long pants and a long-sleeve T-shirt, for sure, and I remember wondering about that because it was a warm, sunny day. I never did see what he was driving because I left before he did and there was a number of trucks and cars in the lot. A busy time. Folks coming in, buying and selling fresh-caught seafood."

"In your opinion, would someone have to know that area to dispose of a body there?" Scarpetta asks.

"After dark? Lord. I don't know anybody who goes in creeks like that after dark. I wouldn't. But that don't mean it didn't happen. Whoever did it isn't like regular people anyhow. Couldn't be, to do something like that to a little child."

"Did you notice any disturbance in the grass, the mud, the oyster bed when you found him?" Scarpetta asks.

"No, ma'am. But if somebody put the body there the night before during low tide, then during high tide the water would have smoothed out the mud just like when a wave goes over the sand. He would have been underwater for a while, but stayed put because of all that tall grass he was in. And the oyster bed, you wouldn't want to step on that anyhow. Would step over it or go around it as best you can. Nothing much hurts worse than a cut from an oyster shell. You step in the middle of them and lose your balance, you can get mighty cut up."

"Maybe that's what cut you up," Marino says. "You fell in the oyster bed."

Scarpetta knows cutting injuries made by a blade when she sees them, and says, "Mr. Grant, there are houses set back from the marshland, and long piers, one not far from where you found him. Possible he could have been transported by car, then carried over a pier, let's say, and ended up where he was found?"

"I can't imagine anybody climbing down

the ladder of one of them old piers, especially after dark, while carrying a body and a flashlight. And you sure would have to have a powerful flashlight. A man can sink up to his hips in that mud, suck the shoes right off your feet. Would think there would have been muddy footprints on the pier, assuming he climbed back up and left that way after he done it."

"How do you know there weren't any muddy footprints on the pier?" Marino asks him.

"The man from the funeral home told me so. I was waiting in the parking lot until they brought in the body, and he was there talking to the police."

"This would be Lucious Meddick again," Scarpetta says.

Bull nods. "He spent a lot of time talking to me, too, wanting to know what I had to say. I didn't tell him much."

A knock on the door and Rose walks in, sets a mug of coffee on the table next to Bull, her hands shaking. "Cream and sugar," she says. "Sorry it took so long. The first pot overflowed, grounds everywhere."

"Thank you, ma'am."

"Anybody else need anything?" Rose looks around, takes a deep breath, looks more exhausted and paler than she did earlier.

Scarpetta says. "Why don't you go home? Get some rest."

"I'll be in my office."

The door shuts and Bull says, "I'd like to explain my situation, if you don't mind."

"Go ahead," Scarpetta says.

"I had me a real job until three weeks ago." He stares down at his thumbs, slowly twiddles them in his lap. "I'm not gonna lie to you. I got in trouble. You can look at me and tell that much. And I didn't fall in no oyster bed." He meets Marino's eyes again.

"In trouble for what?" Scarpetta asks.

"Smoking weed and fighting. I never really smoked the weed, but I was going to."

"Now, ain't that nice," Marino says. "It just so happens one of the requirements we got in this joint is anybody wants to work here has to smoke weed and be violent and find at least one dead body of somebody murdered. Same requirements for gardeners and handymen at our personal residences."

Bull says to him, "I know how it sounds. But it's not like that. I was working at the port."

"Doing what?" Marino asks.

"Called a heavy-lift mechanic helper. That was my job title. Mainly, I did whatever my supervisor told me. Helped take care of equipment, lifting and carrying. Had to be able to talk on the radio and fix things, do whatever. Well, when I was signed off the clock one night, I decided to slip off near some of these old containers you find in the shipyard. The ones I'm talking about aren't used anymore, sort of banged up and off to the side. You drive by on Concord Street and you can see what I mean, right there on the other side of the chain-link fence. It'd been a long day, and to tell you the truth, me and my wife had words that morning so I was in a mood, so I decided to smoke me some weed. It wasn't something I made a habit of, can't even remember the last time I did it. I hadn't lit up yet when all a sudden this man come out of nowhere from near the railroad tracks. He cut me up bad, real bad."

He pushes up his sleeves, holds out his muscular arms and hands, turning them, displaying more long slashes, pale pink against his dark black skin.

"Did they catch who did it?" Scarpetta asks.

"Don't think they tried real hard. The police accused me of fighting, said I'd probably got into it with the man who sold me the weed. I never said who that was, and I know it wasn't him who cut me. He don't even work at the port. After I got out of the emergency room, I spent a few nights in jail until I went before the judge, and the case got dismissed because there was no suspect and no weed was found, either."

"Really. So why did they accuse you of possessing marijuana if none was found?" Marino says.

"Because I told the police I was getting ready to smoke weed when it happened. I had rolled me one and was about to light it when the man came after me. Maybe the police just never found it. I don't think they was all that interested, truth is. Or maybe the man who cut me took it, I don't know. I don't go near weed no more. Don't touch a drop of liquor, either. Promised my wife I wouldn't."

"The port fired you," Scarpetta assumes.

"Yes, ma'am."

"What is it you think you could help us with around here, exactly?" she asks.

"Whatever you need. Nothing I'm above doing. The morgue don't scare me. I got no trouble with dead people."

"Maybe you can leave me your cell phone number or whatever is the best way to get hold of you," she says.

He pulls a folded piece of paper out of a back pocket, gets up and politely places it on her desk. "Got it all right here, ma'am. Call me anytime."

"Investigator Marino will show you out. Thank you so much for your help, Mr. Grant." Scarpetta gets up from her desk and carefully shakes his hand, mindful of his injuries.

Seventy miles southwest on the resort island of Hilton Head, it is overcast, and a warm wind gusts in from the sea.

Will Rambo walks the dark, empty beach, headed to a destination. He carries a green tackle box and shines a Surefire tactical light wherever he likes, not really needing it to find his way. The light is powerful enough to blind someone, at least for seconds, and that's enough, assuming a situation requires it. Blasts of sand sting his face and click against his tinted glasses. Sand swirls like gauzy dancing girls.

And the sandstorm roared into Al Asad like a tsunami and swallowed the Humvee and him, swallowed the sky, the sun, swal-

lowed everything. Blood spilled through Roger's fingers, and his fingers looked as if they had been painted bright red, and the sand blasted and stuck to his bloody fingers as he tried to tuck his intestines back in. His face was panicky and shocked like nothing Will had ever seen, and he could do nothing about it except to promise his friend he would be all right and help him tuck his intestines back in.

Will hears Roger's shrieks in the gulls wheeling over the beach. Screams of panic and pain.

"Will! Will! Will!"

The screams, piercing screams, and the roar of sand.

"Will! Will! Please help me, Will!"

It was some time after that, after Germany. Will returned stateside to the Air Force base in Charleston, and then to Italy, different parts of Italy where he grew up. He wandered in and out of blackouts. He went to Rome to face his father because it was time to face his father, and it seemed like a dream to sit amid the stenciled palmette design and trompe l'oeil moldings of the dining room of Will's boyhood summer home at the Piazza Navona. He drank red wine with his father, wine as red as blood, and was irritated by the noise of tourists below the open windows, silly tourists no smarter than pigeons, throwing coins into Bernini's Fontana dei Quattro Fiumi and taking photographs, water constantly splashing.

"Making wishes that never come true. Or if they do, too bad for you," he commented to his father, who didn't understand but kept looking at him as if he were a mutant.

At the table beneath the chandelier, Will could see his face in the Venetian mirror on the far wall. It wasn't true. He looked like Will, not like a mutant, and he watched his mouth move in the mirror as he recounted to his father that Roger wished to be a hero when he returned from Iraq. His wish came true, Will's mouth said. Roger returned home a hero in a cheap coffin in the belly of a C5 cargo plane.

"We didn't have goggles or protective gear or body armor or anything," Will told his father in Rome, hoping he would understand but knowing he wouldn't.

"Why did you go if all you do is complain?"

"I had to write you to send batteries for our flashlights. I had to write you for tools because every screwdriver broke. The cheap shit they gave us," Will's mouth said in the mirror. "We had nothing unless it was cheap shit because of goddamn lies, the goddamn lies politicians tell."

"Then why did you go?"

"I was fucking told to, you foolish man."

"Don't you dare talk like that! Not in this house, where you will treat me with respect. I didn't choose that fascist war, you did. All you do is complain like a baby. Did you pray over there?"

When the wall of sand slammed into them and Will couldn't see his hand in front of his face, he prayed. When the explosion from the roadside bomb flipped the Humvee on its side and he couldn't see and the wind screamed as if he were inside the engine of a C17, he prayed. When he held Roger, he prayed, and when he could no longer endure Roger's pain, he prayed, and that was the last time he prayed.

"When we pray we are really asking ourselves—not God—for help. We're asking for our own divine intervention," Will's mouth in the mirror told his father in Rome. "So I don't need to pray to some god on a throne. I'm God's Will because I'm my own Will. I don't need you or God because I'm God's Will."

"When you lost your toes, did you also lose your mind?" his father said to him in Rome, and it was an ironic thing to say in the dining room where on a gilded console below the mirror was a stone foot of antiquity with all of its toes. But then, Will had seen dismembered feet over there after suicide bombers drove into crowded places, so he supposed to be missing a few toes was better than to be a whole foot missing everything else.

"That's healed now. But what do you know?" he said to his father in Rome. "You never came to see me all those months in Germany or Charleston or the years before. You've never been to

Charleston. I've been here in Rome countless times, but never for you, even if you thought otherwise. Except this time, because of what I have to do, a mission, you see. I was allowed to live so I can relieve others of their suffering. Something you would never understand because you're selfish and useless and don't care about anyone except yourself. Look at you. Rich and uncaring and cold."

Will's body got up from the table, and he watched himself walk to the mirror, to the gilded console beneath it. He picked up the stone foot of antiquity as the fountain below the window splashed and the tourists were noisy.

He carries the tackle box, a camera slung over his shoulder as he walks the beach in Hilton Head to carry out his mission. He sits and opens the tackle box, and takes out a freezer bag full of special sand, then small vials of pale violet glue. With the flashlight, he illuminates what he's doing as he squeezes the glue over the palmar surfaces of his hands. He plunges them one at a time into his bag of sand. He holds up his hands in the wind and the glue dries quickly and he has sandpaper hands. More vials, and he does the same thing with the bottoms of his bare feet, careful to completely cover the pads of his seven toes. He drops the empty vials and what's left of the sand back into his tackle box.

His tinted glasses look around and he turns off the flashlight.

His destination is the *No Trespassing* sign planted in the beach at the end of the long wooden boardwalk that leads to the fenced-in backyard of the villa.

Chapter 7

The parking lot behind Scarpetta's office.

It was the cause of much contention when she started her practice, and neighbors filed formal objections to almost every request she made. She got her way with the security fence by obscuring it with evergreens and Cherokee roses, but she lost out on the lighting. At night the parking lot is much too dark.

"So far I see no reason not to give him a try. We really could use somebody," Scarpetta says.

Palmettos flutter and the plants bordering her fence stir as she and Rose walk to their cars.

"I have no one to help me in my garden, for that matter. I can't distrust everybody on the planet," she adds.

"Don't let Marino push you into something you might regret," Rose says.

"I do distrust him."

"You need to sit down with him. I don't mean at the office. Have him over. Cook for him. He doesn't mean to hurt you."

They have reached Rose's Volvo.

"Your cough is worse," Scarpetta says. "Why don't you stay home tomorrow."

"I wish you'd never told him. I'm surprised you told any of us."

"I believe it was my ring that said something."

"You shouldn't have explained it," Rose says.

"It's time Marino faces what he's avoided for as long as I've known him."

Rose leans against her car as if she is too tired to stand on her own, or maybe her knees are hurting. "Then you should have told him a long time ago. But you didn't, and he held out hope. The fantasy festered. You don't confront people about their feelings, and all it does is make things . . ." She coughs so hard she can't finish her sentence.

"I think you're getting the flu." Scarpetta presses the back of her hand against Rose's cheek. "You feel warm."

Rose pulls a tissue out of her bag, dabs her eyes, and sighs. "That man. I can't believe you'd even consider him." She's back to Bull.

"The practice is growing. I must get a morgue assistant, and I've given up hoping for somebody already trained."

"I don't think you've tried very hard or have an open mind." The Volvo is so old, Rose has to unlock the door with the key. The interior light goes on, and her face looks drawn and tired as she slides into the seat and primly arranges her skirt to cover her thighs.

"The most qualified morgue assistants come from funeral homes or hospital morgues," Scarpetta replies, her hand on top of the window frame. "Since the biggest funeral home business in the area happens to be owned by Henry Hollings, who also happens to use the Medical University of South Carolina for autopsies that are his jurisdiction or subcontracted to him, what luck do you think I might have if I called him for a recommendation? The last damn thing our local coroner wants is to help me succeed."

"You've been saying that for two years. And it's based on nothing."

"He shuns me."

"Exactly what I was saying about communicating your feelings. Maybe you should talk to him," Rose says.

"How do I know he's not the one responsible for my office and home addresses suddenly getting mixed up on the Internet?"

"Why would he wait until now to do that? Assuming he did."

"Timing. My office has been in the news because of this child abuse case. And Beaufort County asked me to take care of it instead of calling Hollings. I'm involved in the Drew Martin investigation and just came back from Rome. Interesting timing for someone to deliberately call the Chamber of Commerce and register my practice, listing my home address as the office address. Even pay the membership fee."

"Obviously, you had them remove the listing. And there should be a record of who paid the fee."

"A cashier's check," Scarpetta says. "All

anyone could tell me is the caller was a woman. They removed the listing, thank God, before it ended up all over the Internet."

"The coroner isn't a woman."

"That doesn't mean a damn thing. He wouldn't do his dirty work himself."

"Call him. Ask him point-blank if he's trying to run you out of town. Run all of us out of town, I should say. It seems you have a number of people to talk to. Starting with Marino." She coughs, and as if on command, the Volvo's interior light goes out.

"He shouldn't have moved here." Scarpetta stares at the back of her old brick building, small, with one floor and a basement she converted into a morgue. "He loved Florida," she says, and that reminds her of Dr. Self again.

Rose adjusts the air-conditioning, turns the vents to blow cold air on her face, and takes another deep breath.

"Are you sure you're all right? Let me follow you home," Scarpetta says.

"Absolutely not."

"How about we spend some time together tomorrow? I'll cook dinner. Prosciutto and figs and your favorite drunk pork roast. A nice Tuscan wine. I know how much you like my ricotta and coffee crème."

"Thank you, but I have plans," Rose says, her voice touched by sadness.

The dark shape of a water tower on the southern tip of the island, or the toe, as it is called.

Hilton Head is shaped like a shoe, like the shoes Will saw in public places in Iraq. The white stucco villa that belongs to the *No Trespassing* sign is worth at least fifteen million dollars. The electronic blinds are down, and she is probably on the couch in the great room watching another movie on the retractable screen that covers an expanse of glass facing the sea. From Will's perspective, outside looking in, the movie plays backward. He scans the beach, scans the nearby empty houses. The dark, overcast sky hangs low and thick as the wind gusts in fierce fits and starts.

He steps up on the boardwalk and follows it toward the gate that separates the outside world from the backyard as images on the big movie screen flash backward. A man and woman fucking. His pulse quickens as he walks, his sandy footsteps quiet on the weathered boards, actors flashing backward on the movie screen. Fucking inside an elevator. The volume is low. He can barely hear the thudding and moans, those sounds that sound so violent as characters fuck in Hollywood, and then there is the wooden gate, and it is locked. He climbs over it and goes to his usual place at the side of the house.

Through a space between the window and the shade he has watched her on and off for months, watched her pace and cry and pull out her hair. She never sleeps at night, is afraid of the night, afraid of storms. She watches movies all night and into the morning. She watches movies when it rains, and if there's thunder, she turns the volume up very loud, and when the sun is bright, she hides from it. Usually she sleeps on the black leather wraparound couch where she's now stretched out, propped up by leather pillows, a blanket over her. She points the remote control and backs up the DVD, returning to the scene where Glenn Close and Michael Douglas are fucking in the elevator.

The houses on either side are obscured

by tall borders of bamboo and trees, nobody home. Empty because the rich owners don't rent them out and aren't here and haven't been here. Families often don't start using their expensive beach homes until after their children are out of school for the year. She wouldn't want other people here, and no neighbors have been here all winter. She wants to be alone and is terrified of being alone. She dreads thunder and rain, dreads clear skies and sunlight, doesn't want to be anywhere anymore under any conditions whatsoever.

That's why I have come.

She backs up the DVD again. He's familiar with her rituals, lying there in the same soiled pink sweatsuit, backing up movies, re-playing certain scenes, usually people fuck-ing. Now and then she goes out by the pool for a smoke and to let her pitiful dog out of his crate. She never picks up after him, the grass full of dried shit, and the Mexican yardman who comes every other week doesn't pick up the shit, either. She smokes and stares at the pool while the dog wanders about the yard, sometimes baying his deep, throaty howl, and she calls out to him.

"Good dog," or more often "Bad dog," and "Come. Come here right now!" Clapping her hands.

She doesn't pet him, can scarcely bear to look at him. Were it not for the dog, her life would be unbearable. The dog understands none of it. It's unlikely he remembers what happened or understood it at the time. What he knows is the crate in the laundry room where he sleeps and sits up and bays. She thinks nothing of it when he bays as she drinks vodka and takes pills and pulls out her hair, the routine the same day after day after day.

Soon I'll hold you in my arms and carry you back through the inner darkness to the higher realm, and you'll be separated from the physical dimension that's now your hell. You will thank me.

Will keeps up his scan, making sure no one sees him. He watches her get up from the couch and walk drunkenly to the slider to go out for a smoke and, as usual, she forgets the alarm is set. She jumps and swears when it wails and hammers, and she stumbles to the panel to shut it off. The phone rings, and she rakes her fingers through her thinning dark hair, saying something, then she yells and slams down the receiver. Will gets low to the ground behind shrubbery, doesn't move. In minutes the police come, two officers in a Beaufort County sheriff's cruiser. Will watches invisibly as the officers stand on the porch, not bothering to go inside because they know her. She forgot her password again, and the alarm company dispatched the police again.

"Ma'am, it's not a good idea to use your dog's name, anyway." One of the officers tells her the same thing she's been told before. "You should use something else for your password. A pet's name is one of the first things an intruder tries."

She slurs. "If I can't remember the damn dog's name, how can I remember something else? All I know is the password's the dog's name. Oh, hell. Buttermilk. There, now I remember it."

"Yes, ma'am. But I still think you should change it. Like I said, it's not good to use a pet's name, and you never remember it anyway. There must be something you'll remember. We have a fair number of burglaries around here, especially this time of year, when so many of the houses are empty."

"I can't remember a new one." She can barely talk. "When it goes off, I can't think."

"You sure you're all right being alone? Is there anyone we can call?"

"I have no one anymore."

Eventually, the cops drive off. Will emerges from his safe place and, through a window, watches her reset the alarm. One, two, three, four. The same code, the only one she can remember. He watches her sit back down on the couch, crying again. She pours herself another vodka. The moment is no longer right. He follows the boardwalk back to the beach.

Chapter 8

The next morning, eight o'clock, Pacific Daylight Time. Lucy eases to a stop in front of the Stanford Cancer Center.

Whenever she flies her Citation X jet to San Francisco and rents a Ferrari for the hour's drive to see her neuroendocrinologist, she feels powerful, the way she feels at home. Her tight jeans and tight T-shirt show off her athletic body and make her feel vital, the way she feels at home. Her black crocodile boots and titanium Breitling Emergency watch with its bright orange dial make her feel she's still Lucy, fearless and accomplished, the way she feels when she's not thinking about what's wrong with her.

She rolls down the window of the red F430 Spider. "Can you park this thing?" she asks the valet in gray who tentatively approaches her at the entrance of the modern brick-and-glass complex. She doesn't recognize him. He must be new. "It's Formula One shift, these paddles on the steering wheel. Right for shifting up, left for down, both at the same time for neutral, this button for reverse." She notes the anxiety in his eyes. "Well, okay, I admit it's kind of complicated," she says, because she doesn't want to belittle him.

He's an older man, probably retired and bored, so he's parking cars at the hospital. Or maybe someone in his family has cancer or did. But it's obvious he's never driven a Ferrari and may never have seen one up close. He eyes it as if it just landed from outer space. He wants no part of it, and that's a good thing when one doesn't know how to drive a car that costs more than some houses.

"I don't think so," the valet says, transfixed by the saddle leather interior and red "start" button on the carbon-fiber steering wheel.

He steps around the back of the car and looks at the engine under glass and shakes his head. "Now, that's something. A convertible, I guess. Must blow you around a lot when you got the top down, as fast as it must go, I guess," he says. "I got to admit that's something. Why don't you just pull it right over there." He shows her. "Best spot in the house. That really is something." Shaking his head.

Lucy parks, grabs her briefcase and two large envelopes containing magnetic resonance films that reveal the most devastating secret of her life. She pockets the Ferrari key, slips the valet a hundred-dollar bill, says very seriously but winks at him, "Guard it with your life."

The cancer center is the most beautiful medical complex, with expansive windows and miles of polished wooden floors, everything open and full of light. The people who work here, many of them volunteers, are unfailingly polite. Last time she had an appointment, a harpist was perched in the corridor gracefully plucking and strumming "Time After Time." This afternoon the same lady is playing "What a Wonderful World." What a joke, and as Lucy walks fast, looking at no one, a baseball cap pulled low over her eyes, she realizes there's no music anyone could play that wouldn't make her feel cynical or depressed right now.

The clinics are open areas, perfectly appointed in earth tones, no art on the walls, just flat-screen TVs that show soothing nature scenes: meadows and mountains, leaves in the fall, snowy woods, giant redwood trees, the red rocks of Sedona, accompanied by the gentle sounds of flowing streams and pattering rain and birds and breezes. Live potted orchids are on tables, the lighting soft, the waiting areas never crowded. The only patient in Clinic D when Lucy reaches the check-in desk is a woman wearing a wig and reading *Glamour* magazine.

Lucy quietly tells the man behind the counter she's here to see Dr. Nathan Day, or Nate, as she calls him.

"Your name?" With a smile.

Lucy quietly tells him the alias she uses. He types something on his computer, smiles again and reaches for the phone. In less than a minute, Nate opens the door and motions for Lucy to come inside. He hugs her, always does. "It's great to see you. Looking fantastic." He talks as they walk to his office.

It's small, not at all what one might expect of a Harvard-trained neuroendocrinologist considered one of the most outstanding in his field. He has a cluttered desk, a computer with a large video screen, an overflowing bookcase, multiple light boxes mounted on walls where in most offices there might be windows. There's a couch and one chair. Lucy hands over the records she brought with her.

"Lab work," she says. "And the scan you looked at last time, and the most recent one."

He settles behind his desk, and she sits on the couch. "When?" As he opens the envelopes, then reads her chart, not a word of it stored electronically, the paper file kept in his personal safe, identified by code, her name not listed anywhere.

"Blood work was two weeks ago. Most recent scan a month ago. My aunt's looked, says I look good, but then considering what she looks at most of the time," Lucy says.

"She's saying you don't look dead. That's a relief. And how's Kay?"

"She likes Charleston, but I'm not sure it likes her. I like it okay. . . . Well, I'm always motivated by places that are a bad fit."

"Which is most places."

"I know. Lucy the freako. I trust we're still undercover. Seems like it, since I gave my alias to that same what's-his-name at the desk and he didn't question it. Democratic majority notwithstanding, privacy's a joke."

"Don't get me started." He peruses her lab report. "You know how many patients I have who would self-pay if they could afford it just to keep their information out of databases?"

"Good thing. If I wanted to hack into your database, I could probably do it in five minutes. The Feds might take an hour, but they've probably already been in your database. And I haven't. Because I don't believe in violating a person's civil rights unless it's for a good cause."

"That's what *they* say."

"They lie and are stupid. Especially the FBI."

"Still topping your Most Wanted List, I see."

"They fired me for no good cause."

"And to think you could be abusing the Patriot Act and getting paid for it. Well, not much. What computer stuff are you selling for multimillions these days?"

"Data modeling. Neural networks that take input data and basically perform intelligent tasks the way our brains do. And I'm fooling around with a DNA project that could prove interesting."

"TSH excellent," he says. "Free T-four fine, so your metabolism's working. I can tell that without a lab report. You've lost a little weight since I saw you last."

"Maybe five pounds."

"Looks like you've gained muscle mass. So you've probably lost a good ten pounds of fat and water weight from bloating."

"Eloquently put."

"How much are you working out?"

"The same."

"I'll note that as obligatory, although it's probably obsessive. Liver panel's fine. And your prolactin level's great, down to two-point-four. What about your periods?"

"Normal."

"No white, clear, or milky discharge from your nipples? Not that I expect lactation with a prolactin level this low."

"Nope. And don't get your hopes up. I'm not letting you check."

He smiles, makes more notes in her record.

"Sad part is, my breasts aren't as big."

"There are women who'd pay a lot of money for what you've got. And do," he says matter-of-factly.

"They're not for sale. In fact, I can't even give them away these days."

"That I know isn't true."

Lucy is no longer embarrassed, can talk about anything with him. In the beginning, it was a different story, a horror and humiliation that a benign pituitary macroadenoma—a brain tumor—was causing an overproduction of the hormone prolactin that fooled her body into thinking she was pregnant. Her periods stopped. She gained weight. She didn't have galactorrhea, or begin to produce milk, but had she not discovered what was wrong when she did, that would have been next.

"Sounds like you're not seeing anyone." He slides her MR films out of their envelopes, reaches up, and attaches them to light boxes.

"Nope."

"How's your libido?" He dims the lights in the office and flips on the light boxes, illuminating films of Lucy's brain. "Dostinex is sometimes called the sex drug, you know. Well, if you can get it."

She moves close to him and looks at her films. "I'm not having surgery, Nate."

She stares dismally at the somewhat rectangular-shaped region of hypointensity at the base of the hypothalamus. Every time she looks at one of her scans, she feels there must be a mistake. That can't be her brain. A young brain, as Nate calls it. Anatomically, a great brain, he says, except for one little glitch, a tumor about half the size of a penny.

"I don't care what the journal articles say. No one's cutting on me. How do I look? Please tell me okay," she says.

Nate compares the earlier film to the new one, studies them side by side. "Not dramatically different. Still seven to eight millimeters. Nothing in the suprasellar cistern. A little shift left to right from the infundibulum of the pituitary stalk." He points with a pen. "Optic chiasm is clear." Points again. "Which is great." He puts down the pen and holds up two fingers, starts with them together, then moves them apart to check her peripheral vision. "Great," he says again. "So almost identical. The lesion isn't growing."

"It isn't shrinking."

"Have a seat."

She sits on the edge of the couch. "Bottom line," she says, "it's not gone. It hasn't burned out from the drug and become necrotic, and it never will, right?"

"But it's not growing," he repeats himself. "The medication did shrink it some and is containing it. All right. Options. But what do you want to do? Let me say that just because Dostinex and its generic have been linked to heart valve damage, I'm not sure you need to worry. The studies are dealing with people who take it for Parkinson's. At your low dose? You'll probably be fine. The bigger problem? I can write you a dozen prescriptions, but I don't think you'll find a single pill in this country."

"It's manufactured in Italy. I can get it over there. Dr. Maroni said he will."

"Fine. But I want you to get an echocardiogram every six months."

The phone rings. Nate punches in a button, listens briefly, and says to whoever it is, "Thanks. Call security if it seems to get out of hand. Make sure nobody touches it." He hangs up and says to Lucy, "Apparently, someone drove up in a red Ferrari that's attracting quite a lot of attention."

"Kind of ironic." She gets up from the couch. "It's all a matter of perspective, isn't it."

"I'll drive it if you don't want it."

"It's not that I don't want it. It's just nothing feels the same anymore. And that's not entirely bad. Just different."

"That's the thing about what you've got. It's something you don't want. But it's something more than what you had, because maybe it's changed the way you look at things." He walks her out. "I see it every day around here."

"Sure."

"You're doing well." He stops by the door that leads out to the waiting area and there's no one to hear them, just the man behind the desk, who smiles a lot and is on the phone again. "I'd put you in the top ten percent of my patients in terms of how well you're doing."

"Top ten percent. I believe that's a B-plus. I think I started out with an A."

"No, you didn't. You've probably had this thing forever and just didn't know it until it became symptomatic. Are you talking to Rose?"

"She won't face it. I'm trying not to resent her for it, but it's hard. Really, really hard. It's not fair. Especially to my aunt."

"Don't let Rose run you off, because that's probably what she's trying to do for the very reason you just said. She can't face it." He slips his hands into his lab coat pockets. "She needs you. She's certainly not going to talk about it with anyone else."

Outside the Cancer Center, a thin woman with a scarf wrapped around her bald head and two little boys are walking around the Ferrari. The valet rushes over to Lucy.

"They haven't got too close. I've been watching. Nobody has," he says in a low, urgent voice.

She looks at the two little boys and their sick mother, and walks over to the car, remotely unlocking it. The boys and their mother step back, and fear shows on their faces. The mother looks old but probably isn't more than thirty-five.

"I'm sorry," she says to Lucy. "But they're smitten. They haven't touched it."

"How fast can it go?" the older boy asks, a redhead, maybe twelve.

"Let's see, four-ninety horsepower, six speed, a four-point-three-liter V-eight, eighty-five hundred rpm and carbon-fiber rear diffuser panel. Zero to sixty in less than four seconds. Around two hundred miles an hour."

"No way!"

"You ever driven one of these things?" Lucy says to the older boy.

"I've never seen one in person."

"What about you?" Lucy asks his red-headed brother, who is maybe eight or nine.

"No, ma'am." Shyly.

Lucy opens the driver's door and the two redheads crane to get a peek and suck in their breath at the same time.

"What's your name?" she asks the older boy.

"Fred."

"Sit in the driver's seat, Fred, and I'm going to show you how to start this thing."

"You don't have to do that," Mom says to her, and she looks as if she's about to cry. "Honey, don't you hurt anything."

"I'm Johnny," the other boy says.

"You're next," Lucy says. "Get over here next to me and pay attention."

Lucy turns on the battery, makes sure the Ferrari's in neutral. She takes Fred's finger and places it on the steering wheel's red start button. She lets go of his hand. "Hold it in for a few seconds and fire her up." The Ferrari roars awake.

Lucy gives each boy a ride around the parking lot while their mother stands all alone in the middle of it and smiles and waves and wipes her eyes.

Benton records Gladys Self from his office phone inside McLean's Neuroimaging Lab. As is true of her famous daughter, the name Self suits her.

"If you're wondering why that rich daughter of mine doesn't put me in some nice mansion in Boca," Mrs. Self says, "well, sir, I don't want to be in Boca or Palm Beach or anywhere but right here in Hollywood, Florida. In my run-down little oceanfront apartment on the boardwalk."

"Why might that be?"

"To pay her back. Think how that will look when they find me dead in a dump like this someday. Let's see what that does to her popularity." She chortles.

"Sounds like you might have a hard time saying anything nice about her," Benton says. "And I do need several minutes of your praising her, Mrs. Self. Just as I'm going to need a few minutes of your being neutral and then critical."

"Why's she doing this, anyway?"

"I explained it at the beginning of our conversation. She volunteered for a scientific research project I'm conducting."

"That daughter of mine doesn't volunteer for shineola unless there's something she wants out of it. Never known her to do anything for the pure reason of helping others. Hogwash. Ha! A family emergency. She's lucky I didn't get on CNN and tell the world she's lying. Let's see. Wonder what the truth might be. Let me follow the clues. You're one of these police psychologists at what's the name of your hospital? McLean? Oh, that's right. Where all the rich and famous go. Just the sort of place she'd go to if she had to go somewhere, and I know a good reason why. Would knock you out if you knew. Bingo! She's a patient, that's what this is all about!"

"As I've said, she's part of a project I'm conducting." *Dammit.* He warned Dr. Self about this. If he called her mother to make the recording, she might suspect that Dr. Self is a patient. "I'm not allowed to discuss anything about her situation—where she is or what she's doing or why. I can't divulge information about any subjects in our studies."

"I sure could divulge a thing or two to you. I knew it! She's worth studying, all right. What normal person would get on TV and do what she does, twisting people's minds, their lives, like that tennis player who just got murdered. Bet you dollars to donuts Marilyn's somehow to blame for that, had her on her TV show, getting into all this personal information from her for all the world to see. It was embarrassing, can't believe that little girl's family allowed it."

Benton's seen a copy of it. Mrs. Self is right. It was too much exposure and made Drew vulnerable and accessible. Those are the ingredients for being stalked, if she was. It isn't the purpose of his call, but he can't resist probing. "I'm wondering how your daughter happened to get Drew Martin on her show. Did they know each other?"

"Marilyn can get anybody she wants. When she calls me on special occasions, mostly she brags about this celebrity and that. Only the way she says it, they're all lucky to meet her, not the other way around."

"I have a feeling you don't see her very often."

"Do you really think she'd go to the trouble to see her own mother?"

"Now, she's not completely devoid of feelings, is she?"

"As a little girl she could be sweet, I know that's hard to believe. But something went haywire when she turned sixteen. She ran off with some playboy and had her heart broken, came back home and we had quite a time of it. Did she tell you about that?"

"No, she didn't."

"That figures. She'll go on and on about her father killing himself and how horrible I am and all the rest. But her own failures don't exist. That includes people. You'd be surprised if you knew the people she's managed to excommunicate from her life for no good reason except they're inconvenient. Or maybe someone shows a side of her the world's not supposed to see. That's a killable offense."

"I assume you don't mean that literally."

"Depends on your definition."

"Let's start with what's positive about her."

"She tell you she makes everybody sign a confidentiality agreement?"

"Even you?"

"Do you want to know the real reason I

live like this? Because I can't afford her so-called generosity. I live off Social Security and what retirement I got from working all my life. Marilyn never did a damn thing for me and then had the nerve to tell me I had to sign one of these confidentiality agreements, you see. She said if I didn't, I was on my own no matter how old and sick I got. I didn't sign it. And I don't talk about her anyway. But I could. I sure could."

"You're talking to me."

"Well, now, she told me to, didn't she? She gave you my phone number because it suits whatever little selfish purpose she has this time. And I'm her weakness. She can't resist. Just itching to hear what I'll say. Validates her beliefs about herself."

"What I need you to try," Benton says, "is to imagine you're telling her what you like about her. There must be something. For example, 'I've always admired how bright you are' or 'I'm so proud of your success,' et cetera."

"Even if I don't mean it?"

"If you can't say something positive, I'm afraid we can't do this." Which would be fine with him.

"Don't worry. I can lie as well as she can."

"Then the negative. Such as, I wish you were more generous or less arrogant, or whatever comes to mind."

"Easy as pie."

"Finally, neutral comments. The weather, shopping, what you've been doing, things like that."

"Don't trust her. She'll fake it and ruin your study."

"The brain can't fake it," Benton says. "Not even hers."

An hour later. Dr. Self, in a shimmering red silk pants suit and no shoes, is propped up with pillows on her bed.

"I understand your feeling this is unnecessary," Benton says, turning pages in the pale blue *Structured Clinical Interview for DSM-IV Axis 1 Disorders* patient edition.

"Do you need a script, Benton?"

"To keep things consistent in this study, we SCID with the book. Each time for each subject. I'm not going to ask you things that are obvious and irrelevant, such as your professional status."

"Let me help you out," she says. "I've never been a patient in a psychiatric hospital. I don't take any medications. I don't drink too much. I usually sleep five hours a night. How many hours does Kay sleep?"

"Have you lost or gained much weight recently?"

"I maintain my weight perfectly. What does Kay weigh these days? Does she eat a lot when she's lonely or depressed? All that fried food down there."

Benton flips pages. "What about strange sensations in your body or on your skin?"

"Depends on who I'm with."

"Do you ever smell or taste things other people can't smell or taste?"

"I do a lot of things other people can't."

Benton looks up at her. "I don't think the study is a good idea, Dr. Self. This isn't constructive."

"That's not for you to judge."

"Do you think this is constructive?"

"You haven't gotten to the mood chronology. Aren't you going to ask me about panic attacks?"

"Have you ever had them?"

"Sweating, trembling, dizzy, racing heart. Fear I might die?" She gazes thoughtfully at him, as if he's the patient. "What did my mother say on the tape?"

"What about when you first got here?" he

says. "You seemed rather much in a panic over an e-mail. The one you mentioned to Dr. Maroni when you first got here and haven't mentioned since."

"Imagine your little assistant thinking she was going to SCID me." She smiles. "I'm a psychiatrist. It would be like a beginner playing Drew Martin in tennis."

"How are you feeling about what happened to her?" he asks. "It's been on the news that you had her on your show. Some people have suggested the killer may have fixed on her because of . . ."

"As if my show was the only time she was on TV. I have so many people on my show."

"I was going to say because of her visibility. Not her appearance on your show, specifically."

"I'll probably win another Emmy because of that series. Unless what happened . . ."

"Unless what happened?"

"That would be grossly unfair," Dr. Self says. "If the Academy were prejudiced because of what happened to her. As if that has anything to do with the quality of my work. What did my mother say?"

"It's important you don't hear what she says until you're in the scanner."

"I'd like to talk about my father. He died when I was very young."

"All right," says Benton, who sits as far away from her as he possibly can, his back to the desk and the laptop computer on top of it. On a table between them, the recorder runs. "Let's talk about your father."

"I was two when he died. Not quite two."

"And you remember him well enough to feel rejected by him?"

"As you know from studies I presume you've read, infants who aren't breast-fed are more likely to have increased stress and distress in life. Women in prison who can't breast-feed suffer significant compromises in their capacity to nurture and protect."

"I don't understand the connection. Are you implying your mother was in prison at some point?"

"She never held me to her breast, never suckled me, never soothed me with her heartbeat, never had eye contact with me when she fed me with a bottle, with a spoon, a shovel, a backhoe. Did she admit all this when you taped her? Did you ask her about our history?"

"When we tape a subject's mother, we

don't need to know the history of their relationship."

"Her refusal to bond with me compounded my feelings of rejection, my resentment, made me more prone to blame her for my father's leaving me."

"You mean his dying."

"Interesting, don't you think? Kay and I both lost our fathers at an early age, and both of us became doctors. But I heal the minds of the living while she cuts up the bodies of the dead. I've always wondered what she's like in bed. Considering her occupation."

"You blame your mother for your father's death."

"I was jealous. Several times I walked in on them while they were having sex. I saw it. From the doorway. My mother giving her body to him. Why him and not me? Why her and not me? I wanted what they gave to each other, not realizing what that meant, because certainly I didn't want oral or genital sex with my parents and didn't understand that part of it, what they did as things progressed. I probably thought they were in pain."

"At not quite two, you walked in on them

more than once and remember it?" He has placed the diagnostic manual under his chair, is taking notes now.

She readjusts her position on the bed, makes herself more comfortable and provocative, making sure Benton is aware of her body's every contour. "I saw my parents alive, so vital, and then in the blink of an eye he was gone. Kay, on the other hand, witnessed her father's long, lingering death from cancer. I lived with loss and she lived with dying and there's a difference. So you see, Benton, as a psychiatrist, my purpose is to understand my patient's life, while Kay's is to understand her patient's death. That must have some effect on you."

"We're not here to talk about me."

"Isn't it wonderful that the Pavilion doesn't adhere to rigid institutional rules? Here we are. Despite what happened when I was admitted. Has Dr. Maroni told you about coming into my room, not this one, the first one? Shutting the door, loosening my gown? Touching me? Was he a gynecologist in a former career? You seem uncomfortable, Benton."

"Are you feeling hypersexual?"

"So now I'm having a manic episode." She

smiles. "Let's see how many diagnoses we can conjure up this afternoon. That's not why I'm here. We know why I'm here."

"You said it was because of the e-mail you discovered while you were taking a break at the studio. Friday before last."

"I told Dr. Maroni about the e-mail."

"From what I understand, all you told him is you'd gotten one," Benton says.

"If it were possible, I might suspect all of you hypnotically lured me here because of that e-mail. But that would be something out of a movie or a psychosis, wouldn't it?"

"You told Dr. Maroni you were terribly upset and feared for your life."

"And then I was given drugs against my will. Then he fled to Italy."

"He has a practice there. Is always in and out, especially this time of year."

"The Dipartimento di Scienze Psichiatriche at the University of Rome. He has a villa in Rome. He has an apartment in Venice. He's from a very wealthy Italian family. He's also the clinical director of the Pavilion, and everyone does as he says, including you. Before he left the country, we should have sorted through what happened after I checked in."

" 'Checked in'? You seem to refer to McLean as if it's a hotel."

"Now it's too late."

"Do you really believe that Dr. Maroni touched you inappropriately?"

"I believe I've made that patently clear."

"So you do believe it."

"Everybody here would deny it."

"We absolutely wouldn't. If it were true."

"Everybody would deny it."

"When the limousine brought you to admissions, you were quite lucid but agitated. Do you remember that? Do you remember talking to Dr. Maroni in the admissions building and telling him you needed a safe refuge because of an e-mail and would explain later?" Benton asks. "Do you remember becoming provocative with him both verbally and physically?"

"You have quite the bedside manner. Perhaps you should go back to the FBI and use rubber hoses and whatnot. Perhaps break into my e-mail and my homes and my bank accounts."

"It's important you remember what you were like when you first got here. I'm trying to help you do that," he says.

"I remember him coming into my room here at the Pavilion."

"That was later on—in the evening—when you suddenly became hysterical and incoherent."

"Brought on by drugs. I'm very sensitive to drugs of any sort. I never take them or believe in them."

"When Dr. Maroni came into your room, a female neuropsychologist and a female nurse were already there with you. You continued to say that something wasn't your fault."

"Were you there?"

"I wasn't."

"I see. Because you act as if you were."

"I've read your chart."

"My chart. I suppose you fantasize about selling it to the highest bidder."

"Dr. Maroni asked you questions while the nurse checked your vitals, and it became necessary to sedate you by intramuscular injection."

"Five milligrams Haldol, two milligrams Ativan, one milligram Cogentin. The infamous five-two-one chemical restraint used on violent inmates in forensic units. Imagine.

My being treated like a violent prisoner. I remember nothing after that."

"Can you tell me what wasn't your fault, Dr. Self? Did it have to do with the e-mail?"

"What Dr. Maroni did wasn't my fault."

"So your distress had nothing to do with the e-mail that you said was your reason for coming to McLean?"

"This is a conspiracy. All of you are in on it. That's why your comrade Pete Marino contacted me, isn't it? Or maybe he wants out. He wants me to rescue him. Just like I did in Florida. What are you people doing to him?"

"There's no conspiracy."

"Do I see the investigator peeking out?"

"You've been here for ten days. And told no one the nature of this e-mail."

"Because it's really about the person who has sent me a number of e-mails. To say *an e-mail* is misleading. It's about a person."

"Who?"

"A person Dr. Maroni could have helped. A very disturbed individual. No matter what he's done or hasn't done, he needs help. And if something happens to me, or to someone else, it's Dr. Maroni's fault. Not mine."

"What might be your fault?"

"I just said nothing would be."

"And there's no e-mail you can show me that might help us understand who this person is and perhaps protect you from him?" he says.

"It's interesting, but I'd forgotten you work here. I was reminded when I saw the ad for your research study posted in admissions. Then, of course, Marino said something when he e-mailed me. And that's not *the* e-mail. So don't get excited. He's so bored and sexually frustrated working for Kay."

"I'd like to talk to you about any e-mails you've received. Or sent."

"Envy. That's how it starts." She looks at him. "Kay envies me because her own existence is so small. So desperately envious she had to lie about me in court."

"And you're referring to . . . ?"

"Mainly her." Hatred coils. "I'm perfectly objective about what happened in that gross example of litigious exploitation and never took it personally that you and Kay—mainly Kay—were witnesses, making the two of you—mainly her—champions of that gross example of litigious exploitation." Hatred coils coldly. "I wonder how she'd feel if she knew you're in my room with the door shut."

"When you said you needed to talk to me alone in the privacy of your room, we made an agreement. I would record our sessions in addition to taking notes."

"Record me. Take your notes. You'll find them useful someday. There's much you can learn from me. Let's discuss your experiment."

"Research study. The one you volunteered for, got special permission for, and I advise against. We don't use the word *experiment*."

"I'm curious why would you wish to exclude me from your experiment unless you have something to hide."

"Frankly, Dr. Self, I'm not convinced you meet the criteria."

"Frankly, Benton, it's the last thing you want, now, isn't it? But you have no choice because your hospital is far too shrewd to discriminate against me."

"Have you ever been diagnosed as bipolar?"

"I've never been diagnosed as anything but gifted."

"Has anybody in your family ever been diagnosed as bipolar?"

"What all this will prove in the end, well, that's your business. That during various mood states the dorsolateral prefrontal cortex of the brain is going to *light up,* given appropriate external stimuli. So what. PET and fMRI have clearly demonstrated there is an abnormal blood flow in the prefrontal regions and decreased activity in the DLPFC in people who are depressed. So now you throw violence into the mix, and what will you prove, and why does it matter? I know your little experiment wasn't approved by the Harvard University Committee on Use of Human Subjects."

"We don't conduct studies that aren't approved."

"These healthy control subjects. Are they still healthy when you're done? What happens to the not-so-healthy subject? The poor wretch with a history of depression, schizophrenia, bipolar or other disorder, who also has a history of hurting themselves or others or trying to, or obsessively fantasizing about it."

"I take it Jackie briefed you," he says.

"Not quite. She wouldn't know the dorsolateral prefrontal cortex from a small cod. Studies of how the brain responds to maternal criticism and praise have been done before. So now you throw violence into the mix, and what will you prove, and why does it matter? You show what's different about the brains of violent versus nonviolent individuals and what does it prove, and what does it matter? Would it have stopped the Sandman?"

"The Sandman?"

"If you looked at his brain, you'd see Iraq. And then what? Would you magically extract Iraq and he'd be fine?"

"Is the e-mail from him?"

"I don't know who he is."

"Might he be the disturbed person you referred to Dr. Maroni?"

"I don't understand what you see in Kay," she says. "Does she smell like the morgue when she comes home? But then, you're not there when she comes home."

"Based on what you've said, you got the e-mail several days after Drew's body was found. A coincidence? If you have information about her murder, you need to tell me," Benton says. "I'm asking you to tell me. This is very serious."

She stretches her legs and with her bare foot touches the table between them. "If I kicked this recorder off the table and it broke, what then?"

"Whoever killed Drew will kill again," he says.

"If I kicked this recorder"—she touches it with her bare toe and moves it a little—"what might we say and what might we do?"

Benton gets up from his chair. "Do you want someone else murdered, Dr. Self?" He picks up the recorder but doesn't turn it off. "Haven't you been through this before?"

"And there it is," she says from the bed. "That's the conspiracy. Kay will lie about me again. Just like before."

Benton opens the door. "No," he says. "It will be much worse this time."

Chapter 9

Eight p.m. in Venice. Maroni refills his wine-glass and smells the unpleasant canal smell below his open window as daylight wanes. Clouds are piled halfway up the sky in a thick, frothy layer, and along the horizon is the first touch of gold.

"Manic as hell." Benton Wesley's voice is clear, as if he is here instead of in Massachusetts. "I can't be clinical or appropriate. I can't sit there and listen to her manipulations and lies. Get someone else. I'm done with her. I'm handling it badly, Paulo. Like a cop, not a clinician."

Dr. Maroni sits before his apartment window, drinking a very nice Barolo that is being spoiled by this conversation. He can't get away from Marilyn Self. She has invaded his hospital. She has invaded Rome. Now she has followed him to Venice.

"What I'm asking is if I can remove her from the research study. I don't want to scan her," Benton says.

"Certainly I won't tell you what to do," Dr. Maroni replies. "It's your study. But if you want my recommendation? Don't piss her off. Go ahead and scan her. Make it a pleasant experience and just assume the data is no good. Then she's gone."

"What do you mean 'gone'?"

"I see you haven't been informed. She's been discharged and is leaving after the scan," Dr. Maroni says, and through his open shutters, the canal is the color of green olives and as smooth as glass. "Have you talked with Otto?"

"Otto?" Benton says.

"Captain Poma."

"I know who he is. Why would I talk to him about this?"

"I had dinner with him last night in Rome. I'm surprised he hasn't contacted you. He's on his way to the U.S. In the air as we speak."

"Jesus Christ."

"He wants to talk to Dr. Self about Drew Martin. You see, he feels sure she has information and isn't coming forward with it."

"Please tell me you didn't."

"I didn't. He knows anyway."

"I don't see how that's possible," Benton says. "Do you realize what she'll do if she thinks we told anybody she's a patient here?"

A water taxi slowly rumbles past, and water laps against Dr. Maroni's apartment.

"I assumed he got the information from you," he says. "Or Kay. Since both of you are members of the IIR and are investigating Drew Martin's murder."

"He certainly didn't."

"What about Lucy?"

"Neither Kay nor Lucy knows Dr. Self is here," Benton says.

"Lucy is good friends with Josh."

"Jesus Christ. She sees him when she's scanned. They talk about computers. Why would he tell her?"

Across the canal, a seagull on a rooftop cries like a cat, and a tourist tosses bread to it, and the bird cries more.

"What I'm saying is hypothetical, of course," Dr. Maroni says. "I suppose it entered my mind because he calls her often when the computer's down or there's some other problem he can't fix. You see, it's too much for Josh to be an MRI tech and the IT."

"What?"

"The question is where she'll go and what further trouble she'll cause."

"New York, I assume," Benton says.

"You'll tell me when you know." Dr. Maroni drinks. "This is all hypothetical. I mean about Lucy."

"Even if Josh told her, are you making the leap that she then told Captain Poma, who she doesn't even know?"

"We need to monitor Dr. Self when she leaves," Dr. Maroni says. "She's going to cause trouble."

"What is all this cryptic talk? I don't understand," Benton says.

"I can see that. It's a shame. Well, no great matter. She'll be gone. You'll tell me where she goes."

"No great matter? If she finds out someone told Captain Poma she's a patient at McLean or was a patient here, it's a HIPAA violation. She'll cause trouble, all right, which is exactly what she wants."

"I have no control over what he tells her

or when. The Carabinieri's in charge of the investigation."

"I don't understand what's going on here, Paulo. When I did the SCID, she told me about the patient she referred to you," Benton says, frustration in his voice. "I don't understand why you didn't tell me."

Along the canal, apartment facades are muted pastel shades, and brick is exposed where the plaster is worn away. A polished teak boat passes beneath an arched brick bridge, and the captain stands, and the bridge is very low, and his head almost touches it. He works the throttle with his thumb.

"Yes, she did refer a patient to me. Otto has asked me about it," Dr. Maroni says. "Last night I told him what I know. At least, what I'm at liberty to say."

"It would have been nice if you'd told me."

"Now I'm telling you. If you hadn't brought it up, I still would be telling you. I saw him several times in the space of several weeks. Last November," Dr. Maroni says.

"He calls himself the Sandman. According to Dr. Self. Does that sound familiar?"

"I know nothing about the name Sandman."

"She says that's how he signs his e-mails," Benton says.

"When she called my office last October and asked me to see this man in Rome, she didn't supply me with any e-mails. She never said anything about him calling himself the Sandman. He never mentioned the name when he saw me in my office. Twice, I believe. In Rome, as I've said. I have no information that would lead me to conclude he's killed anyone, and I told Otto the same thing. So I can't give you access to his file or my evaluation of him, and I know you understand this, Benton."

Dr. Maroni reaches for the decanter and refills his glass as the sun settles into the canal. Air blowing through the open shutters is cooler, and the canal smell isn't as strong.

"Can you give me any information about him at all?" Benton asks. "Any personal history? A physical description? I know he was in Iraq. That's all I know."

"I couldn't if I wanted to, Benton. I don't have my notes."

"Meaning there could be important information in them."

"Hypothetically," Dr. Maroni says.

"Don't you think you should check?"

"I don't have them," Dr. Maroni says.

"You don't have them?"

"Not in Rome, is what I mean," he says from his sinking city.

Hours later, the Kick 'N Horse Saloon, twenty miles north of Charleston.

Marino sits across the table from Shandy Snook, both of them eating chicken-fried steak with biscuits, gravy, and grits. His cell phone rings. He looks at the number on the display.

"Who is it?" she says, sipping a bloody Mary through a straw.

"Why can't people leave me alone?"

"Better not be what I think it is," she says. "It's seven-damn-o'clock, and we're eating dinner."

"I ain't here." Marino pushes a button to silence the phone, acts like it doesn't bother him.

"Yeah." She loudly slurps up the last of her drink, reminding him of Drano unclogging a sink. "Nobody home."

Inside the saloon's Feed Troff, Lynyrd Skynyrd's booming through the speakers, the Budweiser neon signs are lit up, ceiling fans slowly turn. Saddles and autographs fill the walls, and models of motorcycles and rodeo horses and ceramic snakes decorate windowsills. The wooden tables are packed with bikers. More bikers are outside on the porch, everybody eating and drinking and getting ready for the Hed Shop Boys concert.

"Son of a bitch," Marino mumbles, staring at the cell phone on the table, at the wireless Bluetooth earpiece next to it. Ignoring the call is impossible. It's her. Even though the display says *Restricted,* he knows it's her. By now she's bound to have seen what's on the desktop of his computer. He's surprised and irritated it's taken this long. At the same time, he feels the thrill of vindication. He imagines Dr. Self wanting him like Shandy does. Wearing him out like Shandy does. For a solid week, he's gotten no sleep.

"Like I always say, the person's not going to get any deader, right?" Shandy reminds him. "Let the Big Chief take care of it for once."

It's her. Shandy doesn't know it. Assumes it's some funeral home. Marino reaches for his bourbon and ginger, keeps glancing at his cell phone.

"Let her take care of it for once," Shandy rants on. "Fuck her."

Marino doesn't answer, his tension growing as he swirls what's left of his drink. Not answering Scarpetta's calls or returning them makes his chest tight with anxiety. He thinks about what Dr. Self said and feels deceived and abused. His face heats up. For the better part of twenty years, Scarpetta has made him feel he's not good enough, when maybe the problem is her. *That's right. It's probably her.* She doesn't like men. *Hell, no.* And all these years she's made him feel the problem is him.

"Let the Big Chief take care of whoever the latest stiff is. She's got nothing better to do," Shandy says.

"You don't know a thing about her or what she's doing, either."

"You'd be surprised what I know about her. Better watch it." Shandy motions for another drink.

"Better watch what?"

"You sticking up for her. Because it sure is getting on my nerves. Like maybe you keep forgetting who I am in your life."

"After a whole week."

"Just remember, baby. It's not *on call*. But *at her beck and call*," she says. "Why should you? Why should you always jump when she says it? Jump! Jump!" She snaps her fingers and laughs.

"Shut the fuck up."

"Jump! Jump!" She leans forward so he can see what's inside her silk vest.

Marino reaches for his phone, reaches for his earpiece.

"Truth is?" She's not wearing a bra. "She treats you like you're nothing more than an answering service, a flunky, a nobody. I'm not the first person who's said it."

"I don't let anybody treat me like that," he says. "We'll see who the nobody is." He thinks of Dr. Self and imagines himself on international TV.

Shandy reaches under the table, and he can see down her vest, see as much as he wants. She rubs him.

"Don't," he says, waiting and getting anxious and angry.

Pretty soon, other bikers will find excuses to walk past so they can take in the sight of her leaning against the table just right. He watches her do it, and her breasts swell and her cleavage deepens. She knows how to lean into a conversation so anybody interested can imagine a mouthful of her. A big guy with a big gut and a chain attached to his wallet slowly gets up from the bar. He takes his time walking to the men's room, taking in the view, and Marino feels violent.

"You don't like it?" Shandy rubs him. "'Cause it sure feels to me like you do. Remember last night, baby? Like a damn teenager."

"Don't," he says.

"Why? Am I giving you a hard time?" says Shandy, who prides herself on her way with words.

He moves her hand. "Not now."

He returns Scarpetta's call. "Marino here," he says curtly, as if he's talking to a stranger, so Shandy won't know who it is.

"I need to see you," Scarpetta says to him.

"Yeah. What time?" Marino acts like he doesn't know her, and he's aroused and jealous as bikers wander past the table, looking at his dark, exotic girlfriend exposing herself.

"As soon as you can get here. To my house," Scarpetta's voice says in his earpiece, and her tone is one he's not accustomed to, and he senses her fury like an approaching storm. She's seen the e-mails, he's sure of it.

Shandy gives him a *who are you talking to?* look.

"Yeah, I guess so." Marino feigns irritation, glancing at his watch. "Be there in a half-hour." He hangs up, says to Shandy, "A body coming in."

She looks at him as if trying to read the truth in his eyes, as if for some reason she knows he's lying. "Which funeral home?" She leans back in her chair.

"Meddicks'. Again. What a squirrel. Must do nothing but drive that damn hearse morning, noon, and night. What we call an ambulance chaser."

"Oh," she says. "That sucks." Her attention wanders to a man in a flame-pattern do-rag, his boots low in the heel. He pays no attention to them as he walks past their table to the ATM.

Marino noticed him when they got here earlier, has never seen him before. He watches him get a pitiful five bucks out of the ATM while his mutt of a dog sleeps curled up in a chair at the bar. The man hasn't petted him once or even asked the bartender for a treat for him—not so much as a bowl of water.

"I don't know why it's got to be you," Shandy starts in again, but her voice is different. Quieter, colder, the way she gets with the first frost of spite. "When you think of all you know and all you've done. The big-shot homicide detective. You ought to be the boss, not her. Not her dyke niece, either." She drags the last of a biscuit through white gravy smeared on her paper plate. "The Big Chief's kind of turned you into the Invisible Man."

"I told you. Don't talk about Lucy like that. You don't know shit."

"Truth is truth. I don't need you to tell me. Everyone in this bar knows what kind of saddle she rides."

"You can shut up about her." Marino angrily finishes his drink. "You keep your mouth shut about Lucy. Me and her go back to when she was a kid. I taught her how to drive, taught her how to shoot, and I don't want to hear another word. You got it?" He wants another drink, knows he shouldn't, has already had three bourbons, strong ones. He lights two cigarettes, one for Shandy, one for him. "We'll see who's invisible."

"Truth is truth. You had a real career before the Big Chief started dragging you around everywhere. And why'd you tag along as usual? I know why." She gives him one of her accusatory looks, blows out a stream of smoke. "You thought she might want you."

"Maybe we should move," Marino says. "Go to a big city."

"Me move with you?" She blows out more smoke.

"What about New York?"

"We can't ride our bikes in New Damn York. No way I'm moving to a place swarming like a beehive with all those stuck-up damn Yankees."

He gives her his sexiest look and reaches under the table. He rubs her thigh because he's terrified of losing her. Every man in this bar wants her, and he's the one she's picked. He rubs her thigh and thinks about Scarpetta and what she'll say. She's read Dr. Self's e-mails. Maybe she's realizing who he is and what other women think of him.

"Let's go to your place," Shandy says.

"How come we never go to your place? You afraid to be seen with me or something? Like maybe you live around rich people and I'm not good enough?"

"I have to decide whether I'm going to keep you. See, I don't like slavery," she says. "She's gonna work you to death like a slave, and I know all about slaves. My great-grandfather was a slave, but not my daddy. Nobody told him what the hell to do."

Marino holds up his empty plastic cup, smiles at Jess, who's looking mighty fine this evening in tight jeans and a tube top. She appears with another Maker's Mark and ginger, sets it in front of him. She says, "You riding home?"

"Not a problem." He winks at her.

"Maybe you should stay in the campground. I got an empty camper back there." She has several in the woods behind the bar, in case patrons aren't safe to ride.

"I couldn't be better."

"Bring me another." Shandy has a bad habit of barking orders at people who don't have her status in life.

"I'm still waiting on you to win the bike build-off, Pete." Jess ignores Shandy, talks mechanically, slowly, her eyes on Marino's lips.

It took a while for him to get used to it. He's learned to look at Jess when he talks, is never too loud, never exaggerates his speech. He's hardly aware of her deafness anymore and feels a special closeness to her, maybe because they can't communicate without looking at each other.

"One hundred and twenty five thousand dollars cash for first place." Jess draws out the staggering amount.

"I'm betting River Rats is going to get it this year," Marino says to Jess, knowing she's just messing with him, maybe flirting a little. He's never built a bike or entered any contest, and never will.

"And I'm betting on Thunder Cycle." Shandy inserts herself in that snotty way Marino hates. "Eddie Trotta's so damn hot. He can *trotta* into my bed anytime he wants."

"Tell you what," Marino says to Jess, putting his arm around her waist, looking up at her so she can see him talking. "One of these days, I'll have big bucks. I won't need to win a bike build-off or work a shit job."

"He ought to quit his shit job, doesn't earn enough to make it worth his while—or worth my while," Shandy says. "He's nothing but a squaw to the Big Chief. Besides, he doesn't need to work. He's got me."

"Oh, yeah?" Marino knows he shouldn't say it, but he's drunk and hateful. "What if I told you I got an offer to go on TV in New York?"

"As what? A commercial for Rogaine?" Shandy laughs as Jess tries to read what's being said.

"As a consultant for Dr. Self. She's been asking me." He can't stop himself, should change the subject.

Shandy looks genuinely startled, blurts, "You're lying. Why would she care a shit about you?"

"We got a history. She wants me to go to work for her. I've been thinking about it, maybe would have accepted right away, but that would mean moving to New York and leaving you, babe." He puts his arm around her.

She pulls away. "Well, looks like her show's on its way to being a comedy."

"Put our guest over there on my tab," Marino says with loud largesse, nodding and pointing at the man in the flame do-rag sitting next to his dog at the bar. "He's having a rough night. Got five lousy bucks to his name."

The man turns around and Marino gets a good look at a face pitted with acne scars. He has the snake eyes that Marino associates with people who have done time.

"I can pay for my own damn beer," the man in the flame do-rag says.

Shandy continues complaining to Jess, not bothering to look at her face, so she may as well be talking to herself.

"Don't appear to me like you can pay for much of anything, and I apologize for my southern hospitality," Marino says, loud enough for everyone in the bar to hear.

"I don't think you should go anywhere." Jess looks at Marino, at his drink.

"There's room for only one woman in his

life, and one of these days he's gonna figure that out," Shandy says to Jess and anybody else listening. "Without me, what's he got, anyway? Who do you think gave him that fancy necklace he's wearing?"

"Fuck you," the man in the do-rag says to Marino. "Fuck your mother."

Jess walks over to the bar, crosses her arms. She says to the man in the do-rag, "We talk polite in here. I think you better leave."

"What?" he says loudly, cupping a hand behind his ear, mocking her.

Marino's chair scrapes back and in three long strides he is between them. "You say you're sorry, asshole," Marino says to him.

The man's eyes touch his like needles. He crumples the five-dollar bill he got out of the ATM, drops it on the floor, crushes it beneath his boot as if he's putting out a cigarette. He smacks the dog's butt, heads to the door as he says to Marino, "Why don't you come out here like a man? I got something to say to you."

Marino follows him and his dog across the dirt parking lot to an old chopper, probably put together in the seventies, a four-speed with a kick start, flame paint job, something funny-looking about the license tag.

"Cardboard," Marino realizes out loud. "Homemade. Now, ain't that sweet. Tell me what you got to say."

"Reason I'm here tonight? Got a message for you," the man in the do-rag says. "Sit!" he yells at the dog, and it cowers, flattens on its belly.

"Next time send a letter." Marino grabs him by the front of his dirty denim jacket. "It's cheaper than a funeral."

"You don't let go of me, I'll get you later in a way you won't like. There's a reason I'm here and you better listen."

Marino takes his hands off him, aware that everyone in the saloon has moved out on the porch, watching. The dog remains flat on his belly, cowering.

"That bitch you work for ain't welcome in these parts and would be smart to go back where she come from," the man in the do-rag says. "Just passing along a word of advice from someone who can do something about it."

"What'd you call her?"

"Say this much, that bitch's got some set of tits." He cups his hands and licks the air. "If she don't leave town, I'll find out just how nice."

Marino kicks the chopper hard and it thuds to the dirt. He grabs his forty-caliber Glock out of the back of his jeans and points it between the man's eyes.

"Don't be stupid," the man says, as bikers start yelling from the porch. "You shoot me, your worthless life's over and you know it."

"Hey! Hey! Hey!"

"Whoa, now!"

"Pete!"

Marino feels as if the top of his head is floating off as he stares at the spot between the man's eyes. He racks back the slide, chambering a round.

"You kill me, you may as well be dead, too," the man in the do-rag says, but he's scared.

Bikers are on their feet, shouting. Marino is vaguely aware of people venturing into the parking lot.

"Pick up your piece-of-shit bike," Marino says, lowering the gun. "Leave the dog."

"I ain't leaving my damn dog!"

"You're leaving him. You treat him like shit. Now get out of here before I give you a third eye."

As the chopper roars away, Marino clears the chamber, tucks the pistol back into his waistband, unsure what just came over him and terrified by it. He pets the dog and it stays flat on its belly and licks his hand.

"We'll find someone nice to take care of you," Marino says to him as fingers dig into his arm. He looks up at Jess.

"I think it's time you deal with this," she says.

"What are you talking about?"

"You know what. That woman. I warned you. She's beating you down, making you feel like a nothing, and look what's happening. In one short week you've turned into a wild man."

His hands are shaking badly. He looks at her so she can read his lips. "That was stupid, wasn't it, Jess. Now what?" He pets the dog.

"He'll be the saloon dog, and if that man comes back, it won't be good for him. But you better be careful now. You've started something."

"You ever seen him before?"

She shakes her head.

Marino notices Shandy on the porch, by the railing. He wonders why she hasn't left the porch. He almost killed someone and she's still on the porch.

Chapter 10

Somewhere a dog barks in the near dark, and the barking becomes more insistent.

Scarpetta detects the distant carbureted *potato-potato-potato* rhythm of Marino's Roadmaster. She can hear the damn thing blocks away on Meeting Street, heading south. Moments later it roars through the narrow alleyway behind her house. He's been drinking. She could hear it in his voice when she talked to him on the phone. He's being obnoxious.

She needs him sober if they're going to have a productive conversation—perhaps the most important one they've ever had.

She begins making a pot of coffee as he turns left on King Street, then another left into the narrow driveway she shares with her unpleasant neighbor, Mrs. Grimball. Marino rolls the throttle a few times to announce himself and kills the engine.

"You got something to drink in there?" he says as Scarpetta opens the front door. "A little bourbon would be nice. Wouldn't it, Mrs. Grimball!" he shouts up at the yellow frame house, and a curtain moves. He locks the bike's front fork, slips the key in his pocket.

"Inside, now," Scarpetta says, realizing he's far more intoxicated than she thought. "For God's sake, why did you find it necessary to ride down the alley and yell at my neighbor?" she says as he follows her to the kitchen, his booted footsteps loud, his head almost touching the top of each door frame they pass through.

"Security check. I like to make sure nothing's going on back there, no lost hearses, no homeless people hanging out."

He pulls out a chair, sits, slumped back. The odor of booze is powerful, his face bright red, his eyes bloodshot. He says, "I can't stay long. Got to get back to my woman. She thinks I'm at the morgue."

Scarpetta hands him a coffee, black. "You're going to stay long enough to sober up, otherwise you're not going anywhere near your motorcycle. I can't believe you got on it in your condition. That's not like you. What's wrong with you?"

"So I had a few. Big deal. I'm fine."

"It *is* a big deal, and you're *not* fine. I don't care how well you supposedly handle alcohol. Every drunk driver thinks he's fine right before he ends up dead or maimed or in jail."

"I didn't come here to be lectured to."

"I didn't invite you over to have you show up drunk."

"Why did you invite me? To rag on me? To find something else wrong with me? Something else not up to your high-horse standards?"

"It's not like you to talk this way."

"Maybe you've just never listened," he says.

"I asked you to come over in hopes we could have an open and honest conversation, but it doesn't appear this is a good time. I have a guest room. Maybe you should go to sleep and we'll talk in the morning."

"Seems as good a time as any." He yawns and stretches, doesn't touch his coffee. "Talk away. Either that or I'm out of here."

"Let's go into the living room and sit in front of the fire." She gets up from the kitchen table.

"It's seventy-five friggin' degrees outside." He gets up, too.

"Then I'll make it nice and chilly in here." She goes to a thermostat and turns on the air-conditioning. "I've always found it easier to talk in front of a fire."

He follows her into her favorite room, a small sitting area with a brick fireplace, heart-of-pine floors, exposed beams, and plaster walls. She places a chemical log on the grate and lights it, and pulls two chairs close and switches off the lamps.

He watches flames burn the paper wrapping off the log and says, "I can't believe you use those things. Original this, original that, and then you use fake logs."

Lucious Meddick drives around the block and his resentment festers.

He saw them go inside after that asshole investigator thundered up on his motorcycle drunk and disturbed the neighbors. *Daily double*, Lucious thinks. He's blessed because he's been wronged and God is making it up to him. Setting out to teach her a lesson, Lucious has caught both of them, and he slowly noses his hearse into the un-lighted alleyway, worrying about another flat tire, and getting angrier. He snaps the rubber band hard as his frustration spikes. Voices of dispatchers on his police scanner are a dis-tant static he can decipher in his sleep.

They didn't call him. He drifted past a fatal car crash on William Hilton Highway, saw the body being loaded into a competitor's hearse—an old one—and again Lucious was ignored. Beaufort County is her turf now, and nobody calls him. She's blackballed him be-cause he made a mistake about her address. If she thought that was a violation of her pri-vacy, she doesn't know the meaning.

Filming women through a window at night is nothing new. Surprising how easy it is and how many of them don't bother with curtains or blinds, or leave them open just a tiny inch or two, thinking *Who's going to look? Who's going to get down behind the shrubbery or climb up in a tree to see?* Lucious, that's who. See how the snotty lady doctor likes watching herself in a home movie that people can gawk at for nothing and never know who took it. Better still, he'll get both of them in the act. Lucious thinks of the hearse—nowhere near as nice as his—and the car wreck, and the unfairness of it is unendurable.

Who was called? Not him. Not Lucious, even after he radioed the dispatcher and said he was in the area, and she came back and told him in her snippy, terse tone that she hadn't called him and what unit was he? He said he wasn't a unit and she told him in so many words to stay off the cop channels and, for that matter, off the air. He snaps the rubber band until it stings like a whip. He bumps over pavers, past the iron gate behind the lady doctor's carriage garden, and spots a white Cadillac blocking his way. It's dark back here. He snaps the rubber band and swears. He recognizes the oval bumper sticker on the Cadillac's rear bumper.

HH for Hilton Head.

He'll just leave his damn hearse right here. Nobody drives through this damn alley anyway, and he has a mind to call in the Cadillac and laugh while the police give the driver a ticket. He gleefully thinks about YouTube and the trouble he's about to cause. That damn investigator is in that damn bitch's pants. He saw them walk into the house, sneaking and cheating. He has a girl, that sexy thing he was with in the morgue, and Lucious saw them carrying on when they weren't paying attention. From what he hears, Dr. Scarpetta has a man up north. Isn't that something. Lucious makes a fool of himself, promoting his business, telling the rude investigator that he—Lucious Meddick—would appreciate referrals from him and his boss, and their response? To disrespect him. To discriminate. Now they have to pay.

He turns off the engine and the lights and gets out as he glares at the Cadillac. He opens the back of the hearse and an empty stretcher is clamped to the floor, a stack of neatly folded white sheets and white body pouches on top of it. He finds the camcorder, and extra batteries in a utility box he keeps in back, and shuts the tailgate and stares at the Cadillac, walks past it, considering the best way to get close to her house.

Someone moves behind the glass of the driver's door, just the faintest hint of something dark inside the dark car, shifting. Lucious is happy as he turns on the camcorder to see how much memory is left, and the darkness inside the Cadillac shifts again, and Lucious walks around the back of it and films the license plate.

Probably some couple making out, and

he gets excited thinking about it. Then he's offended. They saw his headlights and didn't get out of the way. Disrespect. They saw him park his hearse in the dark because he couldn't get past, and they couldn't have been more inconsiderate. They'll be sorry. He raps his knuckles against the glass, about to scare them but good.

"I got your plate number." He raises his voice. "And I'm calling the damn police."

The burning log crackles. An English bracket clock on the mantle *tick-tocks*.

"What's really going on with you?" Scarpetta says, watching him. "What's wrong?"

"You're the one who asked me here. So I assume something's wrong with you."

"Something's wrong with us. How about that? You seem miserable. You're making me miserable. This past week has been out of control. Do you want to tell me what you've done and why?" she says. "Or do you want me to tell you?"

The fire crackles.

"Please, Marino. Talk to me."

He stares at the fire. For a while, neither of them talk.

"I know about the e-mails," she says. "But

then, you probably already know that, since you asked Lucy to check out the alleged false alarm the other night."

"So you have her snoop around my computer. So much for trust."

"Oh, I don't think it's a good idea for you to say anything about trust."

"I'll say what I want."

"The tour you gave your girlfriend. All of it was caught on camera. I've seen it. Every minute of it."

Marino's face twitches. Of course he knew the cameras and microphones were there, but she can tell it didn't occur to him that he and Shandy were being watched. Certainly, he would have known their every action and word was being captured, but most likely he assumed that Lucy would have no reason to review the recordings. He was right about that. She wouldn't have had a reason. He was confident he would get away with it, and that makes what he did even worse.

"There are cameras everywhere," she says. "Did you really think no one would find out what you did?"

He doesn't answer.

"I thought you cared. I thought you cared about that murdered little boy. Yet you unzipped his pouch and played show-and-tell with your girlfriend. How could you do such a thing?"

He won't look at her or respond.

"Marino. How could you do such a thing?" she asks him again.

"It was her idea. The tape should have showed you that," he says.

"A tour without my permission is bad enough. But how could you let her look at bodies? Especially his."

"You saw the tape from when Lucy was spying on me." He glowers at her. "Shandy wouldn't take no for an answer. She wouldn't get out of the cooler. I tried."

"There's no excuse."

"Spying. I'm sick of it."

"Betrayal and disrespect. I'm sick of it," Scarpetta says.

"I've been thinking of quitting anyway," he goes on in a nasty tone. "If you stuck your nose in my e-mails from Dr. Self, you ought to know I got better opportunities than hanging out here with you for the rest of my life."

"Quit? Or are you hoping I'll fire you? Because that's what you deserve after what you did. We don't give tours of the morgue and make a spectacle of the poor people who end up there."

"Jesus, I hate the way women overreact to everything. Get so damn emotional and irrational. Go ahead. Fire me," he says thickly, over-enunciating, the way people do when they try too hard to sound sober.

"This is exactly what Dr. Self wants to happen."

"You're just jealous because she's a hell of a lot more important than you."

"This isn't the Pete Marino I know."

"You ain't the Dr. Scarpetta I know. Did you read what else she said about you?"

"She said quite a lot about me."

"The lie you live. Why don't you finally admit to it? Maybe that's where Lucy got it. From you."

"My sexual preference? Is that what you're so desperate to know?"

"You're afraid to admit it."

"If what Dr. Self implied were true, I certainly wouldn't be afraid of it. It's people like her, people like you, who seem to be afraid of it."

He leans back in his chair, and for an instant, he seems near tears. Then his face turns hard again as he stares at the fire.

"What you did yesterday," she says, "isn't the Marino I've known all these years."

"Maybe it is and you just never wanted to see it."

"I know it isn't. What's happened to you?"

"I don't know how I got here," he says. "I look back on it and see this guy who did good as a boxer for a while, but I didn't want to have mush for a brain. Got sick of being a uniform cop in New York. Married Doris, who got sick of me, had a sicko son who's dead, and I'm still chasing sicko assholes. I'm not sure why. Never have been able to figure out why you do what you do, either. You probably won't tell me." Sullenly.

"Maybe because I grew up in a house where nobody talked to me in a way that conveyed anything I needed to hear or made me feel understood or important. Maybe because I watched my father die. Every day, that's all any of us watched. Maybe I've spent the rest of my life trying to understand the thing that defeated me as a child. Death. I don't think there are simple or even logical reasons for why we're who we are and do what we do." She looks over at him, but he doesn't look at her. "Maybe there's no simple or even logical answer that explains your behavior. But I wish there were."

"In the old days, I didn't work for you. That's what's changed." He gets up. "I'm having a bourbon."

"More bourbon isn't what you need," she says, dismayed.

He isn't listening, and he knows his way to the bar. She hears him open a cabinet and get out a glass, then another cabinet and a bottle. He walks back into the room with a tumbler of liquor in one hand, the bottle in the other. An uneasiness starts in the pit of her stomach, and she wants him to leave but can't send him out in the middle of the night drunk.

He sets the bottle on the coffee table and says, "We got along pretty good all those years in Richmond when I was the top detective and you was the chief." He lifts his glass. Marino doesn't sip. He takes big swallows. "Then you got fired and I quit. Since then, nothing's turned out the way I thought. I liked the hell out of Florida. We had a kick-ass training facility. Me in charge of investigations, good pay, even had my own celebrity shrink. Not that I need a shrink, but I lost weight, was in great shape. Was doing really good until I stopped seeing her."

"Had you continued to see Dr. Self, she would have decimated your life. And I can't believe you don't realize that her communicating with you is nothing but manipulation. You know what she's like. You saw what she was like in court. You heard her."

He takes another swallow of bourbon. "For once there's a woman more powerful than you, and you can't stand it. Maybe can't stand my relationship with her. So you got to bad-mouth her because what else can you do. You're stuck down here in no-man's-land and about to become a housewife."

"Don't insult me. I don't want to fight with you."

He drinks, and his meanness is wide awake now. "My relationship with her is maybe why you wanted us to move from Florida. I'm seeing it now."

"I believe Hurricane Wilma is why we moved from Florida," she says, as the feeling in her stomach gets worse. "That and my need to have a real office, a real practice, again."

He drains his glass, pours more.

"You've had enough," she says.

"You got that right." He lifts his glass, takes another swallow.

"I think it's time I call a cab to take you home."

"Maybe you should start a real practice somewhere else and get the hell out of here. You'd be better off."

"You're not the judge of where I'd be better off," she says, watching him carefully, fire-light moving on his big face. "Please don't drink anymore. You've had enough."

"I've had enough, all right."

"Marino, please don't let Dr. Self drive a wedge between you and me."

"I don't need her to do that. You done it on your own."

"Let's don't do this."

"Let's do." Slurring, swaying a bit in his chair, a gleam in his eyes that's unnerving. "I don't know how many days I got left. Who the hell knows what's going to happen. So I don't intend to waste my time in a place I hate, working for someone who don't treat me with the respect I deserve. Like you're better than me. Well, you're not."

"What do you mean by how many days you've got left? Are you telling me you're sick?" she says.

"Sick and tired. That's what I'm telling you."

She's never seen him this drunk. He's

swaying on his feet, pouring more bourbon, spilling it. Her impulse is to take the bottle away from him, but the look in his eyes stops her.

"You live alone and it ain't safe," he says. "It's not safe, you're living here in this little old house alone."

"I've always lived alone, more or less."

"Yeah. What the fuck's that say about Benton? Hope you two have a nice life."

She's never seen Marino this drunk and hateful, and she doesn't know what to do.

"I'm in a situation where I got to make choices. So now I'm gonna tell you the truth." He spits as he talks, the glass of bourbon perilously tilted in his hand. "I'm bored as hell working for you."

"If that's how you feel, I'm glad you're telling me." But the more she tries to soothe him, the more inflamed he gets.

"Benton the rich snob. *Doctor* Wesley. So because I ain't a doctor, lawyer, or Indian chief, I'm not good enough for you. Tell you one goddamn thing, I'm good enough for Shandy, and she's sure as hell not what you think. From a better family than yours. She didn't grow up poor in Miami with some blue-collar grocery store worker just off the boat."

"You're very drunk. You can sleep in the guest room."

"Your family's no better than mine. Just-off-the-boat Italians with nothing but cheap macaroni and tomato sauce to eat five nights a week," he says.

"Let me get you a cab."

He slams his glass down on the coffee table. "I think it's a real good idea for me to get on my horse and ride." He grabs a chair to steady himself.

"You're not going anywhere near that motorcycle," she says.

He starts walking, knocks against the door frame as she holds on to his arm. He almost drags her toward the front door as she tries to stop him, implores him not to go. He digs in a pocket for his motorcycle key and she snatches it out of his hand.

"Give me my key. I'm saying it real polite."

She clenches it in her fist behind her back, in the small foyer at the front door. "You're not getting on your bike. You can hardly walk. You're taking a cab or staying here tonight. I'm not going to let you kill yourself or somebody else. Please listen to me."

"Give it to me." He stares at her with flat eyes, and he's a huge man she no longer knows, a stranger who might physically hurt her. "Give it to me." He reaches behind her and grabs her wrist and she is shocked by fear.

"Marino, let go of me." She struggles to free her arm, but it may as well be in a vise. "You're hurting me."

He reaches around and grabs her other wrist, and fear turns to terror as he leans into her, his massive body pressing her against the wall. Her mind races with desperate thoughts of how to stop him before he goes any further.

"Marino, let go of me. You're hurting me. Let's go sit back down in the living room." She tries to sound unafraid, her arms painfully pinned behind her. He presses hard against her. "Marino. Stop it. You don't mean this. You're very drunk."

He kisses her and grabs her, and she turns her head away, tries to push his hands away, struggles and tells him no. The motorcycle key clatters to the floor as he kisses her and she resists him and tries to make him listen. He rips open her blouse. She tells him to stop, tries to stop him as he tears at her clothes. She tries to push away his hands, and tells him he's hurting her, and then she doesn't struggle with him anymore because he's somebody else. He isn't Marino. He's a stranger attacking her inside her house. She sees the pistol in the back of his jeans as he drops to his knees, hurting her with his hands and mouth.

"Marino? This is what you want? To rape me? Marino?" She sounds so calm and unafraid, her voice seems to come from outside her body. "Marino? Is this what you want? To rape me? I know you don't want that. I know you don't."

He suddenly stops. He releases her, and the air moves and is cool on her skin, wet from his saliva and chafed and raw from his violence and his beard. He covers his face with his hands and hunches forward on his knees and hugs her around her legs and begins to sob like a child. She slides the pistol out of his waistband as he cries.

"Let go." She tries to move away from him. "Let me go."

On his knees, he covers his face with his hands. She drops out the pistol's magazine and pulls back the slide to make sure there isn't a round in the chamber. She tucks the gun in the drawer of a table by the door and picks up the motorcycle key. She hides it and the magazine inside the umbrella stand. She helps Marino up, helps him back to the guest bedroom off the kitchen. The bed is small, and he seems to fill every inch of it as she makes him lie down. She pulls off his boots and covers him with a quilt.

"I'll be right back," she says, leaving the light on.

In the guest bath, she fills a glass with water and shakes four Advil tablets from the bottle. She covers herself with a robe, her wrists aching, her flesh raw and burning, the memory of his hands and mouth and tongue sickening. She bends over the toilet and gags. She leans against the edge of the sink and takes deep breaths and looks at her red face in the mirror and seems as much a stranger to herself as he is. She splashes herself with cold water, washes out her mouth, washes him away from every place he touched. She washes away tears, and it takes a few minutes to get control of herself. She returns to the guest room where he's snoring.

"Marino. Wake up. Sit up." She helps him, plumps pillows behind him. "Here, take these and drink the entire glass of water. You need to drink a lot of water. You're going to feel like hell in the morning, but this will help."

He drinks the water and takes the Advil, then turns his face to the wall as she brings him another glass. "Turn off the light," he says to the wall.

"I need you to stay awake."

He doesn't answer her.

"You don't have to look at me. But you must stay awake."

He doesn't look at her. He stinks like whisky and cigarettes and sweat, and the smell of him reminds her and she feels her soreness, feels where he has been and is nauseated again.

"Don't worry," he says thickly. "I'll leave and you won't ever have to see me. I'll vanish for good."

"You're very, very drunk and don't know what you're doing," she says. "But I want you to remember it. You need to stay awake long enough so you'll remember this tomorrow. So we can get past it."

"I don't know what's wrong with me. I almost shot him. I wanted to so bad. I don't know what's wrong with me."

"Who did you almost shoot?" she says.

"At the bar," he says in his drunken gabble. "I don't know what's wrong with me."

"Tell me what happened at the bar."

Silence as he stares at the wall, his breathing heavy again.

"Who did you almost shoot?" she asks loudly.

"He said he'd been sent."

"Sent?"

"Made threats about you. I almost shot him. Then I come over here and acted just like him. I should kill myself."

"You're not going to kill yourself."

"I should."

"That will be worse than what you just did. Do you understand me?"

He doesn't answer. He doesn't look at her.

"If you kill yourself, I won't feel sorry for you and I won't forgive you," she says. "Killing yourself is selfish, and none of us will forgive you."

"I'm not good enough for you. I never will be. Go on and say it and get it over with once and for all." He talks as if he has rags in his mouth.

The phone on the bedside table rings, and she picks it up.

"It's me," Benton says. "You saw what I sent? How are you?"

"Yes, and you?"

"Kay? Are you all right?"

"Yes, and you?"

"Christ. Is someone there?" he says, alarmed.

"Everything's fine."

"Kay? Is someone there?"

"We'll talk tomorrow. I've decided to stay home, work in the garden, ask Bull to come over and help."

"You're sure? You sure you're okay with him?"

"I am now," she says.

Four o'clock in the morning, Hilton Head. Crashing waves spread white foam on the beach as if the heaving sea is frothing at the mouth.

Will Rambo is quiet on the wooden steps, and he walks the length of the boardwalk and climbs over the locked gate. The faux-Italianate villa is stucco with multiple chimneys and archways, and a sharply pitched red barrel-tile roof. In the back are copper lights, and a stone table with a clutter of filthy ashtrays and empty glasses, and not so long ago, her car key. Since then, she has used the spare, although she drives infrequently.

Mostly, she goes nowhere, and he is silent as he moves about, and palmetto trees and pines sway in the wind.

Trees waving like wands, casting their spell over Rome, and flower petals blowing like snow along Via D'Monte Tarpeo. Poppies were blood-red, and wisteria draped over ancient brick walls was purple like bruises. Pigeons bobbed along steps, and women fed feral cats Whiskas and eggs from plastic plates among the ruins.

It was a fine day for walking, and the tourist traffic wasn't heavy, and she was a little drunk but at ease with him, happy with him. He knew she would be.

"I would like you to meet my father," he said to her as they sat on a wall and looked at feral cats, and she remarked repeatedly that they were pitiful stray cats, inbred and deformed, and someone should save them.

"Not stray but feral. There's a difference. These feral cats want to be here and would rip you apart if you tried to rescue them. They aren't something discarded or hurt with nothing to look forward to but darting from garbage can to garbage can

and hiding under houses until someone catches them and puts them to sleep."

"Why would someone put them to sleep?" she asked.

"Because they would. That's what would happen once they're removed from their haven and end up in unsafe places where they are hit by cars and chased by dogs and constantly endangered and wounded beyond repair. Unlike these cats. Look at them, all alone, and no one dares go near them unless they allow it. They want to be exactly where they are, down there in the ruins."

"You're weird," she said, nudging him. "I thought so when we met, but you're cute."

"Come on," he said, and he helped her up.

"I'm too warm," she complained, because he had draped his long, black coat around her and made her wear a cap and his dark glasses, even though the day wasn't cold or sunny.

"You're very famous, and people will stare," he reminded her. "You know they will, and we can't have people staring."

"I need to find my friends before they think I've been kidnapped."

"**Come on. You must see the apartment. It's quite spectacular. I'll drive you there because I can tell you're tired, and you can call your friends and invite them to join us, if you like. We'll have some very fine wine and cheeses.**"

Then darkness, as if a light went out in his head, and he woke up to scenes in brilliant broken pieces, like brilliant broken pieces of a shattered stained-glass window that once told a story or a truth.

The stairs on the north side of the house haven't been swept, and the door leading into the laundry room hasn't been opened since the housekeeper was here last, almost two months ago. On either side of the stairs are hibiscus bushes, and behind them through a pane of glass he can see the alarm panel and its red light. He opens his tackle box and withdraws a saddle-grip glass cutter with a carbide tip. He cuts out a pane of glass and sets it on the sandy dirt behind the bushes as the puppy inside his crate begins to bay, and Will hesitates, quite calm. He reaches inside and unlocks the deadbolt, then opens the door and the alarm begins to beep, and he enters the code to silence it.

He's inside a house he has watched for many months. He's imagined this and planned it at such great length that finally, the act of doing it is easy and perhaps a little disappointing. He squats and wiggles his sandy fingers through the spaces in the wire crate and whispers to the basset hound, "It's all right. Everything's going to be all right."

The basset hound stops baying, and Will lets the dog lick the back of his hand, where there is no glue and no special sand.

"Good boy," he whispers. "Don't worry."

His sandy feet carry him from the laundry room toward the sound of the movie playing again in the great room. Whenever she smokes outside, she has a bad habit of leaving the door open wide as she sits on the steps and stares at the black-bottom pool that is a gaping wound, and some of the smoke drifts inside as she sits there and smokes and stares at the pool. The smoke has permeated whatever it touches, and he smells the stale stench and it gives a flinty edge to the air, a hard, gray matte finish like her aura. It is sickly. A near-death aura.

The walls and ceiling are washed with ocher and umber, the colors of the earth, and the stone floor is the color of the sea.

Every doorway is an arch, and there are huge pots of acanthus that are limp and brown because she hasn't been watering them properly, and there is dark hair on the stone floor. Head hair, pubic hair, from when she paces about, sometimes nude, ripping at her hair. She's asleep on the couch, her back to him, the bald spot on the top of her head pale like a full moon.

His bare, sandy feet are quiet, and the movie plays. Michael Douglas and Glenn Close are drinking wine to an aria from *Madama Butterfly* playing on the hi-fi. Will stands in the arch and watches *Fatal Attraction*, knows all of it, has seen it many, many times, has watched it with her through the window without her knowing. He hears the dialogue in his head before the characters are saying it, and then Michael Douglas is leaving, and Glenn Close is angry and rips off his shirt.

Ripping, tearing, desperate to get at what was underneath. He had so much blood on his hands he couldn't see the color of his skin as he tried to tuck Roger's intestines in, and the wind and sand blasted both of them and they could barely see or hear each other.

She sleeps on the couch, too drunk and

drugged to hear him come in. She doesn't feel his specter floating near her, waiting to carry her away. She will thank him.

"Will! Help me! Please help me! Oh, please, God!" Screaming. "It hurts so bad! Please don't let me die!"

"You're not going to die." Holding him. "I'm here. I'm here. I'm right here."

"I can't stand it!"

"God will never give you more than you can bear." His father always saying that, ever since Will was a boy.

"It isn't true."

"What isn't true?" His father asked him in Rome as they drank wine in the dining room and Will was holding the stone foot of antiquity.

"It was all over my hands and my face, and I tasted it, tasted him. I tasted as much of him as I could to keep him alive in me because I promised he wouldn't die."

"We should go outside. Let's go have a coffee."

Will turns a knob on the wall, turns up the surround sound until the movie is blaring, and then she's sitting up, and then she's screaming, and he can barely hear her screams over the movie as he leans close to her, puts a sandy finger to her lips, shaking his head, slowly, to hush her. He refills her glass with vodka, hands it to her, and nods for her to drink. He sets the tackle box, flashlight, and camera on the rug and sits next to her on the couch and looks deeply into her bleary, bloodshot, panicky eyes. She has no eyelashes, has pulled all of them out. She doesn't try to get up and run. He nods for her to drink, and she does. Already she's accepting what must happen. She will thank him.

The movie vibrates the house and her lips say, "Please don't hurt me."

She was pretty once.

"Shhhhh." He shakes his head, hushing her again with his sandy finger, touching her lips, pressing them hard against her teeth. His sandy fingers open the tackle box. Inside are more bottles of glue and glue remover, and the bag of sand, and a black-handled six-inch double-edged wallboard saw and reciprocating saw blade, and various hobby knives.

Then the voice in his head. Roger crying, screaming, bloody froth bubbling from his mouth. Only it isn't Roger crying out, it's the woman begging with bloody lips, "Please don't hurt me!"

As Glenn Close tells Michael Douglas to

fuck off, and the volume vibrates the great room.

She panics and sobs, shaking like someone having a seizure. He pulls his legs up on the couch, sits cross-legged. She stares at his sandpaper hands and sandpaper bottoms of mangled bare feet and the tackle box, the camera on the floor, and the realization of the inevitable seizes her blotchy, puffy face. He notices how unkempt her nails are and is overwhelmed by that same feeling he gets when he spiritually embraces people who are suffering unbearably and he releases them from their pain.

He can feel the subwoofer in his bones.

Her raw, bloody lips move. "Please don't hurt me, please, please don't," and she cries and her nose runs and she wets her bloody lips with her tongue. "What do you want? Money? Please don't hurt me." Her bloody lips move.

He takes off his shirt and khaki pants, neatly folds them, places them on the coffee table. He takes off his underwear, places it on top of his other clothes. He feels the power. It spikes through his brain like an electric shock, and he grabs her hard around the wrists.

Chapter 11

Dawn. It looks like it might rain.

Rose gazes out a window of her corner apartment, the ocean gently lapping against the seawall across Murray Boulevard. Near her building—once a splendid hotel—are some of the most expensive homes in Charleston, formidable waterfront mansions she has photographed and arranged in a scrapbook that she peruses from time to time. It's almost impossible for her to believe what's happened, that she's living both a nightmare and a dream.

When she moved to Charleston, her one request was that she live close to the water.

"Close enough to know it's there" is how she described it. "I suspect this will be the last time I'll follow you anywhere," she said to Scarpetta. "At my age, I don't want a yard to bother with, and I've always wanted to live on the water, but not a marsh with that rotten-egg smell. The ocean. If only I could have the ocean at least close enough to walk to it."

They spent a lot of time looking. Rose ended up on the Ashley River in a run-down apartment that Scarpetta, Lucy, and Marino renovated. It didn't cost Rose a penny, and then Scarpetta gave her a raise. Without it, Rose couldn't afford the lease, but that fact was never mentioned. All Scarpetta said was that Charleston is an expensive city compared to other places they've lived, but even if it wasn't, Rose deserved a raise.

She makes coffee and watches the news and waits for Marino to call. Another hour passes, and she wonders where he is. Another hour, and not a word, and her frustration grows. She's left several messages for him saying she can't come in this morning and could he drop by to help her move her couch? Besides, she needs to talk to him. She told Scarpetta she would. Now's as good a time as any. It's almost ten. She's called his cell phone again, and it goes straight to voicemail. She looks out the open window, and cool air blows in from beyond the seawall, the water choppy and moody, the color of pewter.

She knows better than to move the couch herself but is impatient and irked enough to do it. She coughs as she ponders the folly of a feat that would have been manageable not all that long ago. She wearily sits and loses herself in memories of last night, of talking and holding hands and kissing on this same couch. She felt things she didn't know she could feel anymore, all the while wondering how long it can last. She can't give it up, and it can't last, and she feels a sadness so deep and dark that there's no point in trying to see what's in it.

The phone rings, and it's Lucy.

"How did it go?" Rose asks her.

"Nate says hello."

"I'm more interested in what he said about you."

"Nothing new."

"That's very good news." Rose moves to the kitchen counter and picks up the television remote control. She takes a deep breath. "Marino's supposed to come by to move my couch, but as usual . . ."

A pause, then Lucy says, "That's one of the things I'm calling about. I was going to drop by to see Aunt Kay and tell her about my appointment with Nate. She doesn't know I went. I always tell her after the fact so she doesn't go crazy worrying. Marino's bike is parked at her house."

"Was she expecting you?"

"No."

"What time was this?"

"Around eight."

"Impossible," Rose says. "Marino's still in a coma at eight. At least these days."

"I went to Starbucks, then headed back to her house around nine, and guess what? I pass his potato-chip girlfriend in her BMW."

"You sure it was her?"

"Want her plate number? Her DOB? What's in her bank account—not much, by the way. Looks like she's gone through most of her money. Not from her dead rich daddy, either. Tells you something he left her nothing. But she makes a lot of deposits that don't make sense, spends it as fast as she gets it."

"This is bad. Did she see you when you were coming back from Starbucks?"

"I was in my Ferrari. So unless she's blind in addition to being a vapid twat. Sorry . . ."

"Don't be. I know what a twat is, and no doubt she fits the bill. Marino has a special homing device that leads him directly to twats."

"You don't sound good. Like you can hardly breathe," Lucy says. "How about I come over a little later and move the couch?"

"I'll be right here," Rose says, coughing as she hangs up.

She turns on the television in time to see a tennis ball kick up a puff of red dust off the line, Drew Martin's serve so fast and out of reach, her opponent doesn't even try. CNN plays footage from last year's French Open, the news about Drew going on and on. Replays of tennis and her life and death. Over and over again. More footage. Rome. The ancient city, then the small cordoned-off construction site surrounded by police and yellow tape. Emergency lights pulsing.

"What else do we know at this time? Are there any new developments?"

"Rome officials continue to be tight-lipped. It would appear there are no leads and no suspects, and this terrible crime continues to be shrouded in mystery. People here ask why. You can see them laying flowers at the edge of the construction site where her body was found."

More replays. Rose tries not to watch. She's seen all of it so many times, but she continues to be mesmerized by it.

Drew slicing a backhand.

Drew charging the net and slamming a lob so hard it bounces into the stands. The crowd jumping to its feet and wildly cheering.

Drew's pretty face on Dr. Self's show. Talking fast, her mind jumping from one subject to the next, excited because she'd just won the U.S. Open, called the Tiger Woods of tennis. Dr. Self leaning into the interview, asking questions she shouldn't ask.

"Are you a virgin, Drew?"

Laughing, blushing, hiding her face with her hands.

"Come on." Dr. Self smiling, so damn full of herself. "This is what I'm talking about, everyone." To her audience. "Shame. Why do we feel shame when we talk about sex?"

"I lost my virginity when I was ten," Drew says. "To my brother's bicycle."

The crowd going crazy.

"Drew Martin dead at sweet sixteen," an anchor says.

Rose manages to push the couch across the living room and shove it against the wall. She sits on it and cries. She gets up and paces and weeps, and moans that death is wrong and violence is unbearable and she hates it. Hates it all. In the bathroom, she retrieves a prescription bottle. In the kitchen, she pours herself a glass of wine. She takes a tablet and washes it down with wine, and moments later, coughing and barely able to breathe, she washes down a second tablet. The telephone rings and she is unsteady when she reaches for it, dropping the receiver, fumbling to pick it up.

"Hello?"

"Rose?" Scarpetta says.

"I shouldn't watch the news."

"Are you crying?"

The room's spinning. She's seeing double. "It's just the flu."

"I'm coming over," Scarpetta says.

Marino rests his head against the back of the seat, his eyes masked by dark glasses, his big hands on his thighs.

He's dressed in the same clothes he had on last night. He slept in them, and it looks like it. His face is a deep red hue, and he has the stale stench of a drunk who hasn't bathed in a while. The sight and smell of him brings back memories that are too awful to describe, and she feels the rawness, the soreness of flesh he should never have seen or touched. She wears layers of silk and cotton, fabrics gentle to her skin, her shirt buttoned at the collar, her jacket zipped up. To hide her injuries. To hide her humiliation. Around him, she feels powerless and naked.

Another awful silence as she drives. The car is filled with the aromas of garlic and sharp cheese, and he has his window open.

He says, "The light hurts my eyes. I can't believe how much the light's killing my eyes."

He has said this numerous times, offering an answer to an unasked question of why he won't look at her or take off his dark glasses despite the overcast sky and rain. When she made coffee and dry toast barely an hour ago and brought it to him in bed, he groaned as he sat up and held his head. Unconvincingly, he asked, "Where am I?"

"You were very drunk last night." She set

the coffee and toast on the bedside table. "Do you remember?"

"If I eat anything, I'll puke."

"Do you remember last night?"

He says he doesn't remember anything after riding his motorcycle to her house. His demeanor says he remembers all of it. He continues to complain about feeling sick.

"I wish you didn't have food back there. Now's not a good time for me to smell food."

"Too bad. Rose has the flu."

She parks in the lot next to Rose's building.

"I sure as shit don't want to get the flu," he says.

"Then stay in the car."

"I want to know what you did with my gun." He has said this several times as well.

"As I've told you, it's in a safe place."

She parks. On the backseat is a box filled with covered dishes. She stayed up all night cooking. She cooked enough tagliolini with fontina sauce, lasagna Bolognese, and vegetable soup to feed twenty people.

"Last night you were in no condition to have a loaded gun," she adds.

"I want to know where it is. What did you do with it?"

He walks slightly ahead of her, not bothering to ask if he can carry the box.

"I'll tell you again. I took it from you last night. I took your motorcycle key. Do you remember my taking your key away from you because you insisted on riding your motorcycle when you could barely stand up?"

"That bourbon in your house," he says as they walk toward the whitewashed building in the rain. "Booker's." As if it's her fault. "I can't afford good bourbon like that. It goes down so smooth, I forget it's a-hundred-and-twenty-something proof."

"So I'm to blame."

"Don't know why you got something that strong in your house."

"Because you brought it over New Year's Eve."

"Someone may as well have hit me over the head with a tire iron," he says as they climb steps and the doorman lets them in.

"Good morning, Ed," Scarpetta says, aware of the sound of a TV inside his office off the lobby. She hears the news, more coverage of Drew Martin's murder.

Ed looks toward his office, shakes his head, and says, "Terrible, terrible. She was a nice girl, a real nice girl. Saw her just here right before she got killed, tipped me twenty dollars every time she came through the door. Terrible. Such a nice girl. Acted like a normal person, you know."

"She was staying here?" Scarpetta says. "I thought she always stayed at the Charleston Place Hotel. At least that's what's been in the news whenever she's in this area."

"Her tennis coach has an apartment here, hardly ever in it, but he's got one," Ed says.

Scarpetta wonders why she's never heard about that. Now isn't the time to ask. She's worried about Rose. Ed pushes the elevator button and taps the button for Rose's floor.

The doors shut. Marino's dark glasses stare straight ahead.

"I think I got a migraine," he says. "You got anything for a migraine?"

"You've already taken eight hundred milligrams of ibuprofen. Nothing else for at least five hours."

"That don't help a migraine. I wish you hadn't had that stuff in the house. It's like someone slipped me something, like I was drugged."

"The only person who slipped you something is yourself."

"I can't believe you called Bull. What if he's dangerous?"

She can't believe he'd say such a thing after what happened last night.

"I sure as hell hope you don't ask him to help in the office next," he says. "What the hell does he know? He'll just get in the way."

"I can't think about this right now. I'm thinking about Rose right now. And maybe this would be a good time for you to worry about somebody besides yourself." Anger begins to rise, and Scarpetta walks quickly along a hallway of old white plaster walls and worn blue carpet.

She rings the bell to Rose's apartment. No answer, no sound inside except the TV. She sets the box on the floor and tries the bell again. Then again. She calls her cell phone, her landline. She hears them ringing inside, then voicemail.

"Rose!" Scarpetta pounds on the door. "Rose!"

She hears the TV. Nothing but the TV.

"We've got to get a key," she says to Marino. "Ed has one. Rose!"

"Fuck that." Marino kicks the door as hard as he can, and wood splinters and the burglar chain breaks, brass links clinking to the floor as the door flies open and bangs against the wall.

Inside, Rose is on the couch, motionless, her eyes shut, her face ashen, strands of long, snowy hair unpinned.

"Call nine-one-one now!" Scarpetta puts pillows behind Rose to prop her up as Marino calls for an ambulance.

She takes Rose's pulse. Sixty-one.

"They're on their way," Marino says.

"Go to the car. My medical bag's in the trunk."

He runs out of the apartment, and she notices a wineglass and a prescription bottle on the floor, almost hidden by the skirt of the couch. She's stunned to see that Rose has been taking Roxicodone, a trade name for oxycodone hydrochloride, an opioid analgesic that's notoriously habit-forming. The prescription of one hundred tablets was filled ten days ago. She takes the top off the bottle and counts the fifteen-milligram green tablets. There are seventeen left.

"Rose!" Scarpetta shakes her. She's warm and sweating. "Rose, wake up! Can you hear me! Rose!"

Scarpetta goes to the bathroom and returns with a cool washcloth, places it on Rose's forehead, and holds her hand, talking to her, trying to rouse her. Then Marino is back. He looks frantic and frightened as he hands Scarpetta the medical bag.

"She moved the couch. I was supposed to do it," he says, his dark glasses staring at the couch.

Rose stirs as a siren sounds in the distance. Scarpetta takes a blood pressure cuff and a stethoscope from her medical bag.

"I promised to come over and move it," Marino says. "She moved it by herself. It was over there." His dark glasses look at an empty space near a window.

Scarpetta pushes up Rose's sleeve, slides the stethoscope on her arm, wraps the cuff just above the bend in the arm, tight enough to stop blood flow.

The siren is very loud.

She squeezes the bulb, inflates the cuff, then opens the valve to release the air slowly as she listens to the blood beating its way along the artery. Air hisses quietly as the cuff deflates.

The siren stops. The ambulance is here.

Systolic pressure eighty-six. Diastolic pressure fifty-eight. She moves the diaphragm over Rose's chest and back. Respiration is depressed, and she's hypotensive.

Rose stirs, moves her head.

"Rose?" Scarpetta says loudly. "Can you hear me?"

Her eye lids flutter open.

"I'm going to take your temperature." She places a digital thermometer under Rose's tongue and in seconds it beeps. Temperature ninety-nine-point-one. She holds up the bottle of pills. "How many did you take?" she asks. "How much wine did you drink?"

"It's just the flu."

"You move the couch yourself?" Marino asks her, as if it matters.

She nods. "Overdid it. That's all."

Rapid footsteps and the clatter of paramedics and a stretcher in the hallway.

"No," she protests. "Send them away."

Two EMTs in blue jumpsuits fill the doorway and push the stretcher inside. On top of it is a defibrillator and other equipment.

Rose shakes her head. "No. I'm all right. I'm not going to the hospital."

Ed appears in the doorway, worried, looking in.

"What's the problem, ma'am?" One of the

EMTs, blond with pale blue eyes, comes over to the couch and looks closely at Rose. He looks closely at Scarpetta.

"No." Rose is adamant, waving them off. "I mean it! Please go away. I fainted. That's all."

"That's not all," Marino says to her, but his dark glasses are staring at the blond EMT. "I had to bust the damn door down."

"And you better fix it before you leave," Rose mutters.

Scarpetta introduces herself. She explains that it seems Rose mixed alcohol with oxycodone, was unconscious when they got here.

"Ma'am?" The blond EMT leans closer to Rose. "How much alcohol and oxycodone did you have, and when did you take it?"

"One more than usual. Three tablets. And just a little bit of wine. Half a glass."

"Ma'am, it's very important you're honest with me about this."

Scarpetta hands him the prescription bottle and says to Rose, "One tablet every four to six hours. You took two more than that. And you're on a high dose already. I want you to go to the hospital just to make sure everything's all right."

"No."

"Did you crush them or chew them or swallow them whole?" Scarpetta asks, because when the tablets are crushed, they dissolve more quickly and the oxycodone is more rapidly released and absorbed.

"I swallowed them whole, just like I always do. My knees were aching something awful." She looks at Marino. "I shouldn't have moved the couch."

"If you won't go with these nice EMTs, I'll take you," Scarpetta says, aware of the blond EMT's stare.

"No." Rose adamantly shakes her head.

Marino watches the blond EMT watch Scarpetta. Marino doesn't protectively move close to her as he would have done in the past. She doesn't address the most disturbing question—why Rose is on Roxicodone.

"I'm not going to the hospital," Rose says. "I'm not. I mean it."

"It looks like we're not going to need you," Scarpetta says to the EMTs. "But thanks."

"I heard you lecture a few months back," the blond EMT says to her. "The child fatality session at the National Forensic Academy. You lectured."

His name tag reads *T. Turkington.* She has no recollection of him.

"What the hell were you doing there?" Marino asks him. "The NFA's for cops."

"I'm an investigator for the Beaufort County Sheriff's Department. They sent me to the NFA. I'm a graduate."

"Now, ain't that strange," Marino says. "Then what the hell are you doing here in Charleston, riding around in an ambulance?"

"My days off, I work as an EMT."

"This ain't Beaufort County."

"Can use the extra pay. Emergency medicine's good supplemental training for my real job. I have a girlfriend here. Or did." Turkington is easygoing about it. To Scarpetta, he says, "If you're sure everything's all right in here, we'll be on our way."

"Thanks. I'll keep my eye on her," Scarpetta replies.

"Nice to see you again, by the way." His blue eyes fix on her, and then he and his partner are gone.

Scarpetta says to Rose, "I'm taking you to the hospital to make sure nothing else is wrong."

"You're not taking me anywhere," she says. "Would you please go find me a new door?" she says to Marino. "Or a new lock or whatever it takes to fix the mess you made."

"You can use my car," Scarpetta says, tossing him the keys. "I'll walk home."

"I need to get into your house."

"It will have to wait until later," she says.

The sun slips in and out of smoky clouds, and the sea heaves against the shore.

Ashley Dooley, a South Carolinian born and bred, has taken off his Windbreaker and tied the sleeves around his big belly. He points his brand-new camcorder at his wife, Madelisa, then stops filming when a black-and-white basset hound appears from the sea oats on the dune. The dog trots to Madelisa, his droopy ears dragging in the sand. He presses against her legs, panting.

"Oh, look, Ashley!" She squats and pets him. "Poor baby, he's shaking. What's the matter, honey? Don't be scared. He's still a puppy."

Dogs love her. They seek her out. She's never had a single dog growl at her or do anything but love her. Last year, they had to put Frisbee to sleep when he got cancer. Madelisa hasn't gotten over it, won't forgive Ashley for refusing treatment because of the expense.

"Move over there," Ashley says. "You can

have the dog in the film if you want. I'll get all these fancy houses in the background. Holy shit, look at that one. Like something you'd see in Europe. Who the hell needs something that big?"

"I wish we could go to Europe."

"I tell you, this camcorder's something."

Madelisa can't stand to hear about it. Somehow he could afford thirteen hundred dollars for a camcorder but couldn't spare a dime for Frisbee.

"Look at it. All those balconies and a red roof," he's saying. "Imagine living in something like that."

If we lived in something like that, she thinks, *I wouldn't mind you buying fancy camcorders and a plasma-screen TV, and we could have afforded Frisbee's vet bills.* "I can't imagine," she says, posing in front of the dune. The basset hound sits on her foot, panting.

"I hear there's a thirty-million-dollar one down that way." He points. "Smile. That's not a smile. A big smile. Think it's owned by someone famous, maybe the man who started Wal-Mart. Why's that dog panting so much? It's not that hot out here. And he's shivering, too. Maybe he's sick, could have rabies."

"No, pumpkin, he's shaking like he's scared. Maybe he's thirsty. I told you to bring a bottle of water. The man who started Wal-Mart's dead," she adds, as she pets the basset hound and scans the beach, doesn't notice anybody nearby, just a few people in the distance, fishing. "I think he's lost," she says. "I don't see anybody around who might be his owner."

"We'll look for it, get some footage."

"Look for what?" she asks, the dog pressed against her legs, panting, shaking. She checks him, noting he needs a bath and his claws need clipping. Then something else. "Oh, my goodness. I think he's hurt." She touches the top of the dog's neck, looks at blood on her finger, begins parting his fur, looking for a wound, not finding one. "Now, that's strange. How'd he get blood on him? There's some more of it, too. But it doesn't look like he's hurt. Now that's just yucky."

She wipes her fingers on her shorts.

"Maybe there's a carcass of a chewed-up cat somewhere." Ashley hates cats. "Let's keep walking. We've got our tennis clinic at two and I'm gonna need some lunch first. We got any of that honey-baked ham left?"

She looks back. The basset hound sits in the sand, panting, staring at them.

"I know you have a spare key in that little box you bury in your garden under that pile of bricks behind the bushes," Rose says.

"He's hung over as hell, and I don't want him riding his motorcycle with a damn forty-caliber pistol jammed in the back of his jeans," Scarpetta says.

"How did it end up at your house to begin with? How did he end up there, for that matter?"

"I don't want to talk about him. I want to talk about you."

"Why don't you get off the couch and pull up a chair. It's hard for me to talk when you're practically sitting on top of me," Rose says.

Scarpetta carries over a dining room chair, sets it down, and says, "Your medication."

"I haven't been stealing pills from the morgue, if that's what you're implying. All those pitiful people who come in with dozens of prescription bottles, because why? Because they don't take them. Pills don't fix a damn thing. If they did, those people wouldn't end up in the morgue."

"Your bottle has your name on it and the name of your physician. Now, I can look him up or you can tell me what kind of doctor he is and why you're seeing him."

"An oncologist."

Scarpetta feels as if she's been kicked in the chest.

"Please. Don't make this harder for me," Rose says. "I was hoping you wouldn't find out until it was time to pick out an acceptable urn for my ashes. I know I did something I shouldn't." She catches her breath. "Was in such a state, got so upset, and was aching all over."

Scarpetta takes her hand. "Funny how we get ambushed by our feelings. You've been stoical. Or dare I use the word *stubborn*? Now today you have to reckon with it."

"I'm going to die," Rose says. "I hate doing this to everyone."

"What kind of cancer?" Holding Rose's hand.

"Lung. Before you start thinking it's from all that secondary smoke I was exposed to in the early days when you puffed away in your office . . ." Rose starts to say.

"I wish I hadn't. I can't tell you how much I wish that."

"What's killing me has nothing to do with you," Rose says. "I promise. I come by it honestly."

"Non–small cell or small cell?"

"Non–small."

"Adenocarcinoma, squamous?"

"Adenocarcinoma. Same thing my aunt died from. Like me, she never smoked. Her grandfather died of squamous. He did smoke. I never in a million years imagined I'd get lung cancer. But then it's never occurred to me I'd die. Isn't it ridiculous." She sighs, the color slowly returning to her face, the light to her eyes. "We look at death every day and it doesn't change our denial about it. You're right, Dr. Scarpetta. I guess today it hit me from behind. I never saw it coming."

"Maybe it's about time you call me Kay."

She shakes her head.

"Why not? Aren't we friends?"

Rose says, "We've always believed in boundaries, and they've served us well. I work for someone I'm honored to know. Her name is Dr. Scarpetta. Or Chief." She smiles. "I could never call her Kay."

"So now you're depersonalizing me. Unless you're talking about someone else."

"She's someone else. Someone you really

don't know. I think you have a much lower opinion of her than I do. Especially these days."

"Sorry, I'm not this heroic woman you just described, but let me help what little I can—get you to the best cancer center in the country. Stanford Cancer Center. Where Lucy goes. I'll take you. We'll get you any treatment you . . ."

"No, no, no." Rose shakes her head again slowly, side to side. "Now be quiet and listen to me. I've consulted all sorts of specialists. Do you remember last summer I went on a three-week cruise? A lie. The only cruise I went on was from one specialist to another, and then Lucy took me to Stanford, which is where I got my doctor. The prognosis is the same. My only choice was chemo and radiation, and I refused."

"We should try anything we possibly can."

"I'm already in stage three-B."

"It's spread to the lymph nodes?"

"Lymph nodes. And bone. Well on its way to being stage four. Surgery's impossible."

"Chemotherapy and radiotherapy, or even just radiation therapy by itself. We've got to try. We can't just give up like this."

"In the first place, there's no *we*. It's *me*.

And no. I won't put myself through it. I'll be damned if I'm going to have all my hair fall out and be sick and miserable when I know this disease is going to kill me. Sooner rather than later. Lucy even said she would get me marijuana so the chemo wouldn't make me as sick. Imagine me smoking pot."

"Obviously, she's known about this for as long as you have," Scarpetta says.

Rose nods.

"You should have told me."

"I told Lucy, and she's a master of secrets, has so many I'm not sure any of us know what's really true. What I didn't want is this very thing. To make you feel bad."

"Just tell me what I can do." As grief tightens its grip.

"Change what you can. Don't ever think you can't."

"Tell me. I'll do anything you want," Scarpetta says.

"It's not until you're dying that you begin to realize all the things in life you could have changed. This I can't change." Rose taps her chest. "You have the power to change almost anything you want."

Images from last night, and for an instant, Scarpetta imagines she smells him, feels him, and she struggles not to show how devastated she is.

"What is it?" Rose squeezes her hand.

"How can I not feel terrible?"

"You were just thinking about something, and it wasn't me," Rose says. "Marino. He looks awful and is acting odd."

"Because he got shit-face drunk," Scarpetta says, anger in her voice.

" 'Shit-face.' Now, that's a term I haven't heard you use. But then I'm getting rather vulgar myself these days. I actually used the word *twat* this morning when I was talking to Lucy on the phone—referring to Marino's latest. Who Lucy happened to pass in your neighborhood around eight. When Marino's motorcycle was still parked in front of your house."

"I have a box of food for you. It's still in the hall. Let me get it and I'll put it away."

A coughing fit, and when Rose removes the tissue from her mouth, it is spotted with bright red blood.

"Please let me take you back to Stanford," Scarpetta says.

"Tell me what happened last night."

"We talked." Scarpetta feels her face turn red. "Until he was too drunk."

"I don't believe I've ever seen you blush."

"A hot flash."

"Yes, and I have the flu."

"Tell me what to do for you."

"Let me go about my business as usual. I don't want to be resuscitated. I don't want to die in a hospital."

"Why don't you move in with me?"

"That's not going about my business as usual," Rose says.

"Will you at least give me permission to talk to your doctor?"

"There's nothing else for you to know. You asked what I want, and I'm telling you. No curative treatment. I want palliative care."

"I have an extra room in my house. Small as it is. Maybe I should get a bigger place," Scarpetta says.

"Don't be so selfless it makes you selfish. And it's selfish if you make me feel guilty and just plain horrible because I'm hurting everyone around me."

Scarpetta hesitates, then says, "Can I tell Benton?"

"You can tell him. But not Marino. I don't want you telling him." Rose sits up, places her feet on the floor. She takes both of Scarpetta's hands. "I'm no forensic pathologist," she says. "But why are there fresh bruises on your wrists?"

The basset hound is still right where they left him, sitting in the sand near the *No Trespassing* sign.

"See, now, this just isn't normal," Madelisa exclaims. "Been sitting here for more than an hour, waiting for us to come back. Here, Droopy. You sweet little thing."

"Honey, that's not his name. Now, don't be naming him. Look at his tag," Ashley says. "See what his real name is and where he lives."

She stoops down, and the basset hound ambles over to her, presses against her, licks her hands. She squints at the tag, doesn't have her reading glasses. Ashley doesn't have his, either.

"I can't see it," she says. "What little I can make out. Nope, doesn't look like there's a phone number. I didn't bring my phone, anyhow."

"I didn't, either."

"Now, that's dumb. What if I twisted my ankle out here or something? Somebody's barbecuing," she says, sniffing, looking around, noticing a wisp of smoke rising from the back of the huge white house with the balconies and red roof—one of the few houses she's seen with a *No Trespassing* sign. "Now, why aren't you running off to see what's cooking?" she says to the basset hound, stroking his floppy ears. "Maybe we could go out and buy us one of those little grills and cook out tonight."

She tries to read the dog's tags again, but it's hopeless without her glasses, and she imagines rich people, imagines some millionaire grilling on the patio of that huge white house set back from the dune, partially hidden by tall pines.

"Say hello to your old-maid sister," Ashley says, filming. "Tell her how luxurious our town house is here on Millionaire Row in Hilton Head. Tell her next time we're staying in a mansion like that one where they're barbecuing."

Madelisa looks down the beach in the direction of their town house, unable to see it through thick trees. She returns her attention to the dog and says, "I bet he lives in the house right there." Pointing to the white European-looking mansion where someone is barbecuing. "I'll just go on over there and ask."

"Go right on. I'll wander a little bit, filming. Saw a few porpoises a minute ago."

"Come on, Droopy. Let's go find your family," Madelisa says to the dog.

He sits in the sand and won't come. She tugs his collar, but he's not going anywhere. "Okay, then," she says. "You stay put and I'll find out if that big house is where you're from. Maybe you got out and they don't know it. But one thing's for sure. Someone's missing you something awful!"

She hugs and kisses him. She heads off across the hard sand, gets to the soft sand, walks right through sea oats, even though she hears it's illegal to walk on the dunes. She hesitates at the *No Trespassing* sign, bravely steps up on the wooden boardwalk, heading to the huge white house where some rich person, maybe a celebrity, is cooking on the grill. Lunch, she supposes, as she keeps looking back, hoping the basset hound doesn't run off. She can't see him on the other side of the dune. She doesn't see him on the beach, either, just Ashley, a small figure, filming several dolphins rolling through the water, their fins cutting through the waves, then dipping out of sight again. At the end of the boardwalk is a wooden gate, and she's surprised it isn't locked. It isn't completely shut.

She walks through the backyard, looking everywhere, calling out "Hello!" She's never seen such a big pool, what they call a black-bottom pool, trimmed with fancy tile that looks like it came from Italy or Spain or some other exotic faraway place. She looks around, calling out "hello," pauses curiously at the smoking gas grill where a slab of raggedly cut meat is charred on one side, bloody-raw on top. It occurs to her that the meat is strange, doesn't look like steak or pork, certainly not like chicken.

"Hello!" she calls out. "Anybody home?"

She bangs on the sun porch door. No answer. She walks around to the side of the house, supposing whoever is cooking might be somewhere over there, but the side yard is empty and overgrown. She peers through a space between the blinds and the edge of a big window and sees an empty kitchen, all stone and stainless steel. She's never seen a kitchen like that except in magazines. She notices two big dog bowls on a mat near the butcher block.

"Hello!" she yells. "I think I have your dog!

Hello!" She moves along the side of the house, calling out. She climbs up steps to a door, next to it a window missing a pane of glass. Another pane is broken. She thinks about hurrying back to the beach, but inside the laundry room is a big dog crate that's empty.

"Hello!" Her heart beats hard. She's trespassing, but she's found the basset hound's home and she's got to help. How would she feel if it were Frisbee and someone didn't bring him back?

"Hello!" She tries the door and it opens.

Chapter 12

Water drips from live oaks.

In the deep shadows of yew and tea olive trees, Scarpetta arranges broken pieces of pottery in the bottoms of pots to help with drainage so the plants don't rot. The warm air is steamy from a hard rain that suddenly started and just as suddenly stopped.

Bull carries a ladder over to an oak tree that spreads its canopy over most of Scarpetta's garden. She begins tamping potting soil into the pots and tucks in petunias, then parsley, dill, and fennel, because they attract butterflies. She relocates fuzzy silver lamb's ears and artemisia into better spots where they will catch the sun. The scent of wet, loamy earth mingles with the pungency of old brick and moss as she moves rather stiffly—from years of unforgiving tile floors in the morgue—to a brick post overgrown with hollyfern. She starts diagnosing the problem.

"If I pull this fern out, Bull, I might damage the brick. What do you think?"

"That's Charleston brick, probably two hundred years old, my guess." From the top of the ladder. "I'd pull a little, see what happens."

The fern peels off without complaint. She fills a watering can and tries not to think about Marino. She feels sick when she thinks about Rose.

Bull says, "Some man came through the alley on a chopper right before you got here."

Scarpetta stops what she's doing, stares up at him. "Was it Marino?"

When she got home from Rose's apartment, his motorcycle was gone. He must have driven her car to his house and gotten a spare key.

"No, ma'am, it wasn't him. I was up on the ladder limbing the loquats, could see the man on the chopper over the fence. He didn't see me. Maybe nothing." The clippers snap, and side shoots called suckers fall to the ground. "Anybody been bothering you, 'cause I'd like to know about it."

"What was he doing?"

"Turned in and rode real slow about halfway, then turned around and went back. Looked to me like he had on a do-rag, maybe orange and yellow. Hard to tell from where I was. His chopper had bad pipes, rattled and spit like something about to quit. You should tell me if I should know something. I'll be looking."

"You ever seen him before around here?"

"I'd recognize that chopper."

She thinks about what Marino told her last night. A biker threatened him in the parking lot, said something bad would happen to her if she didn't leave town. Who would want her gone so badly as to pass on a message like that? The local coroner sticks in her mind.

She asks Bull, "You know much about the coroner here? Henry Hollings?"

"Only his funeral home business been in the family since the War, that huge place behind a high wall over there on Calhoun, not too far from here. I don't like the thought of someone bothering you. Your neighbor sure is curious."

Mrs. Grimball is looking out the window again.

"She watches me like a hawk," Bull says. "If I might say so, she's got an unkindness about her and don't mind hurting people."

Scarpetta goes back to work. Something's eating the pansies. She tells Bull.

"There's a bad rat problem around here," he replies. It seems prophetic.

She examines more damaged pansies. "Slugs," she decides.

"You could try beer," Bull says with snaps of the pole cutter. "Put out saucers of it after dark. They crawl in it, get drunk, and drown."

"And the beer attracts more slugs than you had before. I couldn't drown anything."

More suckers rain down from the oak tree. "Saw some raccoon droppings over there." He points with the pole clipper. "Could be them eating the pansies."

"Raccoons, squirrels. Nothing I can do about it."

"There is, but you won't. You sure don't like to kill nothing. Kind of interesting when I think what you do. Would assume nothing much would bother you." He talks from up in the tree.

"It seems what I do causes everything to bother me."

"Uh-huh. That's what happens when you know too much. Those hydrangeas over where you are. Put some rusty nails around them and they'll turn a pretty blue."

"Epsom salts will work, too."

"Hadn't heard that."

Scarpetta looks through a jeweler's lens at the back of a camellia leaf, notes whitish scales. "We'll prune these, and because there are wound pathogens, we're going to have to disinfect before using the tools on anything else. I need to get the plant pathologist here."

"Uh-huh. Plants has diseases just like people."

Crows begin to fuss in the canopy of the live oak he's trimming. Several of them suddenly flap off.

Madelisa stands paralyzed like that lady in the Bible who didn't do what God said and He turned her into a pillar of salt. She's trespassing, breaking the law.

"Hello?" she calls out again.

She musters up the courage to walk out of

the laundry room and into the grand kitchen of the grandest house she's ever seen, still calling out "Hello!" and not sure what to do. She's scared in a way she's never felt before and should get out of here as fast as she can. She begins to wander, gawking at everything, feeling like a burglar, worrying she's going to get caught—now or later— and go to jail.

She should leave, get out. Do it now. The hair pricks up on the back of her neck as she continues calling out "Hello!" and "Anybody home?" and wondering why in the world the house is unlocked with meat on the grill if no one's here. She begins to imagine she's being watched as she wanders, something warning her that she ought to run as fast as she can out of this house and get back to Ashley. She has no right to wander around being nosy but can't help it now that she's here. She's never seen a house like this and can't figure out why nobody is answering her, and she's too curious to turn back, or feels like she can't.

She passes through an arch into a tremendous living room. The floor is blue stone, looks like gemstone, and is arranged with gorgeous Oriental rugs, and there are huge exposed beams and a fireplace big enough to roast a pig. A movie screen is pulled down over an expanse of glass that faces the ocean. Dust drifts in the beam of light from the overhead projector, the screen lit up but blank, and there's no sound. She looks at the wraparound black leather sofa, puzzled by the neatly folded clothing on top of it: a dark T-shirt, dark pants, a pair of men's Jockey briefs. The big glass coffee table is cluttered with packs of cigarettes, prescription bottles, an almost empty fifth of Grey Goose vodka.

Madelisa imagines someone—probably a man—drunk and depressed or sick, maybe explaining why the dog got out. Someone was in here not long ago, drinking, she thinks, and whoever it was started cooking on the grill and seems to have vanished. Her heart pounds. She can't shake the feeling she's being watched, and she thinks, *My Lord, it's cold in here*.

"Hello? Anybody home?" she calls out hoarsely.

Her feet seem to move on their own as she explores in awe, and fear hums inside her like electricity. She should leave. She's trespassing like a burglar. Breaking and entering. She's going to get in trouble. She feels something looking at her. The police will be looking at her, all right, if and when they find out, and she's getting panicky, but her feet won't listen. They keep moving her from one place to the next.

"Hello?" she calls out, her voice cracking.

Beyond the living room, off to the left of the foyer, is another room, and she hears running water.

"Hello!"

She hesitantly follows the sound of running water, can't seem to stop her feet. They keep right on, and she finds herself in a large bedroom with fancy, formal furniture and drawn silk curtains and pictures all over the walls. A beautiful little girl with a very pretty, happy woman who must be her mother. The little girl joyous in a wading pool with a puppy—the basset hound. The same pretty woman crying, sitting on a couch talking to the famous talk-show psychiatrist Dr. Self, big cameras rolled in close. The same pretty lady posing with Drew Martin and a handsome man with olive skin and very dark hair. Drew and the man are in tennis clothes, holding racquets on a tennis court somewhere.

Drew Martin's dead. Murdered.

The pale blue duvet on the bed is messy. On the black marble floor near the head of the bed are clothes that seem to have been dropped there. A pink jogging suit, a pair of socks, a bra. The sound of running water gets louder as her feet move toward it, and Madelisa tells her feet to run the other way but they won't. *Run*, she tells them as they walk her into a bathroom of black onyx and copper. *RUN!* She slowly takes in the wet, bloody towels in the copper sink, the bloody saw-toothed knife and bloody box cutters on the back of the black toilet, the neat stack of clean, pale rose linens on top of the hamper.

Behind tiger-striped curtains drawn around the copper tub, water runs, splashing on something that doesn't sound like metal.

Chapter 13

After dark. Scarpetta shines her flashlight on a stainless-steel Colt revolver in the middle of the alley behind her house.

She hasn't called the police. If the coroner is involved in this latest turn of sinister events, then calling the police might make matters worse. No telling who he has in his pocket. Bull has quite a story, and she doesn't know what to think. He says when the crows flapped off from the oak tree in her garden, he knew that had meaning, so he told her an untruth, said he had to go on home, when what he intended to do was some sneaking—that's how he put it. He tucked himself behind shrubbery between her two sets of gates and waited. He waited the better part of five hours. Scarpetta had no idea.

She went about her business. Finished what she was doing in the garden. Took a shower. Worked in her upstairs office. Made phone calls. Checked on Rose. Checked on Lucy. Checked on Benton. All the while, she didn't know Bull was hiding between the two sets of gates behind the house. He says it's like fishing. You don't catch anything unless you fool the fish into thinking you've left for the day. When the sun was lower and the shadows longer and Bull had been sitting on dark, cool bricks between the gates all afternoon, he saw a man in the alleyway. The man walked right up to Scarpetta's outer gate and tried to squeeze his hand through it to unlock it. When that didn't work, he started to climb the ironwork, and that's when Bull swung the gate open and got into it with him. He thinks it's the man who was on the chopper, but whoever it was, he was up to something serious, and when they got into the scuffle, the man dropped his gun.

"Stay right here," she tells Bull in the dark alley. "If one of the neighbors comes out or anyone shows up for any reason, no one gets near anything. No one touches anything. Fortunately, I don't think anybody can see what we're doing."

The beam of Bull's flashlight probes the uneven bricks as she returns to her house. She climbs the stairs to the second story, and in a few minutes is back in the alley with her camera and crime scene case. She takes photographs. She pulls on latex gloves. She picks up the revolver, opens the cylinder, and ejects six thirty-eight-caliber cartridges, placing them in one paper bag, the gun in another. She seals them with bright yellow evidence tape that she labels and initials with a Sharpie.

Bull continues to search, his flashlight bobbing as he walks, stops, crouches, then walks some more, all of it very slowly. A few more minutes pass, and he says, "There's something here. I think you better look."

She walks over to him, watching where she steps, and about a hundred feet from her gates on the leaf-littered asphalt is a small gold coin attached to a broken gold chain. They blaze in the beam of her flashlight, the gold as bright as the moon.

"You were this far away from my gates

when you struggled with him?" she says with doubt. "Then why's his gun way over there?" She points toward the dark shapes of her gates and garden wall.

"Hard to tell where I was," he says. "Things like that happen fast. I didn't think I was way over here, but I can't say it as a fact."

She looks back toward her house. "From here to there is pretty far," she says. "You sure you didn't chase him after he dropped the gun?"

"All I can say," Bull says, "is a gold chain with a gold coin isn't going to lie around out here long. So I could have chased him and it got broke when we tussled. I didn't think I chased him, but when you got life and death going on, time and distance don't always measure right."

"They don't always," she agrees.

She pulls on fresh gloves and picks up the broken necklace by a small area of the chain. Without a lens, she can't tell what type of coin it is, can make out only a crowned head on one side, a wreath and the number 1 on the other.

"So it probably broke off when I started tussling with him," Bull decides, as if he's convinced himself. "Sure hope they don't make you turn all this over to them. The police, I mean."

"There's nothing to turn over," she says. "So far, there's no crime. Just a scuffle between you and a stranger. Which I don't intend to mention to anyone. Except Lucy. We'll see what we can do in the labs tomorrow."

He's already been in trouble. He's not getting into trouble again, especially on her account.

"When folks find a gun lying around, they supposed to call the police," Bull says.

"Well, I'm not going to." She packs up what she carried outside.

"You're fretting they'd think I was involved in something and haul me off. Don't you get in a mess because of me, Dr. Kay."

"No one's hauling you anywhere," she says.

Gianni Lupano's black Porsche 911 Carrera is permanently located in Charleston, no matter how seldom he's here.

"Where is he?" Lucy asks Ed.

"Haven't seen him."

"But he's still in town."

"I talked to him yesterday. He called and asked me to get maintenance up there because his air-conditioning wasn't working right. So while he was out, and I don't know where he went, they changed the filter. He's a private one. I know about his coming and going because he gets me to start his car once a week so the battery don't go dead." Ed opens a foam to-go box, and his small office smells like french fries. "You mind? Don't want it to get cold. Who told you about his car?"

"Rose didn't know he has a place in the building," Lucy says from the doorway, watching the lobby, seeing who walks in. "When she found out, she figured who he is and told me she's seen him driving an expensive sports car that she thought was a Porsche."

"She's got a Volvo as old as my cat."

"I've always loved cars, so Rose knows a lot about them, whether she likes it or not," Lucy says. "Ask her about Porsche, Ferrari, Lamborghini, she'll tell you. Around here, people don't rent Porsches. Maybe a Mercedes but not a Porsche like he's got. So I figured he might keep it here."

"How's she doing?" Ed sits at his desk, eating a cheeseburger from the Sweetwater Cafe. "That was a bad time of it earlier."

"Well," Lucy says. "She's not feeling all that great."

"I had the flu shot this year. Got the flu twice, plus a cold. It's like giving you candy so you don't get a cavity. Last time I'm doing it."

"Was Gianni Lupano here when Drew was murdered in Rome?" Lucy asks. "I was told he was in New York, but that doesn't mean it's true."

"She won the tournament here on a Sunday, the middle of the month." He wipes his mouth with a paper napkin, picks up a big soda, and sucks on the straw. "I know that night Gianni left Charleston, because he asked me to look after his car. Said he didn't know when he'd be back, then all of a sudden, here he is."

"But you haven't seen him."

"Almost never do."

"You talk to him on the phone."

"That's usually it."

"I don't understand it," Lucy says. "Other than Drew playing the *Family Circle* Cup, why would he be in Charleston? The tournament's what? One week a year?"

"You'd be surprised the people who got places in the area. Movie stars, even."

"His car have a GPS?"

"It's got everything. That's some car."

"I need to borrow the key."

"Oh." Ed sets the cheeseburger back in the container. "I can't do that."

"Don't worry. I'm not going to drive it, just need to check something, and I know you won't say a word about it."

"I can't give you the key." He's stopped eating. "He ever found out . . ."

"I need the key for ten minutes, fifteen at the most. He'll never find out, I promise."

"Maybe you could start her up while you're at it. No harm in it." He rips open a packet of ketchup.

"Will do."

She goes out a back door and finds the Porsche in a secluded corner of the parking lot. She turns on the engine and opens the glove box to check the registration. The Carrera is a 2006 and registered to Lupano. She turns on the GPS, checks the history of the stored destinations, and writes them down.

The rapid respiration of the magnet keeping cool.

Inside the MRI suite, Benton looks through glass at Dr. Self's sheet-draped feet. She's on a sliding table inside the bore of the fourteen-ton magnet, her chin taped down to remind her not to move her head, which is against a coil that will receive the radio frequency pulses necessary to image her brain. Over her ears is a set of gradient-damping headphones. Through them, a little later, when the functional imaging starts, she'll hear the audiotape of her mother's voice.

"So far, so good," he says to Dr. Susan Lane. "Except for her fun and games. I'm awfully sorry she's kept everybody waiting." To the tech: "Josh? How about you? Awake?"

"Can't tell you how much I've been looking forward to this," Josh says from his console. "My little girl's been throwing up all day. Ask my wife how much she'd like to kill me right now."

"Never known one person to bring such happiness into the world." Benton means Dr. Self, the eye of the storm. He looks through glass at her feet, catches a glimpse of stockings. "She's wearing hose?"

"You're lucky she's wearing anything. When I brought her in, she insisted on taking everything off," Dr. Lane says.

"I'm not surprised." He's careful. Although Dr. Self can't hear them unless they use the intercom, she can see them. "Manic as hell. Has been since she got here. Been a productive stay. Ask her. She's as sane as a judge."

"I did ask her about anything metal, asked if she had on an underwire bra," Dr. Lane says. "Told her the scanner has a magnetic pull sixty thousand times greater than the earth's and nothing ferrous can be near it, and bra burning would have a different meaning if there was underwire and she didn't tell us. She said she did, was quite proud of the fact, and went on and on about the—*ah-hmmm*—burden of having large breasts. Of course, I told her she had to take off the bra, and she said she preferred to take off everything and asked for a johnny."

"I rest my case."

"So she has on a johnny, but I did convince her to keep her pants on. And her stockings."

"Good job, Susan. Let's get this over with."

Dr. Lane pushes the talk button of the intercom and says, "What we're going to do now is start with some localizing images—structural imaging, in other words. This first part is going to last about six minutes, and you're going to hear some rather loud, strange noises that the machine makes. How are you doing?"

"Can we start, please?" Dr. Self's voice.

Intercom off, and Dr. Lane says to Benton, "You ready for the PANAS?" Positive and Negative Affect Scales rating.

Benton pushes the intercom button again and says, "Dr. Self, I'm going to start with a series of questions about how you're feeling. And I'll be asking you these same questions several other times during our session, all right?"

"I know what a PANAS is." Her voice.

Benton and Dr. Lane exchange glances, their facial expressions relaxed, revealing nothing as Dr. Lane says sarcastically, "Wonderful."

Benton says, "Ignore it. Let's just do this."

Josh looks at Benton, ready to start. Benton thinks of his conversation with Dr. Maroni and the implied accusation that Josh told Lucy about their VIP patient, and then Lucy told Scarpetta. It still puzzles Benton. What was Dr. Maroni trying to say? As he looks at Dr. Self through the glass, something comes to him. The file that isn't in Rome. The Sandman's file. Maybe it's here at McLean.

A monitor displays vital signs remotely relayed by Dr. Self's finger holder and a blood pressure cuff. Benton says, "BP one twelve over seventy-eight." He writes it down. "Pulse seventy-two."

"What's her pulse ox?" Dr. Lane asks.

He tells her that Dr. Self's arterial oxyhemoglobin saturation—or the measurement of oxygen saturation in her blood—is ninety-nine. Normal. He presses the intercom button to start the PANAS.

"Dr. Self? Are you ready for a few questions?"

"Finally." Her voice over the intercom.

"I'll ask questions, and I want you to rate what you're feeling on a scale of one to five. One means you feel nothing. Two means you feel a little. Three is moderately, four is very much, and five is extremely. Make sense?"

"I'm familiar with a PANAS. I'm a psychiatrist."

"It appears she's a neuroscientist, too," Dr. Lane comments. "She's going to cheat this part of it."

"I don't care." Benton presses the intercom button and goes through the questions, the same ones he'll ask her several more times during the testing. Is she feeling upset, ashamed, distressed, hostile, irritable, guilty? Or interested, proud, determined, active, strong, inspired, excited, enthusiastic, alert? She assigns a rating of *one* to all of them, claiming she feels nothing.

He checks her vitals and writes them down. They are normal, unchanged.

"Josh?" Dr. Lane indicates it's time.

The structural scan begins. What sounds like loud hammering, and images of Dr. Self's brain are displayed on Josh's computer screen. They don't reveal much. Unless there is some gross pathology, such as a tumor, they will see nothing until later, when thousands of images captured by the MRI are analyzed.

"We're ready to begin," Dr. Lane says over the intercom. "You all right in there?"

"Yes." Impatient.

"The first thirty seconds, you're not going to hear anything," Dr. Lane explains. "So be silent and relax. Then you're going to hear an audiotape of your mother's voice, and I want you to just listen. Be completely still and just listen."

Dr. Self's vitals remain the same.

An eerie sonar sound that brings to mind a submarine as Benton looks at Dr. Self's blanketed feet on the other side of the glass.

"*The weather here's been perfectly wonderful, Marilyn.*" The recorded voice of Gladys

Self. *"I haven't even bothered with the air conditioner—not that it works. Rattles like a huge insect. I just keep the windows and doors open because the temperature isn't so bad right now."*

Although this is the neutral set, the most innocuous one of all, Dr. Self's vital signs have changed.

"Pulse seventy-three, seventy-four," Benton says, writing it down.

"I'd say this isn't neutral for her," Dr. Lane says.

"I was thinking of all those gorgeous fruit trees you used to have when you lived down here, Marilyn, the ones the Department of Agriculture had to cut down because of the citrus canker. I love a pretty yard. And you'd be pleased to know that silly eradication program has pretty much ground to a halt because it doesn't work. Such a shame. Life is all about timing, isn't it?"

"Pulse seventy-five, seventy-six. Pulse ox ninety-eight," Benton says.

". . . The darnedest thing, Marilyn. This submarine going back and forth all day about a mile offshore. Has a little Ameri-

**can flag waving from the whatever you
call it. The tower where the periscope is?
Must be the war. Back and forth, back and
forth, some kind of practice, the little flag
waving. I say to my friends, practice for
what? Did anybody tell them they don't
need submarines in Iraq . . . ?"**

The first neutral set ends, and during a
thirty-second recovery period, Dr. Self's
blood pressure is taken again. It's gone up
to one sixteen over eighty-two. Then her
mother's voice again. Gladys Self talks
about where she likes to shop these days in
South Florida, and the never-ending construction, high-rises sprouting up everywhere, she says. A lot of them empty
because the real estate market has gone to
hell. Mainly because of the war in Iraq. What
it's done to everyone.

Dr. Self reacts the same way.

"Wow," Dr. Lane says. "Something's certainly got her paying attention. Just look at
her pulse ox."

It's dropped to ninety-seven.

Her mother's voice again. Positive comments. Then the criticism.

". . . You were a pathological liar, Mari-

lyn. From the time you could talk, I never could get the truth out of you. Then later? What happened? Where did you get those morals of yours? Not from anyone in this family. You and your dirty little secrets. It's disgusting and reprehensible. What happened to your heart, Marilyn? If only your fans knew! Shame on you, Marilyn . . ."

Dr. Self's oxygenated blood has dropped ninety-six percent, her breathing more rapid, shallower, and audible through the intercom.

". . . The people you threw away. And you know what and who I mean. You lie as if it's the truth. That's what's worried me all your life, and it will catch up with you one of these days . . ."

"Pulse one hundred and twenty-three," Dr. Lane says.

"She just moved her head," Josh says.

"Can the motion software correct for it?" Dr. Lane asks.

"I don't know."

". . . And you think money solves everything. Send your widow's mites and it absolves you of responsibility. Pay people off. Oh, we'll see. One of these days you'll reap what you sow. I don't

want your money. I have drinks in the tiki bar with my friends and they don't even know who you are to me . . ."

Pulse one hundred and thirty-four. Oxygenated blood down to ninety-five. Her feet are restless. Nine seconds left. Mother talks, activating neurons in her daughter's brain. Blood flows to those neurons, and with the increase of blood is an increase in deoxygenated blood that is detected by the scanner. Functional images are captured. Dr. Self is in physical and emotional distress. It isn't an act.

"I don't like what's going on with her vitals. That's it. No more," Benton says to Dr. Lane.

"I agree."

He gets on the intercom. "Dr. Self. We're going to stop."

From a locked cabinet inside the computer lab, Lucy retrieves a tool kit, a thumb drive, and a small black box as she talks to Benton on the phone.

"Don't ask questions," he says. "We just finished a scan. Better put, had to abort one. I can't tell you about it, but I need something."

"Okay." She sits in front of a computer.

"I need you to talk to Josh. I need you to get in."

"To do what?"

"A patient is having her e-mails forwarded to the Pavilion's server."

"And?"

"And also on the same server are electronic files. One for an individual who saw the Pavilion's clinical director. You know who I mean."

"And?"

"And he saw a person of interest in Rome last November," Benton says over the phone. "All I can tell you is this patient of interest served in Iraq, seems he's a referral from Dr. Self."

"And?" Lucy logs on to the Internet.

"Josh just finished the scan. The one aborted. On a person who's leaving tonight, meaning no more forwarded e-mails. Time is of the essence."

"Still there? The person who's leaving?"

"Right now, yes. Josh has already left, has a sick baby at home. Is in a hurry."

"If you give me your password, I can access the network," Lucy says. "That will make it easier. But you're going to be down for about an hour."

She reaches Josh on his cell phone. He's in his car, driving away from the hospital.

That's even better. She tells him Benton can't get into his e-mail, there's something going on with the server, she has to fix it immediately, sounds like it will take some time. She can do it remotely, but she needs the system administrator password unless he wants to turn around and handle it himself. He sure doesn't want to do that, starts talking about his wife, their baby. Okay, it would be great if Lucy could take care of it. They work on technical problems all the time, and it would never occur to him that her intention is to access a patient's e-mail account and Dr. Maroni's private files. Even if Josh suspected the worst, he would assume she would just hack in, wouldn't ask. He knows her abilities, how she makes her money, for God's sake.

She doesn't want to hack into Benton's hospital. And it would take too long. An hour later, she calls Benton back. "Don't have time to look," she says. "Leave that up to you. I forwarded everything. And your e-mail's up."

She leaves the lab and rides off on her Agusta Brutale motorcycle and is overwhelmed by anxiety and anger. Dr. Self is at

McLean. She has been for almost two weeks. *Goddamn it.* Benton has known it.

She rides fast, the warm wind slapping her helmet, as if trying to bring her to her senses.

She understands why Benton couldn't say a word, but it's not right. Dr. Self and Marino e-mailing each other, and all the while she's under Benton's nose at McLean. He doesn't warn Marino or Scarpetta. He doesn't warn Lucy as the two of them watch Marino on camera in the morgue, giving Shandy a tour. Lucy making comments about Marino, about his e-mails to Dr. Self, and Benton just listens, and now Lucy feels stupid. She feels betrayed. He doesn't mind asking her to break into confidential electronic files, but he can't tell her that Dr. Self is a patient and is sitting in her private room at the very private Pavilion, paying three thousand fucking dollars a day to fuck everyone.

Sixth gear, tucked in, and passing cars on the Arthur Ravenel Jr. Bridge with its soaring peaks and vertical cables that remind her of the Stanford Cancer Center, of the lady playing incongruous songs on her harp. Marino may have been messed up already, but he didn't bargain for the chaos Dr. Self could cause. He's too simple to comprehend a neutron bomb. Compared to Dr. Self, he's a big, dumb kid with a slingshot in his back pocket. Maybe he started it by sending her an e-mail, but she knows how to finish something. She knows how to finish him.

Racing past shrimp boats docked in Shem Creek, crossing the Ben Sawyer Bridge to Sullivan's Island, where Marino lives in what he said at one time was his dream home—a tiny, run-down fishing shack on stilts, with a red metal roof. The windows are dark, not even a porch light on. Behind the shack, a very long pier cuts through the marsh and ends at a narrow creek that snakes to the Intracoastal Waterway. When he moved here, he bought a drift boat and enjoyed exploring the creeks and fishing or just cruising and drinking beer. She's not sure what happened. *Where did he go? Who's living in his body?*

The patch of a front yard is sandy and dappled with spindly weeds. Under the shack, she picks her way through an assortment of junk. Old ice chests, a rusting grill, crab pots, rotting fishnets, garbage cans that smell like a swamp. She climbs warped wooden steps and tries the paint-peeled door. The lock is flimsy, but she doesn't want to pry it open. Better to take the door off the hinges and get in that way. A screwdriver, and she's inside Marino's dream house. He has no alarm system, always says his guns are alarming enough.

She pulls the string of an overhead bulb, and in the harsh glare and uneven shadows, she looks around to see what's changed since she was here last. When was that? Six months ago? He's done nothing new, as if he stopped living here after a while. The living room is a bare wooden floor with a cheap plaid couch, two straight-back chairs, a big-screen TV, a home computer and printer. Against a wall is a kitchenette, a few empty beer cans and a bottle of Jack Daniel's on the counter, lots of cold cuts and cheese and more beer inside the refrigerator.

She sits at Marino's desk and from the USB port of his computer removes a two-hundred-and-fifty-six-megabyte thumb drive attached to a lanyard. She opens her tool kit and selects needle-nose pliers, a screwdriver pen, a battery-powered drill—as tiny as one a jeweler might use. Inside the small black box are four unidirectional microphones, each no more than eight millimeters in size, or about the size of a baby aspirin. Pulling the plastic casing off the thumb drive, she removes the shaft and the lanyard, and embeds a microphone, its metal mesh top unnoticeable in the small hole where the lanyard originally was attached. The drill makes a quiet hum as it bores a second hole in the base of the casing, where she inserts the ring of the lanyard, reattaching it.

Next she digs into a pocket of her cargo pants and pulls out another thumb drive—the one she retrieved from the lab—and inserts it into the USB port. She downloads her own version of a spyware application that will relay Marino's every keystroke to one of her e-mail accounts. She scrolls through his hard drive, looking for documents. Almost nothing except the e-mails from Dr. Self that he copied onto his computer at the office. No big surprise. She doesn't imagine him sitting around writing professional journal articles or a novel. He's bad enough about doing paperwork. She plugs his thumb drive back into the port and begins a quick walk around, opening drawers. Cigarettes, a couple *Playboy* magazines, a .357-magnum Smith &

Wesson, a few dollars and loose change, receipts, junk mail.

She's never figured out how he fits inside the bedroom, where the closet is a rod attached between the walls at the foot of the bed, clothes jammed and sloppily hung, other items on the floor, including his huge boxer shorts, socks. She spots a lacy red bra and panties, a studded black leather belt and a crocodile one, way too small to be his, a plastic butter tub filled with condoms and cock rings. The bed is unmade. God knows when the linens were washed last.

Next door is a bathroom the size of a phone booth. A toilet, a shower, a sink. Lucy checks the medicine cabinet, finds the expected toiletries and hangover remedies. She removes a bottle of Fiorinal with Codeine prescribed to Shandy Snook. It's almost empty. On another shelf is a tube of Testroderm, prescribed to someone she's never heard of, and she enters the information on her iPhone. She reattaches the door to its hinges and makes her way down the dark, rickety stairs. The wind has kicked up, and she hears a faint noise coming from the pier. She slips out her Glock, listening, shining the light in the direction of the noise, but the beam falls short, the length of the pier dissolving into solid darkness.

She climbs stairs that lead to the pier, old with curling boards, some of them missing. The smell of pluff mud is strong, and she begins to swat at no-see-ums and remembers what an anthropologist told her. It's all about your blood type. Pests like mosquitos like type O. That would be her, but she's never been sure how a no-see-um can smell her blood type if she isn't bleeding. They swarm around her, attacking her, even biting her scalp.

Her footsteps are quiet as she walks and listens, hearing a bumping sound. The flashlight moves over weathered wood and bent rusty nails, and a breeze touches the marsh grass, whispers through it. The lights of Charleston seem distant in the sulfur-smelling, humid air, the moon elusive behind thick clouds, and at the end of the pier, she looks down at the source of the disconcerting sound. Marino's bass boat is gone, and bright orange bumpers rock against pilings in dull thuds.

Chapter 14

Karen and Dr. Self on the front steps of the Pavilion in the almost-dark.

A porch light that isn't too bright, and Dr. Self slides a folded piece of paper out of her raincoat pocket. She opens it, gets out a pen. In the woods beyond them, the high-pitched static of insects. The faraway cry of coyotes.

"What's that?" Karen asks Dr. Self.

"Whenever I have guests on my shows, they sign one of these. It simply gives me permission to have them on the air. To talk about them. No one can help you, Karen. That's clear, isn't it?"

"I feel a little better."

"You always do. Because they program you. Just as they tried to program me. It's a conspiracy. That's why they made me listen to my mother."

Karen takes the waiver from her, tries to read it. There's not enough light.

"I'd like to share our wonderful conversations and the insights from them that might help my millions of viewers around the world. I need your permission. Unless you'd rather I use an alias."

"Oh, no! I'd be very happy for you to talk about me and use my real name. And even be on your show, Marilyn! What conspiracy? Do you think it includes me?"

"You need to sign this." She gives Karen the pen.

Karen signs it. "If you'll let me know if you're going to talk about me so I can watch. I mean, if you do. Do you think you really will?"

"If you're still here."

"What?"

"It can't be my first show, Karen. My first one is about Frankenstein and shocking experiments. Being drugged against my will. Subjected to torment and humiliation in the magnet. Let me repeat, a huge magnet, while I listened to my mother, while they forced me to hear her voice lying about me, blaming me. It could be weeks before you're on my show, you see. I hope you're still here."

"You mean the hospital? I'm leaving first thing in the morning."

"I mean here."

"Where?"

"Do you still want to be in this world, Karen? Or did you ever want to be in it? That's really the question."

Karen lights a cigarette with trembling hands.

"You saw my series on Drew Martin," Dr. Self says.

"It's so sad."

"I should tell everyone the truth about her coach. I certainly tried to tell her."

"What did he do?"

"Have you ever taken a look at my website?"

"No. I should have." Karen sits hunched over on the cold stone step, smoking.

"How would you like to be on it? Until we can get you on my show?"

"Be on it? You mean, you tell my story on it?"

"Briefly. We have a section called *Self Talk*. People blog, tell their stories, and write to each other. Of course, some of them can't write very well, and I have a team of people who edit, rewrite, take dictation, interview. Remember when we first met? I gave you my card?"

"I still have it."

"I want you to send your story to the e-mail address on that card, and we'll post it. What an inspiration you can be. Unlike poor Dr. Wesley's niece."

"Who?"

"She's not really his niece. She has a brain tumor. Not even my tools can cure somebody of that."

"Oh, my. That's awful. I suppose a brain tumor could make somebody crazy, and there's no help for them."

"You can read all about her when you log on. You'll see her story and all the blogs. You'd be astonished," Dr. Self says from one step above her, the breeze in her favor, the smoke drifting the other way. "Your story? Quite a message it will send. How many times have you been hospitalized? At least ten. Why the failure?"

Dr. Self imagines herself asking her audience this as cameras move in tight on her face—one of the most recognizable faces on earth. She loves her name. Her name is part of her incredible destiny. Self. She's always refused to give it up. She wouldn't change her name for anyone, and she would never share it, and anybody who doesn't want it is condemned because the unforgivable sin isn't sex. It's failure.

"I'll be on your show anytime. Please call me. I can be there at a moment's notice," Karen keeps saying. "As long as I don't have to talk about . . . I can't say it."

But even back then, when Dr. Self's fantasies were the most vivid, when her thinking became magical and the premonitions began, she never dreamed of what would happen.

I'm Dr. Marilyn Self. Welcome to Self on Self. SOS. Do you need help? At the beginning of each show, to the wild applause from a live audience as millions watch from all over the world.

"You won't make me tell it, will you? My

family will never forgive me. It's why I can't stop drinking. I'll tell you if you don't make me say it on TV or on your website." Karen is lost in her drivel.

Thank you, thank you. Sometimes Dr. Self can't get the audience to stop clapping. *I adore all of you, too.*

"My Boston terrier, Bandit. I let her out late one night and forgot to let her back in because I was so drunk. It was wintertime."

Applause that sounds like a hard rain, like a thousand hands clapping.

"And the next morning I found her dead by the back door, and the wood was all clawed up from her scratching on it. My poor little Bandit with her short little fur. Shivering, crying, and barking, I'm sure. Scratching to get back in because it was freezing cold." Karen weeps. "And so I just kill off my brain so I don't have to think. They said I have all these white areas and widening of . . . well, and the atrophy. Way to go, Karen, I say. You're killing off your brain. You can see it. Plain as day, you can see I'm not normal." She touches her temple. "It was right up there on the light box in the neurologist's office, big as all outdoors, my abnormal brain. I'm never going to be normal. I'm almost sixty, and what's done is done."

"People are unforgiving about dogs," Dr. Self says, lost in herself.

"I know I am. What can I do to get over it? Please tell me."

"People with mental disease have peculiarities in the shape of their skulls. Lunatics have very contracted or deformed heads," Dr. Self says. "Maniacs have soft brains. Such scientific insights gleaned from a study done in Paris in 1824, which concluded that out of one hundred idiots and imbeciles examined, only fourteen had normal heads."

"Are you saying I'm an imbecile?"

"Sound all that different from what the doctors here have been telling you? That your head is somehow different, meaning you are somehow different?"

"I'm an imbecile? I killed my dog."

"These superstitions and manipulations have been around for centuries. Measuring the skulls of people locked up in lunatic asylums and dissecting the brains of idiots and imbeciles."

"I'm an imbecile?"

"Today, they put you in some magic

tube—a magnet—and tell you your brain is deformed, and they make you listen to your mother." Dr. Self stops talking as a tall figure walks toward them with purpose in the dark.

"Karen, if you don't mind, I need to talk to Dr. Self," Benton Wesley says.

"Am I an imbecile?" Karen says, getting up from the step.

"You're not an imbecile," Benton says kindly.

Karen says good-bye to him. "You were always nice to me," she says to him. "I'm flying home and won't be back," she says to him.

Dr. Self invites Benton to sit next to her on the steps, but he won't. She senses his anger, and it's a triumph, yet one more.

"I'm feeling much better," she says to him.

He's transformed by shadows pushed back by lamps.

She's never seen him in the dark, and the realization is fascinating.

"I wonder what Dr. Maroni would say right now. I wonder what Kay would say," she says. "Reminds me of spring break at the beach. A young girl notices a glorious young man, and then? He notices her. They sit in the sand and wade in the water and splash each other and do everything they desire until the sun comes up. They don't care that they're wet and sticky with salt and each other. Where did the magic go, Benton? Getting old is when nothing's enough and you know you'll never feel magic again. I know what death is, and so do you. Sit next to me, Benton. I'm glad you want to chat before I go."

"I talked to your mother," Benton says. "Again."

"You must like her."

"She told me something very interesting that's caused me to retract something I said to you, Dr. Self."

"Apologies are always welcome. From you, they're quite an unexpected treat."

"You were right about Dr. Maroni," Benton says. "About your having sex with him."

"I never said I had sex with him." Dr. Self goes cold inside. "When would that have happened? In my goddamn room with a goddamn view? I was drugged. I couldn't have had sex with anyone unless it was against my will. He drugged me."

"I'm not talking about now."

"While I was unconscious, he opened my gown and fondled me. He said he loved my body."

"Because he remembered it."

"Who said I had sex with him? Did that goddamn bitch say that? What would she know about what happened when I checked in? You must have told her I'm a patient. I'll sue you. I said he couldn't help himself, couldn't resist, and then he fled. I said he knew what he'd done was wrong and so he fled to Italy. I never said I had sex with him. I never told you that. He drugged me and took advantage of me, and I should have known he would. Why wouldn't he?"

It excites her. It did then and it still does, and she had no idea it would. At the time she chided him but didn't tell him to stop. She said, "Why is it necessary to examine me so enthusiastically?" And he said, "Because it's important I know." And she said, "Yes. You should know what isn't yours." And he said as he explored, "It's like a special place you once visited and haven't seen in many years. You want to find out what's changed and what hasn't and whether you could live it again." And she said, "Could you?" And he said, "No." Then he fled, and that was the worst thing he did, because he'd done it before.

"I'm talking about a very long time ago," Benton says.

Water laps quietly.

Will Rambo is surrounded by water and the night as he rows away from Sullivan's Island, where he left the Cadillac in a secluded spot an easy walk from where he borrowed the bass boat. He has borrowed it before. He uses the outboard engine when needed. When he wants quiet, he rows. Water laps. In the dark.

Into the Grotta Bianca, the place he took the first one. The feeling, the familiarity, as fragments come together in a deep cavern in his mind among dripstones of limestone, and moss where sunlight touched. He walked her beyond the Column of Hercules into an underworld of stone corridors with prisms of minerals and the constant sound of water dripping.

That dreamlike day they were all alone except once, when he let excited schoolchildren pass in their jackets and hats, and he said to her, "Noisy like a swarm of bats." And she laughed and said she was

having fun with him, and she grabbed his arm and pressed against him, and he felt the softness of her against him. Through silence, only the sound of water dripping. He took her through the Tunnel of Snakes beneath chandeliers of stone. Past translucent curtains of stone into the Corridor of the Desert.

"If you left me here, I would never find my way out," she said.

"Why would I leave you? I'm your guide. In the desert, you can't survive without a guide unless you know your way."

And the sandstorm rose up in a mighty wall, and he rubbed his eyes, trying not to see it in his mind that day.

"How do you know the way? You must come here often," she said, and then he left the sandstorm and was back in the cave, and she was so beautiful, pale and well defined, as if carved of quartz, but sad because her lover had left her for another woman.

"What makes you so special you can know a place like this?" she said to Will. "Three kilometers deep into the earth and an endless maze of wet stone. How horrible to be lost in here. I wonder if anyone's ever gotten lost in here. After hours, when they turn out the lights, it must be pitch-black and cold as a cellar in here."

He couldn't see his hand in front of his face. All he saw was bright red as they were sandblasted until he thought he would have no skin left.

"Will! Oh, God! Help me, Will!" Roger's screams became the screams of the schoolchildren a corridor away, and the roar of the storm stopped.

Water dripped and their footsteps sounded wet. "Why do you keep rubbing your eyes?" she asked.

"I could find my way even in the dark. I can see very well in the dark and came here often when I was a child. I'm your guide." He was very kind, very gentle with her because he understood her loss was more than she could bear. "See how the stone's translucent with light? It's flat and strong like tendons and sinews, and crystals are the waxy yellow of bone. And through this narrow corridor is the Dome of Milano, gray, damp, and cool like the tissue and vessels of a very old body."

"My shoes and the cuffs of my pants

are spattered with wet limestone, like whitewash. You've ruined my clothes."

Her complaints irritated him. He showed her a natural pond scattered with green coins on the bottom, and wondered aloud if anyone's wishes had come true, and she tossed a coin in and it plashed and sank to the bottom.

"Make all the wishes you want," he says. "But they never come true, or if they do, too bad for you."

"That's a terrible thing to say," she said. "How can you say that it would be bad if a wish came true? You don't know what I wished. What if my wish was to make love to you? Are you a bad lover?"

He didn't answer her as he got angrier, because if they made love, she would see his bare feet. The last time he made love was in Iraq, a twelve-year-old girl who screamed and cried and pounded him with small fists. Then she stopped and went to sleep, and he has never felt anything about it because she had no life, nothing to look forward to except the endless destruction of her country, and endless deaths. Her face fades from his mind as water drips. He holds the pistol in his hand as Roger screams because the pain is too much.

In the Cave of the Cupola, stones were round like skulls, and water dripped, dripped, dripped, as if it had rained, and then there were formations of stony frost and icicles and spurs that glowed like candlelight. He told her not to touch them.

"If you touch them, they turn black like soot," he warned.

"The story of my life," she said. "Whatever I touch turns to shit."

"You will thank me," he said.

"For what?" she said.

In the Corridor of the Return, it was warm and humid, and water ran down the walls like blood. He held the pistol and was one finger away from the end of all he knew about himself. If Roger could thank him, he would.

A simple thanks, and doing it again isn't needed. People are ungrateful and take away whatever has meaning. Then one doesn't care anymore. One can't.

A red-and-white-striped lighthouse, built soon after the War, is isolated three hundred feet offshore and no longer has a beacon.

Will's shoulders burn from rowing, and his

buttocks ache on the fiberglass bench. It's hard work because his payload weighs almost as much as the flat-bottom boat, and now that he's close to his place, he won't use the outboard motor. He never does. It makes noise, and he wants no noise, even if there is no one to hear it. No one lives here. No one comes here except during the day, and then only in nice weather. Even then, no one knows this place is his. The love of a lighthouse and a bucket of sand. How many little boys own an island? A glove and a ball, and a picnic and camping. All gone. Dead. The forlorn passage in a boat to the other side.

Across the water are the lights of Mount Pleasant, and the lights of James Island and Charleston. Southwest is Folly Beach. Tomorrow will be warm and cloudy, and by late afternoon, the tide will be low. The boat scrapes over oyster shells as he drags it onto the beach.

Chapter 15

Inside the forensic photography lab, early the next morning. It is Wednesday now.

Scarpetta sets up what she might need, the science this time simple. From cabinets and drawers she retrieves ceramic bowls, paper, and foam cups, paper towels, sterile swabs, envelopes, modeling clay, distilled water, a bottle of gun blue (a selenium dioxide solution that turns metal surfaces a dark blue/black), a bottle of RTX (ruthenium tetroxide), tubes of superglue, and a small aluminum pan. She attaches a macro lens and a remote shutter release to a digital camera mounted on a copy stand, and covers a countertop with thick brown paper.

Although she has a choice of which concoctions to use so latent prints will show themselves on nonporous surfaces, such as metal, the standard fare is fuming. No magic, just chemistry. Superglue is composed almost entirely of cyanoacrylate, an acrylic resin that reacts to the amino acids, glucose, sodium, lactic acid, and other chemicals exuded from skin pores. When superglue vapors come in contact with a latent print (not visible to the unaided eye), a chemical reaction forms a new composite—one hopes, a very durable and visible white ridge detail.

Scarpetta ponders her approach. DNA swabbing, but not in this lab, and it shouldn't be done first and doesn't need to be first because neither RTX nor superglue destroys DNA. Superglue, she decides, and she removes the revolver from its paper bag and writes down the serial number. She opens the empty cylinder and plugs both ends of the barrel with wads of paper towel. From another bag, she retrieves the six .38 special live rounds, setting them upright inside a fuming chamber, which is nothing more than a heat source inside a glass tank. From a wire anchored across the length of it, she suspends the revolver by its trigger guard. She places a cup of warm water inside for humidity, squeezes superglue into a small aluminum pan, and covers the fuming chamber with a lid. She turns on an exhaust fan.

Another pair of fresh gloves, and she picks up the plastic bag with the gold coin necklace inside. The gold chain is a very likely source of DNA, and she bags that separately and labels it. The coin is a possible source of DNA but also of fingerprints, and she holds it lightly by its edges and looks at it through a lens as she hears the biometric lock of the lab's front door. Then Lucy walks in. Scarpetta can feel her mood.

"I wish we had a program that does photo recognition," Scarpetta says, because she knows when not to ask questions about how Lucy is feeling and why.

"We do," Lucy says, avoiding her eyes. "But you have to have something to compare it with. Very few police departments have searchable databases of mug shots, and those that do? Doesn't matter. Nothing's integrated. Whoever this asshole is, we'll probably have to ID him some other way. And I don't necessarily mean the asshole on the chopper who supposedly showed up in your alley."

"Then who do you mean?"

"I mean whoever was wearing the necklace and had the gun. And I mean you don't know it wasn't Bull."

"That wouldn't make any sense."

"Sure as hell would if he wanted to seem like a hero. Or hide something else he's up to. You don't know who had the gun or necklace, because you never saw whoever lost them."

"Unless the evidence indicates otherwise," Scarpetta says, "I'll take him at his word and feel grateful that he put himself in harm's way to protect me."

"Believe what you want."

Scarpetta looks at Lucy's face. "I believe something's wrong."

"I'm just pointing out that the alleged altercation between him and whoever this guy on a chopper is wasn't witnessed. That's all."

Scarpetta checks her watch. She walks over to the fuming chamber. "Five minutes. That should do it." She removes the lid to bring the process to a halt. "We need to run the serial number of the revolver."

Lucy moves close, looks inside the glass

tank. She puts on gloves, reaches inside, and detaches the wire and retrieves the revolver. "Ridge detail. A little. Here on the barrel." She turns the gun this way and that, sets it down on the paper-covered countertop. She reaches back inside the tank and plucks out the cartridges. "A few partials. I think there's enough minutiae." She sets them down, too.

"I'll photograph them, and perhaps you can scan in the photos so we can get the characteristics and have them run on IAFIS."

Scarpetta picks up the phone, calls the fingerprints lab, explains what they're doing.

"I'll work with them first to save time," Lucy says, and she isn't friendly. "Lose the color channels so the white's inverted to black and get them run ASAP."

"Something's the matter. I guess you'll tell me when you're ready."

Lucy doesn't listen. Angrily, "Garbage in, garbage out."

Her favorite point to make when she's cynical. A print is scanned into IAFIS, and the computer doesn't know if it's looking at a rock or a fish. The automated system doesn't think. It knows nothing. It overlays the characteristics of one print on top of the matching characteristics of another print, meaning if characteristics are missing or obscured or haven't been correctly encoded by a competent forensic examiner, there's a good chance a search will come to nothing. IAFIS isn't the problem. People are. Same is true of DNA. The results are only as good as what's collected and how it's processed and by whom.

"You know how rare it is when prints are even rolled properly?" Lucy rants on. Her tone bites. "You get some Deputy Bubba in a jail taking all these ten-print cards, still doing centuries-old shitty ink-and-roll, and they're all dumped into IAFIS and are crap, when they wouldn't be if we were using biometric optical live scanning. But no jail's got money. No money for anything in this fucking country."

Scarpetta leaves the gold coin inside its transparent plastic envelope and looks at it under a lens. "You want to tell me why you're in such an awful mood?" She's afraid of the answer.

"Where's the serial number so I can enter the gun into NCIC?"

"That piece of paper over there on the counter. Have you been talking to Rose?"

Lucy gets it, sits before a computer terminal. Keys start clicking. "Called to check on her. She said you need checking on."

"A U.S. one-dollar piece," Scarpetta says of the magnified coin so she doesn't have to say anything else. "Eighteen seventy-three." And she notices something she's never seen before in unprocessed evidence.

Lucy says, "I'd like to test-fire this in the water tank and run ballistics on it through NIBIN."

The National Integrated Ballistic Identification Network.

"See if the revolver's been used in any other crime," Lucy says. "Although you're not considering what happened a crime yet and don't want to involve the police."

"As I've explained"—Scarpetta doesn't want to sound defensive—"Bull struggled with him and knocked the gun out of his hands." She studies the coin, adjusting the magnification. "I can't prove the man in question on the chopper was there to harm me. He never trespassed, just tried."

"So Bull says."

"If I didn't know better, I'd think this coin has already been superglued for prints." Through the lens, Scarpetta examines what looks like pale white ridge detail on front and back.

"What do you mean, if you didn't know better? You don't know better. You don't know anything about it or where it's been or anything except Bull found it behind your house. Who lost it's another story."

"Sure looks like a polymer residue. Like superglue. I don't understand," Scarpetta says, carrying the plastic-protected coin to the copy stand. "A lot of things I don't understand." She glances up at Lucy. "I guess when you're ready to talk to me, you will." She takes off her gloves, puts on new ones and a face mask.

"Sounds like all we need to do is photograph them. No gun blue or RTX." Lucy refers to the ridge detail on the coin.

"At most, maybe black powder. But I suspect we won't need even that." Scarpetta adjusts the camera mounted on the copy stand's column. She manipulates the arms of the four lights. "I'll photograph it. Then everything can go to DNA."

She tears off a section of brown paper for the copy stand's base, removes the coin from its envelope, and sets it down heads up. She cuts a foam cup in half, places one funnel-shaped half over the coin. Home-made tent lighting to minimize glare, and the ridge detail is much more visible. She reaches for the remote shutter release and starts taking pictures.

"Superglue," Lucy says. "So maybe it's evidence from a crime and somehow ended up in circulation again, so to speak."

"That certainly would explain it. Don't know if it's right, but it would explain it."

Keys rapidly click. "Gold one-dollar piece." Lucy says. "American, eighteen seventy-three. See what I can find about that." Hits more keys. "Why would someone take Fiorinal with codeine? And what is it, exactly?"

"Butalbital plus codeine phosphate, aspirin, caffeine," Scarpetta says, carefully turning the coin so she can photograph the other side. "A strong narcotic pain reliever. Often prescribed for severe tension headaches." The camera's shutter shuts. "Why?"

"What about Testroderm?"

"A testosterone gel you rub into your skin."

"You ever heard of a Stephen Siegel?"

Scarpetta thinks for a moment, can't come up with anyone, the name completely unfamiliar. "Not that I recall."

"The Testroderm was prescribed by him,

and it just so happens he's a slimeball proctologist in Charlotte, where Shandy Snook is from. And it just so happens that her father was a patient of this proctologist, which would suggest Shandy knows him and is able to get prescriptions when she wants them."

"Where was this prescription filled?"

"A pharmacy on Sullivan's Island, where it just so happens Shandy has a two-million-dollar house in the name of an LLC," Lucy says, typing again. "Maybe it would be a good idea for you to ask Marino what the hell's going on. I think all of us ought to be worried."

"What worries me most is how angry you are."

"I think you don't know what I'm like when I'm really angry." Lucy taps on the keyboard, rapid, hard, angry taps. "So Marino's all nice and doped up. Illegally. Probably slathering on testosterone gel like it's suntan lotion and popping pills like crazy to help with his hangovers because he's suddenly turned into a raging drunk King Kong." Loudly tapping keys. "Probably suffering priapism and could have a fucking heart attack. Or become so aggressive he's out of control when he's already out of control because of the booze.

Amazing the effect one person can have on another in one short week."

"Clearly this new girlfriend is very bad news."

"I don't mean her. You had to tell him your news."

"Yes, I did. I had to tell him. And you and Rose," Scarpetta quietly says.

"Your gold coin's worth about six hundred dollars," Lucy says, closing a file on the computer. "Not including the chain."

Dr. Maroni sits before the fire in his apartment south of San Marco, the domes of the basilica dreary in the rain. People, mostly the locals, have on green rubber boots, while the tourists wear cheap yellow ones. In no time, the water rises above the streets of Venice.

"I simply heard about the body." He talks on the phone to Benton.

"How? At first the case wasn't important. Why would you hear of it?"

"Otto told me."

"You mean Captain Poma."

Benton is determined to distance himself from the captain, can't even bring himself to use his first name.

Dr. Maroni says, "Otto called about something else and mentioned it."

"Why would he know? There wasn't much in the news at first."

"He knew because he's Carabiniere."

"And that makes him omniscient?" Benton says.

"You're resentful of him."

"What I am is puzzled," Benton says. "He's a medico legale with the Carabinieri. And it was the national police, not the Carabinieri, that had jurisdiction in the case. And as usual, this is because the national police got to the scene first. When I was a kid, that was called having *dibs*. In law enforcement, it's called *unheard-of*."

"What can I say? It's the way things are done in Italy. Jurisdiction depends on who arrives at the scene first, or who's called. But that's not what's making you so irritable."

"I'm not irritable."

"You're telling a psychiatrist you're not irritable." Dr. Maroni lights his pipe. "I'm not there to see your affect, but I don't need to. You're irritable. Tell me why it matters how I found out about the dead woman near Bari?"

"Now you're implying I'm not objective."

"What I'm implying is you feel threatened by Otto. Let me try to explain the sequence of events more clearly. The body was found on the side of the Autostrade outside Bari, and I thought nothing of it at first when I heard about it. No one knew who she was, and it was believed she was a prostitute. The police speculated the killing was connected to Sacra Corona Unita—the Puglia mafia. Otto said he was quite happy the Carabinieri wasn't involved, because he wasn't fond of dealing with gangsters. In his words, there's nothing redeeming about victims who are as corrupt as their killers. I believe it was a day later when he informed me he'd spoken to the forensic pathologist at the Sezione di Medicina Legale in Bari. It appeared the victim was a missing Canadian tourist last seen at a discotheque in Ostuni. She was quite drunk. She left with a man. A young woman fitting the same description was seen the next day at Grotta Bianca in Puglia. The White Cave."

"Again, Captain Poma is omniscient, and it seems the entire world reports to him."

"Again, you sound resentful of him."

"Let's talk about the White Cave. We have

to assume this killer makes symbolic associ-
ations," Benton says.

"The deeper levels of consciousness," Dr.
Maroni says. "Buried childhood memories.
Suppressed memories of trauma and pain.
We might interpret the exploration of a cave
as his mythological journey into the secrets
of his own neuroses and psychoses, his
fears. Something terrible happened to him,
and it probably predates what he thinks is
the terrible thing that happened to him."

"What do you remember about his physical
description? Did people who claimed to have
seen him with the victim in the disco, the cave,
or elsewhere give a physical description?"

"Young, wearing a cap," Dr. Maroni tells
him. "That's it."

"That's it? Race?"

"In both the disco and the cave, it was
very dark."

"In your patient notes—right here, I'm
looking at them—your patient mentioned
meeting a Canadian woman in a disco. He
said this the day after her body was found.
Then you never heard from him again. What
was his race?"

"He's white."

"You say in your notes he indicated he

had, and I quote, 'left the girl on the roadside in Bari.'"

"At that time, it wasn't known that she was Canadian. She was unidentified. It was assumed she was a prostitute, as I said."

"When you found out she was a Canadian tourist, you didn't make a connection?"

"Naturally, I was worried. But I had no proof."

"Yes, Paulo, protect the patient. Nobody gave a shit about protecting the Canadian tourist, whose only crime was to have a little too much fun at a disco and meet someone she obviously liked and thought she could trust. Her vacation in southern Italy ends with an autopsy in a cemetery. She's lucky she wasn't buried in a pauper's grave."

"You are very impatient and upset," Dr. Maroni says to him.

"Maybe now that you have your notes in front of you, Paulo, your memory will be jogged."

"I didn't release these notes to you. I can't imagine how you got them." He has to say that repeatedly, and Benton has to play along.

"If you store patient notes in an electronic format on the hospital server, you might want to leave the file-sharing function off," Benton says over the line. "Because if someone figures out what hard disk these very confidential files are on, they can be accessed."

"The Internet is a treacherous place."

"The Canadian tourist was murdered almost a year ago," Benton says. "Same type of mutilation. Tell me how it is you didn't think of that case—didn't think of your patient—after what was done to Drew Martin? Chunks of flesh cut from the same area of the body. Nude, dumped in a place where it will be discovered quickly and shockingly. And no evidence."

"It doesn't appear he rapes them."

"We don't know what he does. Especially if he forces them to sit in a tub of cold water for God knows how long. I'd like to get Kay on the line. I called her right before I called you. Hopefully, she's at least glanced at what I sent."

Dr. Maroni waits. He stares at the image on his screen as rain falls hard beyond his apartment and the canal rises. He opens the shutters far enough to see that the water is more than a foot deep on the sidewalks. He's grateful he has no need to go out today.

Flooding is not the adventure for him that it seems to be for the tourists.

"Paulo?" Benton is back. "Kay?"

"I'm here."

"She has the files," Benton says to Dr. Maroni. "You're looking at the two photographs?" he says to Scarpetta. "And the other files?"

"What he did to Drew Martin's eyes," she says right off. "No evidence of this with the woman murdered near Bari. I'm looking at her autopsy report. In Italian. I'm making out what I can. And I'm wondering why you have the autopsy report included in the file of this patient, the Sandman, I presume?"

"Clearly, he calls himself that," Dr. Maroni says. "Based on Dr. Self's e-mails. And you've looked at some of them?"

"I'm looking now."

"Why the autopsy report was in your patient's file," Benton reminds him. "The Sandman's file."

"Because I was concerned. But I had no proof."

"Asphyxia?" Scarpetta questions. "Based on petechiae, and an absence of other findings."

"Possible she could have been a drowning?" Dr. Maroni asks, the files Benton forwarded to him printed and on his lap. "Possible Drew was, too?"

"No, Drew absolutely wasn't. She was strangled with a ligature."

"The reason I think of a drowning is the tub in Drew's case," Dr. Maroni says. "And now this latest photograph of the woman in the copper tub. But I understand if I'm wrong."

"You're wrong about Drew. But victims in tubs prior to death—or what we unfortunately assume is death—I agree. We have to consider drowning if we have no evidence otherwise. I will tell you with certainty," Scarpetta repeats, "that Drew didn't drown. But this doesn't mean the victim from Bari didn't. And we can't know what's happened to this woman in the copper tub. We can't say she's even dead, although I'm afraid of it."

"She looks drugged," Benton says.

"I strongly suspect the three women in question have that in common," Scarpetta says. "The victim in Bari was compromised, based on her alcohol level, which was three times the legal limit. Drew's was more than twice the legal limit."

"Compromises them so he can control them," Benton says. "So nothing would hint to you the victim in Bari was drowned? Nothing at all on the report? What about diatoms?"

"Diatoms?" Dr. Maroni asks.

"Microscopic algae," Scarpetta says. "First, someone would have had to check, which isn't likely if drowning isn't suspected."

"Why would it be? She was found alongside a road," Dr. Maroni says.

"Second," Scarpetta says, "diatoms are ubiquitous. They're in water. They're airborne. The only examination that might yield significant information is if bone marrow or internal organs are examined. And you're right, Dr. Maroni. Why would they have been? As for the victim in Bari, I'm suspicious she may have been a victim of opportunity. Perhaps the Sandman—from now on I'll refer to him as that . . ."

"We don't know how he referred to himself back then," Dr. Maroni says. "My patient certainly never mentioned this name."

"I'll call him the Sandman for the sake of clarity," Scarpetta says. "Perhaps he was cruising bars, discos, tourist attractions, and it was her tragic misfortune to be in the wrong place at the wrong time. Drew Martin, on the other hand, doesn't strike me as random."

"We don't know that, either." Dr. Maroni smokes his pipe.

"I think I do know that," she says. "He began writing e-mails to Dr. Self about Drew Martin last fall."

"Assuming he's the killer."

"He sent Dr. Self the photograph of Drew in the tub that he took within hours of her murder," Scarpetta says. "In my book, that makes him the killer."

"Please tell me more about her eyes," Dr. Maroni says to her.

"Based on this report, the killer didn't remove the Canadian victim's eyes. Drew's eyes were removed, the sockets filled with sand, the eyelids glued shut. Thankfully, based on what I know, it appears this was done postmortem."

"Not sadism but symbolism," Benton says.

"The Sandman sprinkles sand in your eyes and makes you go to sleep," Scarpetta says.

"This is the mythology I point out," Dr. Maroni says. "Freudian, Jungian, but relevant. We ignore the *depth psychology* of this case at our own peril."

"I'm not ignoring anything. I wish you hadn't ignored what you knew about your patient. You worried he might have something to do with the tourist's murder and said nothing," Benton says.

Debating. Hinting of mistakes and blame. The three-way conversation continues as the city of Venice floods. Then Scarpetta says she is in the middle of work at the labs, and if there is nothing more they need from her, she'll get off the phone. She does, and Dr. Maroni resumes his defense.

"That would have been a violation. I had no proof, no evidence whatsoever," he says to Benton. "You know the rules. What if we ran to the police every time a patient makes violent allusions or references to violent acts that we have no reason to believe are true? We'd be reporting patients to the police daily."

"I think your patient should have been reported, and I think you should have asked Dr. Self more about him."

"I think you're not an FBI agent who can arrest people anymore, Benton. You're a forensic psychologist at a psychiatric hospital. You're on the faculty of Harvard Medical School. Your first loyalty is to the patient."

"Maybe I'm not capable of that anymore. After two weeks of Dr. Self, I don't feel the same about anything. Including you, Paulo.

You protected your patient, and now at least two other women are dead."

"If he did it."

"He did."

"Tell me what Dr. Self did when you confronted her with these images. The one of Drew in the tub. The room looks Italian and old," Dr. Maroni says.

"It would be in Rome or near Rome. It would have to be," Benton says. "We can assume she was murdered in Rome."

"And then this second image?" He clicks on a second file that was in Dr. Self's e-mail. A woman in a tub, this one copper. She appears to be in her thirties, with long, dark hair. Her lips are swollen and bloody, her right eye swollen shut. "What did Dr. Self say when you showed her this most recent image that the Sandman sent to her?"

"When it was sent, she was in the magnet. When I showed it to her later, it was the first time she'd seen it. Her main concern was we hacked—her word—into her e-mail and that we'd violated her legal rights, and we'd violated HIPAA because Lucy was the hacker—Dr. Self's accusation—and that means outsiders knew Dr. Self was a patient at McLean. How did Lucy get blamed, by the way? I wonder."

"Curious she would, without hesitation, be blamed. I agree."

"Have you seen what Dr. Self posted on her website? Supposedly a confessional by Lucy, talking freely about her brain tumor. It's everywhere."

"Lucy did that?" Dr. Maroni is surprised. This he didn't know.

"She most assuredly didn't. I can only assume Dr. Self somehow discovered that Lucy comes to McLean for regular scans, and as part of her insatiable appetite to harass, she contrived this confessional on her website."

"How is Lucy?"

"How do you think?"

"What else did Dr. Self say about this second image? The woman in the copper tub. We have no idea who she is?"

"So someone must have planted in Dr. Self's mind that Lucy got into her e-mail. Very strange."

"The woman in the copper tub," Dr. Maroni says again. "What did Dr. Self say when you confronted her on the steps in the dark?

That must have been something." He waits. Relights his pipe.

"I never said she was on the steps."

Dr. Maroni smiles and puffs smoke as the tobacco in the pipe's bowl glows. "Again, when you showed this to her, what did she say?"

"She asked if the image is real. I said we can't know without seeing the files on the computer of the person who sent it. But it looks genuine. I don't see the telltale signs of something that's been tampered with. A missing shadow. An error in perspective. Lighting or weather that doesn't make sense."

"No, it doesn't look tampered with," Dr. Maroni says, studying it on his screen as the rain falls beyond his shutters and canal water splashes against stucco. "As much as I know about such a thing."

"She insisted it could be a sick ruse. A sick joke. I said Drew Martin's photo is real, and it was more than a sick joke. She's dead. I voiced my concern that the woman in this second photo is also dead. It seems someone is talking to Dr. Self indiscriminately, and not just about this case. I wonder who."

"And she said?"

"And she said it wasn't her fault," Benton says.

"And now that Lucy has gotten us this information, she might know . . ." Dr. Maroni starts to say, but Benton gets there first.

"Where they're sent from. Lucy's explained it. Having access to Dr. Self's e-mail made it possible to trace the IP address of the Sandman. Just more proof she doesn't care. She could have traced the IP address herself or gotten someone else to do it. But she didn't. It probably never entered her mind. It traces to a domain in Charleston, specifically, the port."

"This is most interesting."

"You're so wide open and effusive, Paulo."

"I'm not sure what you mean by that. 'Wide open and effusive'?"

"Lucy talked to the port's IT, the guy who manages all of the computers, the wireless network, and so on," Benton says. "What's important, according to her, is the Sandman's IP doesn't correspond to any MAC at the port. That's the Machine Address Code. Whatever computer the Sandman is using to send his e-mails, it doesn't seem to be one at the port, meaning it's unlikely he's an employee there. Lucy has pointed out several possible scenarios. He could be someone in and out of the port—on a cruise ship, a cargo ship—and when he docks, he hijacks the port's network. If that's the case, he must work for a cruise ship or cargo vessel that's been in Charleston at the port whenever he's sent Dr. Self e-mails. Every one of his e-mails—all twenty-seven that Lucy found in Dr. Self's inbox—were sent from the port's wireless network. Including this one she just got. The woman in the copper tub."

"Then he must be in Charleston now," Dr. Maroni says. "I hope you have the port under surveillance. This may be the way to catch him."

"We must be careful, whatever we do. Can't involve the police right now. He'll be scared off."

"There must be calendars for cruises, for cargo ships. Is there an overlapping of those dates and when he sent e-mails to Dr. Self?"

"Yes and no. Some dates of a particular cruise ship—and I'm talking schedules for embarking and debarking—do correspond with date stamps on the e-mails he sent. But some don't. Which makes me fairly certain he has some reason to be in Charleston, possibly even lives there, and gets access to the port's network by perhaps parking very close to it and hijacking it."

"Now you're leaving me," Dr. Maroni says. "I live in a very old world." He lights his pipe again, and one reason he enjoys a pipe is the pleasure of lighting it.

"Analogous to driving around with a scanner and monitoring people on cell phones," Benton explains.

"I suppose this isn't Dr. Self's fault, either," Dr. Maroni ruefully says. "This killer has been sending e-mails from Charleston since last fall, and she could have known it and told someone."

"She could have told you, Paulo, when she referred the Sandman to you."

"And she knows about this Charleston connection?"

"I told her. I hoped it might prompt her to recall something or divulge other information that might help us."

"And what did she say when you told her that the Sandman has been e-mailing her from Charleston all this time?"

"She said it wasn't her fault," Benton replies. "Then took her limousine to the airport and got on her private plane."

Chapter 16

Applause and music and Dr. Self's voice. Her website.

Scarpetta can't hide her extreme distress as she reads Lucy's bogus confessional article about her brain scans at McLean and why she has them and what it's like to live with it. Scarpetta reads the blogs until it's too much, and Lucy can't help but think her aunt's upset is easier than what she ought to be feeling.

"There's nothing I can do. What's done is done," Lucy says as she scans partial fingerprints into a digital imaging system. "Even I can't un-send things, un-post things, un-anything. One way to look at it is once it's out there, I don't have to dread being outed because of it anymore."

"Outed? That's a telling way to describe it."

"By my definition, having a physical liability is worse than anything else I've been outed for. So maybe it's better to have people finally know and get it over with. Truth is a relief. Better not to hide something, don't you think? Funny thing about people knowing is it opens up the possibility of unexpected gifts. People reaching out when you didn't know they cared. Voices from the past talking to you again. Other voices finally shutting up. Some people finally getting out of your life."

"Who are you referring to?"

"Let's just say I've not been surprised."

"Gift or not. Dr. Self had no right," Scarpetta says.

"You should listen to what you're saying."

Scarpetta doesn't answer her.

"You want to consider how it might be your fault. You know, if I weren't the niece of the infamous Dr. Scarpetta, there wouldn't be the interest. You have this unrelenting need to make everything your fault and try to fix it," Lucy says.

"I can't look at this anymore." Scarpetta logs out.

"That's your flaw," Lucy says. "One I have a hard time with, if you must know."

"We need to find a lawyer who specializes in things like this. Internet libel. Defamation of character on the Internet, which is so un-regulated, it's like a society with no laws."

"Try proving I didn't write it. Try making a case for any of it. Don't focus on me because you don't want to focus on something about yourself. I've left you alone about it all morn-ing, and now it's enough. I can't anymore."

Scarpetta starts clearing off a countertop, putting things away.

"I sit here listening to you talk so calmly on the phone to Benton. To Dr. Maroni. How can you do it and not choke on denial and avoidance?"

Scarpetta runs water in a steel sink near an eyewash station. She scrubs her hands as if she's just done an autopsy instead of work-ing inside a pristinely clean lab where noth-ing much goes on except photography. Lucy sees the bruises on her aunt's wrists. She can try all she likes, but she can't hide them.

"Are you going to protect that bastard for the rest of your life?" Lucy means Marino. "All right. Don't answer me. Maybe the biggest difference between him and me isn't what's obvious. I won't let Dr. Self drive me to doing anything fatal to myself."

"Fatal? I hope not. I don't like it when you use that word." Scarpetta busies herself with repackaging the gold coin and its chain. "What are you talking about? Something fatal."

Lucy takes off her lab coat, hangs it on the back of the shut door. "I'm not going to give her the pleasure of goading me into something that can't be repaired. I'm not Marino."

"We need to get these to DNA immediately." Scarpetta tears off evidence tape to seal envelopes. "I'll hand them over directly to keep the chain of evidence intact, and maybe in thirty-six hours? Maybe less? If there are no unforeseen complications. I don't want the analysis to wait. I'm sure you understand why. If someone came to visit me with a gun."

"I remember that time in Richmond. Christmas, and I was spending it with you, home from UVA, had brought a friend with me. He hit on her right in front of me."

"Which time? He's done that more than once." Scarpetta has an expression on her face that Lucy's never seen before.

Her aunt fills out paperwork, busies herself with one thing after another, anything so she doesn't have to look at her, because she can't. Lucy doesn't recall a time when her aunt seemed angry and shamed. Maybe angry but never shamed, and Lucy's bad feeling gets worse.

"Because he couldn't handle being around women he wanted desperately to impress, and worse than not being impressed, at least in the way he's always wanted, we had no interest in him except in a way he's never been able to handle," Lucy says. "We wanted to relate to him as one person to another, and so what does he do? He tries to grope my girlfriend right in front of me. Of course, he was drunk."

She gets up from the work station and walks over to the counter where her aunt is now preoccupied with removing color markers from a drawer and taking off their caps, testing each one to make sure the ink hasn't been used up or dried out.

"I didn't put up with it," Lucy says. "I fought back. I was only eighteen and I called him on it, and he's lucky I didn't do something worse. Are you going to keep distracting yourself as if somehow that will make it go away?"

Lucy takes her aunt's hands and gently pushes up the sleeves. Her wrists are a bright red. Deep tissue damage, as if she's been clamped hard by iron manacles.

"Let's don't get into this," Scarpetta says. "I know you care." She pulls her wrists away, pulls down her sleeves. "But please leave me alone about it, Lucy."

"What did he do to you?"

Scarpetta sits.

"You'd better tell me everything," Lucy says. "I don't care what Dr. Self did to provoke him, and we both know it doesn't take much. He's gone too far, and there's no going back and there's no exception to the rule. I'll punish him."

"Please. Let me deal with it."

"You aren't, and you won't. You always make excuses for him."

"I'm not. But punishing him isn't the answer. What good will it do?"

"What exactly happened?" Lucy is quiet and calm. But inside she goes numb, the way she gets when she's capable of anything. "He was at your house all night. What did he do? Nothing you wanted, that's for sure, or you wouldn't be bruised. You wouldn't want anything from him anyway, so he forced you, didn't he? He grabbed your wrists. What did he do? Your neck is raw. Where else? What did the son of a bitch do? All the trash he sleeps with, no telling what diseases . . ."

"It didn't go that far."

"How far is *that* far? What did he do." Lucy says it not as a question but as a point of fact that demands further explanation.

"He was drunk," Scarpetta says. "Now we find out he's probably on a testosterone supplement that could make him very aggressive, depending on how much he's using, and he doesn't know the meaning of moderation. His excesses. Too much. Too much. You're right, his drinking this past week, and his smoking. He's never good with boundaries, but now there are none. Well, I suppose it's all been leading up to this."

"All been leading up to this? After all these years, your relationship has been leading up to his sexually assaulting you?"

"I've never seen him like that. He was someone I didn't know. So aggressive and angry, completely out of control. Maybe we should be more worried about him than me."

"Don't start."

"Please try to understand."

"I'll understand better when you tell me what he did." Lucy's voice is flat, the way she sounds when she's capable of anything.

"What did he do? The more you dodge it, the more I want to punish him, and the worse it will be when I do. And you know enough to take me seriously, Aunt Kay."

"He went only so far then stopped and started crying," Scarpetta says.

"How far is 'only so far'?"

"I can't talk about this."

"Really? And if you'd called the police? They'd demand details. You know how it goes. Violated once. Then violated again when you tell all and some cop starts imagining it happening, and secretly gets off on it. These perverts who go from courtroom to courtroom looking for rape cases so they can sit in the back and listen to all the details."

"Why are you going off on this tangent? It has nothing to do with me."

"What do you think would have happened had you called the police and Marino were charged with sexual battery? At the very least? You'd end up in court, and God knows what a spectator sport that would be. People listening to all the details, imagining all of it, as if, in a sense, you were undressed in public, viewed as a sexual object, degraded. The great Dr. Kay Scarpetta naked and manhandled for all the world to see."

"It didn't go that far."

"Really? Open your shirt. What are you hiding? I can see abrasions on your neck." Lucy reaches for Scarpetta's shirt, starts on the top button.

Scarpetta pushes her hands away. "You're not a forensic nurse, and I've heard enough. Don't make me angry with you."

Lucy's own anger begins to work its way to the surface. She feels it in her heart, in her feet, in her hands. "I'll take care of this," she says.

"I don't want you to take care of it. Clearly, you've already broken into his house and searched it. I know how you take care of things, and I know how to take care of myself. What I don't need is some confrontation between the two of you."

"What did he do? What exactly did that drunk, stupid son of a bitch do to you?"

Scarpetta is silent.

"He takes that garbage girlfriend on a tour of your building. Benton and I watch every second of it, can see as plain as day he has a hard-on in the morgue. No wonder. He's a walking hard-on doped up on some hormone gel so he can please that fucking bitch who's less than half his age. And then he does this to you."

"Stop it."

"I won't stop it. What did he do? He rip your clothes off? Where are they? They're evidence. Where are your clothes?"

"Stop it, Lucy."

"Where are they? I want them. I want the clothes you had on. What did you do with them?"

"You're making it worse."

"You threw them out, didn't you?"

"Leave it alone."

"Sexual battery. A felony. And you aren't going to tell Benton or you would have already. And you weren't going to tell me. Rose had to tell me, at least tell me she suspected it. What's wrong with you? I thought you were a strong woman. I thought you were powerful. All my life I've thought it. There. The flaw. Someone who lets him do this and doesn't tell. Why did you let him?"

"And that's what this is about."

"Why did you?"

"That's what this is about," Scarpetta says. "Let's talk about your flaw."

"Don't turn this on me."

"I could have called the police. I was within reach of his gun and could have killed him and it would have been justified. There are a lot of things I could have done," Scarpetta says.

"Then why didn't you?"

"I chose the lesser of evils. It will be all right. All other choices wouldn't have been," Scarpetta says. "You know why you're doing this."

"It's not what I'm doing. It's what you did."

"Because of your mother—my pathetic sister. Bringing one man after another into the house. Worse than male-dependent. She's male-addicted," Scarpetta says. "Do you remember what you asked me once? You asked why men were always more important than you."

Lucy clenches her hands.

"You said any man in your mother's life was more important than you. And you were right. Remember my telling you why? Because Dorothy's an empty vessel. It's not about you. It's about her. You always felt violated because of what went on in your home . . ." Her voice trails off and a shadow turns her eyes a deeper blue. "Did something happen? Something else? Did one of her boyfriends ever act inappropriately with you?"

"I probably wanted attention."

"What happened?"

"Forget it."

"What happened, Lucy?" Scarpetta says.

"Forget it. This isn't about me right now. And I was a little kid. You aren't a little kid."

"I may as well have been. How could I have fought him off?"

They get quiet for a while. The tension between them suddenly goes slack. Lucy doesn't want to fight with her anymore, and she resents Marino as much as she's resented anyone in her life because, for an instant, he made her unkind toward her aunt. She showed no mercy toward her aunt, who did nothing but suffer. He inflicted an injury that can't ever heal, not really, and Lucy just made it worse.

"That wasn't fair," Lucy says. "I just wish I'd been there."

"You can't always fix things, either," Scarpetta says. "You and I are more alike than we're different."

"Drew Martin's coach has been to Henry Hollings's funeral home," Lucy says, because they shouldn't talk about Marino anymore. "The address is stored in his Porsche's GPS.

I can check it out if you'd prefer to stay away from the coroner."

"No," she says. "I think it's time we meet."

An office tastefully furnished with fine antiques and damask draperies pulled back to let the outdoors in. On mahogany-paneled walls are oil portraits of Henry Hollings's ancestors, an array of somber men watching over their past.

His desk chair is swiveled around as he faces the window. Beyond it is yet another perfectly splendid Charleston garden. He doesn't seem aware that Scarpetta is standing in the doorway.

"I have a recommendation I think you just might like." He talks on the phone in a soothing voice with a thick southern cadence. "We have urns made just for that, an excellent innovation most people don't know about. Biodegradable, dissolve in water, nothing ornate or expensive . . . Yes, if you plan on a water committal . . . That's right . . . Scatter his ashes at sea . . . Indeed. You prevent them from blowing everywhere by simply immersing the urn. I understand it might not seem the same. Of course, you can choose whatever's meaningful to you, and I'll assist in any way I can . . . Yes, yes, it's what I recommend . . . No, you don't want them blowing everywhere. How do I put this delicately? Blowing in the boat. That would be unfortunate."

He adds several sympathetic comments and hangs up. When he turns around, he doesn't seem surprised to see Scarpetta. He's expecting her. She called first. If it occurs to him she was listening to his conversation, he doesn't seem concerned or the least bit offended. It disconcerts her that he seems sincerely thoughtful and kind. There's a certain comfort in assumptions, and hers has always been that he is greedy, unctuous, and full of self-importance.

"Dr. Scarpetta." He smiles as he gets up and walks around his perfectly organized desk to shake her hand.

"I appreciate your seeing me, especially on such short notice," she says, choosing the wing chair while he settles on the couch, his choice of where he sits significant. If he wanted to overpower or belittle her, he would remain enthroned behind his massive burlwood partner's desk.

Henry Hollings is a distinguished man in a beautiful hand-tailored dark suit with creased trousers, and a black silk-lined single-button jacket, and a pale blue shirt. His hair is the same silver as his silver silk tie, his face lined but not in a harsh way, the wrinkles indicating that he smiles more than he frowns. His eyes are kind. It continues to disturb her that he doesn't fit the image of the cunning politician she expected, and she reminds herself that that's the problem with cunning politicians. They fool people right before they take advantage of them.

"Let me be forthright," Scarpetta says. "You've had ample opportunity to acknowledge I'm here. It's been almost two years. Let me just say that and we'll move on."

"Seeking you out would have been forward of me," he says.

"It would have been gracious. I'm the new person in town. We have the same agendas. Or should."

"Thank you for your candor. It affords me an opportunity to explain. We tend to be ethnocentric in Charleston, quite skilled at taking our time, waiting to see what's what. I suspect you may have noticed by now that things don't tend to happen speedily. Why, people don't even walk fast." He smiles. "So I've been waiting for you to take the initiative, if you ever made that choice. I didn't think you would. If you'll allow me to explain further? You're a forensic pathologist. Of considerable reputation, I might add, and people such as yourself generally have a low opinion of elected coroners. We're not doctors or forensic experts, as a rule. I expected you would experience some defensive feelings about me when you set up your practice here."

"Then it would seem both of us have made assumptions." She'll give him the benefit of the doubt, or at least pretend.

"Charleston can be gossipy." He reminds her of a Matthew Brady photograph—sitting straight, legs crossed, hands folded in his lap. "A lot of it spiteful and small-minded," he says.

"I'm sure you and I can get along as professionals." She's not sure of any such thing.

"Are you familiar with your neighbor Mrs. Grimball?"

"I mainly see her when she's looking out her window at me."

"Apparently, she complained about a hearse being in the alley behind your house. Twice."

"I'm aware of once." She can't think of a second time. "Lucious Meddick. And a mysterious and erroneous listing of my address, which I'm hoping has been cleared up."

"She made a complaint to people who could have caused you quite a lot of trouble. I got a call about it and interceded. I said I knew for a fact you didn't have body deliveries at your house, and there must be a misunderstanding."

"I'm wondering if you would have told me this if I hadn't happened to call you."

"If I were out to get you, why would I have protected you in this instance?" he says.

"I don't know."

"I happen to think there's plenty of death and tragedy to go around. But not everybody feels the same way," he says. "There's not a funeral home in South Carolina that doesn't want my business. Including Lucious Meddick's. I don't believe for one minute he truly thought your carriage house was the morgue. Even if he read the wrong address somewhere."

"Why would he want to hurt me? I don't even know him."

"That's your answer. He doesn't view you as a source of revenue because, and this is just my guess, you aren't doing anything to help him," Hollings says.

"I don't do marketing."

"If you'll allow me, I'll send an e-mail to every coroner, funeral home, and removal service you might deal with and make sure they have your correct address."

"That's not necessary. I can do it myself." The nicer he is, the less she trusts him.

"Frankly, it's better if it comes from me. It sends the message that you and I are working together. Isn't that why you're here?"

"Gianni Lupano," she says.

His expression is blank.

"Drew Martin's tennis coach."

"I'm sure you know I have absolutely no jurisdiction in her case. No information beyond what's been in the news," Hollings says.

"He's visited your funeral home in the past. At least once."

"If he came here to ask questions about her, I most assuredly would be aware of it."

"He's been here for some reason," she says.

"Might I ask how you can know that for a fact? Perhaps you've heard more Charleston gossip than I have."

"At the very least, he's been in your parking lot, let me put it that way," she says.

"I see." He nods. "I suppose the police or

someone looked at the GPS in his car and my address was in there. And that would lead me to ask if he's a suspect in her murder."

"I imagine everyone associated with her is being questioned. Or will be. And you said 'his car.' How do you know he has a car in Charleston?"

"Because I happen to know he has an apartment here," he says.

"Most people—including people in his building—don't know he has an apartment here. I'm wondering why you do."

"We keep a guest book," he says. "It's always on a podium outside the chapel, so those who attend a wake or a service can sign in. Perhaps he attended a funeral here. You're welcome to look at the book. Or books. Going back as far as you'd like."

"The last two years would be fine," she says.

Shackles attached to a wooden chair inside an interrogation room.

Madelisa Dooley wonders if she'll end up in that room next. For lying.

"A lot of drugs, but we've got everything," Investigator Turkington says as she and Ashley follow him past one unsettling room after another inside the southern branch of the Beaufort County Sheriff's office. "Burglaries, robberies, homicides."

It's larger than she imagined, because it never occurred to her there might be crime on Hilton Head Island. But according to Turkington, there's enough of it south of the Broad River to keep sixty sworn officers, including eight investigators, busy around the clock.

"Last year," he says, "we worked more than six hundred serious crimes."

Madelisa wonders how many of them were trespassing and lying.

"I can't tell you how shocked I am," she nervously says. "We thought it was so safe here, haven't even bothered locking our door."

He leads them into a conference room and says, "You'd be amazed how many people think just because they're rich, they're immune to anything bad happening to them."

It flatters Madelisa that he must assume she and Ashley are rich. She can't think of anybody who's ever thought that about them, and she's happy for a moment until she remembers why they're here. Any minute, this young man in his smart suit and tie will figure out the truth about Mr. and Mrs. Ashley Dooley's economic status. He'll put two and two together when he finds out about their unimpressive North Charleston address and the cheap town house they rented here, so far back in the pine trees one can't even see a hint of the ocean.

"Please have a seat." He pulls out a chair for her.

"You sure are right," she says. "Money certainly doesn't make you happy or cause people to get along." As if she knows.

"That's quite a camcorder you've got there," he says to Ashley. "How much that set you back? At least a thousand." He indicates for Ashley to hand it over to him.

"I don't know why you've got to take it from me," he says. "Why can't you just look at what I got real quick?"

"What I'm still unclear about"—Turkington's pale eyes stare right at her—"is why you went up to that house to begin with. Why you walked right on to that property, even though there's a *No Trespassing* sign."

"She was looking for the owner," Ashley replies, as if he's talking to his camcorder on the table.

"Mr. Dooley, please don't answer for your wife. According to what she told me, you weren't a witness, were out on the beach when she found what she did in the house."

"I don't see why you've got to keep it." Ashley obsesses about his camcorder while Madelisa obsesses about the basset hound all alone in the car.

She left the windows cracked so he could get air, and thank God it's not hot out. Oh, please, don't let him bark. She loves that dog already. *Poor baby.* What he's been through, and she remembers touching the sticky blood on his fur. She can't mention the dog, even if it might help her explain that the only reason she went near house was to find his owner. If the police discover she has that poor, sweet puppy, they'll take him, and he'll end up in the pound and eventually be put to sleep. Just like Frisbee.

"Looking for the owner of the house. So you've said a number of times. I'm still unclear as to why you were looking for the owner." Turkington's pale eyes are fixed on her again, his pen resting on the legal pad he's writing on as he continues to make a record of her lies.

"It's such a beautiful house," she says. "I wanted Ashley to film it but didn't think that was right without permission. So I looked for people out by the pool, looked for anybody who might be home."

"There aren't many people here this time of year, not up there where you were. A lot of those big places are second, third homes for very wealthy people and they don't rent them and it's off-season."

"That's exactly true," she agrees.

"But you assumed someone was home because you said you saw something cooking on the grill?"

"That's exactly right."

"How'd you see that from the beach?"

"I saw smoke."

"You saw smoke from the grill and maybe smelled what was being barbecued." He writes it down.

"That's exactly right."

"What was it?"

"What was what?"

"What was being cooked on the grill?"

"Meat. Pork, maybe. Could have been London broil, I guess."

"And you took it upon yourself to walk right into the house." He makes more notes, then the pen goes still and he looks up at her. "You know, that's the part that I still can't figure out."

It's the part she's had a hard time figuring out, too, no matter how much she's thought about it. What lie can she tell that will have the ring of truth?

"Like I told you over the phone," she says, "I was looking for the owner and then started getting worried. Started imagining some rich old person barbecuing and all of a sudden having a heart attack. Why else would you put something on the grill and then disappear? So I kept calling 'Anybody home?' Then I found the laundry-room door open."

"You mean unlocked."

"Yes, it was."

"The door next to the window where you said a pane of glass was missing and another pane was broken," Investigator Turkington says, writing it down.

"And I went in, knowing I probably shouldn't. But I thought in my head, *What if that rich old person is lying on the floor after having a stroke?*"

"That's the thing—where you make hard choices in life," Ashley says, his eyes jumping back and forth from the investigator to the camcorder. "Don't go in? Or never forgive yourself later when you read in the paper that someone could have used your help."

"Did you film the house, sir?"

"Filmed some porpoises while I was waiting for Madelisa to come back out."

"I asked if you filmed the house."

"Let me think. I guess a little bit. Earlier, with Madelisa in front of it. But I wasn't going to show it to anybody if she couldn't get permission."

"I see. You wanted permission to film the house but filmed it anyway without permission."

"And when we didn't get permission, I erased it," Ashley says.

"Really?" Turkington says, looking at him for a long moment. "Your wife runs out of the house afraid somebody's been murdered in there and it occurs to you to erase part of what you filmed because you failed to get permission from whoever might have been murdered?"

"I know it sounds strange," Madelisa says. "But what matters is I didn't mean any harm."

Ashley says, "When Madelisa ran out and was all upset about what she saw in there, I was desperate to call nine-one-one but didn't have my phone. She didn't have hers, either."

"And you didn't think to use the one in the house?"

"Not after what I saw in there!" Madelisa says. "I felt like he was still in there!"

" 'He'?"

"It was just this awful feeling. I've never been so scared. You don't really think after what I saw I'd stop to use the phone when I could feel something watching me." She rummages through her purse for a tissue.

"So we hurried back to our condo, and she got so hysterical, I had to calm her down," Ashley says. "She just cried like a baby and we missed our tennis clinic. She cried and cried, well into the night. Finally, I said, 'Honey, why don't you sleep on it and let's talk about it again in the morning.' Truth is, I wasn't sure I believed her. My wife here has quite the imagination. Reads all these mystery books, watches all these crime shows, you know. But when she kept on crying, I started to get worried maybe there was something to it. So I called you."

"Not until after another tennis clinic," Turkington points out. "She's still so upset, yet you went to tennis this morning, then back to your condo, showered, changed, and packed the car to head back to Charleston. Then finally got around to calling the police? I'm sorry. I'm supposed to believe this?"

"If it wasn't true, why'd we cut our vacation two days short? We planned it for a whole year," Ashley says. "You'd think you'd get a refund when there's an emergency. Maybe you could put in a word for us with the rental agent."

"If that's why you called the police," Turkington says, "you just wasted your time."

"I wish you wouldn't keep my camcorder. I erased what little bit I filmed in front of the house. There's nothing to see. Just Madelisa in front of it, talking to her sister for maybe ten seconds."

"Now her sister was with you?"

"Talking to her on the camcorder. I don't know what you'd see that's helpful, because I erased it."

Madelisa made him erase it because of the dog. He had filmed her petting the dog.

"Maybe if I saw what you recorded," Turkington says to Ashley, "I would see the smoke rising up from the barbecue. You said that's what you saw from the beach, didn't you? So if you filmed the house, wouldn't the smoke be in it?"

This takes Ashley by surprise. "Well, I don't think I got that part, wasn't aiming my camcorder in that direction. Can't you just watch what's on it and give it back? I mean, most of what's on there is Madelisa and a few porpoises and other stuff I've filmed at home. I don't see why you've got to keep my camcorder."

"We have to be sure there's nothing you recorded that might give us information about what happened, details you might not be aware of."

"Like what?" Ashley says, alarmed.

"Like, for instance, are you telling the truth about your not going inside the house after your wife told you what she did." Investigator Turkington is getting very unfriendly now. "I find it unusual you didn't go in and check out your wife's story for yourself."

"If what she said was true, there's no way I was walking in there," Ashley says. "What if some killer was hiding in there?"

Madelisa remembers the sound of running water, the blood, the clothes, the photograph of the dead tennis player. She envisions the mess in the huge living room, all those prescription bottles and vodka. And the projector turned on with nothing playing on the movie screen. The detective doesn't believe her. She's in for a world of trouble. Breaking and entering. Stealing a dog. Lying. He can't find out about the dog. They'll take him and put him to sleep. She loves that dog. The hell with lies. She'll tell lies all the way to hell for that dog.

"I know this isn't my business," Madelisa says, and it takes all her nerve to ask, "but do you know who lives in that house and if anything bad's happened?"

"We know who lives there, a woman whose name I don't care to divulge. It just so happens she's not home, and her dog and car are gone."

"Her car's gone?" Madelisa's lower lip starts to tremble.

"Sounds like she went somewhere and took her dog, don't you think? And you know what else I think? You wanted a free tour of her mansion and then worried someone might have seen you trespassing. So you made up this wild tale to cover your butts. That was almost clever."

"If you bother to look inside her house, you'll know the truth." Madelisa's voice shakes.

"We did bother, ma'am. I sent a few officers over there to check, and they didn't find anything you supposedly saw. No pane of glass missing from a window by the laundry-room door. No broken glass. No blood. No knives. The gas grill was turned off, clean as a whistle. No sign something had recently been cooked on it. And the projector wasn't on," he says.

In the arrangement office where Hollings and his staff meet with families, Scarpetta sits on a pale gold-and-cream-striped sofa and goes through a second guest book.

Based on everything she's seen so far, Hollings is a tasteful, thoughtful man. The large, thick guest books are bound in fine black leather with lined creamy pages, and because of the magnitude of his business, three to four books a year are required. A tedious search through the first four months of last year's hasn't produced evidence that Gianni Lupano attended a funeral here.

She picks up another guest book and begins to work her way through it, running her finger down each page, recognizing well-known Charleston family names. No Gianni Lupano for January through March. No sign of him for April, and Scarpetta's disappointment grows. Nothing for May or June. Her finger stops at a generous, looping signature easy to decipher. On July 12 of last year, it seems he attended the funeral service of someone named Holly Webster. It appears the attendance was small—only eleven people signed the guest book. Scarpetta writes down each name and gets up from the sofa. She walks past the chapel, where two ladies inside are arranging flowers around a polished bronze casket. Up a flight of mahogany stairs, she returns to Henry Hollings's office. Once again, his back is to the door and he's on the phone.

"Some people prefer to fold the flag in tri-corners and place it behind the person's head," he is saying in his soothing, lilting voice. "Well, certainly. We can drape it over the casket. What do I recommend?" He holds up a sheet of paper. "You seem to be leaning toward the walnut with champagne satin. But also the twenty-gauge steel . . . I sure do know. Everybody says the same thing. . . . It's hard. Just as hard as it can be to make decisions like this. You want me to be honest, I'd go for the steel."

He talks a few minutes longer, turns around, and sees Scarpetta in his doorway again. "Some of these are so hard," he says to her. "Seventy-two-year-old veteran, recently lost his wife, very depressed. Puts a shotgun in his mouth. We did what we could, but no cosmetics or restorative procedures in the world were going to make him viewable, and I know you know what I'm talking about. You can't possibly have an open casket, and the family won't take no for an answer."

"Who was Holly Webster?" Scarpetta asks.

"Such a terrible tragedy." He doesn't hesitate. "One of those cases you never forget."

"Do you remember Gianni Lupano attending her funeral?"

"I wouldn't have known him back then," he oddly says.

"Was he a family friend?"

He gets up from his desk and slides open a cherry cabinet drawer. He looks through files and pulls one out.

"What I have here are details of the funeral arrangements, copies of invoices and such, which I can't let you look at out of respect for the family's privacy. But I can let you look at news clippings." He hands them to her. "I keep them on any death I handle. As you know, the only source of legal records on this will be from police and the medical examiner who worked the case, and the coroner who referred the case here for the autopsy, since Beaufort County doesn't have an ME's office. But then, you know all about that, since he's referring his cases to you now. When Holly died, they weren't using you yet. Otherwise, I suppose this sad situation would have landed in your lap instead of mine."

She detects no hint of resentment. He doesn't seem to care.

He says, "The death occurred at Hilton Head, a very wealthy family."

She opens the file. There are but a few clippings, the most detailed one in Hilton Head's *Island Packet*. According to that account, in the late morning of July 10, 2006, Holly Webster was playing on the patio with her puppy basset hound. The Olympic-size pool was off-limits unless the child was supervised, and on this morning she wasn't. According to the newspaper, her parents were out of town, and friends were staying at the house. No mention of the parents' whereabouts or their friends' names. At almost noon, someone went out to tell Holly it was time for lunch. She was nowhere in sight, the puppy walking back and forth at the edge of the pool, pawing at the water. The little girl's body was discovered at the bottom, her long, dark hair caught in the drain. Nearby was a rubber bone that police believe the child was trying to retrieve for her dog.

Another clipping, a very brief one. Not even two months later, the mother, Lydia Webster, was a guest on Dr. Self's talk show.

"I remember hearing about this case," Scarpetta says. "I believe I was in Massachusetts when it happened."

"Bad news but not big news. The police played it down as best they could. For one reason, resort areas aren't particularly keen on publicizing, shall we say, negative events." Hollings reaches for the phone. "I don't think he'll tell you anything, the ME who did the autopsy. But let's see." He pauses, then, "Henry Hollings here . . . Fine, fine . . . Up to your ears. I know, I know . . . They really do need to get some help for you down there . . . No, haven't been out in my boat for a while. . . . Right . . . I owe you a fishing trip. And you owe me for doing a lecture down there to all those wannabe kids who think death investigations are entertainment . . . The Holly Webster case. I've got Dr. Scarpetta here. Wonder if you would mind talking to her for a minute?"

Hollings hands her the phone. She explains to the MUSC assistant chief medical examiner that she has been called in as a consultant on a case that might have a connection to Holly Webster's drowning.

"What case?" the assistant chief asks.

"I'm sorry but I can't discuss it," she replies. "It's a homicide under investigation."

"Glad you understand the way it works. I can't discuss the Webster case."

What he means is he won't.

"I'm not trying to be difficult," Scarpetta says to him. "Let me go this far out on a limb. I'm here with Coroner Hollings because it appears Drew Martin's tennis coach, Gianni Lupano, attended Holly Webster's funeral. I'm trying to figure out why and can't say more than that."

"Not familiar. Never heard of him."

"That was one of my questions—if you had any idea what connection he might have had with the Webster family."

"No idea."

"What can you tell me about Holly's death?"

"Drowning. Accidental, and nothing to indicate otherwise."

"Meaning no pathognomonic findings. Diagnosis based on circumstances," Scarpetta says. "Mostly based on the way she was found."

"That's correct."

"Would you mind telling me the name of the investigating officer?"

"No problem. Hold on." As computer keys click. "Let me see here. Right, I thought so. Turkington of the Beaufort County Sheriff's Department. You want to know anything else, you need to call him."

Scarpetta thanks him again, gets off the phone, and says to Hollings. "Are you aware that the mother, Lydia Webster, appeared on Dr. Self's talk show not even two months after her child's death?"

"I didn't watch the show, don't watch any of her shows. That woman ought to be shot," he says.

"Any idea how Mrs. Webster ended up on Dr. Self's show?"

"I would guess she has quite a team of researchers who scour the news for material. Line up guests that way. In my opinion, it would have been psychologically destructive for Mrs. Webster to expose herself in front of the world when she hadn't coped with what happened. I understand it was the same sort of situation with Drew Martin," he says.

"You're referring to her appearance on Dr. Self's show last fall?"

"I hear a lot of what goes on around here, whether I want to or not. When she comes to town, she always stays at the Charleston Place Hotel. This last time, not even three weeks ago, she was rarely in her room, certainly never slept there. Housekeeping would come in and find her bed made, no sign of her being there except her belongings, or at least some of them."

"And how might you know all this?" Scarpetta says.

"A very good friend of mine is the head of security. When relatives, friends of the deceased come to town, I recommend the Charleston Place. Providing they can afford it."

Scarpetta recalls what Ed the doorman said. Drew was in and out of the apartment building, always tipped him twenty dollars. Maybe it was more than generosity. Maybe she was reminding him to keep his mouth shut.

Chapter 17

Sea Pines, the most exclusive plantation on Hilton Head Island.

For five dollars, one can buy a day pass at the security gate, and the guards, in their gray-and-blue uniforms, don't demand identification. Scarpetta used to complain about it when she and Benton had a condo here, and the memories of those days are still painful.

"She bought the Cadillac in Savannah," Investigator Turkington is saying as he drives Scarpetta and Lucy in his unmarked cruiser. "White. Which isn't helpful. You got any idea how many white Cadillacs and Lincolns there are around here? Probably two out of three rental cars are white."

"And the guards at the gate don't remember seeing it, maybe at an unusual hour? The cameras pick up anything?" Lucy says from the front seat.

"Nothing useful. You know how it is. One person says maybe they saw it. Another person says no. My thought is he drove it out, not in, so they wouldn't have noticed it anyway."

"Depends on when he took it," Lucy says. "She keep it in the garage?"

"It's been observed parked in her driveway, as a rule. So it would strike me as unlikely he's had it for a while. What?" He glances at her as he drives. "He somehow got hold of her keys, took her car, and she didn't notice?"

"No telling what she noticed. Or didn't."

"You're still sure the worst happened," Turkington starts to say.

"Yes, I am. Based on facts and common sense." Lucy has been bantering with him since he picked them up at the airport and made a smart-aleck comment about her helicopter.

He called it an eggbeater. She called him a Luddite. He didn't know what a Luddite was, still doesn't. She didn't define it for him.

"But that doesn't preclude her having been abducted for ransom," Lucy says. "I'm not saying that's impossible. I don't believe it, but sure, it's possible, and we should do exactly what we're doing. Have every investigative agency looking."

"Sure as hell wish we could have kept it out of the news. Becky says they've been chasing people away from the house all morning."

"Who's Becky?" Lucy asks.

"Chief of crime scene investigation. Like me, she's got a second job as an EMT."

Scarpetta wonders why that matters. Maybe he's self-conscious about needing a second job.

"Then again, I guess you don't have to worry about paying the rent," he says.

"Sure do. It's just mine's a little bit more than yours."

"Yeah, just a little. Can't imagine what those labs are costing you. Or your fifty houses and Ferraris."

"Not quite fifty, and how do you know what I've got?"

"Many departments using your labs yet?" he asks.

"A few. Still under construction, but we've

got the basics. And we're accredited. You get to choose. Us or SLED." South Carolina Law Enforcement Division.

"We're faster," she adds. "If you need something that's not on the menu, we've got friends in high-tech places. Oak Ridge. Y-Twelve."

"I thought they make nuclear weapons."

"That's not all they do."

"You're kidding. They do forensic stuff? Like what?" he asks.

"It's a secret."

"Doesn't matter. We can't afford you."

"Nope, you can't. Doesn't mean we wouldn't help."

His dark glasses appear in the rearview mirror. He says to Scarpetta, probably because he's had enough of Lucy, "You still with us back there?"

He wears a suit the color of cream, and Scarpetta wonders how he stays clean at crime scenes. She picks up on the more important points he and Lucy were discussing, reminds them that no one should assume anything at all, including when Lydia Webster's Cadillac disappeared, because it appears she rarely drove anyway, only on occasion, for cigarettes, booze, some food. Sadly, driving wasn't a good idea. She was too impaired. So the car could have been gone for days, and its disappearance may have nothing to do with the dog's being gone. Then there are the images the Sandman e-mailed to Dr. Self. Both Drew Martin and Lydia Webster were photographed in bathtubs that seem to have been filled with cold water. Both of them look drugged, and what about what Mrs. Dooley saw? This case must be worked as a homicide, no matter what the truth may be. Because—and Scarpetta's been preaching this for more than twenty years—you can't go back.

Then she goes back into her own private place. She can't help it. Her thoughts return to the last time she was in Hilton Head, when she cleared out Benton's condo. It never entered her mind during the darkest of dark times that his murder might have been contrived to hide him from those who certainly would have killed him, given the chance. Where are those would-be hit men now? Did they lose interest, decide he was no longer a threat or worthy of retribution? She's asked Benton. He won't talk about it, says he can't. She rolls down the window of Turkington's car and her ring winks in the sun, but it doesn't reassure her, and the good weather won't last. Later today, yet another storm is supposed to roll in.

The road winds through golf courses, and over short bridges that briefly span narrow canals and small ponds. On a grassy embankment, an alligator looks like a log, and turtles are quiet in the mud, and a snowy egret stands on stick legs in shallow water. The conversation in the front seat is centered on Dr. Self for a while, and light turns to shadow in the shade of huge oak trees. Spanish moss looks like dead, gray hair. Little has changed. A few new houses have been built here and there, and she remembers long walks and salt air and wind, and sunsets on the balcony, and the moment all of it came to an end. She envisions what she believed was him in the charred ruins of the building where he supposedly died. She sees his silver hair and incinerated flesh in the blackened wood and filth from a fire that was still smoldering when she arrived. His face was gone, nothing but burned bone, and his autopsy records were false. She was fooled. Devastated. Destroyed, and she is forever different because of what Benton did—far more different than she is because of Marino.

They park in the driveway of Lydia Webster's sprawling white villa. Scarpetta remembers seeing it before, from the beach, and it seems surreal because of why they're here. Police cars line the street.

"They got the place about a year ago. Some tycoon from Dubai had it before that," Turkington says, opening his door. "Real sad. They'd just finished a massive renovation and moved in when the little girl drowned. I don't know how Mrs. Webster stood being inside the place after that."

"Sometimes people can't let go," Scarpetta says as they walk over pavers toward the double teakwood doors at the top of stone steps. "So they stay embedded in a place and its memories."

"She get this in the settlement?" Lucy asks.

"Probably would have." As if, in truth, there's no doubt she's dead. "Still in the middle of the divorce. Her husband's into hedge funds, investments, whatever. Almost as rich as you are."

"How about we stop talking about that," Lucy says, annoyed.

Turkington opens the front door. Crime

scene investigators are inside. Propped against a stucco wall in the foyer is a window with a broken pane of glass.

"The lady on vacation," Turkington says to Scarpetta. "Madelisa Dooley. According to her statement, the glass was removed from the window when she came in through the laundry room. This pane here." He squats and points to a pane of glass on the bottom right-hand side of the window. "It's the one he removed and glued back. If you look, you can just barely see the glue. I made her think we didn't find the broken glass when officers first looked here. I wanted to see if she changed her story, so I told her the glass wasn't broken."

"I guess you didn't foam it first," Scarpetta says.

"I've heard about that," Turkington says. "We need to start doing it. My theory is, if Mrs. Dooley's got her story right, something went on in the house after she left."

"We'll foam it before it's wrapped up and transported," Scarpetta says, "so we can stabilize the broken glass."

"Help yourself." He walks off toward the living room, where an investigator takes photographs of the clutter on the coffee table and another lifts up cushions from the couch.

Scarpetta and Lucy open their black cases. They put on shoe covers and gloves, and a woman in range pants and a polo shirt with FORENSICS in bold letters on the back walks out of the living room. She's probably in her forties, with brown eyes and short, dark hair. She's petite, and it's difficult for Scarpetta to imagine that a woman so short and slight would want to go into law enforcement.

"You must be Becky," Scarpetta says, and she introduces herself and Lucy.

Becky indicates the window leaning against the wall and says, "The lower-right pane of glass. Tommy must have explained." She means Turkington, and she points a gloved finger. "A glass cutter was used, then the pane was glued back. The reason I noticed?" She's proud of herself. "Sand stuck in the glue. See?"

They look. They can see it.

"So it appears when Mrs. Dooley came in looking for the owner," Becky tells them, "the glass certainly could have been out of the window and on the ground. I find it credible she did what she said. Got the hell out of here, and then the killer straightened up after himself."

Lucy inserts two pressurized containers into a holster that is attached to a mixing gun.

"Creepy to think about," Becky says. "The poor lady was probably in here when he was. She said she felt like somebody was watching her. This that glue spray? I've heard of it. Holds the broken glass in place. What's it made out of?"

"Mostly polyurethane and compressed gas," Scarpetta says. "You taken photographs? Dusted for prints? Swabbed for DNA?"

Lucy photographs the window anyway, with and without a scale.

"Photos, swabs. No prints. We'll see about DNA, but I'd be shocked, as clean as it is," Becky says. "He obviously cleaned the window, the entire window. I don't know how it got broke. Looks like a big bird flew into it. Like a pelican or a buzzard."

Scarpetta begins making notes, documenting areas of damaged glass and measuring them.

Lucy tapes the edges of the window frame and asks, "Which side do you think?"

"I'm thinking this was broken from the inside," Scarpetta says. "Can we turn this? We need to spray the other side."

She and Lucy carefully lift the window and turn it around, so it faces the other way. They lean it against the wall and take more photographs and make more notes while Becky stays out of the way and watches.

Scarpetta says to her, "I need a little help here. Can you stand over here?"

Becky stands next to her.

"Show me on the wall where the broken glass would be if the window were in situ. In a minute, I'll look at where you removed it from, but for now, let's get an idea."

Becky touches the wall. "Course, I'm short," she says.

"About the level of my head," Scarpetta says, studying the broken glass. "This breakage is similar to what I see in car accidents. When the person isn't belted and his head hits the windshield. This area isn't punched out." She points to the hole in the glass. "It simply received the brunt of the blow, and I'm betting there are some glass fragments on the floor. Inside the laundry room. Maybe on the windowsill, too."

"I collected them. You thinking somebody hit their head on the glass?" Becky asks. "Wouldn't you think there'd be blood?"

"Not necessarily."

Lucy tapes brown butcher's paper over one side of the window. She opens the front door and asks Scarpetta and Becky to step outside while she sprays.

"I met Lydia Webster once." Becky keeps talking, and they're on the porch. "When her little girl drowned and I had to come take photographs. I can't tell you what that did to me, since I've got a little girl of my own. Still see Holly in her little purple swimsuit, just floating underwater upside down with her hair caught in the drain. We got Lydia's driver's license, by the way, have the info on an APB, but don't get your fingers crossed on that one. She's about your height. That would be about right if she ran into the glass and broke it. I don't know if Tommy told you, but her wallet was right there in the kitchen. Doesn't look like it was touched. I don't think whoever we're talking about here was motivated by robbery."

Even outside, Scarpetta can smell the polyurethane. She looks out at large live oaks draped with Spanish moss, and a blue

water tower peeking above pines. Two people on bicycles slowly ride past and stare.

"You can come back in." Lucy is in the doorway, taking off her goggles and face mask.

The broken windowpane is covered in
thick yellowish foam.

"So what do we want to do with it?" Becky
asks, her eyes lingering on Lucy.

"I'd like to wrap it up and take it with us,"
Scarpetta says.

"And check it for what?"

"The glue. Anything microscopic that's adhering to it. The elemental or chemical composition of it. Sometimes you don't know
what you're looking for until you find it."

"Good luck fitting a window under a microscope," Becky jokes.

"And I'll also want the broken glass you
collected," Scarpetta says.

"The swabs?"

"Anything you want us to test at the labs.
Can we take a look at the laundry room?"
Scarpetta says.

It is next to the kitchen, and inside to the
right of the door, brown paper has been
taped over the empty space where the window was removed. Scarpetta is careful how
she approaches what is believed to be the

killer's point of entry. She does what she always does—stands outside and looks in, scanning every inch. She asks if the laundry room has been photographed. It has, and it's been checked for footprints, shoe prints, fingerprints. Against one wall are four expensive washers and dryers, and against the opposite wall, an empty dog crate. There are storage closets and a large table. In a corner, a wicker laundry basket is piled with dirty clothes.

"Was this door locked when you got here?" Scarpetta asks of the carved teak door that leads outside.

"No, and Mrs. Dooley says it was unlocked, which is why she was able to walk right in. What I'm thinking is he removed the pane of glass and reached his hand inside. You can see"—Becky walks over to the paper-covered space where the window used to be—"if you removed the glass here, it's easy to reach the deadbolt inside. That's why we tell people not to have keyless deadbolts near glass. Of course, if the burglar alarm was on . . ."

"Do we know it wasn't?"

"It wasn't when Mrs. Dooley walked in."

"But we don't know if it was on or off when he did?"

"I've thought about that. Seems if it was on, the glass breakers," Becky starts to say, then thinks again. "Well, I don't guess cutting the glass would set them off. They're noise-sensitive."

"Suggesting the alarm wasn't on when the other pane of glass was broken. Suggesting he was inside the house at that point. Unless the glass was broken at an earlier time. And I doubt it."

"Me, too," Becky agrees. "Seems like you'd get that fixed to keep the rain and bugs out. Or at least pick up the broken glass. Especially since she kept the dog in there. I'm wondering if maybe she struggled with him. Tried to run for the door to get away. Night before last, she set off her alarm. Don't know if you knew that. This was a fairly regular occurrence, because she'd get so drunk and forget the alarm was on and open the slider, which instantly set it off. Then she couldn't remember her password when the service called her. So we'd get dispatched."

"No record of her alarm going off since then?" Scarpetta says. "Have you had a chance to get the history from the alarm company? For example, when did it go off last? When was it armed and disarmed last?"

"The false alarm I mentioned is the last time it went off."

Scarpetta says, "When the police responded, do they remember seeing her white Cadillac?"

Becky says no. The officers don't remember the car being there. But it could have been in the garage. She adds, "It appears she set the alarm about the time it got dark on Monday, and then it was unset later on at nine or so, then reset it. Then unset it again at four-fourteen the next morning. Meaning yesterday."

"And not reset after that?" Scarpetta says.

"It wasn't. This is just my opinion, but when people are drinking and drugging, they don't keep normal hours. Sleep during the day on and off. Get up at strange hours. So maybe she unset the alarm at four-fourteen to take the dog out, maybe to smoke, and the guy was watching her, maybe had been watching her for a while. Stalking her, I'm saying. For all we know, he may already have cut out the glass and was just waiting back here in the dark. There's bamboo and bushes along this side of the house and no neighbors home, so even with the floodlights on, he could hide back here and no one was going to see him. It's weird about the dog. Where is he?"

"I've got someone checking on that," Scarpetta says.

"Maybe he can talk and solve the case." Joking.

"We need to find him. You never know what might solve a case."

"If he ran off, someone would have found him," Becky says. "It's not like you see basset hounds every day, and people notice loose dogs around here. The other thing is, if Mrs. Dooley was telling the truth, then he must have stayed with Mrs. Webster for a while, maybe kept her alive for hours. The alarm was unset at four-fourteen yesterday, and Mrs. Dooley found the blood and everything around lunchtime—about eight hours later, and he was probably still inside the house."

Scarpetta examines the dirty clothes inside the laundry basket. On top is a T-shirt that is loosely folded, and with a gloved hand, she picks it up and lets it fall open. It's damp and streaked with dirt. She gets up and looks inside the sink. The stainless steel is spotted from splashing water, and a small amount of water is pooled around the drain.

"I'm wondering if he used this to clean the

window," Scarpetta says. "It still feels damp, and it's dirty, as if someone used it as a cleaning rag. I'd like to seal it in a paper bag, submit it to the labs."

"To look for what?" Becky asks that question again.

"If he held this, we might get his DNA. Could be trace evidence. I guess we'd better decide which labs."

"SLED's fine and dandy but will take forever. If you can help us with your labs?"

"That's why we've got them." Scarpetta looks at the alarm keypad near the door that leads into the hallway. "Maybe he disarmed the alarm when he came in. I don't think we should assume he didn't. An LCD touchpad instead of buttons. A good surface for prints. And maybe DNA."

"That would mean he knew her if he unset the alarm. Makes sense when you think about how long he was in the house."

"It would mean he's familiar with this place. It doesn't mean he knew her," Scarpetta says. "What's the code?"

"What we call the 'one, two, three, four, walk right in my door' code. Probably preset, and she never bothered to change it. Let me make sure about the labs before we start receipting everything to you. I need to ask Tommy."

He's in the foyer with Lucy, and Becky asks him about the labs, and he says it's amazing what's going private these days. Some departments are even hiring private cops.

"We will be," Lucy says, handing Scarpetta a pair of yellow-tinted goggles. "We had them in Florida."

Becky gets interested in the hard case open on the floor. She looks at the five flashlight-shaped forensic high-intensity light sources, the nickel nine-volt batteries, the goggles, and multiport charger. "I've been begging the sheriff to get us one of these portable Crime-lites. Each one of them's a different bandwidth, right?"

"Violet, blue, blue-green, and green spectra," Lucy says. "And this handy broad-bandwidth white light"—she picks it up—"with interchangeable filters in blue, green, and red for contrast enhancement."

"Works good?"

"Body fluids, fingerprints, drug residues, fibers, or trace evidence. Yup. Works good."

She selects a violet light in the 400- to 430-nanometer range and she, Becky, and Scarpetta walk into the living room. All the shades are open, and beyond them is the black-bottom pool where Holly Webster drowned, and beyond that dunes, sea oats, the beach. The ocean is calm, and sunlight flashes in the tide like small silver fish.

"There's plenty of footprints in here, too," Becky offers as they look around. "Bare footprints, shoe prints, all of them small, probably hers. It's strange, because there's no evidence he wiped down the floors before he left—like he must have done to the window. So you would think there'd be shoe prints. This shiny stone, what is it? I've never seen blue tiles like this. It looks like the ocean."

"That's probably what it's supposed to look like," Scarpetta says. "Sodalite blue marble, maybe lapis."

"No shit. I had a ring made out of lapis once. I can't believe someone's got a whole floor of it. Hides the dirt pretty good," she says, "but it sure as hell hasn't been cleaned in recent memory. A lot of dust and stuff, the entire house is like that. You shine a flashlight at an angle and you see what I mean. I just don't understand why it doesn't appear he left a single shoe print, not even in the laundry room where he came in."

"I'm going to wander around," Lucy says. "What about upstairs?"

"I don't think she was using the upstairs. Doubt he went up there. It's undisturbed. Just guest rooms, an art gallery, and game room up there. Never seen a house like this. Must be nice."

"Not for her," Scarpetta says, looking at the long, dark hair all over the floor, at the empty glasses and bottle of vodka on the table in front of the couch. "I don't think this place gave her a moment's happiness."

Madelisa hasn't been home an hour when the doorbell rings.

In the past, she wouldn't have bothered to ask who's there.

"Who is it?" she calls out from behind the locked door.

"Investigator Pete Marino from the medical examiner's office," a voice says, a deep voice with an accent that reminds her of the North, of Yankees.

Madelisa suspects what she feared. The lady in Hilton Head is dead. Why else would someone from the medical examiner's office show up here? She wishes Ashley hadn't decided to run errands the minute they got home, leaving her alone after what she'd been through. She listens for the basset hound. Thank goodness he's quiet in the spare bedroom. She opens the front door and is terrified. The huge man is dressed like a motorcycle thug. He's the monster who killed that poor woman, and he followed Madelisa home to kill her next.

"I don't know anything," she says, trying to shut the door.

The thug blocks the door with his foot, walks right into the house. "Easy does it," he says to her, and he opens his wallet, shows her his badge. "Like I said. I'm Pete Marino from the ME's office."

She doesn't know what to do. If she tries to call the police, he'll kill her on the spot. Anybody can buy a badge these days.

"Let's sit down and have us a little talk," he says. "I just got word about your visit to the Beaufort County Sheriff's Department in Hilton Head."

"Who told you about that?" She feels a little better. "Did that investigator get hold of you, and why would he? I told him everything I know. He didn't believe me, anyhow. Who told you where I live? Now, that concerns me. I cooperate with the authorities, and they give out my home address."

"We got a little problem with your story," Pete Marino says.

Lucy's yellow goggles look at Scarpetta.

They are in the master bedroom, and the shades are down. On top of the brown silk bedspread, several stains and smears fluoresce neon green in the high-intensity violet light.

"Could be seminal fluid," Lucy says. "Could also be something else." She scans the bed with the light.

"Saliva, urine, sebaceous oils, sweat," Scarpetta says. She leans close to a large luminescent spot. "I don't smell anything," she adds. "Hold the light right here. Problem is, no telling when the spread was cleaned last. I don't think housekeeping was a priority. Typical of people who are depressed. Bedspread goes to the labs. What we need is her toothbrush, hairbrush. Of course, the tumblers on the coffee table."

"On the back steps, there's an ashtray full of cigarette butts," Lucy says. "I don't think her DNA's going to be a problem. Or her footprints, fingerprints. The problem's him.

He knows what he's doing. These days, everybody's an expert."

"No," Scarpetta says. "They just think they are."

She takes off her goggles, and the green fluorescence on the bedspread disappears. Lucy turns off the Crime-lite and takes off her goggles, too.

"What are we doing?" she says.

Scarpetta is studying a photograph she noticed when they first came into the bedroom. Dr. Self sits on a living-room set, and across from her is a pretty woman with long, dark hair. Television cameras are rolled in close. People in the audience are clapping and smiling.

"When she was on Dr. Self's show," Scarpetta says to Lucy. "But what I wasn't expecting is this other one."

Lydia with Drew Martin and a dark, swarthy man Scarpetta assumes is Drew's coach, Gianni Lupano. The three of them smile and squint in the sun on center court of the *Family Circle* Cup Tennis Center on Daniel Island, a few miles from downtown Charleston.

"So, what's the common denominator?" Lucy says. "Let me guess. Dr. Self-ish."

"Not this past tournament," Scarpetta

says. "Look at the difference in the pictures."
She points to the photograph of Lydia with
Drew. She points to the photograph of Lydia
with Dr. Self. "The marked deterioration.
Look at her eyes."

Lucy turns on the bedroom light.

"When this picture was taken at the *Family Circle* Cup stadium, Lydia certainly didn't
look like someone chronically abusing alcohol and prescription drugs," she says.

"And pulling out her hair," Lucy says. "I
don't understand why anybody does that.
Head hair, pubic hair. Everywhere. That picture of her in the tub? She looks like she's
missing half her hair. Eyebrows, eyelashes."

"Trichotillomania," Scarpetta says.
"Obsessive-compulsive disorder. Anxiety.
Depression. Her life was a living hell."

"If Dr. Self's the common denominator,
then what about the lady murdered in Bari?
The Canadian tourist. There's no indication
she was ever on Dr. Self's show or knew her."

"I think that might be when he got his first
taste of it."

"Taste of what?" Lucy asks.

"Taste of killing civilians," Scarpetta says.

"That doesn't explain the Dr. Self connection."

"Sending photographs to her indicates he's created a psychological landscape and a ritual for his crimes. And it also becomes a game, serves a purpose. Removes him from the horror of what he's doing, because to face the fact that he's sadistically inflicting pain and death might be more than he can bear. So he has to give it a meaning. He has to make it cunning." She retrieves a very unscientific but practical packet of Post-its from her crime scene case. "Rather much like religion. If you do something in the name of God, that makes it okay. Stoning people to death. Burning them at the stake. The Inquisition. The Crusades. Oppressing people who aren't just like you. He's given a meaning to what he does. My opinion, anyway."

She probes the bed with a bright white light, and uses the sticky side of Post-its to collect any fibers, hairs, dirt, or sand she sees.

"Then you don't think Dr. Self is personally significant to this guy? That she's just a prop in his drama? That he just latched on to her because she's there. On the air. A household name."

Scarpetta places the Post-its in a plastic evidence bag and seals it with yellow crime scene tape that she labels and dates with a

Sharpie. She and Lucy begin to fold the bedspread.

"I think it's extremely personal," Scarpetta replies. "You don't place someone in the matrix of your game or psychological drama if it isn't personal. I can't answer the why part of it."

A loud ripping noise as Lucy tears a large sheet of brown paper from its roll.

"For example, he may have never met her. Same thing stalkers do. Or he might have," Scarpetta says. "For all we know, he's been on her show or has spent time with her."

They center the folded spread on the paper.

"You're right. One way or other, it's personal," Lucy decides. "Maybe he kills the woman in Bari and does all but confess it to Dr. Maroni, perhaps thinking Dr. Self will find out. Well, she doesn't. So now what?"

"He feels even more ignored."

"Then what?"

"Escalation."

"What happens when Mother doesn't pay attention to her profoundly disturbed and damaged child?" Scarpetta asks as she wraps.

"Let me think," Lucy says. "The child grows up to be me?"

Scarpetta cuts off a strip of yellow tape and says, "What a terrible thing. Torture and kill women who were guests on your show. Or do it to get your attention."

The sixty-inch flat-screen television talks to Marino. It tells him something about Madelisa that he can use against her.

"That a plasma screen?" he asks. "Must be the biggest one I've ever seen."

She's overweight, with heavy-lidded eyes, and could use a good dentist. Her dentures remind him of a white picket fence, and her hairstylist ought to be shot. She sits on a floral-print couch, her hands fidgety.

She says, "My husband and his toys. I don't know what it is, except big and expensive."

"Must be something watching a game on that thing. Me? I'd probably sit in front of it, never get a damn thing done."

Which is probably what she does. Sit in front of the TV like a zombie.

"What do you like to watch?" he asks.

"I like crime shows and mysteries, because I can usually figure them out. But after what just happened to me, I'm not sure I can watch anything violent ever again."

"Then you probably know a lot about

forensics," Marino says. "Seeing as how you watch all these crime shows."

"I was on jury duty about a year ago and knew more about forensics than the judge did. That doesn't say much about the judge. But I know a few things."

"How about image recovery?"

"I've heard of it."

"As in photographs, videotapes, digital recordings that have been erased."

"Would you like some iced tea? I can make it."

"Not right now."

"I think Ashley's going to pick up some Jimmy Dengate's. You ever had fried chicken from there? He'll be home any minute, and maybe you'd like some."

"What I'd like is for you to quit changing the subject. See, with image recovery, it's next to impossible to totally get rid of a digital image that's on a disk or memory stick or whatever. You can delete stuff all day and we can get it back." This isn't entirely true, but Marino has no compunction about lying.

Madelisa looks like a cornered mouse.

"You know what I'm getting at, don't you?" Marino says, and he's got her where he wants her but he doesn't feel good about it, and he himself isn't quite sure what he's getting at.

When Scarpetta called him a while ago and said Turkington is suspicious about what Mr. Dooley erased because he kept mentioning it during the interview, Marino said he'd get an answer. More than anything right now, he wants to please Scarpetta, make her think something's still worthwhile about him. He was shocked she called him.

"Why are you asking me?" Madelisa says, and she begins to cry. "I said, I don't know anything other than what I already told that investigator."

She continues glancing past Marino toward the back of her small, yellow house. Yellow wallpaper, yellow carpet. Marino's never seen so much yellow. It looks like an interior decorator peed on everything the Dooleys own.

"The reason I bring up image recovery is I understand your husband erased part of what he videotaped out there on the beach," Marino says, unmoved by her tears.

"It was just me standing in front of the house before I had permission. That's the only thing he erased. Of course, I never did get permission, because how could I? It's not that I didn't try. I have manners."

"I really don't give a shit about you and your manners. What I care about is what you're hiding from me and everybody else." He leans forward in the recliner chair. "I know damn well you're not being totally honest with me. Why do I know that? Because of science."

He doesn't know anything of the sort. To recover deleted images from a digital recorder isn't a given. If it can be done at all, the process is painstaking and would take a while.

"Please don't," she begs him. "I'm so sorry, but please don't take him. I love him so much."

Marino has no idea what she's talking about. It occurs to him she means her husband, but he isn't sure.

He says, "If I don't take him, what then? How do I explain it when I leave here and I'm asked?"

"Pretend you don't know about it." She cries harder. "What difference does it make? He didn't do anything. Oh, the poor baby. Who knows what he's been through. He was shaking and had blood on him. He didn't do anything except get scared and escape, and if you take him you know what will happen. They'll put him to sleep. Oh, please, let me keep him. Please! Please! Please!"

"Why did he have blood on him?" Marino asks.

In the master bathroom, Scarpetta shines a flashlight obliquely over an onyx floor the color of tigereye.

"Bare footprints," she says from the doorway. "Smallish. Maybe hers again. And more hair."

"If what Madelisa Dooley says is to be believed, he had to have walked around in here. This is so weird," Becky says as Lucy shows up with a small blue-and-yellow box and a bottle of sterile water.

Scarpetta steps inside the bathroom. She pulls open the tiger-striped shower curtain and shines the light inside the deep copper tub. Nothing, then something catches her attention, and she picks up what looks like a piece of broken white pottery that for some reason was between a bar of white soap and a dish hooked to the side of the tub. She examines it carefully. She gets out her jeweler's lens.

"Part of a dental crown," she says. "Not porcelain. A temporary that somehow got broken."

"I wonder where the rest of it is," Becky says, crouching in the doorway and peering at the floor, turning on her flashlight and shining it in all directions. "Unless it's not recent."

"Could have gone down the drain. We should check the trap. Could be anywhere." Scarpetta thinks she sees a trace of dried blood on what she estimates is almost half of a crown from what she believes is a front tooth. "We have any way of knowing if Lydia Webster has been to the dentist lately?"

"I can check it out. There's not that many dentists on the island. So unless she went elsewhere, it shouldn't be hard to track down."

"It would have to be recent, very recent," Scarpetta says. "I don't care how much you neglect your hygiene, you don't ignore a broken crown, especially on a front tooth."

"Could be his," Lucy says.

"That would be even better," Scarpetta says. "We need a small paper envelope."

"I'll get it," Lucy says.

"I don't see anything. If it broke in here, I don't see the rest of it. I guess it could still be attached to the tooth. I broke a crown once and part of it was still stuck to the little nub that's left of my tooth." Becky looks past Scarpetta, at the copper tub. "Talk about the biggest false-positive on the planet," she adds. "This will be a new one for the books. One of the few times I need to use luminal, and the damn tub and sink are copper. Well, we can forget it."

"I don't use luminol anymore," Scarpetta says, as if the oxidizing agent is a disloyal friend.

Until recently, it was a forensic staple and she never questioned using it to find blood no longer visible. If blood had been washed away or even painted over, the way to know was to mix up a spray bottle of luminol and see what fluoresced. The problems have always been many. Like a dog that wags its tail at all the neighbors, luminol is excited by more than the hemoglobin in blood and is, unfortunately, quite responsive to a number of things: paint, varnish, Drano, bleach, dandelions, thistle, creeping myrtle, corn. And, of course, copper.

Lucy retrieves a small container of Hemastix for a presumptive test, looking for any residue of what may be scrubbed-away blood. The presumptive test says blood might be there, and Scarpetta opens the box of Bluestar Magnum and removes a brown glass bottle and a foil pack, and a spray bottle.

"Stronger, longer-lasting, don't have to use it in total darkness," she explains to Becky. "No sodium perborate tetrahydrate, so it's nontoxic. Can use it on copper because the reaction will be a different intensity, a different color spectrum, and will have a different duration than blood."

She has yet to see blood inside the master bathroom. Despite what Madelisa claimed, the most intense white light revealed not the slightest stain. But this is no longer surprising. By all indications so far, after she fled from the house, the killer meticulously cleaned up after himself. Scarpetta selects the finest setting on the spray bottle's nozzle and pours in four ounces of sterile water. To this she adds two tablets. She gently stirs with a pipette for several minutes, then opens the brown glass bottle and pours in a sodium hydroxide solution.

She begins to spray, and spots and

streaks and shapes and spatters luminesce bright cobalt blue all over the room. Becky takes photographs. A little later, when Scarpetta has finished cleaning up after herself and is repacking her crime scene case, her cell phone rings. It's the fingerprint examiner from Lucy's labs.

"You're not going to believe this," he says.

"Don't ever start a conversation like that with me unless you mean it." Scarpetta isn't joking.

"The print on the gold coin." He's excited, talking fast. "We got a hit—the unidentified little boy who was found last week. The kid from Hilton Head."

"Are you sure? You can't be sure. It makes no sense."

"May not make sense, but there's no doubt about it."

"Don't say that, either, unless you mean it. My first reaction is there's an error," Scarpetta says.

"There's not. I pulled his ten-print card from the prints Marino took in the morgue. I visually verified it. Unquestionably, the ridge detail from the partial on the coin matches the unidentified kid's right thumbprint. There's no mistake."

"A fingerprint on a coin that's been fumed with glue? I don't see how."

"Believe me, I'm with you. We all know the fingerprints of prepubescent kids don't last long enough to fume. They're mostly water. Just sweat instead of the oils, amino acids, and all the rest that comes with puberty. I've never superglued a kid's prints and don't think you could. But this print is from a kid, and that kid is the one in your morgue."

"Maybe that's not how it happened," Scarpetta says. "Maybe the coin was never fumed."

"Had to be. There's ridge detail in what sure looks like superglue, the same as if it had been fumed."

"Maybe he had glue on his finger and touched the coin," she says. "And left his print that way."

Chapter 18

Nine p.m. A hard rain slaps the street in front of Marino's fishing shack.

Lucy is soaking wet as she turns on a wireless receiver minidisc recorder disguised as an iPod. In exactly six minutes, Scarpetta will call Marino. Right now, he is arguing with Shandy, their every word picked up by the multidirectional mike embedded in his computer's thumb drive.

His heavy footsteps, the refrigerator door opening, the swish of a can popped open, probably a beer.

Shandy's angry voice sounds in Lucy's earpiece. ". . . Don't lie to me. I'm warning you. All of a sudden? All of a sudden you decide you don't want a committed relationship? And by the way, who said I'm committed to you? The only fucking thing that ought to be committed is you—to a fucking mental hospital. Maybe the Big Chief's fiancé can give you a discount on a room up there."

He's told her about Scarpetta's engagement to Benton. Shandy's hitting Marino where it hurts, meaning she knows where it hurts. Lucy wonders how much she's used that against him, taunted him about it.

"You don't own me. You don't get to have me until it don't suit you anymore, so maybe I'm getting rid of you first," he yells. "You're bad for me. Making me get on that hormone shit—it's a damn wonder I hadn't had a stroke or something. After barely more than a week. What happens in a month, huh? You picked out a fucking cemetery? Or maybe I'll end up in the fucking penitentiary because I lose my mind and do something."

"Maybe you already did something."

"Go to hell."

"Why would I be committed to an old, fat fuck like you, who can't even get it up without *that hormone shit?*"

"Cut it out, Shandy. I've had it with you putting me down, you hear me? If I'm such a nothing, why are you here? I need some space, time to think. Everything's so fucked up right now. Work's turned to shit. I'm smoking, not going to the gym, drinking too much, doped up. Everything's gone to hell, and all you do is get me in worse and worse trouble."

His cell phone rings. He doesn't answer. It rings and rings.

"Answer it!" Lucy says out loud in the heavy, steady rain.

"Yeah." his voice sounds in her earpiece.

Thank God. He's quiet for a moment, listening, then says to Scarpetta on the other line, "That can't be right."

Lucy can't hear Scarpetta's side of the conversation but knows what's being said. She's telling Marino there were no hits in NIBIN or IAFIS for the serial number of the Colt .38 and any prints or partial prints recovered from the gun and the cartridges that Bull found in her alleyway.

"What about him?" Marino asks.

He means Bull. Scarpetta can't answer that. Bull's prints wouldn't be in IAFIS, because he's never been convicted of a crime, and his being arrested several weeks ago doesn't count. If the Colt is his but isn't stolen or wasn't used in a crime and then ended up back on the street, it wouldn't be in NIBIN. She's already told Bull it would be helpful if he were printed for exclusionary purposes, but he's not gotten around to it. She can't remind him again because she can't get hold of him, and both she and Lucy have tried several times since they left Lydia Webster's house. Bull's mother says he went out in his boat to pick oysters. Why he would do that in this weather is baffling.

"Uh-huh, uh-huh." Marino's voice fills Lucy's ear, and he is walking around again, obviously careful what he says in front of Shandy.

Scarpetta will also tell Marino about the partial print on the gold coin. Maybe that's what she's relaying to him right now, because he makes a sound of surprise.

Then he says, "Good to know."

Then he falls silent again. Lucy hears him pacing. He moves closer to the computer, to the thumb drive, and a chair scrapes across the wooden floor as if he's sitting down. Shandy is quiet, probably trying to figure out what he's talking about and to whom.

"Okay," he finally says. "Can we deal with this later? I'm in the middle of something."

No. Lucy's certain her aunt will force him

to talk about whatever she wants, or at least listen. She's not going to get off the phone without reminding him that within the past week, he started wearing an old Morgan silver dollar on a necklace. It may have no connection to the gold coin necklace that was at least held, at some point, by the dead little boy in Scarpetta's freezer. But where did Marino get his gaudy new necklace? If she's asking him that, he isn't answering. He can't. Shandy's right there listening. And as Lucy stands in the dark, in the rain, and the rain soaks her cap and seeps in around the collar of her slicker, she thinks about what Marino did to her aunt, and that same feeling comes back. A fearless, flat feeling.

"Yeah, yeah, no problem," Marino says. "Like a ripe apple falling from a tree."

Lucy infers that her aunt is thanking him. What an irony, she's thanking him. How the fuck can she thank him for anything? Lucy knows why, but it's still revolting. Scarpetta's thanking him for talking with Madelisa, which resulted in her confessing that she'd taken the basset hound, and then showing him a pair of shorts that had blood on them. The blood had been on the dog. Madelisa wiped it on her shorts, indicating she must have arrived on the scene very soon after someone was injured or killed, because the blood on the dog was still wet. Marino took the shorts. He let her keep the dog. His story, he told her, is that the killer stole the basset hound, probably killed it and buried it somewhere. Amazing how kind and decent he is to women he doesn't know.

Rain is relentless cold fingers drumming the top of Lucy's head. She walks, staying out of view, should Marino or Shandy move close to a window. It may be dark, but Lucy takes no chances. Marino is off the phone now.

"You think I'm so stupid I don't know who the hell you were talking to and that you were making damn sure I had no idea what you're saying? Speaking in riddles, in other words." Shandy is shrieking. "As if I'm so stupid I fall for it. The Big Chief, that's who!"

"It's none of your damn business. How many times I got to tell you that? I can talk to who the hell I want."

"Everything's my business! You spent the night with her, you lying asshole! I saw your damn motorcycle there early the next morning! You think I'm stupid? Was it good? I know you been wanting it half your life! Was it good, you big, fat fuck!"

"I don't know who beat it into your spoiled

rich girl's head that everything in life is your business. But hear this. *It ain't.*"

After more *fuck-yous* and other profanities and threats, Shandy storms out and slams the door. From where she hides, Lucy watches her stride angrily underneath the fishing shack to her motorcycle, angrily ride it through Marino's sliver of a sandy front yard, then loudly speed away toward the Ben Sawyer Bridge. Lucy waits a few minutes, listening to make sure Shandy isn't coming back. Nothing. Just the distant sound of traffic and the loud spattering of the rain. On Marino's front porch, she knocks on the door. He flings it open, his angry face suddenly blank, then uneasy, his expressions running through emotions like a slot machine.

"What are you doing here?" he asks, looking past her, as if worried Shandy might come back.

Lucy walks into a squalid sanctuary she knows better than he thinks. She notices his computer, the thumb drive still in it. Her fake iPod and its earpiece are tucked in a pocket of her slicker. He shuts the door, stands in front of it, looking more uncomfortable by the second as she sits on a plaid couch that smells like mildew.

"I hear you was spying on me and Shandy when we was in the morgue like you're a damn two-legged Patriot Act." He goes first, maybe assuming that is why she's here. "You don't know by now not to try shit like that on me?"

Foolishly, he tries to intimidate her when he knows damn well he's never intimidated her, not even when she was a child. Not even when she was a teenager and he ridiculed—at times mocked and shunned—her for who and what she is.

"I already talked about it with the Doc," Marino goes on. "There's nothing left to say, so don't start in on me."

"And that's all you did with her? Talk to her?" Lucy bends forward, slides her Glock out of her ankle holster and points it at him. "Give me one good reason why I shouldn't kill you," she says with no emotion.

He doesn't answer.

"One good reason," Lucy says it again. "You and Shandy were just fighting like hell. Could hear her screaming all the way out on the street."

She gets up from the couch, walks over to a table, and opens the drawer. She pulls out the Smith & Wesson .357 revolver she saw last night, sits back down, slides her Glock back into her ankle holster. She points Marino's own gun at him.

"Shandy's fingerprints are all over this place. I imagine there's plenty of her DNA in here, too. The two of you fight, she shoots you and speeds off on her bike. Such a pathologically jealous bitch."

She pulls back the revolver's hammer. Marino doesn't flinch. He doesn't seem to care.

"One good reason," she says.

"I don't got a good reason," he says. "Go ahead. I wanted her to and she wouldn't." He means Scarpetta. "She should have. She didn't, so go ahead. I don't give a shit if Shandy gets blamed. I'll even help you out. There's underwear in my room. Help yourself to her DNA. They find her DNA on the gun, that's all they need. Everyone in the bar knows what she's like. Just ask Jess. No one would be surprised."

Then he shuts up. For a moment, the two of them are motionless. Him standing in front of the door, hands down by his sides. Lucy on the couch, the revolver pointed at his head. She doesn't need the larger target of his chest. He is well aware of that fact.

She lowers the gun. "Sit down," she says.

He sits in the chair near his computer. "I guess I should have known she'd tell you," he says.

"I guess it should tell you a lot that she didn't. Not a word to anyone. She continues to protect you. Isn't that something?" Lucy says. "You see what you did to her wrists?"

His answer is a sudden brightening of his bloodshot eyes. Lucy's never seen him cry.

She continues, "Rose noticed. She told me. This morning when we were in the lab, I saw for myself—the bruises on Aunt Kay's wrists. Like I said. What are you going to do about it?"

She tries to push away images of what she imagines he did to her aunt. The idea of him seeing her, touching her, makes Lucy feel far more violated than she would if she had been the victim. She looks at his huge hands and arms, his mouth, and tries to push away what she imagines he did.

"What's done is done," he says. "Plain and simple. I promise she'll never have to be around me again. None of you will. Or you can shoot me just the way you said and get away with it like you always do. Like you have before. You can get away with anything you want. Go ahead. If someone else did to her what I did, I'd kill him. He'd already be dead."

"Pathetic coward. At least tell her you're sorry instead of running away or committing suicide by cop."

"What good would it do to tell her? It's over. That's why I find out about everything after the fact. Nobody called me to go to Hilton Head."

"Don't be a baby. Aunt Kay asked you to go see Madelisa Dooley. I couldn't believe it. It makes me sick."

"She won't ask me nothing again. Not after you being here. I don't want either of you asking me nothing," Marino says. "It's over."

"Do you remember what you did?"

He doesn't answer. He remembers.

"Say you're sorry," she says. "Tell her you weren't so drunk that you don't remember what you did. Tell her you remember and you're sorry and you can't undo it but you're sorry. See what she does. She won't shoot you. She won't even send you away. She's a better person than I am. " Lucy tightens her grip on the gun. "Why? Just tell me why. You've been drunk around her before. You've been alone with her a million times, even in hotel rooms. Why? How could you?"

He lights a cigarette, his hands shaking badly. "It's everything. I know there's no excuse. I've been half crazy. It's everything, and I know it doesn't matter. She came back with the ring and I don't know."

"Yes, you do."

"I should never have e-mailed Dr. Self. She fucked with my head. Then Shandy. Medications. Booze. It's like this monster moved inside of me," Marino says. "I don't know where it came from."

Disgusted, Lucy gets up, tosses the revolver on the couch. She walks past him toward the door.

"Listen to me," he says. "Shandy got me this stuff. I'm not the first guy she's handed it out to. Last one had a hard-on for three days. She thought it was funny."

"What stuff?" Even though she knows.

"Hormone gel. It's been making me crazy, like I want to fuck everyone, kill everyone. Nothing's ever enough for her. I never been with a woman who can't get enough."

Lucy leans against the door, crosses her arms. "Testosterone prescribed by a dirtbag proctologist in Charlotte."

Marino looks baffled. "How did you . . ." His face darkens. "Oh, I get it. You've been in here. That fucking figures."

"Who's the asshole on the chopper, Marino? Who's the jerk you almost killed in the Kick 'N Horse parking lot? The one who supposedly wants Aunt Kay dead or out of town?"

"I wish I knew."

"I believe you do."

"I'm telling the truth, I swear. Shandy must know him. She must be the one trying to run the Doc out of town. The jealous fucking bitch."

"Or maybe it's Dr. Self."

"Hell if I know."

"Maybe you should have checked out your jealous fucking bitch," Lucy says. "Maybe e-mailing Dr. Self to make Aunt Kay jealous was poking a snake with a stick. But I guess you were too busy having testosterone sex and raping my aunt."

"I didn't."

"What do you call it?"

"The worst thing I ever did," Marino says.

Lucy won't take her eyes off his. "How about that silver-dollar necklace you got on? Where'd you get it?"

"You know where."

"Shandy ever tell you about her potato-chip daddy's house getting burglarized not long before she moved here? Burglarized right after he died, matter of fact. Had a coin collection, some cash. All gone. Police suspect an inside job but couldn't prove it."

"The gold coin Bull found," Marino says. "She's never said nothing about a gold coin. The only coin I've seen is this silver dollar. How do you know Bull didn't lose it? He's the one who found that kid, and the coin's got the kid's print on it, right?"

"What if the coin was stolen from Shandy's dead daddy?" Lucy says. "What does that tell you?"

"She didn't kill the kid," Marino says with a hint of doubt. "I mean, she's never said nothing about having kids. If the coin has anything to do with her, she probably gave it to somebody. When she gave me mine, she laughed, said it was a dog tag to remind me I was one of her soldiers. Belonged to her. I didn't know she meant it literally."

"Getting her DNA's a fine idea," Lucy says.

Marino gets up and walks off. He comes back with the red panties. Puts them in a sandwich bag. Hands it to Lucy.

"Kind of unusual you don't know where she lives," Lucy says.

"I don't know nothing about her. That's the damn truth of it," Marino says.

"I'll tell you exactly where she lives. This same island. A cozy little place on the water. Looks romantic. Oh. I forgot to mention, when I checked it out, I happened to notice a bike was there. An old chopper with a cardboard license tag, under a cover in the carport. Nobody was home."

"I never saw it coming. I didn't use to be like this."

"He's not going to come within a million miles of Aunt Kay again. I've taken care of him, because I don't trust you to do it. His chopper's old. A piece of junk with ape-hanger handlebars. I don't think it's safe."

Marino won't look at her now. He says, "I didn't use to be like this."

She opens the front door.

"Why don't you just get the hell out of our lives," she says from his porch, in the rain. "I don't give a shit about you anymore."

The old brick building watches Benton with empty eyes, many of its windows broken out. The abandoned cigar company has no lights, its parking lot completely dark.

His laptop computer is balanced on his thighs as he logs in to the port's wireless network, hijacks it, and waits inside Lucy's black Subaru SUV, a car not generally associated with law enforcement. Periodically, he looks out the windshield. Rain slowly slides down the glass, as if the night is crying. He watches the chain-link fence around the empty shipyard across the street, watches the shapes of containers abandoned like wrecked train cars.

"No activity," he says.

Lucy's voice sounds in his earpiece. "Let's hold tight as long as you can."

The radio frequency is a secure one. Lucy's technological skills are beyond Benton, and he's not naïve. All he knows is she has ways of securing this and that, and scramblers, and she thinks it's great she can spy on others and they can't spy on her. He hopes she's right. About that and a lot of things, including her aunt. When he asked Lucy to send her plane, he said he didn't want Scarpetta to know.

"Why?" Lucy asked.

"Because I'll probably have to sit in a parked car all night, watching the damn port," he said.

It would make matters worse if she knew he was here, just a few miles from her house. She might insist on sitting here with him. To which Lucy offered that he was insane. There was no way Scarpetta would stake out the port with him. In Lucy's words, that's not her aunt's job. She's not a secret agent. She doesn't particularly like guns, even though she certainly knows how to use them, and she prefers to take care of the victims and leave it to Lucy and Benton to take care of everybody else. What Lucy really meant was that sitting out here at the port could be dangerous, and she didn't want Scarpetta doing it.

Funny that Lucy didn't mention Marino. That he could have helped.

Benton sits inside the dark Subaru. It smells new—smells like leather. He watches the rain, and looks past it across the street, and monitors the laptop to make sure the Sandman hasn't hijacked the port's wireless network and logged on. But where would he do it? Not from this parking lot. Not from the

street, because he wouldn't dare stop his
car in the middle of the street and just sit
there sending yet another infernal e-mail to
the infernal Dr. Self, who is probably back in
New York by now inside her Central Park
West penthouse apartment. It's galling. It's
as unfair as anything could possibly be.
Even if, in the end, the Sandman doesn't get
away with murder, Dr. Self most likely will,
and she's as much to blame for the murders
as the Sandman is, because she sat on information, didn't look into it, doesn't care.
Benton hates her. He wishes he didn't. But
he hates her more than he's ever hated anybody in his life.

Rain pummels the roof of the SUV, and
fog shrouds distant streetlights, and he can't
tell the horizon from the sky, the harbor from
the heavens. He can't tell anything from anything in this weather, until something moves.
He sits very still, and his heart kicks as a
dark figure slowly moves along the fence
across the street.

"I've got activity." He transmits to Lucy.
"Anybody on, because I'm not seeing it."

"Nobody's on." Her voice comes back into
his earpiece, and she's confirming that the

Sandman has not logged on to the port's wireless network. "What kind of activity?" she asks.

"At the fence. About three o'clock, not moving now. Holding at three o'clock."

"I'm ten minutes away. Not even."

"I'm getting out," Benton says, and he slowly opens his car door, and the interior light is out. Complete darkness, and the rain sounds louder.

He reaches under his jacket and slides out his gun, and he doesn't shut the car door all the way. He doesn't make a sound. He knows how to do this, has had to do it more times than he'd ever want to remember. He moves like a ghost, dark and silent, through puddles, through the rain. Every other step he stops, and he's sure the person across the street doesn't see him. *What is he doing?* Just standing there by the fence, not moving. Benton gets closer, and the figure doesn't move. Benton can barely see the shape through blowing veils of water, and he can't hear anything but the splashing of the rain.

"You okay?" Lucy's voice in his head.

He doesn't answer. He stops behind a telephone pole and smells creosote. The figure at the fence moves to the left, to the one o'clock position, and he starts to cross the street.

Lucy says, "You ten-four?"

Benton doesn't answer, and the figure is so close, he can see the dark shadow of a face, and the distinct outline of a hat, then arms and legs moving. Benton steps out and points the pistol at him.

"Don't move." He says it quietly in a tone that commands attention. "I've got a nine-mil pointed right at your head, so stand real still."

The man, and Benton feels sure it's a man, has turned into a statue. He doesn't make a sound.

"Step off the road but not toward me. Step to your left. Very slowly. Now drop to your knees and put your hands on top of your head." Then, to Lucy, he says, "I've got him. You can close in."

As if she's a stone's throw away.

"Hold on." Her voice is tense. "Just hold on. I'm coming."

He knows she's far away—too far away to help him if there's a problem.

The man has his hands on top of his head, and he's kneeling on the cracked, wet blacktop, and he says, "Please don't shoot."

"Who are you?" Benton says. "Tell me who you are."

"Don't shoot."

"Who are you?" Benton raises his voice above the sound of the rain. "What are you doing here? Tell me who you are."

"Don't shoot."

"Goddamn it. Tell me who you are. What are you doing at the port? Don't make me ask you again."

"I know who you are. I recognize who you are. My hands are on my head, so there is no need to shoot," the voice says as rain splashes, and Benton detects an accent. "I'm here to catch a killer, just like you. Am I right, Benton Wesley? Please put away your gun. It's Otto Poma. I'm here for the same reason as you. It's Captain Otto Poma. Please put the gun away."

Poe's Tavern, a few minutes' ride from Marino's fishing shack. He could use a beer or two.

The street is wet and shiny black, and the wind carries the smell of the rain and the scent of the sea and the marshes. He is soothed as he rides his Roadmaster through the dark, rainy night, knowing he shouldn't drink, but he doesn't know how to stop himself, and anyway, why does it matter? Ever since it happened, he has a sickness in his soul, a feeling of terror. The beast within has surfaced, the monster has shown himself, and what he's always feared is right in front of him.

Peter Rocco Marino isn't a decent person. As is true of almost every criminal he's caught, he has believed little in life is his fault, that he's inherently good, brave, and well-intentioned, when the truth is quite the reverse. He's selfish, sick, and bad. Bad, bad, bad. That's why his wife left him. That's why his career has gone to hell. That's why Lucy hates him. That's why he's ruined the best thing he ever had. His relationship with Scarpetta is dead. He killed it. Brutalized it. Betrayed her again and again because of something she can't help. She never wanted him, and why would she? She's never been attracted to him. How could she be? So he punished her.

He shifts into a higher gear as he gives his bike more gas. He rides much too fast, rain painful pinpricks against his bare skin, speeding to the strip, as he calls the hangouts of Sullivan's Island. Cars are parked wherever there is space. No bikes, only his, because of the weather. He's chilled, his hands stiff, and he feels unbearable pain and shame, and laced with it is a venomous anger. He unstraps his useless brain bucket of a helmet and hangs it from the handlebars and locks the bike's front fork. His rain gear swishes as he walks inside a restaurant of unpainted worn wood and ceiling fans, and framed posters of ravens and probably every Edgar Allan Poe movie ever made. The bar is crowded, and his heart bumps hard and flutters like a startled bird when he notices Shandy between two men, one of them wearing a do-rag—the man Marino almost shot the other night. She is talking to him, pressing her body against his arm.

Marino stands near the door, dripping rainwater on the scuffed floor, watching, wondering what to do as the wounds inside him swell, and his heart races, feels like horses galloping in his neck. Shandy and the man in the do-rag are drinking beer and shots of tequila and snacking on tortilla chips with chili con queso, the same thing she and Marino always order when they come here. Used to. In days past. Over and out. He didn't use his hormone gel this morning. Threw it away with reluctance as the vile creature inside his darkness whispered mocking things. He can't believe Shandy is so brazen as to come in here with that man, and the meaning is clear. She put him up to threatening the Doc. As bad as Shandy is, as bad as he is, as bad as they are together, Marino's worse.

What they tried to do to the Doc is nothing like what he did.

He approaches the bar without looking in their direction, pretends he doesn't see them, wondering why he didn't spot Shandy's BMW. She's probably parked on a side street, always worried about someone dinging one of the doors. He wonders where the man with the do-rag's chopper is and remembers what Lucy said about it. About it looking dangerous. She did something. She'll probably do something to Marino's bike next.

"Whatcha have, hon? Where you been, anyway?" The bartender looks maybe fifteen, the way all young people look to Marino these days.

He's so depressed and distracted, he can't remember her name, thinks it's Shelly but is afraid to say. Maybe it's Kelly. "Bud Lite." He leans close to her. "Don't look. But that guy over there with Shandy?"

"Yeah, they've been in here before."

"Since when?" Marino asks as she slides a draft beer his way and he slides back a five.

"Two for the price of one. So you got another one coming, hon. Oh, gosh. On and off for as long as I've worked here, hon. The past year, I guess. I don't like either one of 'em, and that's 'tween you and me. Don't ask his name. I don't know. He's not the only one she comes in here with. I think she's married."

"No shit."

"I hope you and her are taking a time out. For good, hon."

"I'm done with her," Marino says, drinking his beer. "It was nothing."

"Nothing but trouble, my guess," Shelly or Kelly says.

He feels Shandy's stare. She's stopped talking to the man in the do-rag, and now Marino has to wonder if she's been having sex with him all along. Marino wonders about the stolen coins and where she gets her money. Maybe her daddy didn't leave her anything and she felt she had to steal. Marino wonders about a lot of things and wishes he'd wondered all of them before. She sees him as he lifts his frosty mug, takes a swallow. Her glaring eyes look half crazy. He thinks about walking over to where she's sitting, but he can't bring himself to do it.

He knows they won't tell him anything. He's sure they'll laugh at him. Shandy nudges the man in the do-rag. He looks at Marino and smirks, must think it's real funny, sitting there feeling up Shandy and knowing that all along she's never been Marino's woman. Who the hell else does she sleep with?

Marino yanks off his silver-dollar necklace and drops it in his beer, and it makes a plopping sound and sinks to the bottom. He slides the mug across the bar, and it stops short of them, and he walks out, hoping he'll be followed. The rain has let up, and the pavement is steaming under streetlights, and he sits on the wet seat of his motorcycle and waits, hoping he'll be followed. He watches the front door of Poe's Tavern, waiting and hoping. Maybe he can start a fight. Maybe they can finish it. He wishes his heart would slow down and his chest would stop hurting. Maybe he'll have a heart attack. His heart ought to attack him, as bad as he is. He waits, looking at the door, looking at people on the other side of lighted windows, everybody happy except him. He waits and lights a cigarette and sits on his wet motorcycle in his wet rain gear, smoking and waiting.

He's such a nothing, he can't even make people angry anymore. He can't make anybody fight him. He's such a nothing, he's sitting out here in the rainy dark, smoking and looking at the door, wishing Shandy or the man in the do-rag or both of them would come out and make him feel he still has something worthwhile left in him. But the door doesn't open. They don't care. They aren't scared. They think Marino's a joke. He waits and smokes. He unlocks the front fork of his bike and starts the engine.

He opens the throttle, rubber squealing, and rides fast. He leaves his bike under his fishing shack, leaves the key in the ignition because he doesn't need his motorcycle anymore. Where he's going, he won't be riding motorcycles. He walks fast but not as fast as his heart is going, and in the dark he climbs the steps to his dock and he thinks about Shandy's making fun of his old, rickety dock, saying it's long and skinny and bent like a *stick bug*. He thought she was funny and clever with words when she said that the first time he brought her here, and they'd made love all night. Ten days ago. That's all it was. He has to consider that she set him up, that it's no coincidence she flirted with him the very night of the very day the dead little boy was found. Maybe she wanted to use Marino to get information. He let her. All because of a ring. The Doc got a ring, and Marino lost his mind. His big boots thud loudly on the pier, and its weathered wood shakes beneath the weight of him as no-see-ums swarm around him like something in a cartoon.

At the end of the pier he stops, breathing hard, eaten alive by what feels like a million invisible teeth as tears flood his eyes and his chest heaves rapidly, the way he's seen a man's chest heave right after he's gotten a lethal injection, right before his face turns dusky blue and he dies. It's so dark and overcast, the water and the sky are one, and below him bumpers thud, and water softly laps against pilings.

He cries out something that doesn't seem to come from him as he hurls his cell phone and earpiece as hard as he can. He hurls them so far, he can't hear them land.

Chapter 19

Y-12 National Security Complex. Scarpetta stops her rental car at a checkpoint in the midst of concrete blast barriers and fences topped with razor wire.

She rolls down her window for the second time in the past five minutes and hands over her identification badge. The guard steps inside his booth to make a phone call while another guard searches the trunk of the red Dodge Stratus that Scarpetta was unhappy to find waiting for her at Hertz when she landed in Knoxville an hour ago. She'd requested an SUV. She doesn't drive red. She doesn't even wear red. The guards seem more vigilant than they've been in the past, as if the car makes them wary, and they are already wary enough. Y-12 has the largest stockpile of enriched uranium in the country. Security is unyielding, and she never bothers the scientists here unless she has a special need that has reached, as she puts it, critical mass.

In the back of the car is the brown-paper-wrapped window from Lydia Webster's laundry room, and a small box containing the gold coin that has the unidentified murdered little boy's fingerprint on it. In the far reaches of the complex is a redbrick lab building that looks like all the others, but housed within it is the largest scanning electron microscope on the planet.

"You can pull over right there." A guard points. "And he'll be right here. You can follow him in."

She moves on and parks, waiting for the black Tahoe driven by Dr. Franz, the director of the materials science lab. She always follows him in. No matter how many times she's been here, she not only can't find her way, she wouldn't dare try. Getting lost inside a facility that manufactures nuclear weapons isn't an option. The Tahoe rolls up and turns around, and Dr. Franz's arm waves out his window, motioning for her to proceed. She follows him past nondescript buildings with nondescript names, then the terrain dramatically changes into woods and open fields, and finally the one-story labs known as Technology 2020. The setting is deceptively bucolic. Scarpetta and Dr. Franz get out of their vehicles. She removes the brown-paper-wrapped window from the back, where it was held safely in place with the seat belt.

"What fun things you bring us," he says. "Last time, it was a complete door."

"And we found a bootprint, didn't we—that nobody thought was there."

"There's always a there there." Dr. Franz's motto.

About her age and dressed in a polo shirt and baggy jeans, he isn't what comes to mind when one conjures up the image of a nuclear metallurgical engineer who finds it fascinating to spend his time magnifying a milled tool part or a spider spinneret, or pieces and parts of a space shuttle or a submarine. She follows him inside what would look like a normal lab, were it not for the massive metal chamber supported by four dampening pillars the diameter of trees. The

VisiTech Large Chamber Scanning Electron Microscope—LC-SEM—weighs ten tons, and required a forty-ton forklift to install it. Simply put, it's the biggest microscope on earth, and its original intended use wasn't forensic science but failure analysis of materials such as the metals used in weapons. But technology is technology, as far as Scarpetta is concerned, and by now Y-12 is used to her shameless begging.

Dr. Franz unwraps the window. He places it and the coin on top of a three-inch-thick steel turntable, and begins positioning an electron gun the size of a small missile, and the detectors lurking behind it, lowering them as close as he can to suspect areas of sand and glue and broken glass. With a remote axis control, he slides and tilts. Hums and clicks. Stopping at end stops—or switches—that prevent precious parts from crashing into samples or one another or going over the edge. He closes the door so he can vacuum down the chamber to ten-to-the-minus-six, he explains. Then he'll backfill the rest of it to ten-to-the-minus-two, he adds, and you couldn't open the door if you tried, he says. Showing her. And what they basically have are the conditions of outer space, he explains. No moisture, no oxygen, just the molecules of a crime.

The sound of vacuum pumps and an electrical smell, and the cleanroom begins to heat up. Scarpetta and Dr. Franz leave, shutting an outer door, back in the lab now, and a column of red, yellow, green, and white lights remind them that no human is inside the chamber, because that would be almost instant death. It would be like a space walk without a suit, Dr. Franz says.

He sits before a computer console with multiple large flat video screens, and says to Scarpetta, "Let's see. What magnification? We can go up to two hundred thousand X." They could, but he's being droll.

"And a grain of sand will look like a planet, and maybe we'll discover little people living on it," she says.

"Exactly what I was thinking." He clicks through layers of menus.

She sits next to him, and the big roughing vacuum pumps remind Scarpetta of an MRI scanner, and then the turbo pump kicks in and is followed by a silence that is broken at intervals when the air dryer vents in a huge, heartfelt sigh that sounds like a whale. They wait for a while, and when they get a green light, they begin to look at what the instrument sees as the electron beam strikes an area of window glass.

"Sand," Dr. Franz says. "And what the heck?"

Mingled with the different shapes and sizes of grains of sand that look like chips and shards of stone are spheres with craters that look like microscopic meteorites and moons. An elemental analysis confirms barium, antimony, and lead in addition to the silica of sand.

"Did this case involve a shooting?" Dr. Franz says.

"Not that I know of," Scarpetta answers, and she adds, "It's like Rome."

"Could be environmental or occupational particulate," he supposes. "The highest peak, of course, is silicon. Plus traces of potassium, sodium, calcium, and don't know why, but a trace of aluminum. I'm going to subtract out the background, which is glass." Now he's talking to himself.

"This is similar—very similar—to what they found in Rome." She says it again. "The sand in Drew Martin's eye sockets. Same thing, and I'm repeating myself because I almost can't believe it. Certainly, I don't understand it. What appears to be gunshot residue. And these darkly shaded areas here?" She points. "These strata?"

"The glue," he says. "I would venture to say that the sand isn't from there—from Rome or its surrounds. What about the sand in Drew Martin's case? Since there was no basalt, nothing to indicate volcanic activity, such as you'd expect in that area. So he brought his own sand with him to Rome?"

"I do know it's never been assumed the sand came from there. At least not the nearby beaches of Ostia. I don't know what he did. Maybe the sand is symbolic, has meaning. But I've seen magnified sand. I've seen magnified dirt. And I've never seen this."

Dr. Franz manipulates the contrast and magnification some more. He says, "And now it gets stranger."

"Maybe epithelial cells. Skin?" She scrutinizes what's on the screen. "No mention of that in Drew Martin's case. I need to call Captain Poma. It all depends on what was deemed important. Or noticed. And no matter how sophisticated the police lab, it's not going to have R&D-quality instruments. It's not going to have this." She means the LC-SEM.

"Well, I hope they didn't use mass spec

and digest the entire sample in acid. Or there won't be anything left to retest."

"They didn't," she says. "Solid-phase x-ray analysis. Raman. Any skin cells should still be in the sand over there, but as I said, I'm not aware of it. There's nothing on the report. No one mentioned it. I need to call Captain Poma."

"It's already seven p.m. over there."

"He's here. Well, in Charleston."

"Now I'm more confused. I thought you told me earlier he's Carabiniere. Not Charleston PD."

"He showed up rather unexpectedly. In Charleston last night. Don't ask me. I'm more confused than you are."

She's still stung. It wasn't a pleasant surprise when Benton appeared at her house last night and had Captain Poma with him. For an instant, she was speechless with surprise, and after coffee and soup, they left just as abruptly as they had arrived. She hasn't seen Benton since, and she's unhappy and hurt, and not sure what to say to him when she sees him—whenever that might be. Before she flew here this morning, she considered taking off her ring.

"DNA," Dr. Franz is saying. "So we don't

want to screw this up with bleach. But the signal would be better if we could get rid of skin debris and oils. If that's what this is."

It's like looking at constellations of stars. Do they resemble animals or even a dipper? Does the moon have a face? What is she really seeing? And she pushes Benton from her thoughts so she can concentrate.

"No bleach, and to be safe, we definitely should try DNA," she says. "And although epithelial cells are common in GSR, that's only when a suspect's hands are dabbed with double-sided sticky carbon tape. So what we're seeing, if it's skin, doesn't make sense unless the skin cells were transferred by the killer's hands. Or the cells were already on the windowpane. But what would be peculiar about the latter is the glass was cleaned, wiped off, and we're seeing fibers from that. Consistent with white cotton, and the dirty T-shirt I found in the laundry basket is white cotton, but what does that mean? Not much, really. The laundry room would be a landfill of microscopic fibers."

"At this magnification, everything becomes a landfill." Dr. Franz clicks the mouse, and manipulates and repositions, and the electron beam strikes an area of broken glass.

Beneath the polyurethane foam, which dried clear, cracks look like canyons. Blurred white shapes might be more epithelial cells, and lines and pores are a skin imprint from some part of the body hitting the glass. There are fragments of hair.

"Someone ran into it or punched it?" Dr. Franz says. "That's how it was broken, maybe?"

"Not with a hand or the bottom of a foot," Scarpetta points out. "No friction ridge detail." She can't stop thinking about Rome. She says, "Instead of the GSR having been transferred from someone's hands, maybe it was in the sand."

"You mean before he touched it?"

"Maybe. Drew Martin wasn't shot. We know that for a fact. Yet traces of barium, antimony, lead are in the sand found in her eye sockets." She goes through it again, trying to sort it out. "He put the sand in there and then glued her eyelids shut. So what appears to be GSR could have been on his hands and was transferred to the sand, because certainly he touched it. But what if the GSR is there because it was already there?"

"First time I've ever heard of anybody doing something like that. What kind of world do we live in?"

"I hope it will be the last time we hear of somebody doing something like that, and I've been asking the same question most of my life," she says.

"Nothing to say it wasn't already there," Dr. Franz says. "In other words, in this case"—he indicates the images on the screen—"is the sand on the glue or is the glue on the sand? And was the sand on his hands or were his hands in the sand? The glue in Rome. You said they didn't use mass spec. Did they analyze it with FTIR?"

"I don't think so. It's cyanoacrylate. That's as much as I know," she says. "If we can try FTIR and see what molecular fingerprint we get."

"Fine."

"On the glue from the window and also the glue on the coin?"

"Certainly."

Fourier Transform Infrared Spectroscopy is a simpler concept than the name implies. Chemical bonds of a molecule absorb light wavelengths and produce an annotated spectrum that is as unique as a fingerprint. At first glance, what they find is no surprise. The spectra are the same for the glue used on the window and the glue on the coin: Both are a cyanoacrylate but not one either Scarpetta or Dr. Franz recognizes. The molecular structure isn't the ethylcyanoacrylate of everyday superglue. It's something different.

"Two-octylcyanoacrylate," Dr. Franz says, and the day is running away from them. It's half past two. "I have no idea what that is except, obviously, an adhesive. And the glue in Rome? The molecular structure of that?"

"I'm not sure anyone asked," she says.

Historic buildings softly lit, and the white steeple of Saint Michael's pointing sharply at the moon.

From her splendid room, Dr. Self can't distinguish the harbor and the ocean from the sky because there are no stars. It has stopped raining, but not for long.

"I love the pineapple fountain, not that you can see it from here." She talks to the city lights beyond her window because it's more pleasant than talking to Shandy. "Way down there at the water, below the market. And little children, so many of them underprivileged, splash in it during the summer. I will say, if you have one of those expensive condos, the noise would rather much tarnish your mood. Listen, I hear a helicopter. Do you hear it?" Dr. Self says. "The Coast Guard. And those huge planes the Air Force has. They seem like flying battleships, overhead every other minute, but then you know about those big planes. Wasting more taxpayers' money for what?"

"I wouldn't have told you if I'd thought you'd stop paying me," Shandy says from her chair near a window, where she has no interest in the view.

"For more waste, more death," Dr. Self says. "We know what happens when these boys and girls come home. We know it all too well, don't we, Shandy?"

"Give me what we talked about and maybe I'll leave you alone. I just want what everybody else does. There's nothing wrong with that. I don't give a shit about Iraq," Shandy says. "I'm not interested in sitting here for hours talking about your politics. You want to hear real politics, come hang out at the bar." She laughs in a not-so-nice way. "Now, that's a thought, you at the bar. You on a big ole *hog.*" She rattles ice in her drink. "A Bush-whacker in Bush country."

"Or perhaps you're shrubs."

"Cause we hate A-rabs and queers and

don't believe in flushing little babies down the toilet or selling their pieces and parts to medical science. We love apple pie, buffalo wings, Budweiser, and Jesus. Oh, yeah— and fucking. Give me what I came here for and I'll shut up and go home."

"As a psychiatrist, I've always said *know yourself*. But not so with you, my dear. I recommend you do your best not to know yourself at all."

"One thing's for sure," Shandy says snidely. "Marino sure got over you when he got all over me."

"He did exactly what I predicted. He thought with the wrong head," Dr. Self says.

"You may be as rich and famous as Oprah, but all the power and glory in the world can't turn on a man like I do. I'm young and sweet and know what they want, and I can keep going as long as they can and make them go a lot longer than they ever dreamed they could," Shandy says.

"Are you talking about sex or the Kentucky Derby?"

"I'm talking about you being old," Shandy says.

"Perhaps I should have you on my show. Such fascinating questions I could ask. What men see in you. What magical musk you must exude to keep them following you like your own rounded ass. We'll display you just as you are right now, in black leather pants as tight as the peel on a plum, and a denim jacket with nothing under it. Of course, your boots. And the pièce de résistance—a do-rag that looks as if it's on fire. Shopworn, to put it kindly, but it belongs to your poor friend who was just in a terrible accident. My audience would find it touching that you wear his do-rag around your neck and say you won't take it off until he gets better. I'm reluctant to tell you that when a head is cracked open like an egg and the brain is exposed to the environment, which includes pavement, it's fairly serious."

Shandy drinks.

"I suspect by the end of an hour—and I don't see a series in this, just one small segment of one show—we'll conclude that you're alluring and pretty with a suppleness and come-hither-ness there's no denying," Dr. Self says. "Likely, you can get away with your base predilections for now, but when you get as old as you think I am, gravity will make you honest. What do I say on my show? Gravity will get you. Life is inclined toward falling. Not standing or flying, indeed, barely sitting. But to fall just as hard as Marino did. When I encouraged you to seek him out after he was foolish enough to seek me out first, the potential plunge seemed rather minimal. Just whatever trouble you could cause, my dear. And just how far could Marino fall, after all, when he's never risen above much of anything to begin with?"

"Give me the money," Shandy says. "Or maybe I should pay you so I don't have to listen to you anymore. No wonder your—"

"Don't say it," Dr. Self snaps at her but with a smile. "We've agreed on who we don't discuss and what names we must never say. It's for your own good. You mustn't forget that part. You have much more to worry about than I do."

"You should be glad," Shandy says. "Truth is? I did you a favor, because now you won't have to deal with me anymore, and you probably like me about as much as you like Dr. Phil."

"He's been on my show."

"Well, get me his autograph."

"I'm not glad," Dr. Self says. "I wish you'd never called with your disgusting news, which you told me so I'd pay you off and help you stay out of jail. You're a smart girl. It's not to my advantage to have you in jail."

"I wish I'd never called. I didn't know you'd stop the checks because . . ."

"Because what for? What would I be paying for? What I was paying for doesn't need my support anymore."

"I shouldn't have told you. But you always said I had to be honest."

"If I did, I've wasted my words," Dr. Self says.

"And you wonder why . . . ?"

"I wonder why you want to annoy me by breaking our rule. There are some subjects we don't bring up."

"I can bring up Marino. And I sure have." Shandy smirks. "Did I tell you? He still wants to fuck the Big Chief. That should bother you, since the two of you are about the same age."

Shandy plows through hors d'oeuvres as if they are Kentucky Fried Chicken.

"Maybe he'd fuck you if you asked him real nice. But he'd fuck her before even me, given the choice. Can you imagine?" she says.

If bourbon were air, there would be nothing left to breathe in the room. Shandy grabbed so much in the Club Level drawing room, she had to ask the concierge for a tray while Dr. Self made a cup of hot chamomile tea and looked the other way.

"She sure must be something special," Shandy says. "No wonder you hate her so much."

It was metaphorical. Everything Shandy represents causes Dr. Self to look the other way, and she'd looked the other way so long, she didn't see the collision coming.

"Here's what we're going to do," Dr. Self says. "You're to leave this very pretty little city and never come back. I know you'll miss your beach house, but since I'm only being polite to call it yours, I predict you'll get over it quickly. Before you pack up, you'll strip it to the bone. Do you remember the stories about Princess Diana's apartment? What happened to it after she died? Carpet and wallpaper torn out, even the lightbulbs removed, her car crushed into a cube."

"No one's touching my BMW or my bike."

"You're to start tonight. Scrub, paint, use bleach. Burn things—I don't care. But not a drop of blood or semen or spit, not an article of clothing, not a single hair or a fiber or a morsel of food. You should go back to Charlotte where you belong. Join the Church of the Sports Bar and worship the god of money. Your erstwhile father was wiser than I. He left you nothing, and certainly I have to leave you something. I have it in my pocket. And then I'm rid of you."

"You're the one who said I should live here in Charleston so I could be . . ."

"And now I have the privilege of changing my mind."

"You can't make me do a fucking thing. I don't give a shit who you are, and I'm tired of you telling me what to say. Or not to say."

"I am who I am and can make you do whatever I please," Dr. Self says. "Now's a good time to be pleasant to me. You asked my help, and here I am. I've just told you what to do so you can get away with your sins. You should say 'Thank you' and 'Whatever you wish is my command' and 'I'll never do anything to upset or inconvenience you again.'"

"Then give it to me. I'm out of bourbon and out of my mind. You make me feel crazier than a shithouse rat."

"Not so fast. We haven't finished our little fireside chat. What did you do with Marino?"

"He's gonzo."

"Gonzo. Then you are well-read, after all. Fiction truly is the best fact, and gonzo journalism is truer than truth. The exception is the war, since fiction got us into it. And that led to what you did, that atrociously horrible thing you did. Amazing to contemplate," Dr. Self says. "You're sitting here right this very minute and in that very chair because of George W. Bush. I'm sitting here because of him, too. Giving you an audience is beneath me, and this really will be the last time I rush to your rescue."

"I'm going to need another house. I can't just move somewhere and not have a house," Shandy says.

"I'm not sure I'll ever get over the irony. I ask you to have a little fun with Marino because I wanted a little fun with the Big Chief, as you call her. I didn't ask for the rest of it. I didn't know the rest of it. Well, now I do. Very few people best me, and no one I've met is worse than you. Before you pack up, clean up, and go wherever people like you go, one last question. Was there ever even a minute when it bothered you? We're not talking poor impulse control, my dear. Not when something so loathsome went on and on and on. How did you look at it day after day? I can't even look at a mistreated dog."

"Just give me what I came here for,

okay?" Shandy says. "Marino's gone." She refrains from saying *gonzo* this time. "I did what you told me . . ."

"I didn't tell you to do the thing that's forced me to come to Charleston when I have infinitely better things to do. And I'm not leaving until I know you are."

"You owe me."

"Shall we add up what you've cost me over the years?"

"Yeah, you owe me because I didn't want to keep it and you made me. I'm tired of living your past. Doing shit because it makes you feel better about your own shit. Anytime you could have taken it off my hands, but you didn't want it, either. That's what I finally had to figure out. You didn't want it, either. So why should I suffer?"

"Do you realize this lovely hotel is on Meeting Street, and if my suite faced north instead of east, we could almost see the morgue?"

"She's the one who's a Nazi, and I'm pretty sure he fucked her, not just wanted to, but I mean did it for real. He lied to me so he could spend the night at her house. So how does that make you feel? She must be something, all right. He's got such a thing for her, he'd bark like a dog or use a litterbox if she told him to. You owe me for having to put up with all that. It wouldn't have happened if you hadn't pulled one of your tricks and said, 'Shandy? There's this big, dumb cop, and how about doing me a favor?'"

"You did yourself a favor. You got information I didn't know you needed," Dr. Self says. "So I made a suggestion, but you certainly didn't take me up on it for my sake. It was an opportunity. You've always been so skilled at taking advantage of opportunities. In fact, I'd call you brilliant at it. Now, this wondrous revelation. Maybe it's my reward for all you've cost me. She cheated? Dr. Kay Scarpetta cheated? I wonder if her fiancé knows."

"And what about me? The asshole cheated on me. Nobody does that. All the guys I could have, and that fat fuck cheats on me?"

"Here's what you do about it." Dr. Self slips an envelope out of a pocket of her red silk robe. "You're going to tell Benton Wesley."

"You're a piece of work."

"It's only fair he should know. Your cashier's check. Before I forget." She holds up the envelope.

"So now you're going to play another little game with me."

"Oh, it's not a game, my dear. And I just

happen to have Benton's e-mail address," Dr. Self says. "My laptop's on the desk."

Scarpetta's conference room.

"Nothing unusual," Lucy says. "Looked the same."

"The same?" Benton asks. "The same as what?"

The four of them are gathered around a small table in what was a servants' quarters, quite possibly occupied by a young woman named Mary, a slave set free who wouldn't leave the family after the War. Scarpetta has gone to much trouble to know the history of her building. Right now she wishes she'd never bought it.

"I will ask again," says Captain Poma. "Has there been a difficulty with him? Perhaps a problem with his job?"

Lucy says, "When doesn't he have difficulty with any job?"

No one's heard from Marino. Scarpetta has called him half a dozen times, maybe more, and he hasn't called her back. On her way here, Lucy stopped by his fishing shack. His motorcycle was parked underneath it, but his truck was gone. He didn't answer the door. He wasn't there. She says she looked through a window, but Scarpetta knows better. She knows Lucy.

"Yes, I'd say so," Scarpetta says. "I'd say he's been unhappy. Misses Florida and is sorry he moved here, and probably doesn't like working for me. This isn't a good time to dwell on the trials and troubles of Marino."

She feels Benton's eyes on her. She makes notes on a legal pad and checks other notes she's already made. She checks preliminary lab reports even though she knows exactly what they say.

"He hasn't moved," Lucy says. "Or if he did, he left all his stuff behind."

"And you saw all this through a window?" Captain Poma says, and he's very curious about Lucy.

He's been watching her since everyone assembled in this room. He seems slightly amused by her, and her response is to ignore him. The way he looks at Scarpetta is the way he looked at her in Rome.

"Seems like a lot to see through a window," he says to Scarpetta, even though he's talking to Lucy.

"He hasn't gone into his e-mail, either," Lucy says. "He might suspect I'm monitoring it. Nothing between him and Dr. Self."

"In other words," Scarpetta says, "he's off the radar screen. Completely."

She gets up and pulls down window shades because it's dark. It's raining again, and has been since Lucy picked her up in Knoxville, when the mountains looked like they weren't there because it was so foggy. Lucy had to divert wherever she could, flying very slowly, following rivers and finding lower elevations. It was luck, or perhaps God's good grace, that they weren't stranded. Search efforts have been halted, except those conducted on the ground. Lydia Webster hasn't been found alive or dead. Her Cadillac hasn't been seen.

"Let's organize our thoughts," Scarpetta says, because she doesn't want to talk about Marino. She's afraid Benton will sense how she feels.

Guilty and angry, and increasingly afraid. It appears Marino has pulled a disappearing stunt, got in his truck and drove away without a warning, without any effort to repair the damage he's done. He's never been facile with words, and he's never made much effort to understand his complicated emotions, and this time what he needs to fix exceeds his capacity to cope. She's tried to dismiss him, to not give a damn, but he's like the persistent fog. Thoughts of him obscure what's around her, and one lie becomes another. She told Benton her bruises are from the hatchback of her SUV accidentally shutting on her wrists. She hasn't undressed in front of him.

"Let's try to make some sense of what we know," she says to everyone. "I would like to talk about the sand. Silica—or quartz, and limestone, and with high magnification, fragments of shells and coral, typical of sand in subtropical areas like this. And most interesting and perplexing of all, the components of gunshot residue. In fact, I'm just going to call it gunshot residue, because we can't figure out any other explanation for barium, antimony, and lead to be present in beach sand."

"If it's beach sand," Captain Poma says. "Maybe it isn't. Dr. Maroni says the patient who came to see him claimed to have just returned from Iraq. I would expect gunshot residue in many areas of Iraq. Maybe he brought sand back from Iraq because he became demented over there, and the sand is a reminder."

"We didn't find gypsum, and gypsum's common in desert sand," Scarpetta says.

"But it really depends on what area of Iraq, and I don't believe Dr. Maroni knows the answer to that."

"He didn't tell me exactly where," Benton says.

"What about his notes?" Lucy asks.

"It's not in them."

"Sand in different regions of Iraq has different compositions and morphology," Scarpetta says. "It all depends on how sediment was deposited, and although a high saline content doesn't prove the sand is from a beach, both samples we have—from Drew Martin's body and Lydia Webster's house—have a high saline content. In other words, salt."

"I think what's important is why sand is so important to him," Benton says. "What does sand say about him? He calls himself the Sandman. Symbolic of putting people to sleep? Maybe. A type of euthanasia that might be related to the glue, to some medical component? Maybe."

The glue. Two-octylcyanoacrylate. Surgical glue, primarily used by plastic surgeons and other medical practitioners to close small incisions or cuts, and in the military to treat friction blisters.

Scarpetta says, "The surgical glue might be what he had because of whatever it is he does and whoever he is. Not simply symbolism."

"Is there an advantage?" Captain Poma asks. "Surgical glue instead of everyday superglue? I'm not so familiar with what plastic surgeons do."

"Surgical glue is biodegradable," she says. "It's noncarcinogenic."

"A healthy glue." He smiles at her.

"You might say that."

"Does he believe he's relieving suffering? Maybe." Benton resumes, as if ignoring them.

"You said it's sexual," Captain Poma points out.

He's dressed in a dark blue suit and a black shirt and black tie and looks as if he stepped out of a Hollywood premiere or an ad for Armani. What he doesn't look like is someone who belongs in Charleston, and Benton doesn't seem to like him any more than he did in Rome.

"I didn't say it was only sexual," Benton replies. "I said there's a sexual component. I will also say he may not be aware of it, and we don't know if he assaults his victims sexually, only that he tortures them."

"And I'm not sure we know that for a fact."

"You saw the photographs he sent to Dr. Self. What do you call it when someone forces a woman to sit naked in a tub of cold water? And possibly dunks her?"

"I don't know what I'd call it, because I wasn't there when he did it," Captain Poma says.

"Had you been, I suppose we wouldn't be here, because the cases would be solved." Benton's eyes are like steel.

"I find it rather fantastic to think he's relieving their suffering," Captain Poma says to him. "Especially if your theory is correct and he tortures them. It would seem he causes suffering. Not relieves it."

"Obviously, he causes it. But we're not dealing with a rational mind, only an organized one. He's calculating and deliberate. He's intelligent and sophisticated. He understands breaking and entering and leaving no evidence. He possibly engages in cannibalism, and possibly believes he's one with his victims, makes them part of him. That he has a significant relationship with them and is merciful."

"The evidence." Lucy is far more interested in that. "Do you think he knows there's gunshot residue in the sand?"

"He might," Benton says.

"I seriously doubt it," Scarpetta says. "Very seriously. Even if the sand comes from some battlefield, so to speak, someplace meaningful to him, that doesn't mean he knows the elemental composition. Why would he?"

"Point well taken. I should say it's likely he brings the sand with him," Benton says. "It's very likely he brings his own tools and cutting instruments with him. Whatever he brings with him isn't purely utilitarian. His world is rife with symbols, and he's acting on impulses that make sense only when we understand these symbols."

"I really don't care about his symbols," Lucy says. "What I care most about is he e-mailed Dr. Self. That's the lynchpin, in my opinion. Why her? And why hijack the port's wireless network? Why climb over the fence—we'll assume. And use an abandoned container? Like he's cargo?"

Lucy was her usual self. She climbed the shipyard's fence earlier tonight and looked around because she had a hunch. Where could one hijack the port's network without being seen? She got her answer inside a banged-up container where she discovered a table and a chair and a wireless router.

Scarpetta has thought a lot about Bull, about the night he decided to smoke weed near abandoned containers and got cut up. Was the Sandman there? Did Bull get too close? She wants to ask him but hasn't seen him since they searched the alley together and found the gun and the gold coin.

"I left everything in place," Lucy says. "Hoping he wouldn't know I was there. But he might. I can't say. He's not sent any e-mails from the port tonight, but he hasn't for a while."

"What about the weather?" Scarpetta asks, mindful of the time.

"Should clear by midnight. I'm stopping by the lab, then heading to the airport," Lucy says.

She gets up. Then Captain Poma does. Benton stays in his chair, and Scarpetta meets his eyes, and her phobias return.

He says to her, "I need to talk to you a minute."

Lucy and Captain Poma leave, and Scarpetta shuts her door.

"Maybe I should start. You showed up in Charleston with no announcement," she says. "You didn't call. I hadn't heard from you in days, and then you walk in unexpectedly last night with him . . ."

"Kay," he says, reaching for his briefcase and placing it on his lap. "We shouldn't be doing this right now."

"You've barely talked to me."

"Can we . . . ?" he starts to say.

"No, we can't put this off until later. I can scarcely concentrate. I have to get to Rose's apartment building, have so much to do, too much to do, and everything's disintegrating and I know what you want to talk to me about. I can't tell you how I feel. Maybe I really can't. I don't blame you if you've made a decision. I certainly understand."

"I wasn't going to suggest we put this off until later," Benton says. "I was going to suggest we stop interrupting each other."

This confuses her. That light in his eyes. She's always believed what's in his eyes is only for her, and now she's afraid it isn't and never was. He's looking at her, and she looks away.

"What do you want to talk to me about, Benton?"

"Him."

"Otto?"

"I don't trust him. Waiting for the Sandman to show up to send more e-mails? On foot? In the rain? In the dark? Did he tell you he was coming here?"

"I suppose someone informed him of what's been happening. A connection of the Drew Martin case with Charleston, with Hilton Head."

"Maybe Dr. Maroni's been talking to him," Benton considers. "I don't know. He's like a phantom." He means the captain. "All over the damn place. I don't trust him."

"Maybe I'm the one you don't trust," she says. "Maybe you should say it and get it over with."

"I don't trust him at all."

"Then you shouldn't spend so much time with him."

"I haven't. I don't know what he does or where. Except I think he came to Charleston because of you. It's obvious what he wants. To be the hero. To impress you. To make love to you. I can't say I'd blame you. He's handsome and charming, I'll give him that."

"Why are you jealous of him? He's so small compared to you. I've done nothing to warrant it. You're the one who lives up there and leaves me alone. I understand your not wanting to be in this relationship anymore. Just tell me and get it over with." Scarpetta looks at her left hand, at the ring. "Should I take it off?" She starts to take it off.

"Don't," Benton says. "Please don't. I don't believe you want that."

"It's not a matter of what I want. It's what I deserve."

"I don't blame men for falling in love with you. Or wanting you in bed. Do you know what happened?"

"I should give you the ring."

"Let me tell you what happened," Benton says. "It's about time you knew. When your father died, he took some of you with him."

"Please don't be cruel."

"Because he adored you," Benton says. "How could he not? His beautiful little girl. His brilliant little girl. His good little girl."

"Don't hurt me like this."

"I'm telling you a truth, Kay. A very important one." The light in his eyes again.

She can't look at him.

"From that day forward, a part of you decided it was too dangerous to notice the way someone looks at you if he adores you or wants you sexually. If he adores you and dies? You believe you can't endure that again. Sexually wants you? Then how do you work with cops and DAs if you think they're imagining what's under your clothes and what they might do with it?"

"Stop it. I don't deserve this."

"You never did."

"Just because I choose not to notice doesn't mean I deserve what he did."

"Never in a million years."

"I don't want to live here anymore," she says. "I should give you back the ring. It was your great-grandmother's."

"And run away from home? Like you did when you had no one left but your mother and Dorothy? You ran away without going anywhere. Lost in learning and accomplishment. Running fast, too busy to feel. Now you want to run away like Marino just did."

"I should never have let him into the house."

"You have for twenty years. Why wouldn't you have that night? Especially when he was so drunk and dangerous to himself. One thing you are is kind."

"Rose told you. Maybe Lucy."

"An e-mail from Dr. Self, indirectly. You and Marino are having an affair. I found out the rest of it from Lucy. The truth. Look at me, Kay. I'm looking at you."

"Promise me you won't do anything to him. And make it worse, because then you'll be like him. This is why you've avoided me, didn't tell me you were coming to Charleston. Have scarcely called me."

"I haven't avoided you. Where do I start? There's so much."

"What else?"

"We had a patient," he says. "Dr. Self befriended her—I use the word loosely. She basically called this patient an imbecile, and from Dr. Self, it wasn't name-calling or a joke. It was a judgment, a diagnosis. It was worse because Dr. Self said it, and the patient was going home where she wasn't safe. She went to the first liquor store she could find. It appears she drank nearly a fifth of vodka, and she hanged herself. So I've been dealing with that. And so much else you don't know about. That's why I've been distant. Not talked to you much these past several days."

He snaps open the clasps of his briefcase and lifts out his laptop.

"I've been very reluctant to use the hospital's phones, their wireless Internet, been very careful on every front. Even the home front. One reason I wanted to get out of there. And you're about to ask me what's going on, and I'm about to tell you I don't know. But it's got to do with Paulo's electronic files. The ones Lucy got into because he left them surprisingly vulnerable to anyone who might want to get into them."

"Vulnerable if you knew where to look. Lucy isn't exactly anyone."

"She was also limited because she had to get into his computer remotely as opposed to having access to the actual machine." He turns on his laptop. He inserts a CD into the drive. "Come closer."

She moves her chair flush against his and looks at what he's doing. Momentarily, he has a document on his screen.

"The notes we've already looked at," she says, recognizing the electronic file that Lucy found.

"Not quite," Benton says. "With all due respect to Lucy, I have access to a few bright people, too. Not as bright as she is, but they'll do in a pinch. What you're looking at is a file that's been deleted and then recovered. It's not the file you saw, the one Lucy found after tricking the system admin password out of Josh. That particular file was several copies removed from this. Several later."

She taps the down arrow and reads. "It looks the same."

"The text isn't what's different. It's this." He touches the file name at the top of the screen. "Do you notice the same thing I did when Josh first showed me this?"

"Josh? I hope you trust him."

"I do, and for a good reason. He did the same thing Lucy did. Got into something he shouldn't, and birds of a feather. Thankfully, they're allies and he forgives her for duping him. In fact, he was impressed."

"File name's MSNote-ten-twenty-one-oh-six," Scarpetta says. "From which I assume MSNotes are the initials of the patient and the notes Dr. Maroni made. And ten-twenty-one-oh-six is October twenty-first, two thousand six."

"You just said it. You said MSNotes and the file name is MSNote." He touches the screen again. "A file that's been copied at least once, and inadvertently the name got changed. A typo. I don't know how, exactly. Or maybe it was deliberate, so he didn't keep copying over the same file. I do that sometimes if I don't want to lose an earlier draft. What's important is that when Josh recovered every deleted file pertaining to the patient of interest, we find the earliest draft was written two weeks ago."

"Maybe it's just the earliest draft he stored on that particular hard drive?" she suggests. "Or maybe he opened the file two weeks ago and saved it, which would have changed the date stamp? But I suppose that begs the question of why would he have looked at those notes before we even knew he had seen the Sandman as a patient? When Dr. Maroni left for Rome, we'd never heard of the Sandman."

"There's that," Benton says. "And there's the fabrication of the file. Because it is a fabrication. Yes, Paulo wrote those notes right before he left for Rome. He wrote them the very day Dr. Self was admitted to McLean on April twenty-seventh. In fact, several hours before she arrived at the hospital. And the reason I can say this with a reasonable degree of certainty is because Paulo may have emptied his trash, but even those deletions aren't gone. Josh recovered them."

He opens another file, this one a rough draft of the notes Scarpetta is familiar with, but in this version, the patient's initials aren't MS but WR.

"Then it would seem to me Dr. Self must have called Paulo. We assume that, anyway, because she couldn't just show up at the hospital. Whatever she told him over the phone inspired him to begin writing these notes," Scarpetta says.

"Another sign of fabrication," Benton says. "Using a patient's initials for a file name. We're not supposed to do that. Even if you do stray from protocol and good judgment, it doesn't make sense he changed his patient's initials. Why? To rename him. Why? To give him an alias? Paulo knows better than to do any such thing."

"Maybe the patient doesn't exist," Scarpetta says.

"Now you see what I'm leading up to," Benton says. "I don't think the Sandman was ever Paulo's patient."

Chapter 20

Ed the doorman is nowhere to be seen when Scarpetta walks into Rose's apartment building at almost ten. It's drizzling, and the dense fog is lifting, and clouds are rushing across the sky as the front moves out to sea.

She steps inside his office and looks around. There isn't much on the desk: a Rolodex, a notebook with *Residents* on the cover, a stack of unopened mail—Ed's and two other doormen's—pens, a stapler, personal items such as a plaque with a clock on it, an award from a fishing club, a cell phone, a ring of keys, a wallet. She checks the wallet. Ed's. He's on duty tonight with what appears to be three dollars to his name.

Scarpetta walks out, looks around, still no sign of Ed. She returns to his office and thumbs through the *Residents* book until she finds Gianni Lupano's apartment on the top floor. She takes the elevator, and listens outside his door. Music is playing, but not loudly, and she rings the bell, and she hears someone moving around. She rings the bell again and knocks. Footsteps and the door opens and Scarpetta is face-to-face with Ed.

"Where's Gianni Lupano?" She walks past Ed, into the surround sound of Santana.

Wind blows through a window open wide in the living room.

Ed's eyes are panicked as he talks frantically. "I didn't know what to do. This is so terrible. I didn't know what to do."

Scarpetta looks out the open window. She looks down and can't make out anything in the dark, just dense shrubbery and a sidewalk and the street beyond. She steps back and glances around a lavish apartment of marble and pastel-painted plaster, ornate molding, Italian leather furniture, and bold art. Shelves are filled with handsomely bound old books that some interior decorator probably bought by the yard, and an entire wall is occupied by an entertainment center too elaborate for a space this small.

"What's happened?" she says to Ed.

"I get this call maybe twenty minutes ago." Excitedly. "First he says, 'Hey, Ed, you start my car?' And I said, 'Yeah, why do you ask?' And I was nervous about it."

Scarpetta notices what must be half a dozen tennis rackets in cases propped against the wall behind the couch, a stack of tennis shoes still in their boxes. On a glass coffee table with an Italian glass base is a stack of tennis magazines. On the cover of the one on top is Drew Martin, about to pound a lob.

"Nervous about what?" she asks.

"That young lady, Lucy. She started his car because she wanted to look at something, and I was afraid he somehow found out. But that wasn't it, I don't guess, because then he said, 'Well, you've always taken such good care of it, I want you to have it.' And I said, 'What? What are you talking about, Mr. Lupano? I can't take your car. Why are you trying to give away that beautiful car?' And then he said, 'Ed, I'll write it down on a piece of paper so people know I gave you the car.' So I hurried up here as fast as I could and found the door unlocked, like he wanted to make it easy for anyone to get inside. And then I found the window open."

Walking toward it and pointing, as if Scarpetta can't see it for herself.

She calls nine-one-one as they run down the hallway. She tells the operator someone may have jumped out a window and gives the address. On the elevator, Ed continues to talk disjointedly about searching Lupano's apartment just to make sure, and he found the piece of paper but left it where it was, on the bed, and he kept calling out for him and he was about to call the police but Scarpetta showed up.

In the lobby, an old woman with a cane clicks her way across marble. Scarpetta and Ed rush past, and out of the building. They run through the dark around the corner, stopping directly below Lupano's open window. It is filled with light at the top of the building. Scarpetta shoves through a tall hedge, branches snapping and scratching, and finds what she feared. The body is nude and contorted, limbs and neck at unnatural angles against the brick side of the building, blood glistening in the dark. She presses two fingers against the carotid and feels no pulse. She repositions the body flat on its back and begins CPR. When she looks up, she wipes blood off her face, off her mouth. Sirens wail, blue and red lights flashing blocks away on East Bay. She gets to her feet and pushes back through the hedge.

"Come here," Scarpetta says to Ed. "Take a look and tell me if that's him."

"Is he . . . ?"

"Just look."

Ed pushes through the bushes, then crashes back through them.

"My God in heaven," he says. "Oh, no. Oh, Lord."

"Is it him?" she asks, and Ed nods yes. In the back of her mind, it bothers her that she just did mouth-to-mouth without protection. "Right before he called you about his Porsche, you were where?"

"Sitting at my desk." Ed is scared, his eyes darting. He's sweating and keeps wetting his lips and clearing his throat.

"Did anyone else come inside the building maybe about that time, or maybe a little before he called?"

Sirens wail as police cars and an ambulance stop on the street, red and blue light pulsing on Ed's face. "No," he says. Except for a few of the residents, he says, he saw no one.

Doors slam, radios chatter, diesel engines rumble. Police and EMTs get out of their vehicles.

Scarpetta says to Ed, "Your wallet's out on the desk. Maybe you'd taken your wallet out, then you got the call? Am I right?" Then she says to a plainclothes cop, "Over there." She points to the hedge. "Came from up there." She points to the lighted open window on the top floor.

"You're that new medical examiner." The detective looks at her, doesn't seem entirely sure.

"Yes."

"You pronounced him?"

"That's for the coroner to do."

The detective starts walking toward the bushes as she confirms that the man—Lupano, it seems—is dead. "I'll need a statement from you, so don't go anywhere," he calls back to her. Bushes crack and rustle as he pushes through them.

"I don't understand what all this is about. My wallet," Ed says.

Scarpetta moves out of the way so the

EMTs can get through with their stretcher and equipment. They head to the far corner of the building so they can maneuver behind the hedge instead of breaking through it.

"Your wallet's on your desk. Right there with the door open. Is that your habit?" she asks Ed.

"Can we talk inside?"

"Let's give our statements to the investigator over there," she says. "Then we'll talk inside."

She notices someone heading toward them on the sidewalk, a woman in a housecoat. The woman is familiar, then becomes Rose. Scarpetta intercepts her in a hurry.

"Don't come over here," Scarpetta says.

"As if there's anything I haven't seen." Rose looks up at the lighted open window. "That's where he lived, isn't it?"

"Who?"

"What would you expect after what happened?" she says, coughing, taking a deep breath. "What did he have left?"

"The question is timing."

"Maybe Lydia Webster. It's all over the news. You and I both know she's dead," Rose says.

Scarpetta just listens, wondering the obvious. Why would Rose assume Lupano might be affected by what has happened to Lydia Webster? Why would Rose know he's dead?

"He was quite full of himself when we met," Rose says, staring toward the dark shrubbery beneath the window.

"I wasn't aware you'd ever met him."

"Just once. I didn't know it was him until Ed said something. He was talking to Ed in the office when I saw him quite a long time ago. Rather rough-looking. I thought he was a maintenance person, had no idea he was Drew Martin's coach."

Scarpetta looks down the dark sidewalk, notices Ed is talking to the detective. Paramedics are loading the stretcher inside the ambulance as emergency lights flash and cops poke around with their flashlights.

"Drew Martin comes along only once in a lifetime. What was left for him?" Rose says. "Possibly nothing. People die when there's nothing left for them. I don't blame them."

"Come on. You shouldn't be out here in the damp air. I'll walk you back inside," Scarpetta says.

They round the corner of the building as Henry Hollings comes down the front steps. He doesn't look in their direction, walking fast and with purpose. Scarpetta watches him dissolve into the darkness along the seawall, toward East Bay Street.

"He got here before the police did?" Scarpetta says.

"He lives only five minutes from here," Rose says. "He has a quite a place on the Battery."

Scarpetta stares in the direction Hollings headed. On the harbor's horizon, two lighted ships look like yellow LEGOs. The weather is clearing. She can see a few stars. She doesn't mention to Rose that the Charleston County coroner just walked past a dead body and didn't bother to look. He didn't pronounce him. He didn't do anything. Inside the building, she gets on the elevator with Rose, who does a poor job disguising how much she doesn't want Scarpetta with her.

"I'm fine," Rose says, holding open the doors, the elevator not going anywhere. "It's back to bed for me. I'm sure people want to talk to you out there."

"It's not my case."

"People always want to talk to you."

"After I make sure you're safely inside your apartment."

"Since you're here, maybe he assumed you'd take care of it," Rose says as the doors shut and Scarpetta presses the button for her floor.

"You mean the coroner." Even though Scarpetta has yet to mention him or point out that he inexplicably left without doing his job.

Rose is too breathless to talk as they follow the corridor to her apartment. She stands before the door and pats Scarpetta's arm.

"Open the door and I'll leave," Scarpetta says.

Rose gets out her key. She doesn't want to open the door with Scarpetta standing there.

"Go on inside," Scarpetta says.

Rose doesn't. The more reluctant she is, the more stubborn Scarpetta gets. Finally, Scarpetta takes the key from her and lets them in. Two chairs have been pulled up to the window that overlooks the harbor, and between them on a table are two wineglasses and a bowl of nuts.

"The person you've been seeing," Scarpetta says, inviting herself inside. "Henry Hollings." She shuts the door and looks into Rose's eyes. "That's why he hurried out of here. The police called him about Lupano and he told you, then left so he could come back without anyone knowing he was already here."

She moves to the window as if she might see him on the street. She looks down. Rose's apartment isn't very far from Lupano's.

"He's a public figure and has to be careful," Rose says, sitting on the couch, exhausted and pale. "We're not having an affair. His wife is dead."

"That's the reason he's sneaking?" Scarpetta sits next to her. "I'm sorry. That doesn't make sense."

"To protect me." A deep breath.

"From what?"

"If it got out the coroner was seeing your secretary, somebody might make something of it. Certainly, it would end up in the news."

"I see."

"No, you don't," Rose says.

"Whatever makes you happy makes me happy."

"Until you visited him, he assumed you hated him. That hasn't helped," Rose says.

"Then it's my fault for not giving him a chance," Scarpetta says.

"I couldn't assure him otherwise, now, could I? You've assumed the worst about him, just as he's assumed the worst about you." Rose struggles to breathe, and she's getting worse. The cancer is destroying her right before Scarpetta's eyes.

"It will be different now," she says to Rose.

"He was so happy you came to see him," Rose says, reaching for a tissue, coughing. "That's why he was here tonight. To tell me all about it. He talked of nothing else. He likes you. He wants the two of you to work together. Not against each other." She coughs some more, the tissue speckled with blood.

"Does he know?"

"Of course. From the start." She gets a pained expression on her face. "In that little wineshop on East Bay. It was instant. When we met. Started talking about burgundy versus Bordeaux. As if I know. Out of the blue, he suggests we try a few. He didn't know where I work, so it wasn't that. He didn't learn I work for you until later."

"It doesn't matter what he knew. I don't care."

"He loves me. I tell him not to. He says if you love someone, that's the way it is. And who can say how long any of us will be here. That's how Henry explains life."

"Then I'm his friend," Scarpetta says.

She leaves Rose, and finds Hollings talking to the detective, the two of them near the shrubbery where the body was found. The ambulance and fire truck are gone, nothing parked nearby except an unmarked car and a cruiser.

"I thought you'd ducked out on us," the detective says as Scarpetta walks toward them.

She says to Hollings, "I was making sure Rose got safely back into her apartment."

"Let me bring you up to speed," Hollings says. "Body's en route to MUSC and will be autopsied in the morning. You're welcome to be present and participate in any way you see fit. Or not."

"Nothing so far to indicate it's anything other than a suicide," the detective says. "Except it bothers me he's got no clothes on. If he jumped, why did he take all his clothes off?"

"You might get your answer from toxicology," Scarpetta says. "The doorman says Lupano sounded intoxicated when he called him not long before he died. I think all of us have seen enough to know that when people decide to commit suicide, they can do a number of things that seem illogical, even suspicious. By chance did you find clothes inside that might be what he took off?"

"Got a few guys up there right now. Clothes on his bed. Jeans, shirt. Nothing unusual about that part of it. No sign anybody else was in there with him when he went out the window."

"Ed say anything about seeing a stranger come inside the building tonight?" Hollings asks her. "Or perhaps someone who showed up to visit Lupano? And I will tell you, Ed's a real stickler about letting people in."

"I didn't get that far with him," Scarpetta says. "I did ask him why he had his wallet out and in plain view on his desk. He says it was on his desk when he got the call from Lupano and rushed upstairs."

"He's ordered a pizza," the detective says. "That's what he told me, said he'd just gotten a hundred-dollar bill out of his wallet when Lupano called. Ed did order a pizza. From Mama Mia's. Was a no-show, and the guy left. I have trouble with the part about him having a hundred-dollar bill. Did he think some pizza deliverer was going to have change?"

"Maybe you should ask him who called first."

"That's a good idea," Hollings says. "Lupano's known for his flashy lifestyle, for having expensive tastes and carrying around a lot of cash. If he came back to the building during Ed's shift, Ed would know he's home. He places his pizza order, then realizes all he has is three dollars and a hundred-dollar bill."

Scarpetta's not going to tell them that yesterday Lucy was inside Lupano's car, looking at his GPS.

She says, "That might be what happened— Ed called Lupano for change. And by this point, Lupano's drunk, maybe drugged, irrational. Ed's concerned and goes upstairs."

"Or maybe he went upstairs to get change," Hollings says.

"Still implying Ed called him first."

The detective walks away and says, "I'm going to ask him."

"I have a feeling you and I have a few matters to clear up," Hollings says to her.

She looks at the sky and thinks about flying.

"How about we find a private place to talk," he says.

Across the street is White Point Gardens, several acres of Civil War monuments, live oak trees, and plugged cannon aimed at Fort Sumter. Scarpetta and Hollings sit on a bench.

"I know about Rose," she says.

"I figured you might."

"As long as you take care of her."

"Seems you do a fine job of that. I had some of your stew earlier tonight."

"Before you left and came back. So no one would realize you were already inside the building," Scarpetta says.

"So you don't mind," he says, as if he needs her approval.

"As long as you're good to her. Because if you're not, I'll do something about it."

"I believe that."

"I need to ask you about Lupano," she says. "I'm wondering if you might have contacted him after I left your funeral home earlier today."

"Might I ask why you'd wonder that?"

"Because you and I talked about him. I asked you why he might have attended Holly Webster's funeral. I think you know what would enter my mind."

"That I asked him about it."

"Did you?"

"Yes."

"It's in the news that Lydia Webster's missing and presumed dead," Scarpetta says.

"He knew her. Very well. We talked for a long time. He was very upset."

"Is Lydia why he's kept an apartment here?"

"Kay—I hope you don't mind if I call you that—I was well aware that Gianni attended Holly's funeral last summer. I couldn't let on that I was. It would have betrayed a confidence."

"I'm growing so weary of people and their confidences."

"I didn't try to obstruct you. If you found out on your own . . ."

"I'm tired of that, too. Finding out on my own."

"If you found out on your own he'd attended Holly's funeral, that was fair enough. So I made the guest books available to you. I understand your frustration. But you'd do the same thing. You wouldn't betray a confidence, now, would you?"

"Depends. That's what I've about decided."

Hollings looks at the lighted windows of the apartment building. He says, "Now I have to worry I'm somehow responsible."

"What confidence?" Scarpetta asks. "Since we're talking about them and you seem to have a secret."

"That he'd met Lydia several years ago when the *Family Circle* Cup used to be played in Hilton Head. They had an affair, an ongoing one, which is why he kept an apartment here. Then that day in July, their punishment. He and Lydia were in her bedroom, you can fill in the rest. No one checked on Holly, and she drowned. They broke up. Her husband left her. She fell apart, completely."

"And he started sleeping with Drew?"

"God knows how many people he's slept with, Kay."

"Why did he continue to keep this apartment? If his affair with Lydia was over."

"Maybe to have a clandestine place to be with Drew. Under the guise of training. Maybe because he said the bright foliage, the weather, the ironwork, and old stucco homes reminded him of Italy. He continued to be a friend to Lydia—this is according to him. Went to see her now and then."

"When was the last time? Did he say?"

"Several weeks ago. He left Charleston after Drew won the tournament here, then came back."

"Maybe I'm just not putting these pieces together very well." Scarpetta's cell phone rings. "Why would he come back? Why didn't he go with Drew to Rome? Or did he? She had the Italian Open and Wimbledon coming up. I've never understood why she suddenly decided to run off with friends instead of training for what could have been the greatest victories of her career. So she goes to Rome? Not to train for the Italian Open. But to party? I don't understand."

Scarpetta doesn't answer her phone. She doesn't even look to see who it is.

"He told me he went to New York right after she won the tournament here. Not even a month ago. Almost impossible to believe."

Her phone stops ringing.

And Hollings says, "Gianni didn't go with Drew, because she'd just fired him."

"She fired him?" Scarpetta says. "Is this known?"

"It's not."

"Why did she fire him?" Her phone rings again.

"Because Dr. Self told her to," Hollings says. "That's why he went to New York. To confront her. To try to get Drew to change her mind."

"I'd better see who this is." Scarpetta answers her phone.

"You need to drop by on your way to the airport," Lucy says.

"It's not exactly on the way."

"Another hour, hour and a half, and I think we can head out. The weather should be fine by then. You need to drop by the labs." Lucy tells Scarpetta where to meet her, and adds, "I don't want to talk about it on the phone."

Scarpetta says she will. To Henry Hollings, she says, "I'm assuming Drew didn't change her mind."

"She wouldn't talk to him."

"And Dr. Self?"

"He did talk to her. In her apartment. Mind you, this is what he told me. And she told him he was bad for Drew, an unhealthy influence, and she would continue to advise her to stay away from him. He got increasingly distraught and angry as he told me all this, and now I see I should have known better. I should have come over here immediately, sat down with him. Done something."

"What else happened with Dr. Self?" Scarpetta asks. "Drew went to New York, then left for Rome the next day. Barely twenty-four hours later, she disappeared and ended up murdered, quite possibly by the same person who murdered Lydia. And I've got to head to the airport. You're welcome to come. If we have any luck, we're going to need you anyway."

"The airport?" He gets up from the bench. "Now?"

"I don't want us to wait another day. Her body's in worse shape every hour."

They start walking.

"Now? And I'm supposed to go with you in the middle of the night, and I have no idea what you're talking about," Hollings puzzles.

"Heat signatures," she says. "Infrared. Any thermal variation is going to show up better in the dark, and maggots can raise the temperature of a decomposing body as much as twenty degrees centigrade. It's been more than two days, because when he left her house, I'm quite sure she wasn't alive. Not based on what we found. What else happened with Dr. Self? Did Lupano tell you anything else?"

They're almost to her car.

"He said he was extraordinarily insulted," Hollings says. "She said very degrading things to him and wouldn't tell him how to find Drew. After he left, he called Dr. Self again. This was supposed to be the greatest moment in his career, and she'd just wrecked it, and then the final blow. She told him Drew was staying with her, had been inside the apartment the entire time he was begging Dr. Self to undo what she'd done. I won't be going with you. You don't need me, and I, well, I want to check on Rose."

Scarpetta unlocks her car as she thinks about the timing. Drew spent the night in Dr. Self's penthouse, and the next day flew to Rome. The day after that, the seventeenth, she disappeared. The eighteenth, her body was found. The twenty-seventh, Scarpetta and Benton were in Rome investigating Drew's murder. That same day, Dr. Self was admitted to McLean, and Dr. Maroni fabricated a file that was supposed to be notes he took when he saw the Sandman as a patient—something Benton feels sure is a lie.

Scarpetta slides behind the wheel. Hollings is a gentleman and isn't going to leave until she starts the engine and locks her door.

She says to him, "When Lupano was inside Dr. Self's apartment, was anybody else there?"

"Drew was."

"I mean, anybody else Lupano knew about?"

He thinks for a moment, says, "There might have been." He hesitates. "He said he ate at her apartment. I think it was lunch. And it seems he made a comment about Dr. Self's chef."

Chapter 21

The Forensic Science Laboratories.

The main building is red brick and concrete with expansive windows that are UV-protected and mirror-finished, so the world outside sees a reflection of itself, and what's inside is protected from prying eyes and damaging rays from the sun. A smaller building isn't finished, and the landscaping is mud. Scarpetta sits in her car and watches a big bay door roll up and wishes hers wasn't so noisy. It adds to the unfortunate ambience of a morgue when the bay door screeches and scrapes like a drawbridge.

Inside, everything is new and pristine,

brightly lighted and painted in shades of white and gray. Some labs she passes are empty rooms, while others are fully equipped. But countertops are uncluttered, work spaces clean, and she looks forward to the day when it feels like someone's home. Of course, it's after hours, but even during them, at most twenty people show up for work, and about half of those followed Lucy from her former labs in Florida. Eventually, she will have the finest private forensic facility in the country, and Scarpetta realizes why that makes her more unsettled than glad. Professionally, Lucy is as successful as anyone can be, but her life is sadly flawed, and so is Scarpetta's. Neither of them adeptly manages to have or sustain personal relationships, and until now, Scarpetta has refused to see that they have this in common.

Despite Benton's kindness, all his talk with her really did was remind her why she needed it. What he said is depressingly true. She's run so fast for fifty years, she has little to show for it beyond an unusual ability to handle pain and stress that results in the very problem she faces. It's much easier to just do her job and live out her days with long, busy hours and long, empty spaces. In fact, if she's honest in examining herself, when Benton gave her the ring it didn't make her feel happy or safe. It symbolizes what scares the hell out of her, and that is whatever he gives, he might take back or realize he didn't mean it.

No wonder Marino finally snapped. Yes, he was drunk and hyped up on hormones, and probably Shandy and Dr. Self helped drive him to it. But if Scarpetta had taken a good look at him all these years, she probably could have saved him from himself and prevented a violation that was hers, too. She violated him, too, because she wasn't a truthful or trustworthy friend. She didn't tell him no until he finally went too far, and she should have told him no some twenty years ago.

I'm not in love with you, and I never will be, Marino. You're not my type, Marino. It doesn't mean I'm better than you, Marino. It just means I can't.

She scripts what she should have said and demands an answer to why she didn't. He might leave her. She might lose his constant presence, as annoying as it sometimes is. She might inflict on him that very thing she has done such a fine job evading: personal rejection and loss, and now she has both and so does he.

The elevator doors open on the second floor, and she follows an empty corridor to a series of labs that are individually sealed off by metal doors and airlocks. In an outer room, she puts on a white disposable gown, a hairnet and cap, shoe covers, gloves, and a face shield. She passes through another sealed area that decontaminates with ultraviolet light, and from there she enters a fully automated lab, where DNA is extracted and replicated—and where Lucy, also in white from head to toe, said to meet her for reasons unknown. She's sitting near a fume hood, talking to a scientist who is covered up, too, and therefore unrecognizable at a glance.

"Aunt Kay?" Lucy says. "I'm sure you remember Aaron. Our interim director."

The face behind the plastic shield smiles and suddenly is familiar, and the three of them sit.

"I know you're a forensic specialist," Scarpetta says. "But I didn't know you had a new position." She asks what happened to the previous lab director.

"Quit. Because of what Dr. Self put on the Internet," Lucy says, anger in her eyes.

"Quit?" Scarpetta asks, baffled. "Just like that?"

"Thinks I'm going to die and scuttled off to take another job. Anyway, he was a jerk, and I'd been wanting to get rid of him. Kind of ironic. The bitch did me a favor. But that's not what we're here to talk about. We've got lab results."

"Blood, saliva, epithelial cells," Aaron says. "Start with Lydia Webster's toothbrush and blood from the bathroom floor. We have a good idea about her DNA, mainly important so we can exclude her. Or identify her eventually." As if there's no doubt she's dead. "Then there's a different profile from the skin cells, the sand and glue recovered from the broken window in her laundry room. And the burglar-alarm keypad. The dirty T-shirt from the laundry basket. All three have her DNA, unsurprisingly. But also a profile from someone else."

"What about Madelisa Dooley's shorts?" Scarpetta asks. "The blood on them."

Aaron says, "Same donor as the three I just mentioned."

"The killer, we think," Lucy says. "Or whoever broke into her house."

"I think we should be careful saying that," Scarpetta says. "There have been other people in her house, including her husband."

"The DNA's not his, and we'll tell you why in a minute," Lucy says.

Aaron says, "What we did was your idea—going beyond the usual profile matching in CODIS and opening up the search by using the DNAPrint technology platform you and Lucy have discussed—an analysis that uses paternity and sibship indices to arrive at a probability of relatedness."

"First question," Lucy says. "Why would her ex-husband leave blood on Madelisa Dooley's shorts?"

"Okay," Scarpetta agrees. "That's a good point. And if the blood is the Sandman's— and to be clear, I'm going to call him that— then he must have injured himself somehow."

"We might know how," Lucy says. "And we're beginning to have an idea of who."

Aaron picks up a file folder. He takes out a report and hands it to Scarpetta.

"The unidentified little boy and the Sandman," Aaron says. "Knowing that each parent donates approximately half of his or her genetic material to their child, we can have an expectation that samples from a parent and a child are going to indicate their relationship. And in the case of the Sandman and the unidentified little boy, a very close family relationship is implicated."

Scarpetta looks at the test results. "I'll say the same thing I did when we got the fingerprint match," she says. "Are we sure there's no mistake? No contamination, for example?"

"We don't make mistakes. Not like that," Lucy says. "You get only one and you're done."

"The boy is the Sandman's son?" Scarpetta wants to make sure.

"I'd like references and investigation, but I certainly suspect it," Aaron replies. "At the very least, as I said, they're closely related."

"You mentioned his being injured," Lucy says. "The Sandman's blood on the shorts? It's also on the broken crown you found in Lydia Webster's bathtub."

"Maybe she bit him," Scarpetta says.

"A very good chance," Lucy says.

"Let's get back to the little boy," Scarpetta says. "If we're implying the Sandman killed his own son, I'm not sure what I think. The abuse went on for a while. The child was being looked after by someone when the Sandman was in Iraq, in Italy, if the information we have is correct."

"Well, I can tell you about the kid's mother," Lucy says. "We do have that reference, unless the DNA on Shandy Snook's underwear came from somebody else. Maybe makes more sense why she was so hot to tour the morgue and look at his body and find out whatever you might know about the case. Find out what Marino might know."

"Have you told the police?" Scarpetta says. "And should I ask how you got her underwear?"

Aaron smiles. Scarpetta realizes why the question could be construed as funny.

"Marino," Lucy says. "And it's sure as hell not his DNA. We have his profile for exclusionary purposes just like we have yours, mine. The police will need more to go on than underwear found on Marino's floor, but even if she didn't beat her son to death, she has to know who did."

"I have to wonder if Marino did," Scarpetta says.

"You saw the recording of him in the morgue with her," Lucy says. "Sure didn't appear to me he had any idea. Besides, he may be a lot of things, but he would never protect someone who did something like that to a kid."

There are other matches. All pointing to the Sandman and revealing another stunning fact: The two sources of DNA recovered from Drew Martin's fingernail scrapings are from the Sandman and someone else who is a close relative.

"Male," Aaron explains. "According to the Italian analysis, ninety-nine percent European. Maybe another son? Maybe the Sandman's brother? Maybe his father?"

"Three sources of DNA from one family?" Scarpetta is amazed.

"And another crime," Lucy says.

Aaron hands Scarpetta another report and says, "A match with a biological sample left in an unsolved crime no one has connected to Drew or to Lydia or to any other case."

"From a rape in 2004," Lucy says. "Apparently, the guy who broke into Lydia Webster's house and probably also murdered Drew Martin raped a tourist in Venice three years ago. The DNA profile from that evidence is in the Italian database, which we decided to search. Of course, there's no suspect to match, because to date they can't enter the profiles of known individuals. In other words, we don't have a name. Just semen."

"By all means, protect the privacy of rapists and murderers," Aaron says.

"News accounts are sketchy," Lucy says. "Twenty-year-old student in Venice, a summer program to study art. Out at a bar late at night, walked back to her hotel near the Bridge of Sighs and was attacked. So far, that's all we know about the case. But since it was worked by the Carabinieri, your friend the captain should have access to the information."

"Possibly the Sandman's first violent crime," Scarpetta says. "At least as a civilian. Assuming it's true this guy served in Iraq. Frequently, a first-time offender leaves evidence and then gets smart. This guy's smart, and his MO has evolved considerably. He's careful about evidence, is ritualistic and much more violent, and after he finishes, his victims aren't alive to tell. Thankfully, it didn't occur to him he might leave his DNA in surgical glue. Does Benton know about this?" she asks.

"Yes. And he knows we've got a problem

with your gold coin," Lucy says, just getting to that. "DNA on it and the chain are the Sandman's, too, and that places him behind your house the night you and Bull found the gun in the alley. I might ask what that implies about Bull. The necklace could have been his. I've asked that question before. We don't have Bull's DNA to tell us."

"That he's the Sandman?" Scarpetta doesn't believe it for a minute.

"I'm just saying we don't have his DNA," Lucy says.

"And the gun? The cartridges?" Scarpetta asks.

"Not the Sandman's DNA on any of those swabs," Lucy says. "But that doesn't necessarily mean anything. His DNA on a necklace is one thing. Leaving it on a gun is another, because he might have gotten the gun from someone else. He might have been careful leaving his DNA or his fingerprints on it because of the story he gave—that the asshole who threatened you is the one who dropped it, when we can't swear that guy ever came near your house. It's Bull's word, because it was unwitnessed."

"You're suggesting that Bull—assuming

he's the Sandman, which I don't believe—
might have deliberately, quote, lost the gun.
But didn't mean to lose his necklace," Scarpetta says. "That doesn't make a whole lot of
sense for two reasons. Why did his necklace
break? And secondly, if he didn't know it
broke and fell off until he found it, why would
he draw my attention to it? Why not just tuck
it into his pocket? I could add the third rather
strange thought of him having a gold coin
necklace to begin with that is reminiscent of
the silver-dollar necklace Shandy gave
Marino."

"It sure would be nice to get Bull's prints,"
Aaron says. "It sure would be nice to swab
him. It sure bothers me he seems to have
disappeared."

"That's it for now," Lucy says. "We're working on cloning him. Going to create a copy of
him in a petri dish so we know who it is," she
says drolly.

"I remember not so long ago waiting
weeks, months for DNA." Scarpetta rues
those days, painfully reminded of how many
people were brutalized and murdered because a violent offender couldn't be identified quickly.

"Ceiling's at three thousand feet, vis three miles," Lucy says to Scarpetta. "We're VFR. I'll meet you at the airport."

Inside Marino's office, his bowling trophies are silhouetted against the old plaster wall, and there is an emptiness in the air.

Benton shuts the door and doesn't turn on the light. He sits in the dark at Marino's desk and for the first time realizes that no matter what he's said, he's never taken Marino seriously or been particularly inclusive. If he's truthful about it, he's always thought of him as Scarpetta's sidekick—an ignorant, bigoted, crass cop who doesn't belong in the modern world, and as a result of that and any number of other factors, is unpleasant to be around and not entirely helpful. Benton has endured him. He's underestimated him in some departments and understood him perfectly fine in others, but failed to recognize the obvious. As he sits at Marino's little-used desk and stares out the window at the lights of Charleston, he wishes he had paid more attention to him, to everything. What he's needed to know is in his reach and has been.

The time in Venice is almost four o'clock in the morning. It's no wonder Paulo Maroni left McLean, and now has left Rome.

"Pronto," he answers his phone.

"Were you asleep?" Benton asks.

"If you cared, you wouldn't be calling. What's going on that you need to call me at this unseemly hour? Some development in the case, I hope?"

"Not a good one, necessarily."

"Then what?" Dr. Maroni's voice has an undercurrent of reluctance, or maybe it's resignation that Benton hears.

"The patient you had."

"I've told you about him."

"You've told me what you wanted to tell me, Paulo."

"What more could I help you with?" Dr. Maroni says. "In addition to what I've said, you've read my notes. I've been a friend and not asked you how that happened. I haven't blamed Lucy, for example."

"You might want to blame yourself. Do you think I haven't figured out that you wanted us to access your patient's file? You left it on the hospital network. You left file-sharing on, meaning anybody who could figure out where it was could get into it. For Lucy, yes, it would be no effort. For you, it was no mistake. You're too smart for that."

"And so you admit Lucy violated my confidential electronic files."

"You knew we'd want to see your patient notes. So you arranged it before you left for Rome. Which was earlier than you planned, by the way. Conveniently, right after you learned that Dr. Self was about to be a patient at McLean. You allowed it. She couldn't have been admitted at the Pavilion if you hadn't allowed it."

"She was manic."

"She was calculating. Does she know?"

"Know what?"

"Don't lie to me."

"It's interesting you would think I might," Dr. Maroni says.

"I've talked to Dr. Self's mother."

"Is she still such an unpleasant woman?"

"I imagine she hasn't changed," Benton says.

"People like her rarely do. Sometimes they burn out as they get older. In her case, she's likely worse. As Marilyn will be. As she already is."

"I imagine she hasn't changed much, either. Although her mother blames her daughter's personality disorder on you," Benton says.

"And we know that's not what happens. She doesn't have a Paulo-induced personality disorder. She came by it honestly."

"This isn't amusing."

"Certainly, it isn't."

"Where is he?" Benton asks. "And you know exactly who I mean."

"In those long-ago days, a person was still a minor at age sixteen. Do you understand?"

"And you were twenty-nine."

"Twenty-two. Gladys would insult me by making me that much older. I'm sure you can understand why I had to leave," Dr. Maroni says.

"Leave or flee? If you ask Dr. Self, it's the latter when she describes your hasty exit of several weeks ago. You were inappropriate with her and fled to Italy. Where is he, Paulo? Don't do this to yourself, and don't do it to anyone else."

"Would you believe it if I told you she was inappropriate with me?"

"It doesn't matter. That's not what I give a goddamn about. Where is he?" Benton says.

"Statutory rape is what they would have

called it, you know. Her mother threatened it and, indeed, wanted to believe Marilyn wouldn't have sex with a man she happened to meet during spring break. She was so beautiful and exciting, and offered her virginity, and I took it. I did love her. I did flee from her, this is true. I recognized she was toxic way back then. But I didn't return to Italy as I led her to believe. I returned to Harvard to finish medical school, and she never knew I was still in America."

"We've done DNA, Paulo. "

"After the baby was born, she still didn't know. I wrote her letters, you see. And had them mailed from Rome."

"Where is he, Paulo? Where's your son?"

"I begged her not to get an abortion, because it's against my religious beliefs. She said if she had the baby, I would have to raise it. And I did the best I could with what turned out to be a miscreant, a devil with a high IQ. He spent most of his life in Italy, and some of his time with her until he turned eighteen. He's the one who is twenty-nine. Perhaps Gladys was playing her usual games. . . . Well. In many ways, he belongs to neither of us and hates both of us. Marilyn more than me, although when I saw him last,

I feared for my safety. Perhaps my life. I thought he was going to attack me with a piece of ancient sculpture, but I managed to soothe him."

"This was when?"

"Right after I got here. He was in Rome."

"And he was in Rome when Drew Martin was murdered. At some point, he returned to Charleston. We know he was just in Hilton Head."

"What can I say, Benton? You know the answer. The tub in the photograph is the very tub in my apartment at Piazza Navona, but then you didn't know I live at Piazza Navona. If you had, you might have asked me questions about my apartment so near the construction site where Drew's body was found. You might have wondered about the coincidence of my driving a black Lancia over here. He probably killed her in my apartment and transported her in my car, not too far. Perhaps a block. In fact, I'm sure he must have. So maybe I would have been better off if he had struck me in the head with that ancient sculpted foot. What he's done is unthinkably reprehensible. But then, he's Marilyn's son."

"He's your son."

"He's an American citizen who didn't want to go to a university and continued his foolishness by joining the American Air Force to be a photographer in your fascist war, where he was wounded. His foot. I believe he did it to himself after he put his friend out of his misery by shooting him in the head. But regardless, if he were unbalanced before he went, he was cognitively and psychologically unrecognizable when he came back. I admit I wasn't the father I should have been. I sent him supplies. Tools, batteries, medical necessities. But I didn't go to see him after it was over. I didn't care. I admit it."

"Where is he?"

"After he joined the Air Force, I washed my hands of him. I admit it. He amounted to nothing. After all that—after my sacrificing so much to keep him on this earth when Marilyn would have had it otherwise—he amounted to nothing. Imagine the irony. I spared his life because the church says abortion is murder, and look what he does. He kills people. He killed them over there because it was his job, and now he kills them because it's madness."

"And his child?"

"Marilyn and her patterns. Once she has a

pattern, try to break it—told the mother to keep him just as I told Marilyn to keep our son. It probably was a mistake. Our son isn't fit to be a father, even if he loves his son very much."

"His little boy is dead," Benton says. "Starved and beaten to death and left in a marsh to be eaten by maggots, crabs."

"I'm sorry to hear it. I never met the child."

"Such compassion you have, Paulo. Where's your son?"

"I don't know."

"You must realize how serious this is. Do you want to go to prison?"

"The last time he was here, I walked him out, and on the street, where it was safe for me to say it, I told him I never wanted to see him again. There were tourists at the construction site where Drew's body was found. There were piles of flowers and stuffed animals. I saw all this as I told him to go away and never come back, and if he didn't honor my wishes, I would go to the police. Then I had my apartment very thoroughly cleaned. And I got rid of my car. And I called Otto to offer my assistance in the case, because it was important for me to know what the police knew."

"I don't believe you don't know where he is," Benton says. "I don't believe you don't know where he stays or lives or—more likely right now—hides. I don't want to go to your wife. I'm assuming she hasn't a clue."

"Please leave my wife out of this. She knows nothing."

"Maybe you know this," Benton says. "Your dead grandson's mother. Is she still with your son?"

"It is like what I had with Marilyn. We sometimes pay a lifelong price for enjoying sex with someone. These women? They get pregnant on purpose, you know. To keep you on a tether. It's a strange thing. They do it and then don't want the child because what they really wanted was you."

"That's not what I asked."

"I've never met her. Marilyn tells me her name is Shandy or Sandy and she's a whore. And stupid."

"Is your son still with her? That's what I asked."

"They had the child in common. But that's it. The same story again. The sins of the father. Events repeating themselves. Now I truly say, I wish my son had never been born."

"Marilyn knows Shandy, obviously," Benton says. "That brings me to Marino."

"I wouldn't know him or what he has to do with this."

Benton tells him. He informs Dr. Maroni of everything except what Marino did to Scarpetta.

"So you'd like me to analyze it for you," Dr. Maroni says. "Based on my knowing Marilyn, based on what you've just said. I would venture a guess that Marino made a very big mistake by sending an e-mail to Marilyn. It woke her up to possibilities, you see, that had nothing to do with why she was at McLean. Now she can get back at the one person she truly hates. Kay, of course. What better way than to torment the people she loves."

"She's the reason Marino met Shandy?"

"My guess. But not the entire reason for why Shandy got so interested in him. There is the boy. Marilyn doesn't know. Or she didn't. She would have told me. For someone to do such a thing would not appeal to Marilyn."

"She has about as much compassion as you do," Benton says. "She's here, by the way."

"You mean New York."

"I mean Charleston. I got an anonymous e-mail with information I won't discuss, and I traced the IP to the Charleston Place Hotel, recognized the Machine Access Code. Guess who's staying there."

"I warn you to be careful what you say to her. She doesn't know about Will."

"Will?"

"Will Rambo. When Marilyn started becoming famous, he changed his name from Willard Self to Will Rambo. He picked Rambo, a nice enough Swedish name. He's anything but a Rambo, and that's at least some of his problem. Will is quite small. He's a good-looking boy but small."

"When she got e-mails from the Sandman, she had no idea it was her son?" Benton says, and it is jarring to hear the Sandman referred to as a boy.

"She didn't. Not consciously. As far as I know, she still doesn't. Not consciously, but what can I say about what she knows in the deep caves of her mind? When she was admitted at McLean and told me about the e-mail, the image of Drew Martin . . ."

"She told you?"

"Of course."

Benton would like to leap through the phone and grab him around the throat. He should go to prison. He should go to hell.

"As I look back, it's tragically clear. Of course, I had a suspicion all along but never mentioned it to her. I mean, from the beginning when she called me with the referral, and Will knew she would do exactly that. He set her up for it. Of course, he had her e-mail address. Marilyn is very generous about an occasional e-mail to people she doesn't have time to see. He started sending these rather bizarre e-mails that he knew would captivate her, because he's just sick enough to understand her perfectly well. I'm sure he was amused when she referred him to me, and then when he called my office in Rome to make an appointment, that, of course, resulted in our having dinner, not a clinical interview. I was concerned about his mental health, but it never occurred to me he might kill someone. When I heard about the murdered tourist in Bari, I was in denial."

"He raped a woman in Venice, too. Another tourist."

"I'm not surprised. Let me guess. After the war began. Each time he was deployed, he got worse."

"Then the case notes weren't really from appointments you had with him. Obviously, he's your son and was never a patient."

"I fabricated the notes. I expected you to guess it."

"Why?"

"So you would do this. Find him yourself, because I could never turn him in. I needed you to ask the questions so I could answer them, and now I have."

"If we don't find him quickly, Paulo, he'll kill again. There must be something else you know. You must have a picture of him?"

"Not a recent one."

"E-mail what you've got."

"The Air Force should have what you need. Perhaps his fingerprints and his DNA. Certainly a photograph. It's better you get such things from them."

"And by the time I go through all those hoops," Benton says, "it will be too goddamn late."

"I won't be back, by the way," Dr. Maroni says. "I'm certain you won't try to bring me back but will leave me alone because I have shown you respect, so you will show me some. It would be futile, anyway, Benton," he says. "I have many friends over here."

Chapter 22

Lucy goes through her pre-start checklist.

Landing lights, Nr switch, OEI limit, fuel valves. She checks the flight instrument indications, sets the altimeter, turns on the battery. She starts the first engine as Scarpetta emerges from the FBO and walks across the tarmac. She slides open the helicopter's back door and sets her crime scene case and camera equipment on the floor, then opens the left front door. She steps up on the skid and climbs in.

Engine one locked into ground idle position, and Lucy fires up engine number two. The whining turbines and *thud-thudding* get louder, and Scarpetta buckles herself into the four-point harness. A linesman trots across the ramp, waving his marshaling wands, and Scarpetta puts her headset on.

"Oh, for God's sake," Lucy says into her mike. "Hey!" As if the linesman can hear her. "We don't need your help. He's gonna be standing there for a while." Lucy opens her door, tries to motion for him to go away. "We're not a plane." She says more things he can't hear. "Don't need your help to take off. Go on now."

"You're awfully tense." Scarpetta's voice sounds inside Lucy's headset. "Any word from other people searching?"

"Nothing. No helicopter up in the Hilton Head area yet, still too foggy there. No luck with the search on the ground. FLIR on standby." Lucy turns on the overhead power switch. "Need about eight minutes for it to cool. Then we're on the go. Hey!" As if the linesman has on a headset, too, and can hear her. "Go away. We're busy. Damn, he must be new."

The linesman stands there, orange wands down by his side, not marshaling anyone anywhere. The tower tells Lucy, "You got the heavy C-seventeen on downwind. . . ."

The military cargo jet is a cluster of big, bright lights and barely seems to move, hangs hugely in the air, and Lucy radios back that she's got it. The "heavy C-seventeen" and its "heavy wingtip vortices" aren't a factor because she wants to head toward downtown, toward the Cooper River bridge. Referring to the Arthur Ravenel Jr. Bridge. Toward whatever she wants. Doing figure-eights if she wants. Barely above the water or the ground if she wants. Because she isn't a plane. That's not how she explains it in radio talk, but it's what she means.

"I called Turkington," she then says to Scarpetta. "Filled him in. Benton called me, so I guess you talked to him and he's filled you in. He should be here any minute, or he'd better be. I'm not sitting here forever. We know who the asshole is."

"We just don't know where he is," Scarpetta says. "I'm supposing we still have no idea where Marino is."

"If you want my opinion, we should be looking for the Sandman, not a dead body."

"Within the hour, everybody will be looking for him. Benton's notified the police, local and military. Somebody's got to look for her. That's my job, and I intend to do it. Did you bring the cargo net? And have we heard any word from Marino? Anything at all?"

"I've got the cargo net."

"The usual gear's in baggage?"

Benton is walking toward the linesman. He hands him a tip and Lucy laughs.

"I suppose every time I ask about Marino, you're going to ignore me," Scarpetta says, as Benton gets closer.

"Maybe you should be truthful with the person you're supposed to marry." Lucy watches Benton.

"What makes you think I haven't been?"

"I wouldn't know what you've done."

"Benton and I have talked," Scarpetta says, looking at her. "And you're right, I should be truthful, and I have been."

Benton slides open the back door and gets in.

"Good. Because the more you trust some-one, the more criminal it is to lie. Including by omission," Lucy says.

The clunking and scraping sounds of Benton putting his headset on.

"I have to get over this," Lucy says.

"I should be the one who needs to get over it," Scarpetta says. "And we can't talk about this now."

"What is it we can't talk about?" Benton's voice in Lucy's headset.

"Aunt Kay's clairvoyance," Lucy says. "She's convinced she knows where the body is. Just in case, I've got the gear and chemicals for decon. And body bags in case we need to slingload. Sorry to be insensitive, but no way a decomp's riding in the back."

"Not clairvoyance. Just gunshot residue," Scarpetta says. "And he wants her found."

"Then he should have made it easier," Lucy says, rolling up the throttles.

"What about the gunshot residue?" Benton asks.

"I have an idea. If you ask what sand around here might have traces of GSR."

"Jesus," Lucy says. "The guy's going to blow away. Look at him. Just standing there with his cones like a zombie referee for the NFL. I'm glad you tipped him, Benton. Poor guy. He's trying."

"Yes, a tip. Only not a hundred-dollar bill," Scarpetta says, as Lucy waits to get on the radio.

Air traffic is almost impossible, because flights have been delayed all day, and now the tower can't keep up.

"When I went off to UVA, what did you

do?" Lucy says to Scarpetta. "Sent me a hundred bucks now and then. *For no reason.* That's what you always wrote at the bottom of the check."

"It wasn't much to do." Scarpetta's voice goes straight into Lucy's head.

"Books. Food. Clothes. Computer stuff."

Voice-activated mikes, and people talk truncated talk.

"Well," Scarpetta's voice says. "It was nice of you. That's a lot of money for someone like Ed."

"Maybe I was bribing him." Lucy leans closer to Scarpetta to check the FLIR's video display. "Ready and waiting," she says. "We're out of here as soon as you'll let us," as if the tower can hear her. "We're a damn helicopter, for Christ's sake. Don't need the damn runway. And we don't need to be vectored. Makes me crazy."

"Maybe you're too cranky to fly." Benton's voice.

Lucy contacts the tower again, and at last is cleared to take off to the southeast.

"Going while the going's good," she says, and the helicopter gets light on its skids. The linesman is marshaling as if he's going to park them. "Maybe he should get a job as a traffic cone," Lucy says, lifting her three-and-a-quarter-ton bird into a hover. "We'll follow the Ashley River a little ways, then turn east, track along the shoreline toward Folly Beach." She hovers at the intersection of two taxiways. "Un-stowing the FLIR."

She switches from *standby* to *on,* and the display turns dark gray, splotched with bright white hot spots. The C-17 does a thunderous touch-and-go, long plumes of white fire blasting from its engines. Lighted window of the FBO. The lights on the runways. All of it surreal in infrared.

"Low and slow, and we'll scan everything along the way. Work in a grid?" Lucy says.

Scarpetta lifts the System Control Unit out of its holder, slaves the FLIR with the searchlight, which she keeps turned off. Gray images and ones hot-white displayed on the video monitor near her left knee. They fly past the port, its different-colored containers stacked like building blocks. Cranes are perched like monster praying mantises against the night, and the helicopter moves slowly over the lights of the city, as if it's floating over them. Ahead, the harbor is black. No stars are out, the moon a charcoal smudge behind thick clouds that are flat on top like anvils.

"Where exactly are we headed?" Benton says.

Scarpetta works the FLIR's trim button, moving images in and out of the screen. Lucy slows to eighty knots and holds the altitude down at five hundred feet.

Scarpetta says, "Imagine what you'd find if you did a microscopic analysis of sand from Iwo Jima. As long as the sand's been protected all these years."

"Away from the surf," Lucy says. "In dunes, for example."

"Iwo Jima?" Benton's voice says, ironically. "We flying to Japan?"

Off Scarpetta's door are the mansions of the Battery, their lights bright white smudges in infrared. She thinks about Henry Hollings. She thinks about Rose. The lights of habitation become spaced farther apart as they near the shore of James Island and slowly fly past it.

Scarpetta says, "A beach environment that's remained untouched since the Civil War. In a place like that, if the sand's protected, you're likely to find gunshot residue. I believe this is it." To Lucy, "Almost below us."

She slows to a near hover and descends

to three hundred feet at the northernmost tip of Morris Island. It is uninhabited and accessible only by helicopter or boat unless the tide is so low one can wade from Folly Beach. She looks down at eight hundred acres of desolate conservation land that during the Civil War was the scene of heavy fighting.

"Probably not much different than it was a hundred and forty years ago," Scarpetta says, as Lucy descends another hundred feet.

"Where the African-American regiment, the Fifty-fourth Massachusetts, was slaughtered," Benton's voice says. "That movie they made about it, what was it called?"

"You look out your side," Lucy says to him. "Tell us if you see anything, and we'll swoop around with the searchlight."

"It was called *Glory*," Scarpetta says. "Not the searchlight quite yet," she adds. "It will interfere with infrared."

The video screen displays mottled gray terrain and a rippled area that is the water, and the water glints like molten lead, flowing to the shore, breaking on the sand in scalloped white ruffles.

"I'm not seeing anything down here but the dark shapes of dunes and that damn lighthouse following us everywhere," Scarpetta says.

"Be nice if they'd restore the beacon so people like us don't crash into it," Lucy says.

"Now I feel better." Benton's voice.

"I'm going to start working a grid. Sixty knots, two hundred feet, every inch of what's down there," Lucy says.

They don't have to work the grid very long.

"Can you hover over there?" Scarpetta points to what Lucy just saw, too. "Whatever we just went past. That beach area. No, no, back that way. Distinct thermal variation."

Lucy noses the helicopter around, and the lighthouse beyond her door is stubby and striped in infrared, and surrounded by the heaving, leaden water in the outer reaches of the harbor. Beyond, a cruise ship looks like a ghost ship with white-fire windows and a long plume from its stack.

"There. Twenty degrees to the left of that dune," Scarpetta says. "I think I see something."

"I see it," Lucy says.

The image is white-hot on the screen in the midst of murky, mottled grayness. Lucy looks down, trying to position herself just right. She circles, going lower.

Scarpetta zooms in, and the shimmering white shape becomes a body, unearthly bright—as bright as a star—at the edge of a tidal creek that glints like glass.

Lucy stows the FLIR and flips a switch to turn on a searchlight as bright as ten million candles. Sea oats flatten to the ground and sand swirls as they land.

A black necktie fluttering in the wind of slowing blades.

Scarpetta looks out her window, and some distance away, in the sand, a face flashes in the strobes, white teeth grimacing in a bloated mass that isn't recognizable as a woman or a man. Were it not for the suit and tie, she wouldn't have a clue.

"What the hell?" Benton's voice in her headset.

"It's not her," Lucy says, flipping off switches. "Don't know about you, but I got my gun. This isn't right."

She turns off the battery, and doors open and they get out, the sand soft beneath their feet. The stench is overwhelming until they get upwind of it. Flashlights probe, pistols are ready. The helicopter is a hulking dragonfly on the dark beach, and the only sound is the surf. Scarpetta moves her light along and stops at wide drag marks that lead to a dune and stop short of it.

"Someone had a boat," Lucy says, and she is moving toward the dunes. "A flat-bottom boat."

The dunes are fringed with sea oats and other vegetation, and roll on for as far as they can see, untouched by the tides. Scarpetta thinks of the battles fought here and imagines lives lost for a cause that couldn't have been more different from the South's. The evils of slavery. Black Yankee soldiers wiped out. She imagines she hears their moans and whispers in the tall grass, and she tells Lucy and Benton not to stray too far. She watches their lights cut through the dark terrain like long, bright blades.

"Over here," Lucy says from the darkness between two dunes. "Mother of God," she says. "Aunt Kay, can you grab face masks!"

Scarpetta opens the baggage compartment and lifts out a large crime scene case. She sets it on the sand and rummages for face masks, and it must be bad for Lucy to ask.

"We can't get both of them out of here." Benton's voice in the wind.

"What the fuck are we dealing with?" Lucy's voice. "Did you hear that?"

Something flapping. Far off in the dunes.

Scarpetta moves toward their lights, and the stench gets worse. It seems to make the air thick, and her eyes burn and she hands out masks and puts one on because it's hard to breathe. She joins Lucy and Benton in a hollow between dunes, at an elevation that makes it impossible to see it from the beach. The woman is nude and badly swollen from days of exposure. She's infested by maggots, her face eaten away, her lips and eyes gone, her teeth exposed. In the beam of Scarpetta's light is an implanted titanium post from where a crown used to be. Her scalp is slipping from her skull, her long hair splayed in the sand.

Lucy wades through sea oats and grass, moving toward the flapping sound that Scarpetta hears, too, and she's not sure what to do, and she thinks of gunshot residue and the sand and this place and wonders what it means to him. He has created his own battlefield. How much more littered with the dead would it have become, had she not found this spot, because of barium, antimony, and lead that he probably knew nothing of, and she feels him. His sick spirit seems to hang in the air.

"A tent," Lucy calls out, and they go to her.

She's behind another dune, and the dunes are dark waves rolling away from them and tangled with undergrowth and grass, and he has made a tented home, or someone has. Aluminum poles and a tarp, and through a slit in a flap that snaps in the wind is a hovel. A mattress is neatly made with a blanket, and there's a lantern. Lucy opens an ice chest with her foot. Inside is several inches of water, and she dips her finger in and announces the water is tepid.

"I've got one spine board in the back of the helicopter," she says. "How do you want to do this, Aunt Kay?"

"We need to photograph everything. Take measurements. Get the police out here right away." There is so much to do. "Any way we can sling two at a time?"

"Not with one spine board."

"I want to look through everything in here," Benton says.

"Then we'll get them in body bags, and you'll have to take one at a time," Scarpetta says. "Where do you want to set them down,

Lucy? Someplace discreet, can't be the FBO where your industrious lineman is probably out there marshaling in mosquitoes. I'll call Hollings and see who can meet you."

Then they are silent, listening to the flapping of the makeshift tent, listening to the swishing of grass, to the soft, wet crashing of waves. The lighthouse looks like a huge, dark pawn in a game of chess, surrounded by the spreading plain of the riffled black sea. He's out there somewhere, and it seems surreal. A soldier of misfortune, but Scarpetta feels no pity.

"Let's do this," she says, and she tries her phone.

Of course, she gets no signal.

"You'll have to try him from the air," she says to Lucy. "Maybe try Rose."

"Rose?"

"Just try her."

"What for?"

"I suspect she'll know where to find him."

They get the spine board and body bags, and plasticized sheets, and what biohazard gear they have. They start with her. She is limp because rigor mortis came and went, as if it gave up stubbornly protesting her death, and insects and tiny creatures like crabs took over. They have eaten away what was soft and wounded. Her face is swollen, her body bloated from bacterial gas, her skin marbled greenish-black in the branched pattern of her blood vessels. Her left buttock and the back of her thigh have been raggedly cut away, but there are no other obvious injuries or signs of mutilation, and no indication of what killed her. They lift her and place her in the middle of the sheet, and then into a pouch that Scarpetta zips closed.

They turn their attention to the man on the beach who has a translucent plastic retainer on his gritted teeth, and around his right wrist, a rubber band. His suit and tie are black, and his white shirt is stained dark from purge fluid and blood. Multiple narrow slits in his jacket front and back suggest he was repeatedly stabbed. Maggots infest his wounds and are a moving mass under his clothes, and in a pants pocket is a wallet that belonged to Lucious Meddick. It doesn't appear the killer was interested in credit cards or cash.

More photographs and notes, and Scarpetta and Benton strap the woman's pouched body—Lydia Webster's pouched body—onto a spine board while Lucy retrieves a fifty-foot line and a net from the back of the helicopter. She hands Scarpetta her gun.

"You need this more than I do," she says.

She climbs in and starts the engines, and blades thud, beating back air. Lights flash, and the helicopter gently lifts and noses around. Very slowly, it rises until the line gets taut and the net with its morbid burden is suspended off the sand. She flies away, and the load gently swings like a pendulum. Scarpetta and Benton head back to the tent. Were it daylight, the flies would be a droning storm and the air would be dense and loud with decay.

"He sleeps here," Benton says. "Not necessarily all the time."

He nudges the pillow with his foot. Beneath it is the border of the blanket, and beneath that, the mattress. A freezer bag keeps a box of matches dry, but paperback books don't seem to mean much to him. They are soggy, the pages stuck together—the sort of obscure family sagas and romance novels one might buy in a drugstore when one wants something to read and doesn't care what it is. Beneath this small makeshift tent is a pit where he built fires, using charcoal and the rusting grate from a grill set on top of rocks. There are root-beer cans. Scarpetta and Benton don't touch anything, and they return to the beach where the helicopter landed, the marks from its skids deep in the sand. More stars are out, and the stench taints the air but no longer crowds it.

"At first you thought it was him. I saw it on your face," Benton says.

"I hope he's all right and didn't do anything foolish," she says. "One more thing that will be Dr. Self's fault. Ruining what all of us had. Driving us apart. You haven't told me how you found out." Getting angry. Old anger and new.

"That's her favorite thing to do. Drive people apart."

They wait near the water, upwind from Lucious Meddick's black cocoon, and the stench is carried away from them. Scarpetta smells the sea and hears it breathe and softly break on the shore. The horizon is black, and the lighthouse warns of nothing anymore.

A little later, in the distance, winking lights, and Lucy flies in and they turn away from blasting sand as she lands. With Lucious Meddick's body securely in the cargo net, they lift off and carry him to Charleston. Police lights throb on the ramp, and Henry Hollings and Captain Poma stand near a windowless van.

Scarpetta walks in front of them. Anger moves her feet. She scarcely listens to a four-way conversation. Lucious Meddick's hearse being found parked behind Hollings's Funeral Home, keys in the ignition. How did it get there unless the killer left it—or maybe Shandy did. Bonnie and Clyde—that's what Captain Poma calls them, then he brings up Bull. Where is he, what else might he know? Bull's mother says he's not home, been saying that for days. No sign of Marino, and now the police are looking for him, and Hollings says the bodies will go straight to the morgue. Not Scarpetta's morgue. The MUSC morgue, where two forensic pathologists are waiting after working most of the night on Gianni Lupano.

"We could use you, if you're willing," Hollings says to Scarpetta. "You found them, so you should work it through. Only if you don't mind."

"The police need to get to Morris Island now and secure the scene," she says.

"Zodiac boats are on the way. I'd better give you directions to the morgue."

"I've been there before. You said the head of security is your friend," she says. "At the Charleston Place Hotel. What's the name?"

As they walk.

Hollings then says, "Suicide. Blunt-force trauma from a jump or a fall. Nothing to indicate foul play. Unless you can charge someone with driving a person to it. In that event, Dr. Self should be indicted. My friend at the hotel, her name's Ruth."

Lights are bright inside the FBO, and Scarpetta steps into the ladies' room to wash her hands and her face and the inside of her nose. She sprays a lot of air freshener and moves into its mist, and she brushes her teeth. When she walks back out, Benton is standing there, waiting.

"You should go home," he says.

"As if I can sleep."

He follows her as the windowless van drives away, and Hollings is talking to Captain Poma and Lucy.

"I've got something I need to do," Scarpetta says.

Benton lets her go. She walks to her SUV alone.

. . .

Ruth's office is near the kitchen, where the hotel has had numerous problems with theft.

Shrimp, in particular. Cunning petty criminals disguised as chefs. She tells one amusing story after another, and Scarpetta listens attentively because she wants something, and the only way to get it is to play audience to the head of security's performance. Ruth is an elegant older woman who is a captain in the National Guard but looks more like a demure librarian. In fact, she looks a little bit like Rose.

"But then, you didn't come see me to hear all this," Ruth says from behind a desk that is likely hotel surplus. "You want to know about Drew Martin, and probably Mr. Hollings told you the last time she stayed here, she was never in her room."

"He did tell me that," Scarpetta says, looking for a gun under Ruth's paisley jacket. "Was her coach ever here?"

"He ate in the Grill now and then. Always ordered the same thing, caviar and Dom Pérignon. Never heard of her being in there, but I don't imagine a professional tennis player would be eating rich food or drinking champagne the night before a big match.

Like I said, she obviously had another life somewhere and was never here."

"You have another famous guest staying here," Scarpetta says.

"We have famous guests all the time."

"I could go door to door and knock."

"You can't get on the secure floor without a key. There's forty suites here. That's a lot of doors."

"My first question is whether she's still here, and I assume the reservation isn't in her name. Otherwise, I'd just call her," Scarpetta says.

"We have twenty-four-hour-a-day room service. I'm so close to the kitchen, I can hear the carts rattle by," Ruth says.

"She's already up, then. Good. I wouldn't want to wake her." Rage. It starts behind Scarpetta's eyes and begins working its way down.

"Coffee every morning at five. She doesn't tip much. We're not crazy about her," Ruth says.

Dr. Self is in a corner suite on the hotel's eighth floor, and Scarpetta inserts a magnetic card into the elevator and minutes later is at her door. She senses her looking through the peephole.

Dr. Self opens the door as she says, "I see someone was indiscreet. Hello, Kay."

She wears a flashy red silk robe, loosely tied around her waist, and black silk slippers.

"What a pleasant surprise. I wonder who told you. Please." She moves to one side to let Scarpetta in. "As fate would have it, they brought two cups and an extra pot of coffee. Let me guess how you found me here at all, and I don't just mean this wonderful room." Dr. Self sits on the couch and tucks her legs under her. "Shandy. It would appear my giving her what she wanted resulted in a loss of leverage. That would be her petty point of view, at any rate."

"I haven't met Shandy," Scarpetta says from a wing chair near a window that offers a view of the lighted old city.

"Not in person, you mean," Dr. Self says. "But I believe you've seen her. Her exclusive tour of your morgue. I think back to those unhappy days in court, Kay, and I wonder how different all of it would have been if the world had known what you're really like. That you give tours of the morgue and turn dead bodies into spectacles. Especially the little boy you skinned and filleted. Why did you cut out his eyes? How many injuries did you need to document before you decided what killed him? His eyes? Really, Kay."

"Who told you about the tour?"

"Shandy bragged about it. Imagine what a jury would say. Imagine what the jury in Florida would have said had they known what you're like."

"Their verdict didn't hurt you," Scarpetta says. "Nothing's hurt you the way you manage to hurt everybody else. Did you hear that your friend Karen killed herself barely twenty-four hours after she left McLean?"

Dr. Self's face brightens. "Then her sad story will have a fitting finale." She meets Scarpetta's eyes. "Don't think I'm going to pretend. What would upset me is if you told me Karen was back in rehab drying out again. The mass of men living lives of quiet desperation. Thoreau. Benton's part of the world. Yet you live down here. How will you manage when you're married?" Her eyes find the ring on Scarpetta's left hand. "Or will you go through with it? The two of you aren't much into commitments. Well, Benton is. A different sort of commitment he deals with up there. His little experiment was a treat, and I can't wait to talk about it. "

"The lawsuit in Florida didn't take anything from you except money that probably was covered by your malpractice insurance. Those premiums must be high. They should be extremely high. I'm surprised any insurance company would carry you," Scarpetta says.

"I've got to pack. Back to New York, back on the air. Did I tell you? A brand-new show all about the criminal mind. Don't worry. I don't want you on it."

"Shandy probably killed her son," Scarpetta says. "I wonder what you're going to do about that."

"I avoided her for as long as I could," Dr. Self says. "A situation very similar to yours, Kay. I knew of her. Why do people entangle themselves in the tentacles of someone poisonous? I hear myself talk, and every comment suggests a show. It's exhausting and exhilarating when you realize you'll never run out of shows. Marino should have known better. He's so simple. Have you heard from him?"

"You were the beginning and the end," Scarpetta says. "Why couldn't you leave him alone?"

"He contacted me first."

"His e-mails were those of a desperately unhappy and frightened man. You were his psychiatrist."

"Years ago. I can scarcely remember it."

"You of all people know how he is, and you used him. You took advantage of him because you wanted to hurt me. I don't care if you hurt me, but you shouldn't have hurt him. Then you tried again, didn't you? To hurt Benton. Why? To pay me back for Florida? I would think you'd have better things to do."

"I'm at an impasse, Kay. You see, Shandy should get what she deserves, and by now Paulo has had a long talk with Benton, am I wrong? Paulo called me, of course. I've managed to make sense of some of the pieces."

"To tell you the Sandman is your son," Scarpetta says. "Paulo called to tell you that."

"One piece is Shandy. The other piece is Will. Yet another piece is Little Will, as I've always called him. My Will came home from a war and walked right into another war far more brutal. Do you think that didn't push him beyond the beyond? Not that he was normal. I'd be the first to say that not even my tools would do any good under his hood. This was about a year, year and a half ago, Kay. He walked in and found his son half starved to death and bruised and battered."

"Shandy," Scarpetta says.

"Will didn't do that. No matter what he's done now, he didn't do that. My son would never harm a child. Shandy probably thought it was very sporting of her to brutalize that boy just because she could. He was a nuisance. She'll tell you that. A colicky baby and a crabby little boy."

"And she managed to hide him from the world?"

"Will was in the Air Force. She kept their son in Charlotte until her father died. Then I encouraged her to move here, and that's when she started abusing him. Severely."

"And she disposed of his body in a marsh? At night?"

"Her? Not hardly. I can't imagine it. She doesn't even own a boat."

"How do you know a boat was used? I don't recall that's been established as a fact."

"She wouldn't know the creeks and tides, would never go out on the water at night. Little secret—she can't swim. Obviously, she would have needed help."

"Does your son have a boat and know the creeks and tides?"

"He used to have one, and loved to take his little boy on 'adventures.' Picnics. Campouts on deserted islands. Discovering never-never lands, just the two of them. So imaginative and wistful—very much a child himself, really. It seems last time he was deployed, Shandy sold a lot of his things. Quite considerate, that one. I'm not sure he even owns a car anymore. But he's resourceful. Light and quick on his feet. And covert, no doubt. Probably learned that over there." She means Iraq.

Scarpetta is thinking about Marino's flat-bottom bass boat with its powerful outboard engine, bow-mount trolling motor, and oars. His boat that he hasn't used for months and doesn't even seem to think about anymore. Especially of late. Especially since Shandy. She would have known about the boat, even if they'd never gone out in it. She could have told Will. Maybe he borrowed it. Marino's boat should be searched. Scarpetta wonders how she will explain all this to the police.

"Who was going to take care of Shandy's little inconvenience? The body. What was my son supposed to do?" Dr. Self says. "That's

what happens, isn't it? One person's sin becomes your own. Will loved his son. But
when Daddy goes marching off to war,
Mommy has to be both parents. And in this
instance, Mommy is a monster. I've always
despised her."

"You've supported her," Scarpetta says.
"Handsomely, I might add."

"Let's see. And you know that? Let me
guess. Lucy's invaded her privacy, probably
knows what she has—or had—in the bank. I
wouldn't have ever known my grandson was
dead if Shandy hadn't called. I suppose the
day the body was found. She wanted money.
More of it. And my advice."

"Is she and what she told you why you're
here?"

"Shandy has managed to do a rather brilliant job of blackmailing me all these years.
People don't know I have a son. They certainly don't know I have a grandson. If these
facts were known, I would be viewed as neg-
lectful. A terrible mother. A terrible grand-
mother. All those things my own dear mother
says about me. By the time I became famous, it was too late to go back and undo
my very deliberate distancing. I had no
choice but to continue it. Mommie Dearest—

and I mean Shandy—kept my secret in exchange for cashier's checks."

"Now you intend to keep her secret safe in exchange for what?" Scarpetta says. "She abused her son to death and you want her to get away with it, in exchange for what?"

"I suppose a jury would love to see the tape of her in your morgue, in your refrigerator, looking at her dead son. The murderer inside your morgue. Imagine what a story that would make. I would say, conservatively say, that you would have no career left, Kay. With that in mind, you should thank me. My privacy ensures your own."

"Then you don't know me."

"I forgot to offer you coffee. Service for two." Smiling.

"I won't forget what you've done," Scarpetta says, getting up. "What you've done to Lucy, to Benton, to me. I'm not sure what you've done to Marino."

"I'm not sure what he did to you. But I know enough. How is Benton handling it?" She refills her coffee. "Such a peculiar thing to consider." She leans back into the pillows. "You know, when Marino was seeing me in Florida, his lust couldn't have been more palpable unless he'd grabbed me and torn off my clothes. It's oedipal and pitiful. He wants to fuck his mother—the most powerful person in his life, and forever and a day he will chase the end of his oedipal rainbow. There was no pot of gold when he had sex with you. At last, at last. Hooray for him. It's a wonder he hasn't killed himself."

Scarpetta stands at the door, staring at her.

"What kind of lover is he?" Dr. Self asks. "Benton, I can see. But Marino? I haven't heard from him in days. Have the two of you worked it out? And what does Benton say?"

"If Marino didn't tell you, who did?" Scarpetta quietly asks.

"Marino? Oh, no. Certainly not. He didn't tell me about your little foray. He was followed to your house from, oh, dear, what's the name of that bar? Another one of Shandy's thugs, this one commissioned to give you serious thoughts about relocating."

"You did that, then. I thought so."

"To help you."

"Do you have so little in your life that you have to overpower people this way?"

"Charleston isn't a good place for you, Kay."

Scarpetta shuts the door behind her. She leaves the hotel. She walks over pavers, past a plashing fountain of horses, and into the hotel's garage. The sun isn't up yet, and she should call the police, but all she can think about is the misery one person can cause. The first shadow of panic touches her in a deserted level of concrete and cars, and she thinks about one remark Dr. Self made.

It's a wonder he hasn't killed himself.

Was she making a prediction or voicing an expectation or hinting at yet another horrible secret she knows? Now Scarpetta can think of nothing else, and she can't call Lucy or Benton. Truth be told, they have no sympathy for him, may even hope he ate his gun or drove off a bridge, and she imagines Marino dead inside his truck at the bottom of the Cooper River.

She decides to call Rose, and gets out her cell phone, but there's no signal, and she walks to her SUV, vaguely aware of the white Cadillac parked next to it. She notices an oval sticker on the rear bumper, recognizes the HH for Hilton Head, and she feels what is happening before she is aware of it, and turns around as Captain Poma rushes out from behind a concrete support. She feels the air move behind her, or she hears it, and he lunges, and she wheels around as something clamps her arm. For a suspended second, a face is level with hers, a young man with a buzz cut and a red, swollen ear, staring wildly. He slams against her car, and a knife clatters at her feet, and the captain is punching him and yelling.

Chapter 23

Bull holds his cap in his hands.

He is stooped over a little in the front seat, mindful that his head touches the roof if he sits up straight, which is what he's prone to do. Bull carries himself with pride, even when he's just been bailed out of the city jail for a crime he didn't commit.

"I sure thank you for the ride, Dr. Kay," he says as she parks in front of her house. "I'm sorry for your trouble."

"Don't keep saying that, Bull. I'm really angry right now."

"I know you are, and I sure am sorry, because it's nothing you did." He opens his door and is slow working his way out of the front seat. "I tried to get the dirt off my boots, but it looks like I messed up your mat a little, so I think I best clean it or at least shake it out."

"Don't apologize anymore, Bull. You've been doing it since we left the jail, and I'm so mad I could spit, and next time something like this happens, if you don't call me right away, I'm going to be mad at you, too."

"Wouldn't want that." He shakes out his mat, and she's getting the idea that he's about as stubborn as she is.

It's been a long day full of painful images, and near misses, and bad smells, and then Rose called. Scarpetta was up to her elbows in Lydia Webster's decomposed body when Hollings appeared at the autopsy table and said he had news and she needed to hear it. How Rose found out, exactly, isn't exactly clear, but a neighbor of hers who knows a neighbor of a neighbor of Scarpetta's—someone she's never met—heard a rumor that the neighbor Scarpetta has met—Mrs. Grimball—had Bull arrested for trespassing and attempted burglary.

He was hiding behind a pittosporum to the left of Scarpetta's front porch, and Mrs. Grimball happened to spot him while she was looking out her upstairs window. It was night-time. Scarpetta can't blame a neighbor for be-ing alarmed by such a sight, unless that neighbor happens to be Mrs. Grimball. Call-ing nine-one-one to report a prowler wasn't enough. She had to embellish her story and claim Bull was hiding on her property, not Scarpetta's, and the long and short of it is Bull—who has been arrested before—went to jail, where he's been since the middle of the week, and where he'd likely still be, had Rose not interrupted an autopsy. After Scar-petta was attacked in a parking garage.

Now Will Rambo is in the city jail, not Bull.

Now Bull's mother can relax. Doesn't have to keep lying, saying he's out picking oysters or just out, period, because the last thing she wants is for him to get fired again.

"I've thawed stew," Scarpetta says, un-locking her front door. "There's plenty of it, and I can only imagine what you've had to eat for the last few days."

Bull follows her into the foyer, and the um-brella stand grabs her attention and she stops and feels terrible. She reaches inside it and pulls out Marino's motorcycle key and the magazine from his Glock, then the Glock itself from a drawer. She feels so unsettled, she almost feels sick. Bull doesn't say anything, but she can feel him wondering about what she just retrieved from the umbrella stand, why those items were in there. It's a moment before she can talk. She locks the key, the magazine, and the pistol inside the same metal box where she keeps the bottle of chloroform.

She warms up stew and homemade bread, and sets a place at the table, and pours a big glass of peach-flavored iced tea and drops in a sprig of fresh mint. She tells Bull to sit down and eat, that she'll be on the upstairs porch with Benton, and to call up to them if Bull needs anything. She reminds him that too much water and the daphne will curl up and die in a week and the pansies need deadheading, and he sits down and she serves him.

"I don't know why I'm telling you this," she says. "You know more about gardening than I do."

"Never hurts to be reminded," he says.

"Maybe we should plant some daphne by the front gate so Mrs. Grimball can smell its lovely fragrance. Maybe it will make her more pleasant."

"She was trying to do the right thing." Bull opens his napkin and tucks it into his shirt. "I shouldn't have been hiding, but after that man on the chopper showed up in the alley with a gun, I've been keeping my eye out. It was a feeling I had."

"I believe in trusting feelings."

"I know I do. There's a reason for them," Bull says, tasting his tea. "And something told me to wait in the bushes that night. I was watching your door, but the funny thing about it is I should have been watching the alley. Since you told me that's where the hearse probably was when Lucious got killed, meaning that killer was back there."

"I'm glad you weren't." She thinks of Morris Island and what they found there.

"Well, I wish I had been."

"It would have been nice if Mrs. Grimball had bothered to call the police about the hearse," Scarpetta says. "She has you thrown in jail and doesn't bother reporting a hearse in my alley late at night."

"I saw him brought into lockup," Bull says. "They locked him up, and he was fussing his ear hurt, and one of the guards asked him what happened to his ear, and he said he got bit by a dog and it's infected and he needs a doctor. There was a lot of talk about him, about his Cadillac with a stolen tag, and I heard a policeman say that man cooked some lady on a grill." Bull drinks his tea. "Been thinking Mrs. Grimball could've seen his Cadillac, and she didn't tell about it any more than she did the hearse. Not to the police, she didn't. Funny how people think one thing they see's important, and something else isn't. You might think to ask if a hearse in the alley at night means somebody died and maybe you should look into it. What if it's somebody you know? She won't like going to court."

"None of us will like it."

"Well, she won't like it the most," Bull says, lifting his spoon but too polite to eat while they're talking. "She'll think she can smart off at the judge. I'd buy me a ticket to see that. Some years back, I was working in this very garden, and I seen her throw a bucket of water on a cat hiding under her house because it just had kittens."

"Don't say anything more, Bull. I can't stand it."

She goes up the stairs, and walks through the bedroom to the small porch that overlooks the garden. Benton is talking on the phone and probably has been ever since she saw him last. He's changed into khakis and a polo shirt, and he smells clean and his hair is damp, and behind him is a trellis of copper pipes she constructed so passionflowers could climb like a lover up to her window. Below is the flagstone patio, and then the shallow pond she fills with an old, leaky hose. Depending on the time of year, her garden is a symphony. Crepe myrtles, camellias, canna lilies, hyacinths, hydrangea, daffodils, and dahlias. She can't plant enough pittosporum and daphne, because anything that has a lovely scent is her friend.

The sun is out, and suddenly she's so tired, her vision is blurry.

"That was the captain," Benton says, putting the phone down on a glass-top table.

"Are you hungry? Can I get you some tea?" she asks.

"How about I get you something?" Benton looks at her.

"Take off your glasses so I can see your eyes," Scarpetta says. "I don't feel like looking into your dark glasses right now. I'm so tired. I don't know why I'm so tired. I didn't used to get this tired."

He takes off his glasses, folds them, and sets them on the table. "Paulo's resigned and not coming back from Italy, and I don't think anything's going to happen to him. The hospital president is doing nothing but damage control because our friend Dr. Self was just on *Howard Stern,* talking about experiments straight out of Mary Shelley's *Frankenstein.* I hope he asks her how big her breasts are and if they're real. Forget it. She'd tell him. She'd probably show him."

"I guess there's nothing about Marino."

"Look. Give me time, Kay. And I don't fault you. We'll work our way past this. I want to touch you again and not think of him. There, I've said it. Yes, it bothers the hell out of me." He reaches for her hand. "Because I feel partly to blame. Maybe more than partly. Nothing would have happened if I'd been here. I'm going to change that. Unless you don't want me to."

"Of course I do."

"I'd be happy if Marino stays away," Benton says. "But I don't wish any harm to him, and I hope nothing has happened to him. I'm trying to accept that you defend him, worry about him, still care about him."

"The plant pathologist is coming in an hour. We have spider mites."

"And I thought what I have is a headache."

"If something's happened to him, especially if he did it to himself, I won't get over it,"

Scarpetta says. "Maybe my worst flaw. I forgive people I care about, and then maybe they do it all over again. Please find him."

"Everybody's trying to find him, Kay."

A long silence, nothing but birds. Bull appears in the garden. He starts uncoiling the hose.

"I need to take a shower," Scarpetta says. "I'm a disgrace, didn't take a shower over there. Wasn't the most private locker room, and I had nothing to change into, why you put up with me I'll never know. Don't worry about Dr. Self. A few months in prison would be good for her."

"She'll film her shows there and make more millions. Some woman inmate will become her slave and knit her a shawl."

Bull waters a bed of pansies, and there's a rainbow in the spray of the hose.

The phone rings again. Benton says, "Oh, God," and answers it. He listens because he's skilled at listening, and, if anything, he doesn't talk enough, and Scarpetta tells him so when she feels lonely.

"No," Benton says. "I appreciate it, but I agree there's no reason for us to be there. I won't speak for Kay, but I don't think we'd do anything but get in the way."

He ends the call and says to her. "The captain. Your knight in shining armor."

"Don't say that. Don't be so cynical. He hasn't earned your wrath. You should be grateful."

"He's on his way to New York. They're going to search Dr. Self's penthouse apartment."

"To find what?"

"Drew was there the night before she flew to Rome. Who else was there? Possibly Dr. Self's son. Probably the man Hollings suggested was the chef. The most mundane answer is often the right one," Benton says. "I had the flight checked. Alitalia. Guess who was on the same flight Drew was?"

"Are you saying she was waiting for him at the Spanish Steps?"

"It wasn't the gold-painted mime. That was a ruse, because she was waiting for Will and she didn't want her friends to know. My theory."

"She'd just ended it with her coach." Scarpetta watches Bull fill the shallow pond. "After Dr. Self brainwashed her to do it. Another theory? Will wanted to meet Drew, and his mother didn't put two and two together and realize he was the one sending the obsessive e-mails signed the Sandman. Inadvertently, she matchmade Drew with her killer."

"One of those details we may never know," Benton says. "People don't tell the truth. After a while, they don't even know it."

Bull stoops down to deadhead pansies. He looks up at the same time Mrs. Grimball is looking down from her upstairs window. Bull pulls a leaf bag close and minds his own business. Scarpetta can see her nosy neighbor lifting a phone to her ear.

"That's it," Scarpetta says as she gets up, smiles, and waves.

Mrs. Grimball looks their way and slides up the window while Benton watches with no expression on his face, and Scarpetta keeps waving as if she has something urgent to say.

"He just got out of jail," Scarpetta calls out. "And if you send him back, I'll burn your house down."

The window quickly shuts. Mrs. Grimball's face disappears from the glass.

"You didn't just say that," Benton says.

"I'll say whatever the hell I want," Scarpetta says. "I live here."